To Cass
I hope
He read! Sincerely,
Alex Disorto

A Separate Heaven

A Separate Heaven

Alex Disanti

Still Waters LTD

A Separate Heaven
Copyright © 2010 Alex Disanti
Published by Still Waters LTD

All rights reserved. No part of this book may be reproduced (except for inclusion in reviews), disseminated or utilized in any form or by any means, electronic or mechanical, including photocopying, recording, or in any information storage and retrieval system, or the Internet/World Wide Web without written permission from the author or publisher.

Cover photographs by David Humphries
Yorkshire, England
www.a-gallery.net

Editor:
Marti Kanna
New Leaf Editing
Seattle, WA
www.newleafediting.com

Book design by:
www.arborbooks.com

Printed in the United States of America

A Separate Heaven
Alex Disanti

1. Title   2. Author   3. Literature/Fiction

Library of Congress Control Number: 2009900319

ISBN 10: 0615273351
ISBN 13: 978-0-615-27335-8

For Susan, Natalie and Ricky

ONE

On October 2, 1980, Dominic Gianelli entered the offices of Carson, Wiehls and Fullerton. A client for only weeks now, his arrival caused a flurry of activity among the staff. Even the most experienced members of the investment firm were on edge. Henry Carson, owner and senior partner, was nervous and unsettled, completely out of character for him, but this was no ordinary client. Gianelli was an enigma, recognized internationally in the business world and his accumulated assets were reported to be prodigious. Little else was known about him, although his penchant for two things, accuracy and privacy, had been evinced at their first meeting. He seemed to have come on the scene quickly, yet his profile revealed more than twenty years of steady, well-planned acquisitions and disposals. With as many European contacts as domestic, he was well respected here in New York. After all, one did not ignore this kind of wealth and, therefore, power.

He was a big man, six-feet, three inches in height, 270 pounds. Immaculately groomed, he had brown eyes and short, dark, slightly thinning hair combed back from his forehead. He seemed, by nature, a rather quiet man with low tolerance for the frivolous or inept. He had an air of confidence that was not lost on those who met him. Gianelli was a man comfortable with himself. When he entered a room, he owned it, and he knew it.

Forty-seven years old, Gianelli had never married, and for the last decade had not given much thought to it. He smoked cigars, never cigarettes, and he drank scotch, favoring Valinch. He enjoyed wine, imported from the regions of Puglia, Campania, and Nero d'Avola, but he was also fond of beer. He played golf and tennis and was a good dancer. His collection of music was extensive.

When he opened the door to the plushly furnished conference room, he was surprised to find a young woman standing at one end of the massive table. He had explained to the partners that he preferred some time to himself, at least half an hour, prior to any meeting, and so far his request had been honored. It was a long-time habit he felt gave him a mental edge, and he liked to study each person as they came into the room. Listening and observing had served him well.

As he entered, the young woman looked up and smiled, but seemed not to know why he was there. "May I help you?"

She was lovely. Dark, shoulder length hair framed a face an artist could have created, with big brown eyes fringed by black lashes. Her nose was straight, rather patrician, her lips full, and she had a beautiful smile. His eyes swept over her, taking in the delicate form, the snug fit of the black dress on her slim body. Her only jewelry was gold earrings and a gold bracelet watch. Dark stockings and black lizard heels completed her outfit.

He crossed the room, extended his hand to her. "Dominic Gianelli. I have a two o'clock appointment."

Her face reddened as she made an obvious effort to collect herself. "Mr. Gianelli…" she began.

In an effort to dispel her embarrassment, he held up one hand and interrupted her apology. "No need, really. And you are…?" He smiled.

Her cheeks flamed again. "Paige, Paige Hamilton."

The name sounded familiar to him. Then he remembered seeing

it in the signature box on the studies. "You're C. P. Hamilton?" He smiled again, warmly.

"Yes." She returned the smile, looked down for a moment, then raised her eyes to his again. "I try to get here an hour or so before our meetings start. It's…more comfortable for me I guess." She bit her lower lip momentarily, then seemed to catch herself, and quit.

He nodded. She was nervous, and a little shy, he thought, and he decided to try to put her at ease. "I know what you mean. I like to show up early myself. It's better than walking into a room full of people, isn't it?"

At the same time, he was looking her over, taking her in from head to toe. As those expressive eyes held his, he noted the slight Cupid's bow in her upper lip, the sensuous lower lip, the small cleft in her chin. Her pale complexion was a startling contrast to the dark eyes and hair. She was of medium height and the top of her head came to just above his chin.

And there was a sweetness about her. He definitely wanted to know her better.

Paige was still trying to collect herself in hopes of appearing professional, mature. Dominic Gianelli. *This* was the client she had heard so much about. There was something so…so magnetic about him. He was good-looking, she thought, a big man, but he carried it well and he had a commanding presence. To say he was well dressed didn't do him justice. The cut of the suit was beautiful, as was the fit. The shirt, the tie, were perfect. His cologne made her want to stay near him. Sharp, well spoken and kind, but a man who knew what he wanted and was accustomed to getting it, she sensed. No wedding band. Then she remembered hearing he wasn't married and felt a wave of relief. She realized he was looking at her expectantly and with some amusement.

She felt her face go hot again. "I'm sorry, what did you say?"

Dominic found it charming that she blushed so easily. "I said, without offending you, I hope, that you seem very young to be an analyst, and I asked how long you've worked here."

"I've been here for two and a half years." She didn't address the age issue.

Ah, she *was* as young as he'd thought—only the young measured in half years.

They were interrupted by Henry Carson, who looked a bit anxious and inquired if everything was all right.

"Fine," Dominic replied. "Miss Hamilton and I were just discussing a few things before we get started."

Carson appeared relieved and took over the conversation, but Dominic thought it was with some disappointment that Paige turned her attention back to her worksheets.

The meeting began promptly at two, and as it progressed, Dominic got to see her in action. He found her impressive. She was poised and spoke clearly. One had to assume she was bright and capable by virtue of her position, but during a forty-minute question-and-answer period, he noticed that not once did she hesitate or refer to the printouts for information, except perhaps for a page number. Ben Rosenzweig, his own consultant, had been exceedingly pleased with the studies.

———

Earlier, as Mr. Wiehls was giving the preliminaries, Paige had found she simply could not stop looking at Dominic Gianelli. Each time he caught her gaze he would smile. Refusing to let her shyness prevail, she forced herself not to look away, but to return the smile.

Now she had gone into what she thought of as "work mode." Her mind was cleared of everything else. This was territory where she excelled, and she knew it well. All eyes were on her, the men listening carefully to what she had to say. Mr. Rosenzweig had only a couple of questions, and she took this as a good sign.

At 3:20 the meeting was over and only the partners and Mr. Gianelli remained, but Paige lingered. When Henry Carson had interrupted her earlier conversation with the client, she had felt a twinge of disappointment. She wanted to know this man. She was *going* to know this man.

She knew that as was often their practice, the partners would have drinks and visit awhile with the client, especially one as important as he. She opened the armoire that served as a liquor cabinet, took out a decanter and glasses, placed them on a heavy silver tray, and set it on the cocktail table in the sitting area.

Mr. Carson had gone in search of his secretary, and, not finding her, returned seeming somewhat perturbed. He thanked Paige for her assistance and dismissed her, but not before she made it clear she would be working in the smaller conference room down the hall should she be needed and would be there until closing. The partners exchanged surprised looks. This was not in keeping with her normal routine. Mr. Gianelli took her hand in his, smiled warmly, and said it was a pleasure to meet her, that her work was outstanding. This pleased her no end, and she let her hand rest in his until he finally released it.

———

They watched as Paige left the room. She moved gracefully, her head up, her back straight.

"A remarkable young woman," Gianelli observed, casually. The partners agreed.

"I'd like to know something about her."

They exchanged cautious glances, and none spoke for a moment. Though little was known about Mr. Gianelli's personal life, his reputation with the ladies was well documented. Henry Carson sipped his drink and leaned back in his chair before responding in clipped sentences. "I've known Paige all her life." He paused, giving Gianelli a meaningful look. "All twenty years, as a matter of fact. Catherine Paige Hamilton. Daughter of Paul Hamilton, a close friend of mine. Investment banker. Well-thought-of fellow. Good family man. Wife's name is Martha.

"Paige was a surprise. Came along later, when the three boys were in their teens. I guess Andrew must have been about seventeen and the twins, John and Matt, about fifteen. When Paige was a toddler,

Martha became ill. Spent a lot of time in and out of private hospitals. I'll say no more than that. So the father and brothers, especially Andrew, pretty much raised Paige. Did a hell of a job.

"Paul expected a lot from his children and he got it. He was strict, especially with Paige. Maybe he was just being protective. I don't know. But don't get me wrong. He's a devoted father. Spent a lot of time with his sons, teaching them to ride, sail, sports—what have you—and when Paige came along they taught her. Kept a schedule no one would envy. Took them to church, wouldn't miss. You won't find four better children anywhere."

At this, Fullerton and Wiehls nodded in agreement. "They're all smart, responsible, well mannered. Their father would entertain no foolishness whatsoever. Paul's fond of saying you can't quarrel with the results, and you sure as hell can't."

Thinking this should satisfy Gianelli's curiosity, he turned the conversation back to the business at hand, but it wasn't long before Gianelli was asking about Paige again and how she had come to work for them.

Carson pursed his mouth and exhaled deeply, resigning himself to this line of conversation. "Well, I have to go back a way for that. When she was about five, Paul put her in St. Agnes's, a Catholic girls' school." Gianelli said he was familiar with St. Ag's, his nieces having attended school there, and Henry continued. "Paige was always bright, exceptionally so. By her fourteenth birthday, St. Ag's insisted she be allowed to test out of high school, and she did.

Paul outlined a curriculum and enrolled her at NYU. In less than three years she had her Bachelor's in economics and market analysis, and a year later her Master's. She wanted to go to work, of course. Problem was, no one would hire her. Too young. You can't have an analyst who looks like a teenager, no matter how smart she is or how many degrees she has. Clients want people like Rosenzweig. That's what they trust, makes them feel secure.

"Still, when Paul asked about her working for us, more as a favor to a good friend than anything else, we put our heads together and decided we would hire her, but she wouldn't office here. Most of the time she works from home. After she's completed several studies and the client is satisfied with what he sees, then we incorporate her into the meetings, which, of course, is why you saw her for the first time today." He paused. "It's worked out well."

At this point Fullerton spoke up. "Worked out *well*, Henry?" Glancing at Gianelli, he smiled sardonically and shook his head. "Truth is, she surprised the hell out of us. She's fucking amazing."

Fullerton was pouring himself a third drink, and was loosening up, a little too much for Carson's taste, so he cleared his throat and said quickly, "She's been a real find, no doubt about it. Far exceeded our expectations. Sharp, quick, accurate. We've had no regrets about our decision. Never a problem, not once."

Wiehls, who had been silent till now, spoke up. "With all that, there's something I find a little … I don't know if sad is the word …." He paused, seeming to consider. "Wistful, maybe. She's different. Not in a bad way, mind you, but she seems to be a loner. She doesn't go out, not to our knowledge, doesn't mix with the others here, even those closer to her age. I know at first some of the juniors asked her out. I don't think she ever went though."

Carson interjected, "Not surprising really, considering her background, but Jack's right, she shows no interest in the young men here. She gets on well enough with everyone, but it's more…" He thought for a moment "…more polite friendliness than anything else. I think she spends most weekends at her parents. Her horse is stabled there. Quite the equestrian actually."

"So she doesn't live with her parents?"

"Nooo." Carson gave a low chuckle. "Not anymore. She wanted to get her own place as soon as we hired her. Of course, her parents felt differently, thought she was too young to be living alone. Paul set forth all kinds of conditions. Damned if she didn't meet them." He paused, poured another drink. "You know what she did? Came in one day and informed me she planned to do some trading, wanted to clear it with me. I told her to check in periodically, let me see how she was doing. Really just wanted to look out for her, you know."

Gianelli nodded.

"She played the market like she'd been doing it for years. Did her homework. Some of what she did was predictable, but still, she had a sense of when to sell. It took her close to two years, but she got her own apartment a few months ago."

At this, Gianelli surprised them by abruptly changing the subject and announcing he was satisfied with the presentation. He asked them to proceed with the acquisitions and to please keep him posted. Thanking them, he shook hands and, almost as an afterthought, inquired, "By the way, there's no problem with my asking Miss Hamilton to dinner, is there? No company policy prohibiting something like that?"

Again, the partners exchanged looks. It was Carson who answered him. "No, no reason. As for company policy, there's no conflict here."

"Very good, then." Gianelli left.

The room was quiet when Carson said, "Well, we're her employers, not her babysitters." The others agreed.

And in the room down the hall, Paige had been waiting anxiously for Gianelli to seek her out. She had to smile. So *this* was what it was all about. She felt such a strong attraction to him, something that had never happened to her before.

Oh, some of the younger brokers had asked her out on occasion, but she simply wasn't interested. To her, they seemed cocky and annoying. It wasn't fair to indict them as a whole, but she had nothing in common with them, and there was nothing about them that made her want to know them better.

Dominic Gianelli was another story. She had been drawn to him immediately. She did not understand why, and she did not care.

When Gianelli tapped lightly on the door and opened it, Paige's back was to him and she was looking out the window. She turned and, seeing him, gave him a warm, appreciative smile, but said nothing.

"I'm not disturbing you?"

"Not at all." She looked at him expectantly.

He had the feeling she had been waiting for him. She was fighting what seemed to be a habit of biting her lower lip, and for some reason, this touched him. She had not taken her eyes off him, and once again his gaze swept over her. He couldn't remember the last time a woman had stirred his interest this way.

Evidently, she was ready to leave. Her purse, a soft-sided briefcase, and a large tote sat near the door.

He was not a man for small talk. "I'd like very much to take you to dinner."

"I'd like that too, thank you."

"Tomorrow evening at seven?"

"Yes."

They exchanged cards after writing their personal phone numbers on them. She lived at the Coronado Arms. He knew the area well and asked if he could offer her a ride home. She refused, saying she had some things she needed to do first.

"We can at least walk down together." He helped her with the tote, noticing it held, among other things, a pair of jeans, sneakers, a sweater and what looked like dance paraphernalia.

At the elevators, Gianelli waited till they could have a car to themselves, and placed his hand on the small of Paige's back as they entered. She could feel its warmth through her dress. They were on a first name basis by the time the elevator reached the lobby, and once again he placed his hand on her back as they walked out into the foyer. Her heart hammered wildly. She felt as if it might pound right out of her chest.

On the street, the evening throng of humanity was everywhere, some with hands jammed into pockets, their heads down and collars up, anxious to get home. Others warily eyed the gray sky, already releasing a sprinkling of white flakes. But Paige didn't care. There could have been a small blizzard and she would have known only that she was with *him*.

There was a silver limo at the curb, parked among the cabs and other vehicles, and he steered her toward it. As they approached, a man exited the driver's side, met them, and opened the doors.

"Paige, this is my driver, Vincente Carlino. Vincente, Paige Hamilton." Vincente took her hand. "Miss Hamilton, my pleasure." She smiled and committed the face and name to memory.

She saw Dominic motion to two men in a smaller car parked behind the limo. Then, glancing at his watch, he turned to her. "As much as I can think of other things I'd rather do, I'd better go. You're certain we can't take you home?"

She thanked him, but again refused, saying she had a couple of stops to make before going home.

"Paige, a favor?"

"Of course." *Of course.*

"Will you promise to take a cab to wherever you're going tonight?"

She smiled. "Of course."

He helped her into a taxi and asked at the last minute, "If I wanted to call you when this meeting is over, how late is too late?"

"Any time is fine. It won't be too late. I'll look forward to it." She felt her face flush, but she got the words out and was pleased with herself.

"I'll talk to you tonight then." He leaned into the cab, and with one hand brushed a few snowflakes from her dark hair, then touched her cheek lightly with his fingertips. "Bye for now."

The hammering in her chest continued.

Dominic spoke briefly to the two men, Leo Manetti and Abramo Buscliano, both members of his security staff. They all left then, the smaller vehicle in pursuit of the taxi.

Three hours passed before Dominic received a call from Manetti reporting that Paige had returned home safely.

"Where did she go?"

"Lotta Java—you know the place—then to a dance studio. Wait a minute...I wrote it down. 'Madame D'Andre's School of Dance.' She helped one of the instructors teach a class of preteens, and when that was over, she stayed for about an hour and just...danced...by herself. Then she took a taxi to her apartment building. At 9:45, we watched the doorman help her with her bags and get on the elevator with her. He was back in the lobby within minutes so it looks like she's in for the night."

"Good. No problems at all, then."

"No, sir."

"You were careful not to let her see you?"

"Of course. She had no idea we were following her."

"Good. That's good. No need to alarm her."

"I understand, sir."

Dominic sighed. He could relax now, knowing she was home—not that he had anticipated a problem. He just hated to think of her out alone, especially at night. Shifting restlessly in his chair, he tried to stay focused, but his thoughts were on her and tomorrow. She had been on his mind all evening.

A coffee shop and a dance studio Manetti had said—those had been her stops on the way home, nothing more. He was glad. That face, the way she moved, the sound of her voice, the things the partners had told him—all this kept running through his mind over the course of the evening. Well, they would start with dinner and see where it went from there.

He was willing to take his time with her. Twenty. She was very young, but the attraction seemed mutual. There was something about her, something in the way she looked at him—it made him feel good. God, how long had it been since he'd taken a woman to dinner, gone on a "date." For years now, he'd had arrangements, women here and there who, for an extravagant price, met his needs. No ties, no messy entanglements. He was a busy man, and for the last ten years had looked for ways to simplify his life, not complicate it. But he had a feeling that Paige Hamilton might indeed do just that. The thought did not displease him.

The meeting finally adjourned, and he would stay in the city that night, as was often his habit during the week. Once at his apartment, he poured a drink, reached for the phone, and dialed her number. It was shortly after midnight. She answered on the second ring. They talked for more than an hour. Finally, it was he who said good night.

Paige, in pajamas that consisted of a white silk tee and boxers, lay in bed hugging a pillow. A smile lit her face. She felt *so* good. It seemed as if tomorrow would never come. There was nothing about Dominic Gianelli she didn't like. She could still feel his hand on her back, smell his cologne as he touched her hair, her cheek. She could feel him all around her, and she loved it. And this was her last thought as she drifted off to sleep.

TWO

Paige awoke on Friday full of excitement in anticipation of her evening with Dominic Gianelli, but after trying on clothes for most of the morning, she was close to despair. She had always had a sense of style, of what was becoming to her. For years she had been able to reach into the closet and pull out any dress, any outfit, and know it would work. She had never bought into fads. Her taste ran to the classic, tailored styles. She favored Ralph Lauren, Pierre Cardin and LaPaglia. Her closets were a vision of organization, shoes, gloves, purses, belts, and jewelry included. Everything had its place.

But today nothing suited her. Nothing was perfect and she wanted perfect! She finally settled on a deep forest green dress with long sleeves, a tight fitted bodice and full skirt. She added gold and emerald earrings and a matching bracelet watch. She chose black leather pumps with three inch heels. She laid her black wool dress coat, black gloves and a small clutch containing a lipstick, a hairbrush, travel size lotion and a package of mints on one end of the loveseat.

In an attempt to calm her nerves, she poured a glass of wine and sipped it as she soaked in the tub for close to an hour. She slathered on moisturizer and body lotion from head to toe, rolled her hair, buffed her nails, and brushed her teeth twice.

She chose a white lace bra and matching panties, then pulled on a half slip and dark thigh-high stockings while she swished mouthwash. She applied mascara, eyeliner and lipstick, the only makeup she ever used. Then, she sprayed a cloud of her favorite perfume and walked through it, letting it drift over her.

She had begun getting ready at three, but it was a quarter to seven by the time she slipped on her dress and shoes and brushed her hair one more time. In the end, she was grateful when the buzzer sounded. She could stop. There was nothing more to decide, no time to change her mind, her dress or anything else.

In the lobby of the Coronado Arms, Dominic met the doorman, Charlie, who was expecting her caller. It was an older building but nice, very well kept. Listed on the market, it would have borne the description of "quiet elegance." Paige's apartment was 17A, one of four on the top floor. When he stepped from the elevator into the hallway, he noted the plush carpet and the ample but subdued lighting from the brass sconces that lined the walls.

He pressed the buzzer, and just before the door opened heard her footsteps, heels clicking on the tile in the entryway. Then she was there, smiling and asking him in. After a brief conversation, he helped her with her coat and they were off.

In the elevator, Paige joked that Charlie was her father's lookout. She wasn't supposed to know, but had figured it out the day she moved in, and there was no denial from Charlie. Dominic was glad to hear it. Already he was protective of her.

Outside, only a smattering of flakes was falling and the wind had quieted. Paige greeted Vincente and settled into the limo beside Dominic.

As the car proceeded cautiously through the wintry night, she inquired about his day. She had this way of listening to what he was saying, giving him her full attention, as if she were committing his every word to memory.

When he asked about her day, she sighed and gave a funny, self-deprecating account of trying to decide what she would wear that night.

He told her she looked beautiful, and this brought forth a smile and a blush.

———

He took her to Harry's on Fifth Avenue, a popular but notably exclusive restaurant. One of his favorites, he said. The maitre d' greeted Dominic by name and showed them to a table in a secluded area where few others were seated. A waiter lit the candles and served them wine. She would later learn that Dominic had his own table there. Looking over the menus—there were three—she asked him to order for her, and she could tell this pleased him.

Conversation came easier than she had expected. They talked in more detail about their families, their work, their likes and dislikes. She learned that he had three sisters as opposed to her three brothers. He was the eldest in his family, she the youngest in hers. She told him about the horse, Fiero, a graduation gift from her parents when she finished at NYU.

Once, during a brief lull, he said, "Name three things you really enjoy." And when she hesitated, he coaxed her, saying, "Quickly! Don't think about it. Just tell me what first comes to mind."

When she told him ballet, music and sailing, he smiled and said they shared some common interests, that he had a sizable music collection and a sailboat.

She learned that his penthouse apartment here in the city was in the adjoining hotel. He also had a house on Long Island and "a place," his words, in Italy. He traveled less now than in previous years, but still spent considerable time in Europe.

The meal was delicious, but lost on Paige, so focused was she on just being with *him*. Dominic ordered an after-dinner liqueur for them, Amaretto Marcati. She liked it, but it could have been anything. They listened to music from a pianist accompanied by a small band. When they played "The Way You Look Tonight," Paige mentioned that it was one of her favorites, and he asked her to dance.

She fit in his arms as if she had been created for that purpose—it felt so right. Her head *did* come to just above his chin. They danced together as if they had done so a hundred times before. When the song ended, Paige asked if they could request others, and they did:

"Harbor Lights," "One in a Million," "I'll Be Seeing You," "So Rare." He seemed surprised and pleased that she knew these songs, and when he asked, she told him she had heard them all her life and they were some of her favorites. They danced for more than an hour. Paige loved being in his arms, and he seemed to share her feelings.

Outside the restaurant, he lit a cigar. No, she didn't mind. He reached for her hand, holding it loosely. They strolled casually, commenting at times on the window displays in the stores. The air was a blend of winter, the city, and the smoke from his cigar. Her feelings were a mixture of excitement and contentment, and he was the source. When he asked if she would like to go to his place and have a drink, she said simply, "I'd love to."

It was on the twenty-third floor, elegantly furnished, very masculine, but beautiful, and spacious, with eleven rooms. The living area opened onto a large terrace that overlooked the city. It had a magnificent view. They stood for several minutes gazing at the multitude of lights before them, the cold night air surrounding them.

She looked up at him, and as if it were the most natural thing in the world to do, he leaned down and kissed her. Then he put his arms around her, drew her to him, and kissed her again, a long, lingering kiss this time.

He took her hand and led her inside to the sofa, where he pulled her down beside him. He held her close, and they kissed again and again. At this point Paige knew only one thing—she wanted him, wanted to be with him. The feelings he stirred within her were so strong they overwhelmed her. He tasted of wine and Amaretto. The fresh scent of soap combined with his cologne and the cigar he had smoked filled her senses. This was a new experience for her and one worth waiting for. She didn't want it to end. Not ever.

As for Dominic, it had been at least twenty years since he had shared kisses like this, and if it had ever been this appealing, he had long forgotten. Paige was so sweet, so responsive. After a while, though, the man in him began signaling for more, and he had to make a decision. Something was eluding him here. He was torn between wanting her to stay the night—and he *did* want her to stay—and an unreasonable and nagging urge to just wait.

Finally, he said, "It's getting late. Shouldn't I be thinking about taking you home?" Sensing she might somehow tie this remark to her age, which seemed to be a sensitive subject, and hoping to take the sting out of it, he tucked a strand of her hair gently behind one ear when he said this, and gave her a little smile. She did not return the smile. Instead, she bit her lower lip, but she never took her eyes from his.

There was a long silence, then, ever so softly, she said, "I don't want to go home." It was barely discernible, but he heard her.

He considered this, then, in a husky voice commanded, "Look at me. Tell me again."

She did, more audibly this time. "I don't want to go home."

His eyes held hers. "Are you sure?"

"I'm sure."

She watched him as he stood up and loosened his tie. Then she suddenly asked for more wine.

Slightly surprised, he filled their glasses and joined her on the sofa. She seemed nervous, a little uncertain, and she was biting her lower lip again. After watching her take several sips, he took her glass and set it beside his on the table. He pulled her to him and kissed her, harder this time.

He slipped his hand under her skirt, feeling the span of warm, young skin between the band of her stockings and her panties. He stroked her thighs and cupped his hand between her legs. She pressed against it, and he could feel her heat through the panties. "Let's get you out of that dress," he said.

She stood up and turned her back to him, one hand raising the sweep of dark hair, exposing her slender neck. Her head was tilted downward, and she was very still. There was something childlike in the gesture, but it was equally sensuous. He unhooked the clasp, then undid the zipper, and the dress slipped from her arms, her waist, and she stepped out of it. He laid it across a chair as he had done with his jacket earlier, and sat down on the sofa again. She had taken off her shoes and stood facing him.

It was intriguing the way she just...just waited. He put his hand on the band of her stocking and she raised her foot, balancing it on the edge of the sofa cushion. He peeled off the stocking and did the same with the other. His fingers found the waistband of her slip, gave a gentle tug, and it lay on the floor, a sliver of soft white silk. She was beautiful and desirable, but somehow fragile. Again, there was something eluding him, something causing him to hesitate, but he couldn't identify it.

He wanted her, and she was, without question, responding to him. She wanted to stay, had said so. Her lips were parted the tiniest bit. She wet them with the tip of her tongue and stood there, watching him watching her.

He pulled her down beside him and held her tightly. His kisses were more demanding now. His hands explored her body. When he reached between her legs this time, his fingers found that tiny spot through the scrap of white lace, and he held her close, stroking it.

He could feel her breath come quickly as she pressed herself into his hand. Her body tensed, gave a slight shudder, then she was still.

Her face was buried in his shoulder now. His lips brushed her cheek, and she turned her face to him again, kissing him, slipping her arms around his neck.

"Good?" His voice was husky, smoky. Her answer: a whispered "yes." Then he was touching her again, his mouth kissing the swell of her breasts above the bra, one hand on the small of her back while the other stroked her through the panties.

He brought her to orgasm once more, then stood up and, taking her hand, led her into the bedroom. Still clad in panties and bra, she watched him as he stripped, never taking her eyes from him.

She stood beside the bed and made no move to undress further, so he sat down and drew her to him. He unhooked the bra, letting it fall to the floor, cupped her breasts in his hands, and rolled each nipple between his thumb and forefinger. Her breathing was quick and uneven. He slid his hands down to the last fragment of lace and took off her panties, revealing the triangle of dark hair.

Bending his head to kiss her there, he felt her stiffen. "No?" She looked uncertain. "It's all right, you can say no...or later...or another time." He was studying her reaction, but rubbing her back gently with one hand as he spoke, letting her know it was okay. He watched her, waiting.

"Another time?" As she said this, she moved into his arms, and in one swift motion he laid her beside him on the bed. He kissed her, drew his hand slowly across her breasts, her midriff, her flat little tummy, and finally between her legs, this time exploring her. With the tip of his middle finger he felt how warm and wet she was, and he drew the moisture upward, caressing her again. Then he slipped his finger into her, deeper this time. Immediately she tensed and held her breath, and he stopped. Carefully, he felt her again.

He sat up on the side of the bed, was quiet for a moment before speaking. "Sweetheart, do you think that maybe, *just maybe*, this was something you should have mentioned to me?" He patted the bed beside him, and after hesitating a moment she scooted over and sat next to him, her leg touching his. He took her hand and held it, and at one point, kissed it. He watched her, waiting. "Hmmmm?" And when she didn't respond, he urged her, not unkindly but firmly, "Can you answer me, please?" This was serious business, but he took care not to sound angry.

She was silent for a moment, then asked. "Are you upset?"

"I think surprised is a better term."

She began drawing her index finger distractedly up and down his thigh. She seemed to be having a hard time meeting his gaze, and he was afraid for a moment she might cry. But then she looked directly at him and asked, "Does it matter?" And there was no sign of tears.

What he did detect was a note of defiance in her voice, and he thought, "So there's fire there too—that's good."

"Does it matter?" he echoed her question. "Well, you've waited. There must be a reason for that."

She answered him without hesitation, with the clarity and honesty found in the young. "Because I never met anyone I wanted to be with until you...and I knew. I just knew."

And there it was. There were some things in life that were meant to be, he thought, and there were moments when this was made known. This was the moment it happened for him. And he, the man who questioned everything, had no more questions.

Later, as she slept curled against him, he would remember her face as he entered her, and the quick intake of her breath. The way, at that very moment, she touched his face, laying the palm of her hand against his cheek, and the look in her eyes…the wonder and trust. There was no mistaking it. The undeniable wonder and trust... he would never forget.

He was forty-seven, and in every sense a man of the world, but he had never experienced the feelings that rose in him tonight. For the rest of his life, he would recall this night in detail, and it would never fail to stir him. She belonged to him now.

Paige awoke to his touch, his finger tracing the outline of her mouth. When she opened her eyes, he kissed her. The clock on the bedside table showed 2:20 A.M.

"Sleepy?"

She shrugged slightly and smiled a little, not quite meeting his gaze. At the same time, she pressed her body close to his and ran her fingers through the hair on his chest.

He kissed the top of her head and again caught the scent of her perfume. Her hair was soft, thick, glossy. Her eyebrows were natural, not thinned out the way so many women wore them, and were a perfect companion to the thick black lashes.

She looked at him now, her dark eyes provocative. She opened her mouth as he kissed her and he pulled her even closer to him. He slid one hand down her back, and let it come to rest on her bottom, then he trailed one finger up and down the cleavage there. Pressing his mouth to her ear he whispered, "Spread your legs." She repositioned herself and did as he asked. He caressed and stroked her until she came, then, using his finger, he worked the wetness toward her bottom.

Repeatedly, he took her just to the brink of satisfaction, then put his finger inside her, delving for the honey-like wetness she exuded, and drew it to her bottom. "I'm going to make you feel really good, Baby, okay? Is that all right?"

Breathlessly, she answered, "Yes."

Yes, and Paige hoped he would hurry. Dominic had been teasing her body to the point that she didn't think she could stand it any longer. His mouth was on hers again. God, she loved the taste of him! He had shifted and was using both hands. It felt *so* good. A small moan escaped her.

"I'll let you come now, Sweetheart. Do you want to come?"

She let out another moan as he manipulated her skillfully. At the height of her desire he slipped the tip of one finger into her bottom and continued massaging her with the other hand. She heard him whisper, "Tell me when, Baby, tell me when."

Then it happened, and it was so intense she cried out, "Now! Oh, now!"

He was smiling, looking pleased. She preferred burying her face in his chest or his shoulder afterward, knowing he had watched her, but he was having none of it this time. "Don't do that. Look at me. This is between us, just us. There's nothing to be embarrassed about, okay?"

"Okay." And she buried her face in his shoulder.

The combination of Paige's shyness and inexperience, coupled with newly found desire and passion moved Dominic, touched him, stirred him no end. His fingers were on her, in her again, and once more a moan escaped her lips, then another and another. After she came, he rolled onto his back and pulled her atop him.

God! She was beautiful! So young, and yet, she responded like a woman, a very passionate woman. "Slow," he said as she lowered herself on him. "Easy." She did as he said, but reached a point where she was obviously not comfortable, and he took over, rolling her onto her back again.

She closed around him, tight but velvety, so warm and so wet. She was moving with him now, meeting his thrusts. Her lips were parted and the desire in her eyes matched his. Then her eyes closed and her hands clutched at his back. "Now!" she cried out, and he could wait no longer. Later, as he held her, she would whisper that it was like the night exploding into a thousand pieces.

Saturday morning found them sleeping soundly. Paige lay on her stomach, he on his side with one arm flung possessively across her back, his hand cupped at her breast. Dominic awoke first, leaned over and whispered, "Wake up, Zucchero," then kissed her cheek.

She turned to him, wrapping her arms around his neck. Her mouth found his and she kissed him, a long, hard kiss.

"Well! A good morning to you too, Miss Hamilton," he said, teasingly.

His eyes drank in the beauty of the tousled dark hair, the expressive eyes, and the full, soft lips. The feel of her in his arms, the way she surrendered herself to him, was something new, even for this man whose sexual encounters were so numerous he had long ago given up remembering with whom or when.

Paige was happy, so happy she thought she might burst from it. Her mouth was bruised and her body deliciously sore from their night of lovemaking. It was wonderful! *He* was wonderful! Thinking of the many things they had done, all new to her, she felt herself blush. She remembered the feel of his hands on her body, touching her, everywhere it seemed, and his voice, different, almost hoarse, as he'd coaxed her, urged her to tell him, "Does that feel good, Baby?" Yes, there had been a couple of awkward moments, but he had guided her through them and she had followed, an oh-so-willing subject. He was watching her now, his eyes warm on her, and he smiled knowingly, as if he knew her thoughts.

Putting her hand on his face, she caressed his cheek lovingly, feeling the prick of morning stubble of his beard.

"Think I need to shave?"

"No."

"Think we need coffee?"

"Yes."

"Do you like ice cream?"

"Yes." She eyed him curiously.

"Have you ever had it for breakfast?"

"Noooo." And she smiled.

"Have you ever wanted to have it for breakfast?"

"Yes." She was laughing now.

"Come on then." He stood up, reached his hand out to her, and pulled her from the bed. It was then she noticed some thready streaks of blood on the sheets and a little that had dried between her legs.

When he saw the blood he took her in his arms and kissed her, gently this time. He told her how special she was and that last night had been wonderful. Before she could become embarrassed, he said they would shower first, have their coffee and ice cream, then change the bed. In the bathroom, he turned on the shower and pulled her in with him. Paige found it a bit awkward at first. Then remembering what he had told her, she tried to relax and not be so self-conscious. He asked her what she would like to do today.

With a little smile, she replied, "I don't want to go home."

He wrapped her in a huge towel and laughed. "Sweetheart, that ship has sailed."

He put on a robe and gave her one to wear, but it was ridiculously large on her, so he told her to look in his closet, pick out a shirt, and wear that. Paige chose a white, well-worn pullover. It came almost to her knees and she had to cuff the sleeves three or four times to get them just below her elbows. She spied his mouthwash and rinsed her mouth, put on lipstick, and brushed her hair.

Paige found Dominic standing by the island in the kitchen, waiting for the coffee to make and smoking a cigar. "Do you mind?" he asked. No, she didn't mind. She never would. Noting the shirt, he told her, "Good choice—one of my favorites." He put his arm around her and pulled her close.

After he poured coffee into two Talavera mugs, he told her to come into the study with him while he checked messages. There, on a beautifully crafted credenza, was an array of equipment—phones, faxes, answering machines. He set his coffee down and positioned her in front of him, with his left arm encircling her waist. She stood quietly with him as he punched buttons and deleted or saved messages, his lips brushing the top of her head with an occasional kiss. This would become a lifelong habit.

When he finished, he held her and whispered, "You're mine now. You know that, don't you?"

"Yes." Just yes.

They ate bowls of sweet cream ice cream and drank coffee. Dominic promised Paige real food later on. She just shrugged and smiled.

"Are you always this agreeable?"

"Only with you."

Laconically, he said. "Works for me, Zucchero."

"Dominic, what does that mean?"

"Sugar, it means sugar."

"I like that. Zucchero."

They changed the sheets and spent the remainder of the day in and out of bed, but mostly in. They ate more ice cream and switched from coffee to wine in the late afternoon. That evening Dominic ordered steak and shrimp, crab-stuffed mushrooms, grilled vegetables, and champagne and strawberries sent up.

Paige, still wearing only his shirt, watched as he filled their plates. She had gone through some of his tapes and put several on to play, everything from Connie Francis and Brook Benton to Van Morrison, Rod Stewart and Bob Seger. He had gotten a kick out of her excitement over his collection. Now she sat cross-legged on an oversized hassock, his shirt punched down between her legs, her plate balanced in her lap.

She was eating only the mushrooms so far and drinking champagne. She seemed quiet, reflective.

"A penny for your thoughts, Zucchero."

"This has been the best twenty-four hours of my life. That's what I'm thinking."

"Come here." She set the plate down, unwound those lovely legs and came to him. As she stood before him, he was struck again by the combination of her beauty and her sweetness, the way she looked at him with such openness and trust, and something akin to gratefulness swept over him. The feelings she evoked, this need he felt to possess her, protect her, were new to him. He had always dealt in reality, in black and white with few areas of gray, and he wasn't accustomed to these feelings. He was not by nature a romantic, but she brought out what there was in him, and somewhere deep inside, he had claimed her. She belonged to him now, and he would *not* let her go.

Holding her hands, he pulled her to him. "You know, I may have to marry you, Sweetheart."

"Okay," she answered softly.

There it was again, the undeniable innocence and trust. "I'm glad it's the best time in your life, Paige." And he meant it.

She leaned into him and kissed him. His hands found her bare bottom and caressed it. God, she stirred him! Her nipples showed erect through the thin fabric of the pullover, and he brushed his mouth lightly across them. Taking her hand, he guided it downward till she could feel him. Her hand trembled slightly as her fingers explored the length of him.

Deciding dinner could wait, he asked, "Do you like cold steak, Sweetheart?"

"Very much."

It was the only answer he needed.

The stereo was playing "One in a Million." How appropriate, Paige thought. How perfect.

Dominic had removed the shirt and was touching her everywhere, his mouth devouring hers. Saturday night was a repeat of the night before: sessions of passion interspersed with a few hours sleep.

It was close to noon when they awoke on Sunday. As they lay contentedly among the tangled bedding, Dominic mused aloud as to whether they should get dressed today. Personally, Paige didn't see the point.

"I think I could live in this bed with you," she told him, rubbing her hand against the even more pronounced stubble of beard.

"We'll move you in today."

"Okay."

They both laughed, but as it turned out, that was exactly what happened.

Around nine Sunday evening, they went to Paige's apartment with plans to see each other again Monday night, but they had no more than stepped off the elevator when Dominic asked if there was any reason they couldn't get what she needed and go back to his place.

Not a reason in the world! She asked him to check her answering machine while she packed.

He called out to her that she had thirteen messages. Astonished, Paige returned to the living room. "Thirteen?"

He laughed and confirmed this. "Should I check them?"

She sensed that he was curious to know who had called. "Of course, please."

The messages, all left, it turned out, by her family, began rather innocuously, but by the ninth call her father was swearing. "Damn it, Paige, where are you? Thoughtless doesn't cover it anymore. We're worried about you. Call us!"

It got worse from there, the final message ending with a threat to notify the police if he didn't hear from her that evening.

Trying to be nonchalant, she grimaced and said, "Uh oh! I guess I'd better call them."

He merely nodded, but he was watching her closely.

Paige called her brothers first, apologizing and assuring them she was fine. She saved her father for last, and she hesitated, standing there, staring at the phone.

"Are you afraid to call your father?"

"No, no, it'll be fine. He's just…easily upset." She knew what was coming and it couldn't get much more humiliating. The last thing she wanted or needed was something that emphasized the difference in their ages. And what could do that more effectively than being openly scolded by her father?

Dominic, eyeing her curiously, smiled and said, "Well, go ahead and get it over with. I promise not to let anything happen to you."

She took a deep breath and dialed the number. Her father answered on the second ring. "Dad?"

Dominic could hear only one side of the conversation, but during the first five minutes Paige seldom finished a sentence without interruption, and her pretty face turned various shades of red as she endured what was obviously a vicious tongue-lashing from her father.

At the outset, she appeared apprehensive, but after making

several attempts to apologize, her attitude changed. She was polite but uninformative, saying only that she had met someone at the office, that he was a client. Actually, they had met last Thursday, and she really liked him.

At this, her cheeks flamed, and she did not look at him. No, she did not wish to discuss it further, and yes, from now on she would remember to call.

As she hung up the phone, she glanced at him, smiled nervously, and bit her lower lip.

He felt bad for her. She was obviously embarrassed. Trying to lighten the moment, he teased her gently. "So you really like me?"

Paige sighed, relieved to have the conversation with her father over and done with. "Yes, I do!" She turned to go back to her room to finish packing, but Dominic reached for her and took her in his arms.

"Well, I like you too, Miss Hamilton. But let's be serious for a moment. Are you afraid to tell him about us? About me?"

Knowing her father wasn't going to take it well, she stretched the truth a little. "Not at all. But I do want more time for...for us." Turning shy, she said, "To me, it's ..it's wonderful. I want as much of this as we can have. Is that all right? Does it make sense?"

"Yes, to both questions, Zucchero." He smiled. "Got everything?"

"Almost."

She changed from her dress into jeans and a sweater, and they finished getting her things together.

In the limo, she snuggled against him contentedly. At his place, they made roast beef sandwiches with creamed horseradish and red onions and drank beer.

Afterward, in the study, he checked his messages, and once again she stood encircled in his arms. As his lips brushed the top of her head, the phrase "heaven on earth" kept running through her mind.

THREE

The Next Four Weeks

Paige was ecstatic. There was no other word for it. She and Dominic spent as much time together as possible, and had settled into a semi routine. Charlie, the doorman, intercepted any work sent to the Coronado Arms. When Dominic went to his office, Vincente would drop her at her apartment and she would do the studies and arrange for a courier. She would check her messages for the times she was needed in the office. That she breezed in and out, purposefully, a secretive smile playing on her lips, was noticed by all. She had always been lovely, but now there was a decided glow about her.

She had an air of confidence she had not previously exhibited. This came about with gentle urging and, at times, rather blunt encouragement from Dominic. Once, when he saw her agonizing over a particularly difficult analysis, he told her, "Just go in there and do what you always do. Make your presentation, and remember, they don't know shit. That's why they need you!" She loved him, *truly* loved him.

Toward the end of the second week, Dominic had to attend a board meeting in L.A. He called her several times during the day and twice to tell her goodnight. At two in the morning the phone woke her from a restless sleep. His voice was husky. "I miss you."

"I miss you, Dom. A lot." Using the shortened form of his name she had recently adapted.

"I'll pick you up on the way in from the airport tomorrow. About four. Okay?"

"Definitely okay."

"Evening in or evening out."

"In, please."

"Good. Go back to sleep, Zucchero. I'll call you in the morning."

"Goodnight, Dom." And so it went.

He took her to the NYC ballet to see their production of Romeo and Juliet. Paige wore a strapless black taffeta dress that hugged her body, then flared to a skirt that ended just a little below the knee. Dyed to match satin heels, diamond drop earrings and a diamond bracelet completed her ensemble. "She's a knockout," he thought. And she was.

During the intermission, they were spotted by Henry Carson and his wife.

Carson had called him earlier in the week and informed him that Paul Hamilton had recently inquired about a client Paige had met and was now dating. According to Carson, he simply pled ignorance in the matter and had said, pointedly, that he did not want to be involved in either his clients' or his employees' personal affairs. Dominic told him that he understood Carson's position and assured him it wouldn't be an issue much longer, since his introduction to the Hamilton family members was imminent.

After visiting briefly with the Carsons, he and Paige returned to their seats, his hand possessively on her back, as always.

They spent the following weekend together aboard his boat, *The Mallorca*. Upon arriving at the marina with Manetti and Buscliano, Paige spied an old Chris-Craft in one of the slips. She told him that she loved the antique wooden boats. Dominic took note of how much she admired it.

His yacht was a sixty-foot Jongert 18D, black hulled with chrome trim. It had an enclosed deckhouse and a complete bar with windows at the stern. White sails loomed high above them, but the boat could also be powered by diesel. It was a magnificent piece of equipment.

Once in open water, Dominic cut the engine and let the boat drift while the four of them ate sandwiches and drank coffee laced with sambuco. That afternoon they spied a pod of humpback whales, and he got as close as he could without disturbing them. The show was spectacular. The huge mammals, known for their breaching and flipper-slapping, did not disappoint them. It was an unexpected treat since the height of the season had passed.

He and Paige and the two bodyguards stood without speaking, just watching. Finally, Buscliano lamented that he didn't have a camera.

"It's so impressive, so awesome. I'm not sure a picture could adequately capture it. Sometimes, you just have to remember the moment and hold on to it. You know, one of those things you keep tucked away but always within reach." This was uttered quietly, poignantly by Paige. The three men exchanged solemn looks. Dominic put his arm around her and kissed the top of her head.

The next time he took her to the marina, docked next to his boat, was a 1929 Chris-Craft, and near the bow, painted on each side, was PAIGE ONE. Paige was obviously overwhelmed when she saw it.

"Want to take a look?" He was enjoying her reaction.

It was a wonderful old boat, a twenty-six foot Model 7 with upswept decks, red leather upholstery and a rare—so Dominic informed her—Chris-Craft A70 V-8 Engine. It was supposed to be the ultimate prewar wooden runabout. She examined the boat with something akin to reverence.

"Can we take it out?"

He pulled the keys from his pocket. "Ready?"

"Ready!" Her eyes were glowing and she looked at him wonderingly. "Dom, is it alright to ask when on earth you found time to do this? We're together almost all the time!"

"I *make* time for the important things, and I think this was time well spent." He had to smile. Paige had that look…as if what he was saying was the most important thing in the world, and she was hanging on to his every word. "But I'm really more interested to know what *you* think."

Her response was everything he had hoped for. "I think it's wonderful, Dom, just wonderful!"

On the open water, he told her forty miles per hour was top speed, but if she wanted something faster they could replace the engine. He caught the look of astonishment that crossed her face before she realized he wasn't serious. Then she laughed. "That was scary!"

He had considered telling her the boat was hers, but she was so affected by the simple fact that it bore her name, something told him anything more would be too much. She kept looking at the boat, then at him, smiling and shaking her head in disbelief.

Paige and Dominic discovered more and more about one another as they talked in depth about their families and shared stories of their childhoods, especially Dominic. He noticed Paige had very little to say about her mother. Well, Henry Carson had told him the mother was ill and in and out of hospitals for years. Dominic would learn more about this later.

The more time he spent with Paige, the more she opened up to him. He was pleased with how much her shyness had diminished over the last three weeks. In their lovemaking, he coaxed her gently, took his time with her. He still thought the way she said "I want you in me" was somehow innocently provocative, but he was now encouraging her to use other words. She was getting there. And last night, when he had pulled her atop him again, this time she had taken it and was able to sit all the way down on him. He knew it hurt her at first, but after a few minutes she seemed to get used to it. Pressing his hand to her belly, he could feel his cock moving inside her. He placed her hand there so she could feel it, too. Finally she tilted forward a little, resting her hands on his chest, and began to move in a slow, circular motion. When he could see that she was close, he told her to tell him when, but this time to say it, really say it.

"Now!"

"Now what? Say it!"

"I'm coming," she whispered. Gripping her wrists to lock her in place against him, he released the passion pent up inside him. Afterward, he asked her, "Good?"

She lay forward on his chest, her head at his chin, with him still inside her. "So good."

Exactly four weeks and two days after their first date, Paige began feeling feverish and her stomach became upset. She realized she was going to start her period. This always created such misery for her at the onset that she usually spent two or three days in bed with a heating pad.

It was Sunday, and she told Dominic she thought she might go back to her apartment that evening, but he talked her into staying the night, saying he would drop her there the next morning on the way to his office. They made love, and while she didn't start her period that night, her back and abdomen were seized with cramps early Monday.

He went up to her apartment with her and stayed a few minutes. She knew he had noticed that her face was flushed and that she wasn't feeling well.

Telling him only that her stomach was upset and she thought she would make some tea, she kissed him good-bye and was grateful when he was on his way.

She swallowed two Pamprin tablets, then made a cup of tea with honey. She peeled off her clothes, went to the bathroom, and drew a tub of water as hot as she could stand it. She lowered herself into the steaming water, which burned her skin but felt good to her back and stomach. Looking down, she saw the cloud of red flow from her body. She sat in the tub until the water began to cool, then stepped out, dried herself, and methodically applied body cream and deodorant.

She put on a pad and her panties, pulled on a sweater and jeans and socks, then brushed her teeth and combed her hair. After grabbing a couple of pillows from her bed and plugging in the heating pad, she lay down on the sofa, covered herself with an afghan, and fell asleep.

Three hours later the phone woke her. Clutching her abdomen, she stumbled across the room and answered with a faint hello.

"Paige?"

"Yes, I'm here." Her voice was strained.

"Paige, are you okay?"

"Yes, my stomach just hurts, Dom. I have to go, Sweetheart."

"What's the matter? "

"Dom, I'll be fine. But I need to lie back down."

"I'm coming over." And he hung up, not giving her the opportunity to protest.

When Dominic arrived, he found Paige curled on the sofa wrapped in a blanket, her arms folded across her abdomen holding a heating pad to it. She was burning up, but insisted she wasn't too warm. When she told him she only had cramps, he finally realized she had started her period. Still, he didn't understand why she was so ill.

"It's always like this for a couple of days, then it gets better. It's normal, really."

Dominic had grown up with three sisters and these monthly episodes weren't alien to him, so he knew this wasn't normal.

"It's always like this?"

"Always, I promise," she said in a reassuring tone.

He offered to get something for her, asked if she wanted to lie down in her bed. She refused, saying she just needed to stay where she was.

After watching her for a moment, he made a decision. "Paige, I have a good friend, Bernardo Rossini. He's a doctor, a woman's doctor. I'm going to call him."

She protested and seemed distressed by the suggestion, but he ignored her and made the call. He briefly explained the situation to his friend and asked if he could come see her. Rossini arrived within the hour.

When Dominic introduced them, Paige evidently felt so bad she didn't even try to sit up. This was not lost on him, and he knew then calling Bernie had been the right thing to do.

Bernie and Dominic had met in school when they were nine and had been friends ever since. Bernie looked at the young woman, in obvious pain, and at the worried face of his friend, and feared this was far more than just a painful period.

Standing over her, he asked, "Are you having your period?" Her faced turned a bright red, but she nodded. "And you're sure that's all it is?"

"Yes."

"Is it always this bad?"

"Yes."

"Have you seen a doctor about it?"

"No." Then, "Well, Dr. Lloyd, when I was fifteen…"

"What did he say?"

"That it was normal. To take the pills, the Pamprin, and use a heating pad."

"I see. And at what age did you have your first period?"

"Fifteen." She was still blushing, and looked away when she answered him.

"That's late. What did Dr. Lloyd say about that?"

"He thought it was because I was a dancer. Thin, low body fat." She grimaced. She tried to straighten her legs and sit up, but soon abandoned the effort and lay back down.

"Do you have a gynecologist?"

"No."

"When was the last time you saw one?"

"I haven't."

"You've never seen one?" He found this surprising, especially considering her age and the times.

"No."

"So no one has examined you since you were fifteen?"

"Dr. Lloyd just talked to me. Actually, to my mother. That's all."

Paige answered his questions, but she looked everywhere except at him, and took long deep breaths as if to try and calm herself. She was obviously uncomfortable and becoming upset.

Dominic motioned Bernie into the kitchen. "What do you think?"

"Lloyd's getting on in years, but I thought he was a better doctor than that! How old is she?"

"Twenty." Bernie guessed his amusement showed, because Dominic added, "Almost twenty-one."

"A little on the young side, isn't she?" He couldn't help but grin. Dominic ignored this and asked what he could do to help her.

"Well, right now all we can do is get through this cycle, but I can give her medications to take from now on that will eliminate most of her discomfort. If she doesn't have a doctor, I guess she's not on the pill or anything."

"No, she's not. She didn't need to be."

Bernie looked at him questioningly. "How long have you been seeing her?"

"A little over four weeks. Look, Bernie, she had never..." He stopped then started over. "I was her first, okay? So no, she's not on the pill. We're not using anything. Now you know that, what are you going to do for her?"

Bernie could see this was not up for discussion, though he was very curious. He couldn't remember the last time his friend had been in a serious relationship, if ever, and this definitely seemed serious. "I'll give her a muscle relaxant and a shot for pain. That'll help. I want to check her abdomen first though."

They went back to the living room.

"Paige?" She opened her eyes. Bernie smiled at her now. "Let's slip your jeans down a bit, okay?" And he reached toward her waist.

"No!" It must have come out more forcefully than she intended, because she blushed and stammered. "I...I mean, no. Not...not now. It's not a good time."

"I'm only going to check your abdomen. Make sure nothing is going on here other than your period." She was clenching the waist of her jeans with both hands. That she was so tense wasn't helping the situation. He backed off, saying, "This is pretty awkward for you, isn't it? Tell you what let's do. Why don't I give you a shot with a muscle relaxant in it? It will stop those spasms. Is that all right?"

She looked at Dominic. "Sounds like a good idea to me, Zucchero."

At this, Bernie looked at his longtime friend. This really was serious! Dominic gave him a conspiratorial smile and a little shrug, as if to acknowledge what he was thinking.

Paige agreed, and Bernie told her to unbutton her pants just enough for him to put the shot in her hip. She did as he asked and rolled over on her side.

Paige knew they wanted to help, but they were talking too much, asking too many questions. All she wanted was to sleep until she felt better. If only they would leave her alone, especially Dominic's friend. Shortly after he gave her the shot though, she'd begun to feel drowsy, and the cramps were definitely easing. The medication had relaxed her. It had also diminished somewhat her lifelong anxiety over doctors.

Dr. Rossini, who'd been watching her, asked, "Better now?"

"Yes, much. Thank you." She bit her lower lip. "Sorry about all the fuss."

He smiled, and his voice was kind. "Not a problem. I have pretty much a closed practice now, made up mostly of clients who have known me for so long they're willing to put up with me. I could use a refresher course in charming new patients. So, you're a dancer?"

Dominic answered for her. "No, she took dancing for years, but she's an analyst."

"She's an analyst?" Bernie couldn't hide his surprise.

Paige laughed at this. "A market analyst, Dr. Rossini."

"Well, even that..." he said, wonderingly. "And you're twenty?"

Paige sighed, and this time it was Dominic who laughed. "It's a long story. We'll tell you another time, okay?"

"Sure, but don't forget. I want to hear this. Paige, feel like letting me check you now?"

"I guess so." She unbuttoned the jeans and Dr. Rossini pulled them down around her hips. It took him only a moment to palp her tummy. Then he pulled her jeans back up and said, "Fine, that's fine."

He suggested she go use the bathroom, put on something comfortable, and go to bed. He would give her a shot for pain, and he would come back that evening to check on her.

It took only minutes for the shot to take effect on Paige. Once Paige was asleep, Dominic and Bernie went into the living room. "She'll probably sleep several hours. Make sure she drinks something when she wakes up, okay?"

Dominic nodded.

Bernie was having a hard time wiping a recurring smile off his face.

Dominic eyed him suspiciously, as if he knew what he was thinking. "What?"

"I think you're smitten, *that's* what." He grinned. "I mean, I don't blame you, but has the phrase 'robbing the cradle' ever crossed your mind?"

"Actually, no, it hasn't. Thanks for coming over, Bern, I appreciate it."

"I can tell when I'm being dismissed. I'll check back after evening rounds, okay?"

"Great. Thanks again."

Dominic picked up an album that lay on the sofa table. It was bound in white leather with gold leaf. Inside, someone had written "Catherine Paige Hamilton, b. February 1, 1960." And under each picture was her age and a description of the event. The album covered the first ten years of her life. Paige looked a lot like her brothers, three handsome young men, almost grown by the time she was born: dark eyes and dark hair, defining brows and lashes.

The photos were an interesting study. Oddly, most of the time she looked so serious, even when she was smiling. At last it came to him—the smile didn't reach her eyes. Often she was posed. It did not surprise him that she had been a beautiful child. A picture he found particularly touching was one with whom he supposed was the eldest brother, Andrew. He was holding her and they were forehead to forehead, their eyes locked on each other. She was four, according to the notation under the photo, and dressed in jeans, sneakers and a hooded sweatshirt.

There were pictures of Paige in leotards and tutus, of her on a pony, then eventually on horses, of her skating, riding a bike, in a swing, sitting on a tree limb, and with her brothers at Christmas,

Thanksgiving, and on her birthday. The last picture was of Paige, in dance costume, sitting on stairs tying the laces of her toe shoes. Her expression was solemn.

Whoever had taken the picture had snapped it just as she looked up. It was a wonderful picture, those dark eyes looking out at him as though they could see him, as if, at any moment she might speak. He closed the album and stood up and stretched.

He went to the bedroom to check on her. She was lying on her side, one hand hanging off the bed, the other tucked under her pillow. She always slept with her mouth slightly open, her lips barely parted. The covers were pulled to above her waist. Her head felt warm, her hairline damp. Drawing back the spread, he found the heating pad. He checked the setting and turned it to low, then drew the covers over her again. After removing his shoes, he stretched out on the bed beside her, put one arm around her, and fell asleep.

Paige awoke at six. It was dusk, and the sky looked like snow again. Dominic lay beside her. She turned toward him and watched him sleep. She felt better. Not terrific, but certainly much better. Lying there, she studied his face. She loved him, loved everything about him.

She wanted to tell him, but didn't know how he would feel about it. She knew, though, that she loved him with all her heart and she wanted only to be with him. He was both possessive and protective of her, but he treated her, loved her, like she was a woman, not a child. He was a bridge to another part of her life, this new part, the man-woman part. She loved the togetherness, loved that he knew every inch of her body, loved how masterfully he wove their hours of shared intimacy. She loved how just thinking about him caused that feeling that started in her chest and went all the way down. And she knew if she felt herself right now, she would be hot and wet. Yes, he was her...her steppingstone...from girl to woman. He had made her a woman.

She kissed him and he stirred, opened his eyes. "Hey, Babe. Feeling better?"

"Much, thanks to you."

"So you forgive me for calling Bernie."

"Yes."

He reached for her. "Well, we can't have you feeling like that. I don't like it. Hungry?"

"A little."

While she went to the bathroom, Dominic ordered dinner for them, French dips and cottage fries. He fixed hot tea for her and opened a beer for himself. He ate his sandwich and half of hers while they watched the news.

Dr. Rossini came by at eight on his way home. He and Dominic drank a beer, as Dominic explained how he and Paige had met. Dr. Rossini had just laid out the injections to give her when the buzzer sounded. Charlie announced that her parents were on their way up.

She was a little scared, and she knew it must have shown, because Dominic took her hand and squeezed it. "I have to meet them sometime, Zucchero. Don't worry about it. Everything will be fine."

She nodded. Of course, it would be all right. He would make it all right. That's what he did.

He opened the door, much to the obvious surprise of her parents, and greeted them. "Hello, I'm Dominic Gianelli." His tone was decisive, confident.

Her father appeared stunned and, acting solely on what she knew was a lifelong habit of good manners, shook Dominic's hand. "Paul Hamilton. This is my wife, Martha."

Dominic took her hand. "Mrs. Hamilton, it's a pleasure to meet you. Paige has told me a lot about you." Her mother smiled uncertainly.

"I'm afraid she's told us nothing of you, if you will forgive my saying so." This, from her father.

Paige saw it was then that they noticed her, clad only in a nightshirt, sitting on the sofa, and the doctor sitting in the chair across from her.

"Paige?" Her father said just her name, but there were many questions in his voice.

Dominic answered smoothly, "Paige isn't feeling well. She was quite ill today. This is my friend, Dr. Rossini. Bernie, Mr. and Mrs.

Hamilton." He continued, "She's feeling better now, but Bernie stopped by to give her a shot to help her rest tonight."

"What's the matter, Paige? Why aren't you well?" Her father's voice showed both caution and concern.

She could feel her face burn. This really wasn't something she wanted to discuss.

Dr. Rossini spoke up. "She's having severe cramping from her period—"

Before he could finish, her mother said, "Oh, that! It's nothing. She'll be better in a few days. Paige, do you have your pills?"

She just nodded.

"Always such a fuss over something so commonplace," her mother continued. "All girls have cramps, some worse than others, that's all."

Paige saw that Dominic was watching her. She looked down at the floor, and did her best to keep her face expressionless.

Bernie cleared his throat. "Well, actually, what your daughter experiences is anything but normal. There's a term for it. Dysmenorrhea. Sometimes it gets better once a woman has children, sometimes not. But if she has to spend several days in bed, then it isn't normal."

There was an uncomfortable silence as her father gazed curiously, first at her mother, then at her. She felt her mother's eyes on her too, but Paige refused to look back at her.

She listened as Bernie continued. "Well, the important thing is, Paige knows something can be done to alleviate the discomfort, so it will be better from now on."

It was then that Dominic sat down beside her on the sofa, put his arm around her, and pulled her close to him. The brief hug and the warm smile he gave her boosted her confidence. She straightened her shoulders and looked defiantly at her parents. She was still a little scared. Confrontations, especially with her father, were rather daunting for her, but with Dominic beside her she knew she could face anything.

Her father was obviously struggling with the situation. She knew Dominic well enough to know he was willing to take a little flack, but only so much. Paige had yet to speak. She took a long breath and stared back at her father as he sat there glaring at them.

Bernie seemed to sense a confrontation coming between the two men, because he said, "Mrs. Hamilton, would you join me in the kitchen for a cup of coffee or tea? I'd enjoy some company, if you don't mind."

Paige watched as her mother responded to Dr. Rossini's invitation. Martha despised any kind of conflict unless she was the initiator. She excused herself and joined him.

Well good, thought Paige, *now whatever has to be said can be said.*

Paul Hamilton was openly sizing up Paige's new friend. He himself was a tall man, but Gianelli towered over him. How old was he? He had to be in his forties, at least. Paul's eyes took in the expensive suit, the European tie, the Italian leather shoes. All quality, no doubt about that. And certainly Gianelli was polite and well spoken, but what on earth was this man doing with his daughter?

The three of them sat in silence for several moments, then, finally, Gianelli opened the conversation. "Mr. Hamilton, I sense that I am not who or what you expected, and I understand your concern."

"Do you now? Mr. Gianelli, may I ask your age?"

"I'm forty-seven. Forty-eight soon, in December."

"And do you know my daughter's age?"

Gianelli smiled at Paige as he said, "Almost twenty-one."

"And you don't find this relevant?"

"No, because she isn't typical; she's special."

You're damn right she's special! Paul thought. But he said only, "All the more reason for my concern. She *is* special. But she's young and inexperienced. She's lived away from home only a few months."

"Dad!"

Paul saw Gianelli silence her with a look, then Gianelli said, "I think Paige is an adult, capable of making adult decisions. She doesn't strike me as moronic or juvenile in any sense. I find her to be a remarkable young woman."

Paul was beginning to understand just how serious this relationship really was. Choosing his words carefully, he said, "Of course she is, but it doesn't change the fact that she's had very few dates and never had a boyfriend."

He could tell his daughter was struggling to remain calm. "You know, Dad, while I don't appreciate your comment, I have to admit it's true. By the same token, the fact that I've never had a *boyfriend*," and she practically spat the word, "wasn't for lack of invitation or opportunity. I simply wasn't interested. You recognized early on that I wasn't compatible with others my age. I was happier spending time with the boys and their friends. You never thought it was a problem then, did you?"

He started to answer, but his daughter cut him off. "Let me finish, please. My lack of experience, Dad, was my choice. And now, *this* is my choice. You and Drew told me I should wait for the right person and the right time. Isn't that what I've done? Exactly as you asked, exactly as you taught me?"

Paul did not answer. She had his attention.

"I can only speak for the way I feel." And now she was blushing, but she faced him squarely. "Dominic makes me very happy. We enjoy so many of the same things. I realize we're still getting to know each other. I haven't introduced you to him because I wanted time for just the two of us. But we have nothing to hide. I wasn't trying to be mysterious or evasive. And in fairness to Dominic, he wanted to meet you. From the beginning, I was the one who insisted we wait. You've done nothing tonight but confirm what I suspected your reaction would be all along. This is my home. And yet, here you sit, uninvited, judging Dominic, questioning his intentions. You don't have that right, Dad. You know nothing about him."

She paused, then said thoughtfully, "I want you to know Dominic, and I want to know his family, too. I do. But it's been so wonderful being together..." With that she turned to Gianelli, and the look that passed between them was not lost on Paul.

"As you can see, he takes very good care of me."

This troubled him. "Paige, I never realized you...felt so poorly. I left that to your mother. I should have known better."

Her face softened a bit and she looked at him sympathetically now. "It's okay, Dad. You didn't know."

Paul did some quick thinking. He was getting nowhere fast

pursuing this tonight. He would back off temporarily, find out later what he needed to know about this man.

"Well, let me say this about tonight, Paige. We were in the city and thought we would stop by, but the visit wasn't meant to be intrusive."

He asked if they would come to dinner Friday evening, and Gianelli accepted.

The Hamiltons left shortly thereafter and Dominic and Paige thanked Bernie profusely for entertaining her mother.

"Okay, but you both owe me," he said. They agreed.

Paige showered, brushed her teeth, and got ready for bed. Then Bernie gave her the injections and said good night. Finally, Dominic showered, checked the setting on the heating pad, and lay down beside her. "You asleep yet, Babe?"

"Not quite." She turned to him and placed her hand on his cheek the way she often did. "I'm sorry about tonight, Dom."

"Don't be. He's your father. You're his only daughter, and his baby, at that. He's allowed to be concerned."

She was silent.

"Right?"

She shrugged and snuggled close against him.

He held her, wanting her, but knowing he wasn't going to do anything about it. Freeing one hand, he began to stroke her cheek and brush through her hair with his fingers. He felt her relax, and within minutes her eyes had closed.

He lay awake thinking about what a strange family they seemed to be, and about Paige, her father, and the confrontation this evening. How those two must have clashed through the years, both of them so strong willed. She had a stubborn streak all right, and the thought made him smile.

Watching her as she slept, he imagined it must have taken everything Hamilton had to manage her, and how, seeing he no longer had control of her must be a jarring realization for him. He sensed Paige would be a formidable opponent, if that was the way her father was going to play it.

He hoped not though. He didn't want her alienated from her family. He believed in family, had strong family ties. But it would be up to the Hamiltons. For her sake, he hoped they would be amenable to the relationship. He could live with it either way.

Well, it would be interesting to see how it played out. But she belonged to him now, and they would have to accept this.

FOUR

Weeks Six and Seven

Friday evening found them at the Hamiltons at 6:30. The house looked similar to what Dominic had imagined, a two-story brick with white columns and charcoal gray shutters. There was a circle drive and a sweeping porch that spanned the front of the house. Lawn chairs and a swing suggested a family atmosphere. Large oaks grew in the well-kept yard that was bordered by neatly trimmed hedges and perennials. It looked like a great place to grow up.

"I see the gang's all here," Paige said lightly upon seeing several cars parked in the drive. She leaned over and kissed him. "Armed and ready?"

"I suppose." He laughed. "Kind of tough on them, aren't you?"

"Oh, not really, I just know them, that's all. One more kiss, please?"

Pulling her to him, he held her close and gave her a meaningful kiss. "More later, Zucchero."

Her answer was a warm and knowing smile.

The door was opened by a small, sixtyish woman with wispy, gray hair and a friendly face. Paige gave her a hug and introduced her as "Molly, who's known us forever."

"So you're the one who's been keeping our girl so busy!" she exclaimed.

"Guilty." He smiled. Already he liked her.

"Well, pick your poison, dearies. The women are in the kitchen and the men in the family room."

"A lot of speculation going on?" This, from Dominic.

Giving him a wicked grin, Molly replied, "Trying to decide how much rope it will take to hang you!"

He played along. "Molly, you're scaring me."

"I doubt that!" She showed them in.

As they entered the spacious foyer, which opened onto numerous rooms, the first thing he saw was an easel holding a portrait of Paige in full dance regalia, one foot perched on the edge of the chair in which she was seated, her other leg extended to the floor. Toes pointed, she was tying the laces on the shoe.

It was similar to the photo he had seen in the album, but she was older here. Once again, she was looking up, as if the camera had caught her by surprise, unsmiling, the large dark eyes unreadable. It was a striking portrait. He thought she must have been around fifteen at the time. A myriad of pictures lined the wall of the staircase, mostly of Paige and her brothers at various stages in their lives.

Dominic met the brothers and found them to be much like their sister in both looks and personality. Andrew—Drew, for short—was the eldest and most serious, and acted more like a parent regarding Paige than a brother, but he supposed that was due to the difference in their ages. Drew's wife, Julia, was friendliest of all and obviously very fond of Paige. Matt's wife, Bitsy, and John's wife, Anne, seemed to be a matched pair, typical former finishing school graduates, now Junior Leaguers, but both were nice.

Shortly after dinner, Paul Hamilton took Dominic aside and asked if he would join him in his study for a moment of private conversation.

The walls of the room, and the desk and credenza, held a multitude of pictures, many of Paige. There were two in particular he immediately coveted, one, in which she was again dressed in the pale pink dance costume, but this time in a formal setting, posed in a French provincial chair. She sat very straight, one hand on the opposite forearm, which rested on the arm of the chair, her feet crossed at the ankles. He had the sensation that she might speak at any moment. The other picture, a smaller one, was displayed on Hamilton's desk. Paige was standing beside a horse, holding the reins. She wore a jacket with a fleece collar, and the wind was blowing strands of her dark hair across her face. This time she was smiling. She looked truly happy. Dominic noticed her father watching him. Any congeniality present during dinner seemed to have vanished.

"Wonderful pictures," he ventured, meeting Hamilton's gaze full on.

Hamilton nodded toward the one on his desk. "Her eighteenth birthday. She had recently graduated from NYU."

Dominic accepted the cigar Hamilton offered, as well as the brandy. Then, seeming to choose his words carefully, her father began. "Mr. Gianelli, I've given a lot of thought to this situation. Would it be my first choice? No, I think not… but…" and he paused here…"I can see my daughter is committed to this…this relationship. Not wishing to alienate her, I don't believe I have any choice but to accept it, at least for now."

Dominic listened in silence, never taking his eyes off Hamilton.

"What I want to know from you is this. How safe is my daughter? I know very little about you. It seems no one knows much about you, but I hear rumblings, innuendoes. Things that pique my curiosity. As for Paige, her feelings for you are obvious. But she's hardly more than a child. What are you going to do about that? Is she someone you will discard once the novelty wears off?" Hamilton paused, then with thinly disguised hostility, blurted, "After all, you can take her virginity only once."

Dominic's voice hardened as he spoke. "Now wait just a minute—"

"No, Mr. Gianelli, you wait just a minute! This is my daughter we're talking about. My daughter, who until a few weeks ago had never even had a serious date, and that's hardly the case now, is it? And don't lie to me, because she told me she spent that first weekend with you!"

"I have no need to lie to you, and I thought we had this conversation the night we met. With all due respect, I didn't force anything on Paige. She made her own decisions—"

"I'm sure you helped." Hamilton's voice dripped with sarcasm, and the more irate he became the calmer and more reasonable Dominic grew. He knew what he did and said this night would set the tone for this relationship. She was Hamilton's daughter. He had to respect Hamilton's feelings up to a point. But he didn't like the accusations and he wasn't going to offer any explanations. In the end, he decided, Hamilton would be his own worst enemy. He didn't doubt that Paige could be equally as stubborn as her father, and he didn't believe he was misreading the girl's feelings for him.

After a long silence, he said thoughtfully, "Paige is very special to me. I would never hurt her, nor would I allow anyone else to hurt her. She is far more than a novelty—your word—which, frankly, I find offensive. I care a great deal for her. On a personal level, I will tell you this relationship was not something I entered into lightly. There were many things I had to consider. I do not for a moment think it acceptable that our relationship estrange Paige from her family. I would never encourage this, but she knows her own mind. I don't think she would choose to alienate her family, but if driven in that direction, and put in the position of feeling she had no choice, I can't speak for what might happen."

It was obvious that his words landed like ice water thrown in Hamilton's face, and Hamilton was making an effort to regain composure. After he calmed somewhat, he said only, "I don't want my daughter hurt."

"Neither do I." There was another long silence.

"Then I guess we understand each other."

"Very well."

Paige looked anxiously at Dominic and her father when they came into the den again, but both faces were noncommittal. Maybe it wasn't so bad, then. The evening had actually gone better than she'd anticipated. Her sisters-in-law, all very curious about Dominic, had seemed impressed and a little in awe of him, she thought. Drew, Matt, and John had thoroughly pleased her by their congeniality toward him. Her mother had flirted a bit with him and her father had seemed determined to make the evening a pleasant one. And later, when she would ask him, Dominic would make light of the discussion in the library and brush it aside.

On the way home, she said, "Well, one down and one to go." They were scheduled for lunch at the Gianellis the next day.

"That's right, Zucchero, it's your turn on the hot seat." And Dominic laughed. "Nervous?"

"Yes."

"Don't be, they'll love you."

And it struck her, and made her somewhat sad, that she could not have said the same thing to him. She was curious about his family and had more than a little trepidation about meeting them. She wished it were easier for her to meet people. She wasn't *painfully* shy, but she was quiet, and often this made others uncomfortable. She hated feeling as if she should talk simply for the sake of talking. Well, she would get through it, one way or another, and she would pray for a nice, uneventful day.

Dominic reached for her hand and squeezed it. "I'm going to take you home and make you forget all about family dinners. Okay?" And he did.

Arriving at the Gianelli's Saturday was quite an experience. Dominic was driving today. They were in the Jag, and though Paige would never have said so, she far preferred it to the limo. It was always nicer when it was just the two of them, but she was wringing her hands by the time he parked the car.

"Enough of that, Zucchero. They're just people, and they're excited about meeting you." With that he held her close and gave her a long kiss. "Now, come on." He took her hand and led her into the house.

First, she met his parents, Victoria and Xavier (who insisted she call him Pop—much later she would settle on Poppa), then all three sisters and their husbands. There were Isabella and Tomas, a doctor; Connie and Mario, and Jackie and Richard. Mario and Richard were owners of a sporting goods store.

Except for height, Dominic did not resemble his father. Xavier was slim, with thick, wavy black hair, and sported a mustache. He was very friendly and had a warm, easy smile. Victoria was also tall, five feet, nine perhaps, with dark hair parted in the center, pulled back from her face, and held with a clasp. She wore a belted black dress, low-heeled pumps, and a lot of jewelry, but it looked right on her, Paige thought.

When they were introduced, Victoria surprised her by hugging her briefly, then holding her at arms-length, and saying how happy they were to finally meet her. Dominic had told them so much about her. Paige wondered, W*hen?*

Isabella, the eldest sister, was a younger version of her mother. Connie and Jackie were shorter and more voluptuous. Lively and vivacious, they too had dark eyes and dark hair. Mario and Richard had the look of athletes, as if they had once been bodybuilders or football players.

There seemed to be children everywhere and of all ages, ranging from nine or ten up into their twenties. Paige thought she would do well to remember the parents today, but she tried to learn who belonged to whom.

After the introductions, Dominic led her into a small area off the formal living room where an older woman was sitting, a glass of wine in hand. Paige was immediately intrigued by her.

She was wearing a gray silk blouse, a colorful paisley skirt—red, gold and purple on a gray background—and a deep purple leather belt with a large gold buckle. She wore several rings on both hands. She had very long fingers—an artist's hands, Paige thought. A large crucifix attached to a strand of rosary beads lay in her lap. It was pewter-colored and embedded with several stones that looked like garnet, cobalt, and maybe topaz.

Her oval face was etched with time, her hair more gray than black. It was easy to see she had once been very beautiful. Like her brother, Xavier, she was tall. She had piercing dark eyes that forced you to look at her. She reminded Paige of the aristocratic women in paintings she had seen in museums. Her demeanor was so...so regal. The chair could easily have been her throne.

"Sophia, may I present Paige Hamilton. Paige, this is my aunt, Sophia Disanti."

Sophia took Paige's hand in both of hers. "Paige, is that correct?" She spoke with an accent.

"Yes."

"What kind of name is that?"

A bit flustered by the question, she hesitated. "I believe it's French. I'm not certain."

"Paige. It feels funny to my tongue, I will have to get used to it. And so, Paige, do you have another name?"

"Catherine. Catherine Paige. "

"Ah, Catherine. Very pretty." She studied the girl's face as she spoke. "But somehow this name Paige suits you, doesn't it." It was not a question.

Paige was silent.

"How old are you, Paige?"

"Twenty." And though she hated herself for it, she could not help but add, "I have my birthday in February, though, so I'll soon be twenty-one."

Sophia, still holding her hand, patted it, and laughed softly. "Someday you will find these birthdays come much too quickly. Twenty is a good age, an acceptable age. Enjoy it."

There was kindness in the comment, and somehow Paige felt she had the aunt's approval.

"Well, Paige, you and I will visit more, but for now you will join the others in the kitchen, yes?" The aunt's tone was cordial, but dismissive.

"It's very nice to have met you, Sophia. I'll look forward to our visit." And she meant it.

Sophia nodded. She watched as her nephew and the young woman left the room, his hand protectively on her back, her face turned up to his, listening attentively as he spoke. The old woman smiled knowingly. So it had finally happened for the nephew. She was pleased.

As in most households, the men and women had separated. The women were preparing lunch. Paige offered to help, and Victoria put her to work slicing tomatoes for the salad. When she had finished, she arranged the condiment trays.

There were several young girls in the kitchen, Connie's and Jackie's daughters. They were a raucous, noisy bunch, but it was fun. There seemed to be several conversations taking place, and all at once. One girl was practicing pirouettes around the kitchen.

"Where do you take?" Paige asked her.

She paused. "Madame D'Andre's."

"I thought I had seen you there." She smiled.

The little girl whispered loudly to her older sister, "I *told* you it was her!"

At this point, four girls ranging in age from nine to fourteen gathered round the counter where Paige was now doing a relish tray.

"Did you take from Madame D'Andre's too?"

"For fourteen years I did."

"Do you teach now? You taught our class not long ago."

"I just help out when I'm needed, but I still like to dance. Where do you go to school?'

"St. Ag's!" They answered in unison.

"Really? That's where I went to school. From kindergarten until I graduated." She was talking to the girls, but she knew the women were listening too. "Is Sister Constantine still there?"

"Yes." All in chorus again, this time, more like a groan.

"Is she still strict?" Paige asked, smiling.

"Yessss!"

"Does she still have that ruler?"

Again, "Yesss!" After much discussion about St. Ag's and which of the sisters were the best teachers, the girls dragged her onto a patio to practice plies and arabesques. Would she show them the proper way to passe releve?

It was too cold to stay long outside, so they returned to the living room, all four girls huddled around her, each wanting to sit next to her.

Connie's youngest, Mallory, wanted to know if she had ever been in trouble at school, this being of great interest to Mallory since she had recently been punished for talking out of turn and failure to turn in homework.

"Well, only once, but that was enough to make me never do it again."

"What did you do?"

With mock seriousness, she said, "If I tell you, you must promise you will never do what I did, and you can't tell anyone. Do you know the secret pledge?" All of them crossed their hearts with a big X, then formed the obligatory "A" with thumbs and forefingers, followed by holding up the first two fingers of the right hand, and swore on St. Agnes.

Paige had to work at not laughing aloud. "All right, then. When I was thirteen—"

"My age," Connie's oldest daughter, Maria, interjected.

"Yes. We were in Sister Constantine's class…" sympathetic groans "…taking a test. The girl who sat across from me—her name was Angela—didn't know some of the answers, so I passed them to her on a slip of paper, but Sister Constantine saw us."

"Our punishment was to polish the railing of the altar, vacuum the kneelers, take up old candles and put out new ones. That kind of thing." They nodded solemnly.

She continued with her story of how she and Angela had found what they thought was wine, and decided to taste it. It was actually brandy that belonged to the father, but they hadn't known the difference, and it wouldn't have mattered anyway.

They found two small glasses and filled them. They didn't like the taste, but it made them feel warm inside, and it made them giggle, so they drank some more. It also made them very sleepy.

Again, it was Maria, who exclaimed, "You fell asleep, Paige?"

She nodded. Jackie's daughter, fourteen-year-old Christina, was shaking her head.

"I'm afraid so. School was dismissed, and eventually our parents called the office. I think they forgot we were in the chapel because they looked everywhere for us, in the classrooms and the dorms. Finally, it was time for evening vespers." The girls' faces expressed their horror. They were enjoying this immensely.

"And that's when they found us. We were in a lot of trouble, but it got even worse because…" she paused for effect here"…we both got very sick to our stomachs."

"You got sick in the church?" Mallory asked, wide-eyed.

As Paige nodded, Christina exclaimed, "Oh man! It's a wonder you lived to tell this!"

This made Paige laugh aloud. "You're right, Christina. We were in so much trouble with everyone. Father Michael, the Reverend Mother, Sister Constantine, our parents. Angela and I were separated and never had another class together. All our privileges were taken away for the rest of the semester and we had to make public apologies. That was just at school. At home, well, let's suffice to say it wasn't easy to sit for a week."

The girls nodded knowingly. Corporal punishment was no stranger to them at school or at home.

Paige smiled. "Come on, we'd better go back to the kitchen. They'll think we're slackers." And the five returned to find Victoria and the others in final preparation for lunch.

In the dining room, the adults were seated at a massive Georgian mahogany table. There was an alcove off this room with another large table where the children were seated. Mallory protested, wanting to sit next to Paige, but was shushed by her grandmother and sent to sit with the others her age.

"Looks like you have a fan." This, from Dominic.

Jackie spoke up. "She has several. Thanks for taking them off our hands awhile, Paige."

"My pleasure. They're lovely girls." The mothers looked pleased.

There was an astonishing amount of food on the table, more courses than she had ever seen served at one meal. She saw Dominic watching her, and he seemed amused. "Just take what you want Paige, you don't have to eat everything." She smiled but felt her face flush, and she bit her lip.

After lunch, Victoria and Isabella shooed everyone away, saying they would clear. The men retired to the den for drinks and cigars. Connie and Jackie had made a run to Connie's house to retrieve some item of apparel Jackie wanted to borrow. Paige was captured by the girls and taken to the game room where some of the older children were playing pool. The girls commandeered her into a game of Yahtzee, but were really more interested in talking, and each had a turn at trying on her earrings.

Eventually, Tom, Isabella's oldest, asked Paige for a game of pool. As they played, she learned that he was twenty-three and was in his last year of college. He was a handsome young man, tall like his parents, and like all the Gianelli's had the obligatory dark eyes and dark hair. He was congenial but very respectful of her, almost formal, she noticed.

Connie's youngest boys, Dimitri and Darius, were twins, a rambunctious pair presently pretending to be bullfighters. Darius had confiscated a red shawl belonging to his grandmother to use as his cape.

Unfortunately for Paige, she managed to step into the path of Dimitri, who was plunging, head down, toward his brother. He hit her in the stomach while running full tilt. It knocked the breath from her and, with both arms folded across her abdomen, she went down on her knees. It was toward the end of her period, but the severe cramping always left her feeling tender inside for several days.

"Dimitri! See what you've done!" It was Tom, now holding her arm and trying to help her stand. She couldn't just yet. "Paige, I'm so sorry. Are you all right?"

She wasn't sure. It felt as if someone had struck her with a bat, but she managed to smile. "It's okay. He didn't mean to do it. He was playing. I'll be fine. I just lost my breath for a moment." And seeing the concern on Tom's face, she repeated, "Really, I'm fine." She stood up and made her way to the kitchen. There she found Victoria and Isabella engaged in conversation while sipping steaming cups of tea. When they saw she had one hand pressed firmly against her abdomen, they expressed concern.

Paige asked Isabella if she would mind showing her to a bathroom, saying only that she might need something, she wasn't sure.

"Of course, dear." Isabella took her upstairs to a large bath complete with sitting area. She told Paige that items of a personal nature could be found in the vanity, and left her alone.

Paige was leaning on the vanity taking slow, deep breaths when Isabella tapped on the door and entered again. "Paige, are you all right? Tom told me what happened. Little heathens!" She smiled apologetically. "Several of us have been victims of the little bull."

"I'm fine, really. I just have problems...each month... and my stomach's a little sore." Feeling nauseous, she asked if she might have a Coke. Isabella went to get one for her and returned with Victoria in tow. So much for an uneventful day!

"Paige, dear, I'm so sorry. Tom said Dimitri literally knocked you down! What can we do?" Victoria insisted she lie down on the sofa.

Paige complied, hoping that and the Coke would quell the nausea. They left her alone to rest, but it was only minutes before there was a knock on the door again, and this time it was Aunt Sophia who entered. How did one ever get used to this constant stream of people?

Sophia pulled a chair close to the sofa, sat down, and felt Paige's forehead. "Well, this is a fine way to treat a guest, isn't it?" Then, "So, you have a hard time with this monthly business, yes?"

News had to travel faster in this family than anything Paige had ever seen, and evidently no subject was considered off limits. "Yes, but Dom's friend, Dr. Rossini, gave me something to take and it helped tremendously. He said from now on things will be much easier."

Neither of them spoke for a few minutes, then Sophia asked, "So, what do you think of our Dominic?"

And Paige never knew what—whether it was something in the aunt's voice or what was in her own heart— that made her reply, "I love him." She hadn't intended to say this, but there it was.

Sophia merely nodded. "I see."

The aching in her abdomen, the still-present nausea, and the realization of what she had just said to this woman she had met only hours ago, were too much for Paige. She closed her eyes and laid one arm across her forehead.

"So you haven't told him?"

Turning to face the aunt, she answered in a slightly fretful tone, "No. Of course not."

"Maybe you should tell him, yes?" she prodded.

"I don't think so...I mean...it's awfully soon, isn't it?" She looked at the aunt, searching her face for the answer.

Sophia shrugged. "Will waiting change what is in your heart?"

"Never."

"How can you be so sure?"

Earnestly, Paige asked, "You know how we met?" Sophia nodded. "When he walked into the room, I knew. Immediately. I liked everything about him. The way he moved, the way he looked, the way he dressed, his voice, just *everything*. I know it sounds...it doesn't matter how it sounds. It's true. I just knew." She smiled at the memory. "I was so afraid he wasn't going to ask me out, but he did—the next night, and...and we've been together ever since."

"I see." The aunt eyed her, a smile playing at the corners of her mouth, and Paige waited. "Bella, shall I tell you something? Did you know our Dominic has never brought a woman home to meet us? Can you imagine that? In all these years? He's known a lot of women, but not one has he brought to us. I think you are very special to my nephew."

At that moment, Dominic, having heard what had happened, appeared. Standing over her, he looked concerned. "I hear Dimitri got you, Zucchero. Are you all right?"

"Yes, of course. Just resting a minute, that's all." What Sophia had told her made her pulse quicken. That he had brought her here today, it had to mean *something*, didn't it?

Sophia watched as her nephew approached Paige, his voice and his expression full of concern over the incident with Dimitri. Dominic knelt and kissed her, and one could not miss the obvious attraction the couple shared. Sophia's heart ached watching the two of them, but it was a welcome and long-awaited ache. This was the first step in fulfilling a prophecy.

Paige was hardly more than a child, but this was not a bad thing. In fact, under the circumstances, it was desirable. Her youth and inexperience touched Sophia. When the girl had spoken of her period, she was obviously embarrassed, two red spots appearing on the pale cheeks, and she had looked away. And Sophia thought this was good. Too many young women would say anything these days, and it did not set well with her. She had to smile, thinking of the girl's apparent misery over her feelings for Dominic. The agonies that accompanied young love!

Sophia had felt an immediate kinship with Paige. This was a sign, and she believed in signs. Others in the family had all but given up on the idea of a wife and children for Dominic, but she knew what *must* be *would* be. The nephew was the only one to carry on for Carlo—it was inevitable—it was Dominic's legacy. And now, this lovely girl would share in the legacy.

Eventually, after Paige had convinced them she was fine, everyone went to the dining room for coffee and dessert. Paige thought the raspberry and Amaretto cheesecake was the best she had ever eaten. When she praised it, she could see Victoria was flattered.

That evening it seemed to take an inordinate amount of time to say goodbye, but finally Dominic and Paige were on their way, and she breathed a sigh of relief.

"Tired, Sweetie?"

"Hmmm, a little maybe. But I had a great time. They're all wonderful."

"Despite the inquisition and the head-butting?" He smiled apologetically. "We seldom have a family gathering that doesn't include an accident or an incident. I guess it's the numbers. The odds are against us."

"They're all wonderful, Dom," she repeated. "And your aunt, she's special, isn't she?"

Fondly, he said, "She was certainly taken with you."

"Sometimes she called me Bella."

"That's a term of endearment." Then, "Where to now?"

It took her a moment to realize he was teasing her. "Well, I *don't* want to go home."

This had become a standing joke between them, and they both laughed.

She leaned across the seat, put her hand in his lap, and asked simply, "Okay?"

He nodded. She unzipped his pants and reached for him, then leaned down and took him in her mouth. She heard the sharp intake of his breath and felt him stiffen more each time she moved further down the shaft of his penis. She sucked him, licked him with her tongue, taking as much of him as far into her mouth as she could. He was a big man and this part of him was no exception.

His hand was on her head, his fingers kneading the back of her neck, and he groaned. "Baby, sit up now." This was the signal, but tonight she ignored it. Tonight was going to be different. She sucked gently as her fingers caressed him. Then, taking more of him into her mouth, she increased the intensity, sucking harder, harder. Suddenly, he pulled the car to the side of the road and shoved it into park.

With both hands, he grabbed her head, pushing it down as he thrust himself further into her mouth. Twice he said, "God, Baby," then, as he came, a loud, "Ahh...ahh...ahhh!"

She lay with her head still in his lap, swallowing repeatedly. It was the first time she had done this.

His fingers were combing gently through her hair. "Come here, Zucchero." And pulling her upright, he folded her in his arms and kissed her.

She pulled her skirt up, guided his hand between her legs. He slipped his fingers inside the lace panties and, finding his target, touched her knowingly. It was only a short time before she whispered, "Now! I'm coming...now!" He kissed her again, then set about putting his clothes in order. When she told him she wanted more, he smiled. "Let's go home, Sweetheart. The night's not over."

She seemed to always want him, no matter how often they made love. And they made love whenever the mood struck them. In the mornings, after work, in the evenings, in the middle of the night, and it was incredible. The things he did to her and had her do for him filled her head at all hours. He could be tender, gently coaxing her one minute, then demanding, wildly passionate the next. And, occasionally, even rough. And she loved it.

She loved the feel of his hands on her, loved having him inside her, fucking her. She could think of it that way now because he had taught her. It wasn't a word she would ever use in any other context, but when they were together, the rules changed—there were none—just whatever brought them pleasure. And nothing gave her more pleasure than pleasing him.

The Seventh Week

Paige was a Hamilton, and to a Hamilton, reserved from birth, few things were worse than unwanted attention.

She had always heard that troubles came in threes. This was one time in her life she believed it. First, there was the thing with her period and her parents showing up, then the embarrassing situation with Dimitri and all the attention that followed, and now this. Today was a special day, exactly seven weeks since they had met, and the fact that both families were now aware of them as a couple was something to be celebrated in her mind. But she awoke with a fever and sore throat. Her head ached. Come to think of it, she ached all over. She sat up on the side of the bed and felt even worse.

"You awake, Zucchero?" Dominic reached for her. She lay back down and turned to him. He kissed her. "Hey, what's this? You're hot as fire."

"I don't know. Flu, maybe." Her voice was hoarse with misery. "I feel awful."

He touched her arms and back. "You have a fever. Stay put, Sweetie. I'm calling Bernie."

———

Bernie stopped by on his way in that morning. He checked Paige and confirmed that she did indeed have the flu. He called in prescriptions for her and said he would see them later in the day

Dominic went to the office for a few hours, and Paige slept while he was gone. She hardly seemed to know when the doctor came by again that evening. Dominic was worried about her, but Bernie assured him she would be better soon, it would just take a few days. The doctor, who was off for a long weekend with his family, told Dominic to make sure she took her pills and drank plenty of fluids, then left.

Dominic stood looking down at her, in fitful sleep in his bed. Her face was flushed, and she mumbled incoherently at times. Every time he woke her, she would insist she was fine, then fall asleep again.

On instructions from Sophia and his mother, he got her up and into a tepid shower, made her drink some juice, and put her back to bed. It was close to midnight when he lay down with her.

Paige, coughing and tossing about restlessly, woke him at 2:40. She was still feverish and her gown was damp. He gave her aspirin and more juice, and they went to sleep again.

At five he awoke and realized she wasn't in bed. He checked the bathroom and found her asleep on the settee. Curled in a ball, she had pulled his bathrobe over her for cover. He put her back to bed and decided to make coffee, shower and dress. He was exhausted.

At seven he called Isabella and made arrangements for her to spend the day with Paige. Tomas would bring her and check on Paige while he was there.

They arrived at nine and sent Dominic on his way, telling him not to worry. It was Friday, and Tomas had a half day at the office. He would return around one and they would stay until Dominic was home again.

———

Isabella poured herself coffee, went to the living room, and watched television for a couple of hours until she heard Paige stirring.

She was surprised to find her up and attempting to get dressed. Well, sort of. The girl had pulled on a pair of jeans but was still wearing her nightshirt. When Isabella asked what she was doing, Paige replied that she had to go home, and she had to do it before Dominic asked her to go.

Isabella was puzzled by the comment. "Why would Dominic ask you to go home, dear?"

With all the wisdom of her twenty years and in the throes of flu and fever, she answered miserably, "Things keep happening. I'm sure he's tired of it. One thing after another. First Dr. Rossini, then my parents. They weren't supposed to come over, but they did. They never asked me. They just showed up. My father insulted Dominic."

Paige was on the floor now, and pulling her sneakers from under the bed. Wearily, she stood with the shoes in her hand, but made no move to put them on. "I wanted to make such a good impression with your family, but there was that embarrassing incident with Dimitri, and now this. I have to go home."

Isabella, trying not to laugh and at the same time attempting to make some sense of what the girl was telling her, said only, "Paige, think about it for a moment. Why would Dominic ask us to stay with you if he wanted to send you home? And why on earth would he introduce you to the family if he was going to stop seeing you?" Paige looked doubtful.

Then, taking another tack, and thinking it would help her see things in a different light, Isabella said, "I don't think you're being fair to Dominic, do you? Shouldn't you at least discuss this with him?"

The girl looked as though she had been slapped, and tears rolled down her face. Stunned by this development, Isabella put an arm around her and coaxed her toward the bed. "Oh, Paige, no, don't cry! I'm just trying to point out…look, you really aren't rational right now, dear. You're sick and that's why you're feeling this way. Don't you remember Dominic telling you he had to go to the office but he would return as soon as he could?"

She shook her head no, the tears coming in streams now.

"Please don't cry, Paige. Everything will be all right. You need to rest."

Tomas arrived in the midst of all this, appearing startled and more than a little concerned to find what was taking place. Isabella took him aside and explained briefly what had happened, whispering to her husband, "Talk to her. See if you can calm her."

Tomas's tone was matter-of-fact, but also reassuring. "Paige, if there's one thing I know about my brother-in-law, it's this: If he didn't want you with him, then you wouldn't be here. I also know he doesn't like other people making his decisions for him. Dominic would be very unhappy with us if he came home and found you gone."

Isabella said gently, "Paige, I thought you cared for Dominic."

"I love him more than anything in the world!" And with that, the dam broke. Paige flopped down on the bed and sobbed into a pillow. Isabella looked helplessly at her husband.

Tomas put his hand on her back now and said softly, "Paige, let's do this. Isabella will help you shower. You'll have something to drink, I'll give you your medicine, and you can rest until Dominic comes home. You're going to feel much better in a day or two. Okay? Can we do that?"

The girl nodded miserably, not looking at all convinced.

It was shortly after lunch when Dominic received the call from Tomas. "Can you talk?"

"Of course. Is everything all right there?"

"Maybe, maybe not. There's one upset young lady here."

"Paige?"

"That's the one."

"Tomas, what's going on?" This, with some annoyance. He did not like guessing games.

"Oh, I think it's mostly the fever, but I also think the girl's in love. Seems she might think you don't share those feelings."

"What?"

"I'm just saying...I thought you should know. She was going to leave until we convinced her otherwise."

"What the hell has happened since I left this morning?"

"Look, I'm just the messenger. Chances are this wouldn't be happening if she weren't sick, but she's one miserable little creature right now. I only know of one person who can make her feel better, so I called him. Only I didn't. Okay?"

After a long pause, Dominic said only, "Okay, thanks."

He managed to stay with it another hour, then adjourned the meeting until Wednesday of the following week. He went to his desk, unlocked a drawer, and took out a small metal case. What was going through her mind, and what had put her in such a state, he wondered? Toying with the box, he thought of what he would do, what he had been thinking about the past two weeks. Yes, it was time.

When he arrived at the apartment, Tomas and Isabella told him in more detail what had taken place. He thanked them for staying with her and sent them on their way. He would take care of her now.

He entered the darkened room, pulled a chair beside the bed, and studied the sleeping form of this lovely girl who had so changed his life in such a short time. As usual, strands of the long dark hair fell across her face as she slept, and he brushed them back with his fingertips, tucking them behind her ear. He leaned down and kissed the warm cheek. "Paige, wake up, Sweetheart."

She opened her eyes, but she was a little slow to focus. "Dom?"

"Yes. How are you feeling? Can you sit up and talk to me for a minute?" She struggled up, then sat there in silence, looking so serious and, at the same time, so vulnerable. Taking her hand, very gently he asked, "What is it, Baby? What's the matter?"

Tears seemed to come from out of nowhere and streamed down her face. "I love you so much I don't know what to do," was all she said, and the tears just kept pouring from the dark eyes. She made no attempt to wipe them.

No one had ever touched him the way she did. The swell of emotion that rose in him whenever he was with her, or just thinking about her, always surprised him. That she was smart and beautiful was a given, but there was more, a sense of goodness and decency about her, an inner beauty that was equal to the other. *And she loved him.*

"Well, then I think the thing for us to do is to get married and spend the rest of our lives together." It was not a question.

At this, she came to him, wrapped her arms around his neck, and buried her face in his shoulder. Sobbing in earnest now, she cried for so long he became concerned. He took out his handkerchief and wiped her eyes, her nose. "Is that a yes, Zucchero?" More tears. "Sweetheart, I'm getting worried. I need an answer. Do I have a yes?"

Finally, she smiled. "Yes." And she was back in his arms.

He held her for a long time. Then, after gently disengaging her, he sat her on the bed and wiped her face again. Her eyes never left his. He pulled his hand away just long enough to open the box and take out the ring. "I want to do this right, Sweetheart, but I must ask you, how important is it that I get down on one knee? I have to tell you it's not something I ever pictured myself doing, but for you...." This, teasingly, but she didn't smile, only shook her head slowly.

"No," she whispered.

"Ah, I owe you big time now, don't I?" He didn't have anything planned, so he said simply, "Paige, I love you, more than I ever knew I could love anyone. Will you marry me?" And without waiting for her response, he slipped the ring on her finger.

Blinking back another rush of tears, she said softly, "Yes. Yes." Then she was in his arms again.

She knew it was not a candlelit dinner with wine and music and her dressed to perfection. It was better than that and it meant so much more. Along with the day they met, Dominic's proposal was to be one of her most treasured memories.

They passed the rest of the evening with Paige sleeping more often than not, but by the next morning her fever had broken and she was better. When Dominic awoke, she was still in his arms.

"Hi." She put her hand on his cheek now, the way she did every morning, and lightly stroked the stubble of beard. "I love you, Dom."

"I love you." Holding her close, he whispered, "I'm not sure one lifetime is enough to spend with you, Zucchero."

Her heart was so full of love for him. She wanted to tell him she needed nothing more than to belong to him, to be everything he wanted in a wife, that her life had begun the day she met him, that every breath she took was special because of him. But she managed to say only, "I would do anything in the world for you, Dom. Anything."

"I know, Sweetheart." He buried his face in the fall of soft, dark hair and kissed the top of her head. "I know."

Dominic and Paige spent Friday and the weekend in the city so she could rest, but Dominic told her that at the first opportunity they would move most of her things to the Long Island house, and they would be staying there more often. He took advantage of the uninterrupted time together to talk to her about several things. He spoke of security and stressed what a priority it was with him and, therefore, must be with her. He hoped she wouldn't find the requirements too restrictive, but he wanted her to realize they were necessary and in place for good reason. He would go into this in greater detail later, but for now, could she please accept it and comply?

She never questioned him. "Of course, just tell me what I should do."

It was simple really. With the exception of family members, she was to go out only with him or be driven by Vincente or security personnel. He would arrange for someone to be available to take her where she needed to go at all times.

They had a lengthy conversation about his business. He explained there was far more than just the investment/acquisition/liquidation part with which she was familiar. In time, he would reveal everything to her in detail, but there was no hurry.

Did she want to continue working after they were married? He preferred she not, but it was up to her. Something could be arranged. She was adamant that she favored being a full-time wife. This was good—he was pleased.

They discussed the upcoming holidays. The following Thursday was Thanksgiving. They would announce their marriage plans then. He asked where she wanted to spend the day, knowing they were obligated to see both families in order to avoid conflict.

He left it to Paige, and she decided they should spend most of the day at the Gianellis and go to her parents' house that evening.

As they prepared for bed Sunday night, he watched as she stepped from the shower and smoothed lotion on her body. As she reached for her nightie, he took it from her and laid it aside. "Come here." He'd made a decision. He was going to take things a step further tonight.

A man with a voracious sexual appetite, he liked variety. He ran his hands over her body—her breasts, her tummy, and between her legs. He slipped his finger inside her, found her warm and slick. He placed his hands on her shoulders and gently pushed her down on her knees.

Her mouth closed around him. She knew what to do. After several minutes, he pulled her to her feet and led her to the bedroom.

Now he lay beside her and began touching her, caressing her everywhere. His mouth was on hers, then on her neck, her breasts, his tongue flicking around her nipples while he fingered her knowingly, skillfully. He took her to the edge, holding her tight as she spiraled off into ecstasy, once, twice.

Afterward, he kissed her, then whispered, "Turn over, Baby."

She lay on her stomach. He pulled two scarves from the bedside table and, taking her wrists, he tied them to the rails on the headboard. He kissed her neck and worked his way down her back. He slid his finger into her and drew the moisture toward her bottom, all the while using his tongue along the cleft of her buttocks. He slipped one hand under her, and his fingers found her and stroked her clit. She began to shift and squirm.

"Does it feel good, Sweetheart?"

She groaned. "Yes. So good." And with that, he slipped his middle finger into her bottom. He would push it in as far as he could, then not quite take it out, and do this while he continued to stroke her. He knew she was close now, focused only on what she was feeling. "Tell me, Baby, tell me when."

And she did.

He was excited, and couldn't wait any longer. He took his cock and rubbed it repeatedly in her, drawing more of the wetness to her bottom each time. He put his cock against the little opening, then pushed himself into her bottom. He heard her gasp. "It's okay, Sweetheart. Breathe. Breathe through your mouth." He saw her hands were gripping the rails now, and this fueled his desire.

"Come on, breathe. It makes it easier to take, Baby. Do it." She took a deep breath, then another, and she relaxed, just a little.

"That's it, Sweetheart, just like that." He worked his way up her slowly, and at the same time reached for her clit and began to stroke her again. As his finger found its target, she moaned...then squirmed, trying to pull away as he pushed himself deeper inside her. This excited him further. Pushing his cock all the way in, he couldn't hold back any longer and he began fucking her.

She cried out only once. God, her ass was so sweet, just like he had known it would be. "Hold it up, Baby, take it." He had waited as long as he could. She was right. It was like the night exploding into a thousand pieces.

Moments later, he pulled himself from her, untied her wrists and wrapped her in his arms. He kissed her over and over again. "Are you all right, Baby?"

"Yes."

"Do you remember what I told you that first night?"

"Yes."

"It still applies."

"We're not doing anything I don't want to do. I promise." Then, " I love you so much, Dom."

"I love you, Angel."

Dominic was drifting off. Paige snuggled against him and, ignoring the throbbing ache in her lower body, fell into a dreamless sleep.

FIVE

Thanksgiving week was an eventful time for them. Paige was in the office for a meeting on Monday, and her ring was immediately noticed. First questions, then rumors flew. Before she left that afternoon, Henry Carson asked to speak to her. Yes, Dominic had given her the ring. No, they had not announced their plans as yet. They intended to tell their families Thanksgiving Day. She hoped he would take this as an indication to keep the information in confidence until then. Carson cleared his throat and said he felt compelled to say something, if she would indulge him a moment. She nodded, guardedly, as if anticipating what was coming.

"Paige, I've known you and your family a long time. This seems so...out of character for you. Are you sure about it? This is an older man...much older than you. You've only known him a few weeks. When it comes right down to it, what do you really know about him?"

Her expression had changed from polite to unreadable, and she gave him a penetrating look. Softly, she asked, "What are you suggesting, Mr. Carson?"

"I'm worried that you don't know what you're getting into, dear."

"What I'm getting into?"

It occurred to him that she had matured substantially since meeting Gianelli. She was more confident, not the subdued, unquestioning young woman she had once been. "I'm afraid I've offended you, dear, without meaning to, of course. I just felt I should express my concern over the matter. Your father already holds us somewhat responsible for this...this situation."

She was silent, her gaze unwavering. When she finally spoke, there was something in her manner that for all the world reminded him of Gianelli. "I can't be offended by your concern for me, Mr. Carson. Quite the opposite. I appreciate it. I really do. It's unfortunate if what you say about my father is true. I'm sorry he put you in that position. I hope, in time, he'll be more accepting of our relationship, but of course this is entirely up to him. I had planned to continue working until Dominic and I were married. If this creates a problem for the firm—"

Carson was quick to interrupt her. "Of course not." He paused. "Are you sure you want to cut your career short, Paige? A promotion to management is easily within your reach before too long."

"Thank you, but I'm sure. We've discussed it and made our decision." She stood and extended her hand to him. "Thank you for your concern, Mr. Carson."

Paige found Vicente waiting to take her to the apartment. She laid her head back on the cushioned seat of the limo and closed her eyes.

So this was how it was going to be. Well, people could think what they would. She didn't care. Nothing was going to spoil her happiness. She was going to marry the man she loved, and she loved Dominic Gianelli. She was glad they were spending most of Thanksgiving Day with his family. She knew they would be accepting. No, more than that, they would be thrilled about the marriage. It would be nice to be with people who would celebrate the occasion before she had to face her own family.

When they arrived, Manetti appeared and took her up to the apartment. In the elevator, Paige asked after his family, and he answered politely but did not pursue conversation. This was going to take some getting used to, but she would do it.

Dominic was waiting for her. "There you are, Zucchero." He embraced Paige and gave her a long kiss.

When he pulled away, she held onto him, saying, "Not so fast."

"Ah, so you missed me." He kissed her again.

"Very much."

Over dinner she told him about the conversation with Henry Carson. He expressed no surprise and said only that she shouldn't let it upset her. People would be more accepting in time.

Taking a sip of her wine, she shrugged and smiled. "They can or they can't. It makes no difference to me. I'm all for them minding their own business and not ours."

"Touché." He hoped, for her sake, that her family would at least be gracious when they announced their plans.

"Dom, it occurred to me today we haven't set a date."

"I've been thinking about it. Let's say December. Is that all right with you?"

She was obviously thrilled. "Yes, it only takes a week or so to get the license, I think."

This startled him; then he laughed. "Sweetheart, not next month. December of next year."

The smile disappeared and she said nothing.

"Paige?"

"Yes?"

"What is it?"

"Nothing. I just...well, that's an awfully long time to wait, isn't it?" She was toying with her food now, her eyes and her attention focused on her plate.

"Not really, and you have a lot to do, my love."

She looked at him now, questioningly.

"You have a wedding to plan."

"Oh."

"Paige?" He was trying not to laugh. She looked so serious he was sure it would offend her if she thought he was amused. "Are you upset, Zucchero?"

"No." The food had now traveled half the circumference of the plate. He took the fork from her and laid it down. "Come here."

She came around the table and stood in the circle of his arms. "Okay, Miss Hamilton, let's talk about what has to happen before we get married. You go first."

"We have to get blood tests and a license?" It was a question.

"Yesss. Eventually we do. But a lot has to happen before we do that. Having been through my sisters' weddings and several others, I think there are things like," and he ticked them off methodically, "deciding on a church, best man, maid of honor, flower girls, ring bearers, ushers, groomsmen, bridesmaids, their attire, flowers, cake, and on and on. Does any of this ring a bell, Sweetheart?"

She shrugged.

He pulled her onto his lap. "Well, I have to think about this. I ask this beautiful woman to marry me. She says yes. I give her a ring. But now she's mad at me."

"I'm not mad," she said, rather grudgingly.

"I don't know, Zucchero. I think you are."

"I'm not. It's just such a long time! Why do we have to wait?"

"Because I don't want to deprive you of anything, Paige. Do you understand? There will be enough opposition to this marriage. You know that, don't you?"

She nodded solemnly. "But I don't care."

"I care, Sweetheart. This should be a special time for you, a happy time. It's a lot of work planning a wedding, but it should be fun for you too. I want you to have the experience, Paige, the parties, the showers, everything."

Again, she nodded. "But what if all that doesn't matter to me, Dom? What if I don't care about those things?"

"I think, given time, you will. Okay? Can you trust me on this? Nothing is going to change. We'll be together just like we have been this past two months. Someday you'll want to tell our children about our wedding. Right? Wouldn't you like to have something to show them other than a license? Hmmm?"

She was thinking. A little smile tugged at the corners of her mouth. "Well, I guess so."

"Okay, then. It's settled."

Paige had noticed that the Gianellis dressed for all occasions, and wore casual attire only on Saturday and sometimes Sunday afternoons. For Thanksgiving Day, she wore an ivory wool sweater dress with long sleeves and a heavy gold chain-link belt. Dominic whistled his approval. He looked so handsome in a dark gray suit, white shirt, and striped tie, which was black and silver with occasional touches of red.

She sat snuggled against him in the car. The scent of his aftershave filled the air, and when she kissed him, he tasted of toothpaste and his cigar. She wanted him. Now. She was never surprised at the extent of the sensuality between them, or of how accepting she was of all aspects of their relationship. He was the only man she had ever known, the only man to ever have touched her. So the things he did, what he expected her to do, were never objectionable to her. She enjoyed their lovemaking, all of it. Even this newest thing. They had done it twice now, and she could tell how much he liked it. And it wasn't without pleasure for her, he made sure of that. It was just different and it hurt, especially at first, but eventually it began to feel good too. She knew she would never refuse him anything.

Thinking about these things, she felt her face flush, and she had that feeling that always started in her breasts and went down to "there."

She knew Dominic had been watching her. She reached for his hand and, taking it in hers, slipped it under her dress, and placed it between her legs.

He seemed surprised, but pleased, and said, "*Now* I know what you've

been thinking about."

She put her mouth to his ear and whispered, "Will you?"

"Will I what?"

"You know."

"I know, but I want you to say it. Tell me what you want. And look at me when you say it."

She put her arms around his neck and kissed him, then she eyed him provocatively and said, "I want you to make me come."

He slipped his hand into her panties and put his finger inside her. He held her close to him, kissing her cheek, her ear, her neck, all the while touching and massaging that sweet spot that brought her such pleasure. He knew her body so well, every inch of it, and he knew exactly what to do to excite and satisfy her.

She was so close, right on the edge. She tensed, holding her breath, wanting to go over it, when he whispered, "You're trying too hard, Baby. It will happen, just let it happen. Breathe, just breathe." She took a breath and the feeling subsided momentarily, then began to build, again taking her to the edge. Another breath and the same thing, but each time it was sweeter, almost unbearable. Then, finally, she was *there*. A little moan escaped her lips. "Oh, oh, Dom." And her body quivered briefly, then was still.

He kissed her, long and hard. "Will that get you through until tonight?"

She smiled, feeling her face grow warm and flushed. "I'm ready to go back home."

He laughed appreciatively. "We'll have a special night, okay?"

"Yes." She was sure it would be.

They arrived at the Gianellis shortly before noon. There seemed to be people everywhere. Paige counted forty-two including Dominic and herself. She was introduced to cousins and Victoria's sister and her family, as well as friends of the older grandchildren.

Five tables were set for dinner and several others for serving. There were five turkeys, one for each table, a multitude of side dishes and so many desserts they could have opened a bakery. Victoria dispatched Paige for more wine glasses from atop a buffet, then asked if she would like to do the napkins.

Isabella watched as Paige expertly folded the napkins and tucked them into each glass. "Very nice, Paige. Where did you learn to do that?"

The girl just smiled and gave a slight shrug of her shoulders. "I think Molly may have shown me." Then she added, "She helps at our house, with cooking and things, and with my mother when she isn't well." She almost never mentioned her mother.

"I see." It was then Isabella noticed the ring. Putting an arm around Paige, she whispered, "Tell me about this beautiful ring, dear."

Eyes shining, Paige whispered back, "Dom asked me to marry him. He asked me last Friday. We're telling everyone today."

Isabella hugged her and asked if they could tell Victoria. Paige nodded.

"Mama, come here, quick!" Victoria came rushing back from the dining room, her expression one of concern.

"Look, Mama, look at the ring!" Isabella beamed, holding Paige's hand out for her mother to inspect. Paige looked very happy.

Victoria hugged and kissed her. "This is wonderful! You rascals, both of you. Why have you not told us?"

"It only happened last Friday, and we wanted to tell everyone at once, so we waited until today."

"When will you be married? Have you set a date?"

Paige looked somber. "Dom says December, next December."

Victoria and Isabella shared a look, then Isabella asked, "Is that bad, dear?"

"It's just such a long time to wait, that's all. Dom says there's a lot to do."

Victoria responded after a moment. "Well, it does take time to prepare for a wedding. And it will pass quickly, dear."

Paige nodded, then said that if they would excuse her, she wanted to tell Sophia before they made their announcement at dinner.

Sophia was playing solitaire in the small sitting area off the living room, where Dominic had first introduced Paige to her.

Upon seeing her, she smiled and said, "Bella, how pretty you look today."

"Thank you. They'll be calling us soon, but I wanted to say hello and tell you something before we go in to eat." Sophia looked at the girl, whose face was radiant with happiness. Her cheeks were pink against the pale complexion, her brown eyes aglow. This could be but one thing.

Paige dropped to her knees and laid her left hand in Sophia's lap. "Dom asked me to marry him."

Deciding to tease her a bit, she asked, "And what was your answer?"

Paige gave her a big smile, then she bit her lower lip. "I said yes."

Sophia put her arms around her and hugged her gently. "You see, things do work out."

"He's making me wait a year though, Sophia." She was serious now.

"A year?"

"A year. It's a long time to wait, don't you think?"

"If Dominic says a year, Bella, he has his reasons. Has he not told you?"

"Well, yes."

"And?"

Paige sighed and there was a tinge of resignation in her voice. "And I guess we'll be getting married next December."

After they had eaten, Xavier rose and asked that everyone remain seated, saying that it was his understanding an important announcement was to be made, at which point Dominic stood and revealed that he had asked Paige to marry him and she had accepted. There was cheering and applause from all the tables, then many hugs and kisses from everyone. Wine was poured and there were several toasts. Then more wine, music and dancing, and still more wine.

By the time they left to go to her parents, Paige seemed to be feeling quite relaxed. When she leaned her head on his shoulder and closed her eyes, Dominic laughed. "Oh no, you don't! I need you alert and sober, Zucchero. Do we need to stop for coffee?" She wrapped her arms around his neck and kissed him fervently. He decided they definitely needed to stop for coffee.

They waited until she had drunk it before proceeding to the Hamiltons. This did not prevent her from falling asleep on the way there, causing him to wonder just how much wine she'd had. He woke her a few minutes before they arrived. She assured him she was fine, just a little tired. She brushed her hair and reapplied her lipstick before getting out of the car.

He would be meeting both sets of grandparents today and Martha's sister and her husband, as well as all the nieces and nephews. It was almost six when they arrived. Paige took him around and introduced to him to the grandparents, exceptionally polite people who had little to say. One had to notice they were a family who stood on formality. So far, the only really close relationships appeared to be between Paige and her brothers.

While everyone was in close proximity, Paige said she had an announcement to make, then told them that Dominic had proposed and she had accepted. It grew very quiet. Paige finally broke the silence by saying lightly, "Well, sometimes people say things like 'congratulations...'"

Julia was the first to speak, then the others followed suit. It was not the clamoring approval they had experienced at his parents, but at least they weren't throwing stones, he thought.

Matt's wife, Bitsy, asked if they had set a date.

"Yes, December of next year." At this, her father nodded affirmatively in Dominic's direction, signifying his approval.

Last Friday, before leaving his office, he had called Paul Hamilton to advise him of what was to take place. Hamilton's displeasure was obvious, but in the end he asked only that the wedding not take place immediately, that they wait at least six months. Dominic had agreed to this stipulation.

The sisters-in-law showed pleasure and excitement for Paige, and he was gratified by this. Her brothers shook his hand and the grandfathers followed suit. Even Martha, a bit giddily, said "Well, Dominic, a son-in-law—this will be something new for us!" He smiled and kissed her cheek.

For Paige's sake, he hoped that over time he would come to enjoy being around her family. They appeared to be good and decent people, for the most part, but he sensed an undercurrent of something dark, something he couldn't quite put his finger on. Maybe it was his imagination, but he didn't think so.

He and Paige managed to get through dinner without anyone noticing they didn't have much appetite after the meal at his parents. The evening was pleasant enough. He fielded several questions about work and his family, his childhood, and where he had gone to school.

After dinner, most of them congregated in the family room and separated into small groups. Paige excused herself for a moment and went to put on some music. Elvis's "I Can't Help Falling in Love with You" filled the room. She came to him, smiling. "Dance, please." He complied.

As they danced, she whispered the words of the song to him, never taking her eyes from his. And he knew, for her, he would be tolerant of the family, or as much so as possible. Her love for him was unmistakable. She was worth any effort.

When "Good Luck Charm" began to play, Andrew cut in, and Dominic stepped back. Julia joined him, and they watched as Paige and her brother went through some intricate steps. "Surprised?" Julia was smiling.

"Somewhat, yes. I knew Paige could dance."

"They all do and they're quite good. I know how you feel though. They're so serious, you don't think about them being people who know how to have fun. You'll like them better as you get to know them."

He merely nodded. He was watching as Andrew pulled Paige close and kissed her forehead as they danced. Julia saw it too and smiled. "They're quite a pair, Dominic. She's like his daughter. He took care of her from the time she was just a baby. He's always looked out for her." Dominic wondered about this comment, but said nothing.

Then, hesitantly, Julia asked, "Dominic, has Paul told you anything at all?"

"About what?"

"About Paige and Martha. The whole family really. What they went through."

"No."

"You need to talk to him. He won't like it, I'm sure. They never speak of it. They like to think it's behind them, and in a sense, it is. But there are things you should know. She's special, Dominic."

He smiled. "I know that."

"I know you think you do, but you really don't." She must have sensed his puzzlement because she smiled apologetically. "It's just not for me to tell you. You should hear it from Paul, but if he won't talk to you, then you need to find out on your own. You strike me as a man of unlimited resources. Use them if you must."

"Couldn't Paige tell me?"

Julia looked alarmed. "Dominic, please, never say anything to Paige. She doesn't remember. At least, that's what everyone believes. I hope it's true. I hope she has no memory of it."

He had no idea what she was talking about, but evidently it was crucial as far as Julia was concerned. "Then I won't ask her."

Paige was making her way toward them. She had danced with all three brothers, then her father. She looked happy. The music started up again and Dominic took her in his arms. She pressed close to him and whispered, "Do you have any idea how much I love you?"

"I think I do, Sweetheart." He kissed her. "And you, Miss Hamilton, do you know how much I love you?"

"No, tell me again, please." This, with a big smile.

When the song had ended they joined Drew and Julia, and the four went to find drinks, then joined Paul and Martha and the grandparents in the living room.

Julia began telling a story about the first time she came home from college with Andrew to meet his family.

Paige groaned. "Not that one, please, Jules!"

Everyone laughed.

"Drew had told me several times he was anxious for me to meet his sister. I was picturing someone who was at least a teenager, since he was twenty-two. We pulled into the drive and I saw this little girl standing on the porch. Drew had the biggest grin on his face. That's when I realized it was his sister. Paige came running toward the car, and Drew jumped out and grabbed her. Then she noticed me. She was *not* thrilled."

With this, she and Paige smiled at each other. Paige leaned her head on Dominic's shoulder, and he put his arm around her as the story continued.

"Drew introduced us, telling her I was his special friend. He asked her to take me to the house while he got our bags. She wasn't happy about it, but she had beautiful manners."

Parents and grandparents were nodding their heads.

"I still remember what she wore that day. Jeans and a white shirt with an outline of a small pale pink horse embroidered on the front. White tennis shoes, socks with white lace peeking out from under the jeans. Her hair was pulled to the side with a pink and white bow. She gave me a tour of the house and showed me to my room, emphasizing that I was staying in the *guest* room. I don't think she planned on me ever returning."

Everyone was laughing now. "It was almost time for dinner. Matt and John held her hand as they came down those stairs—the boys in suits and ties and this little doll in a dress with a black velvet top and a dropped waist. The skirt had three tiers of white crepe ruffles, each ruffle trimmed in black velvet. She was wearing white lace tights and black velvet shoes and had a black velvet ribbon in her hair."

Dominic noticed that Martha listened as if she were hearing the story for the first time.

"Anyway, we sat down to dinner. Drew put her in a dining chair with a big dictionary on the seat to accommodate her size. It was very quiet. As dinner was being served, Paige turned to me and in the most serious voice asked if we'd had a pleasant drive and had I enjoyed the scenery, that fall was such a lovely time of year. I was so surprised to hear a child say something like that, I just sat there."

They were all laughing again. Paul added that they had always treated her as an adult, therefore she acted like one even at that age.

"I managed to say, yes, thank you. Then, she said. 'I trust it was uneventful?' Can you imagine? Not even five yet. And Dominic, I have the pictures that I took that day. I'll show them to you sometime if you'll remind me."

"I'd like that."

Before they left, Paige managed to ask Martha and the sisters-in-law if they, along with Victoria and Dominic's sisters, would help plan the wedding. All seemed pleased and excited at the prospect.

Julia took Dominic aside briefly and said she hoped she had not alarmed him. There were just things he needed to know. For instance, she thought the asthma attacks had something to do with the early years and the situation with Martha.

This was news to Dominic. "Paige has asthma?"

Julia sighed audibly. "Honestly, this family never tells anyone anything."

"What don't we tell?" This, from Paige, who had collected her coat and purse and was pulling on her gloves.

Julia said, almost accusingly, "You've never told Dominic you have asthma?"

It was Paige's turn to be annoyed. "Jules! I haven't even thought about it. I don't remember the last time I had an attack. It's been that long."

"Still, he needs to know, just in case. Do you still keep your inhaler with you and your kit?"

It was coming to the end of a long day, and even Paige seemed short on patience. "They're at my apartment, if I need them."

Seeing her agitation, Dominic remained quiet. Before they left, though, Julia spoke to Drew, and he gave Dominic two kits, each containing an inhaler and an injection to be given in an emergency.

In the car, Paige turned to him immediately. "Dom, I wasn't trying to keep anything from you. It's just been so long since I've had a problem with the asthma, I never thought to tell you."

"It's fine, Zucchero, don't worry about it."

Her annoyance was still evident. "I am *so* ready to go home!"

"Come here."

She slid across the seat and into his arms, remaining there all the way home.

And the night held exactly what he had promised earlier.

Today, December 1, was Dominic's birthday. Paige had two gifts for him. One was already at his parents' house to be opened at the party, and one, more personal, she wanted to give to him when they were alone. The antique gold cigar lighter, a collector's item, was engraved with his initials and the date. And it was something from her that he could carry with him at all times

The model of his sailboat, *The Mallorca*, had been delivered to the Gianelli's. It was beautiful, made of wood and metal, exquisitely crafted down to the last detail. She had put a lot of thought into the gifts and was pleased with her choices.

When Dominic went into the city for a few hours, she stayed

behind, and enjoyed taking her time to dress for the evening. She had decided to wear a long- sleeved, off-the-shoulder black taffeta dress. It was one of his favorites.

Paige was in her bra and panties when Dominic came home.
"I like that outfit."
"Really? I was thinking of changing."
"Never do that, promise me."
Laughing, she said, "I'm losing track of this conversation." She pulled on her stockings and reached for her dress. "Zip me up, please. Then I want to give you one of your presents."
"One of them?" As he closed the zipper and fastened the hook and eye, she stepped into her black heels.
Standing behind her, his hands on her shoulders, he kissed her bare neck. The bodice and sleeves of the dress were tight, the skirt tiered. It fit her like a dream. She was stunning, and she was his.
Opening a dresser drawer, she retrieved a small, beautifully wrapped box. She handed it to him. "Happy birthday, Darling."
He opened the card, which read, "*To Dom, All my love, All my life. Happy Birthday.*"
He removed the ribbon and paper and found a small wooden case. Inside, on a bed of red velvet, was a beautiful, gold cigar lighter. There was intricate scroll work around the top and bottom rims of the lighter. In a small rectangle near the base on both sides were his initials, "DXG," and on the bottom of the lighter, 12/01/80. It was exquisite. *Where* had she found this?
"Now you'll have something with you at all times that I gave you. A little reminder of me."
He smiled down at her. "Thank you, Sweetheart. It's wonderful. You're sure you want me to use this for everyday?"
"Definitely."
"You're the boss." And he replaced the lighter in his pocket with the new one.

It was a fun night at the Gianelli house. As always, there was enough food to feed a small country, and an abundance of wine and liquor. After dinner, the furniture was pushed back to the walls in the family room and everyone danced. The music, spanning at least thirty years, ranged from the McGuire Sisters to the Beatles. Paige danced with Xavier and Tomas a couple of times and once with Bernie Rossini, but the rest of the time only with Dominic. She never tired of dancing with him. It was close to midnight when they served the cake, an elaborate three-tiered affair that was as delicious as it was pretty. Then it was time to open his gifts.

There was a set of wine goblets from his parents, and Paige was touched because they were like those of Victoria's she had openly admired several times. Connie and Mario gave him a box of imported cigars; Jackie and Richard, a windbreaker. From Bernie came a set of black lava ashtrays from Hawaii and matching coasters. Aunt Sophia gave him a leather-bound calendar and appointment book with a pen and pencil set. From the nieces and nephews, came an assortment of men's cologne and after-shave and handkerchiefs. Finally, there was nothing left except the gift from Paige.

Opening it, Dominic said, "Well, what have we here?" It had been wired to the bottom of the crate for shipment, and Poppa and Mario helped cut the box away from the boat. The model stood forty-two inches at its highest point and was fifty-three inches long. The details were exquisite, the sails and rigging identical to the actual boat. The room was quiet except for some soft exclamations. Paige realized she was holding her breath.

Finally, Dominic said, "It's magnificent, Paige. Thank you."

"I'm glad you like it." She felt a little awkward. Everyone remained silent, just watching them. She found herself stating the obvious. "It's supposed to be a replica of *The Mallorca*."

He nodded, still examining the boat. The others had now gathered to get a closer look, commenting on the expertly crafted model.

Isabella told her it was a perfect gift, and asked what made her think of it. Paige could only smile and shrug. "I don't know. I just kept trying to think of something that would be meaningful, something he didn't already have."

During the ride home, Dominic was quiet. Finally, Paige asked, "Is everything okay?"

He patted her hand. "Yes. I'm just annoyed that I can't think of an appropriate way to thank you. Those are remarkable gifts, Paige."

"I think I know how you feel. I felt the same way the day you proposed. About my ring, I mean. It's beautiful and I love it, but I was overwhelmed by…all of it. I wanted so much to tell you what was in my heart, how much you mean to me." She looked away, turning shy, but continued softly. "But that day, the words just wouldn't come.

"I think with some people, it's hard for them to accept anything, especially something meaningful from someone they love. Giving a gift is easy, and the joy you experience in giving it is so rewarding. But accepting is…different. I think you and I are like that, a little different when it comes to being on the receiving end." She paused. "If that makes any sense at all."

He reached for her, and she scooted over next to him and put her head on his shoulder. "Sophia's right, Sweetheart, you *are* an old soul. Tell you what. The way you feel about your ring? That's how I feel about the boat and the lighter."

"You're welcome, Darling."

Upstairs, they showered and readied themselves for bed. Paige reached into a drawer for one of his tee shirts and put it on. He watched, both pleased and amused with her familiarity, that already she considered this her home.

By the time she had brushed her teeth, he was in bed.

Pulling her to him, he groaned. "I'm exhausted, Babe."

"Your birthday lasted most of the night." Paige glanced at the clock. "As a matter of fact, it's lasted into the next day." She kissed him and whispered, "Turn over and I'll rub your back."

And doing so, he said tiredly, "You don't have to say that twice."

She rubbed his neck and shoulders, taking her time, kneading the tension from him. She worked her way down his back and his legs, then spent several minutes rubbing each foot. Finally, she lay down and pulled the covers over them, snuggling against him, her breath soft on his neck as he fell asleep.

When he awoke the next morning, he was tired and his head ached. Paige was sprawled almost crossways in the bed now, a tangle of sheets and pillows and dark hair. He kissed her, but she didn't stir. It was then he noticed the heating pad tucked low against her abdomen. She had started her period.

In the bathroom, her pills were set out on the vanity beside a half-filled glass of water. She would sleep most of the day, he was certain. He showered and shaved and went downstairs.

Paige, at some point, had already made coffee, and there was a bottle of aspirin sitting beside the two mugs. He shook out three tablets, then, coffee in hand, went outside and lit a cigar. It was cold, but there was no wind and the sun was out, a pretty morning. There was a time when he might have stayed as long as an hour there on the porch, drinking coffee, enjoying a smoke, planning his day. But after a few minutes, he felt restless and went back inside. It didn't take him long to realize what was wrong. He missed her.

Paige was still sleeping soundly. After deciding this would be an opportune time take care of some unfinished business, he freshened his coffee and went to his office to call Julia. He asked her for information regarding what they had discussed the previous week. She gave him names of doctors, hospitals, contacts at St. Agnes and, after some hesitation, said he should check the records of the Long Island police and sheriff's departments. "Did you speak to Paul?"

"No, I decided to make inquiries on my own first." He thanked her, saying he would keep what she had told him in strictest confidence. Then he called Rudolfo Santoro, his attorney. He gave him the names of the parties involved, along with the information Julia had provided, and told him he wanted to know everything he could possibly find out about Martha Grace Hamilton and her daughter Catherine Paige Hamilton, and as soon as possible.

After making several calls, he went to check on Paige again. It never occurred to him to wonder about his inclination to take care of her, though he had never done this before, not for anyone. He was a man who accepted who he was, and was not prone to introspection on any level. Always, he did what he had to do. But Paige had brought another dimension to his life. She fulfilled him, made him whole. Sophia called her his gift.

She lay wrapped in a quilt, on her back now, one arm thrown across her forehead, the other across her stomach. Her face was warm and her hairline damp. He sighed, knowing she had the heating pad on high again, and he reset it, turning it to low once more.

Looking down at her, he thought how he knew her so well already. Every inch of her body, down to the little mole on her left shoulder blade, he knew and loved. She was quiet by nature, but the two of them could talk for hours when it suited them, or they could sit watching television or a movie without a word and both be comfortable with this.

That was it, really—they were happy together, comfortable, content. He had found with her what had eluded him, what had been missing in his life. He hoped she would be happy as his wife. Her happiness was important to him. Her life would change, but maybe not so much that she would find it restrictive.

She shopped for apparel mostly through catalogs, which had both pleased and surprised him. "No, I'm not a mall rat," she had told him. "Besides, I find more things I like in the catalogs, and it's not half the hassle." She liked to swim. That was easy. He had pools at each residence. As for her dancing, she liked to go to the studio and work out. Unknown to her, he planned to have mirrors and a barre installed in a spare bedroom at this house and at Villa Disanti, in Salerno.

Maybe it *wouldn't* be too confining for her. She was a pleaser, but he didn't want to take advantage of this any more than he had to. She never complained about anything. It was not in her temperament to whine or nag.

Well, there was one exception: the year-long engagement. At every opportunity, she made her objection known. This amused him no end. She could work it casually into any conversation, and she was a persistent little thing.

He would not change his mind, but he listened patiently to her whenever she broached the subject, her latest idea being the month of June. She could understand waiting a few months, but why a year? What about June? People got married in June. As a matter of fact, there were more weddings in June than in any other month. The stubbornness he had recognized early on had evinced itself several times of late.

The year was necessary, though, partly because of what he had promised her father, but mostly because he wanted her to have time to adjust to the things that would be required of her. He wanted her to know his family and be comfortable with them.

There were anomalies in Paige's relationships with others that had puzzled him at first. He had noticed she would seek out Sophia anytime they were at the house, and she seemed at ease with his mother and Isabella. Jackie and Connie, however, still overwhelmed her a bit, and she was very quiet around his father and Tomas, Mario, and Richard. He finally decided that the lack of a mother, a real mother, in Paige's life had driven her to brave unknown territory with the older women in his family, who did, after all, "mother" her incessantly.

Standing over her, watching her in innocent sleep, he was awash in emotion. He thought of how they shared a love of music and of how she would dance with him, often whispering the words of a song to him. The years between them seemed significant only on the calendar. Bending to kiss her, he whispered, "I love you."

She stirred a little and turned on her side. The phone rang, and he hurried to answer, hoping it wouldn't wake her. It was Tomas. He and Is thought they might like to join them for dinner. Dominic explained that Paige wasn't feeling well, thanked them, and said perhaps another time.

That evening they ate dinner, watched a movie, then played chess until bedtime. Thursday and Friday would be busy days he told her, but they would spend the weekend on the boat and do some sailing and fishing.

Saturday, aboard *The Mallorca*, they had just finished lunch and were rigging their fishing gear again. They weren't having any luck, but didn't care. Paige walked to the bow of the boat and stood, silently watching the waves in the navy water. It was cold, but sunny, a beautiful day. After a while, she ventured, "Dom, I've been thinking about something."

He wasn't surprised. But he said only, "Yes?"

"You know, this thing about waiting so long?"

"Yes." He knew!

"Well, waiting isn't going to change what's in my heart, Dom. What's in *our* hearts." This, earnestly.

"Exactly, my love, exactly!"

He could tell from her expression she realized that, while trying to make her point, she had somehow made his.

She was quiet for a spell, then said softly, "I'm no match for you, am I, Dom?"

He had to smile, but held back his laughter. "No, but you are a worthy contender, my love, and you *do* keep me on my toes."

She stood looking out at the water until he said, "I thought we were fishing."

She came and sat in the chair beside him, still silent. Finally, he spoke. "You know, Sweetheart, as much as I enjoy your innovative thinking and sparring with you about the wedding date, I think we've spent all the time on it we need to spend, okay?"

"Okay."

"You mean that's it?" he said teasingly.

"Of course."

"It's settled?"

"Yes."

"Why am I thinking this was much too easy?"

"I don't know. All you had to do was say so, Dom." Her face was the picture of innocence. "Do I at least get to choose the day?"

He would give her this one. "You do."

"Okay, then, December first."

"My birthday?"

"Yes." And she stated this so firmly, the corners of his mouth twitched, but he managed to hide his amusement.

"December first it is, then."

"Dom?"

"Yes?"

"I've decided on a church. Well, maybe not the exact church itself. I'll need help with that, but I want us to be married in the Catholic Church."

"Are you sure?"

"Yes, I'm sure." Then, "Dom?"

Patiently, he answered, "Yes, love?"

"You *are* Catholic, aren't you?"

He smiled now. "Technically, Paige, yes. I'm Catholic."

"Okay. And your whole family is Catholic, right?"
"That's right, Sweetheart."
"I thought I would talk to Aunt Sophia about it, about the church."
"That's fine, Paige, but I want it to be your decision. Okay?"
"Yes."

December was passing quickly. Christmas was Paige's favorite holiday. She never tired of the lights and decorations, the music, everything it entailed. For Dominic's gift she had chosen an elaborate set of instruments for the *Paige One*. Painstakingly, she selected gifts for his family and her own. By mid-December her list was almost complete:

>Dom-Got It!!!
>Poppa - humidor
>Victoria - crystal pitcher and platter
>Isabella, Connie, and Jackie - gift certificates for spa weekend
>Tomas, Mario and Richard - Yankees season tickets
>Nieces - charm bracelets and personalized Christmas ornaments
>Nephews - gift certificates to Sharper Image and wallets
>Aunt Sophia - antique gold cross
>Dad - Ducks Unlimited jacket
>Drew, Matt and John - antique chess boards
>Jules, Anne and Bitsy - spa gift certificates and Christmas ornaments
>Nieces – custom-made dolls matched to each girl's hair color, eyes, etc.
>Nephews - baseball jackets from their favorite teams
>Grandfathers - windbreakers
>Molly - robe and slippers, favorite candy

> Grandmothers - jewelry boxes and pins
> Vincente - driving gloves and raincoat, tea set for
>   his wife
> Manetti/Buscliano - gloves and designer
>   sunglasses, cheesecake assortment
> Charlie - box of imported cigars, candy for wife
> Mother - ?

It was always hard for Paige to choose a gift for her mother. Even cards were difficult. She was rather ambivalent about the woman. She didn't like her and she didn't dislike her. She knew Martha was her father's wife and her mother, but she didn't know her, not really.

They were very formal with one another, always had been. A few times, when she was a teenager, her mother had tried to be conspiratorially girlish with her—that was how she thought of it—wanting to plan slumber parties, dances and such. It had made Paige uncomfortable. She had never had that kind of relationship with any girl or woman. Even the concept was foreign to her.

When Dominic saw the gift list, he was touched that she had included Vincente and Manny and Buscliano. It was so like her he wasn't even surprised. Noting the question mark by Martha's name, he suggested to her that maybe flowers delivered monthly would be nice. She said it sounded like a good idea to her, and wrote it in.

Dominic was anxious to hear back from Santoro, who was still gathering information. He could not guess what the files would reveal and would not try.

SIX

Christmas 1980

There was a party planned for Saturday, December 20. The Gianelli and the Hamilton families were to meet. The dinner party would be held at Dominic's parent's home. A total of fifty-one people would be there. The week prior to this, Paige helped prepare for the event. Carson, Wiehls and Fullerton had closed for the holidays, so Dominic and Vincente would drop her at the Gianelli's each morning, and she would spend the day. Some evenings he would find her still working, happily hanging, wrapping, arranging. But sometimes she was with Sophia and, according to the others, had been having lengthy discussions with the aunt. He poured a scotch and waited almost an hour before finally disturbing them on this Friday evening.

Paige, in jeans and sweater, her back to him, was sitting cross-legged on the floor decorating a small tree. There were boxes of miniature ornaments scattered around her. Sophia was seated in her favorite chair. A teapot and cups sat on a tray, now pushed to one side on the coffee table. The aunt's expression was one of interest and unmistakable fondness as she listened to what Paige was saying. Neither noticed him when he entered the room.

"Dom told me it had to be my decision." The aunt nodded as Paige continued, emphatically. "That *is* what I want to do. I've given it a lot of thought. I want to marry in the Catholic Church, and I want to raise our children as Catholics. I will be a Gianelli and our children will be Gianellis. I want them to be like the rest of the family, to grow up with their cousins and attend the same schools, go to the same church."

Sophia smiled. Having been instructed by her nephew to listen but neither encourage nor discourage, she replied, "If that's what you want to do, Bella, that's good. But don't forget, your children will have other cousins, Hamilton cousins. How will your parents and grandparents feel about this?"

"I don't know. It's hard for me to imagine them having strong feelings about it. They…we have always been Episcopalians. I don't think anyone in the family has ever belonged to any other church, but they don't make a big deal about it." She was frowning thoughtfully.

"That doesn't mean they don't have feelings about it."

"But it's my decision to make, isn't it? Mine and Dom's? And shouldn't they respect it in the same way I've had to respect their wishes in the past?"

He had to smile at this.

"Well…" his aunt seemed at a loss for words momentarily. "Well, dear, yes, of course."

Paige spoke up again. "And isn't there something in scripture about forsaking all others? Isn't that part of the marriage vows? Am I not supposed to become part of Dominic and his family, his life?" She was very serious.

Sophia skillfully avoided answering. "Well, I can see you have given this a lot of thought. Will you do something for me? Consider it for another month or so. It's not a decision to be made lightly."

Seeing the girl's expression, she added quickly, "And anyone can see you are *not* taking this lightly, Bella. I will give you a book to read, and sometime soon I will introduce you to Father Stefano. I'm sure he'll want to visit with you. Is that all right?"

"Yes, but Sophia?"

"Yes?"

"Why do I feel like every decision I make, someone is trying to talk me out of it?"

Dominic decided to step in and save the aunt another difficult answer. "Because, my love, we all want what's best for you, that's why. So we want you to consider all sides of an issue."

He could see her resisting the urge to jump up and run to him. More than ever she was trying to avoid anything that could be interpreted as childish behavior. But there was no mistaking the joy on her face as she walked toward him.

She kissed him. "Did you see what we did today? We're almost finished. Doesn't it look pretty?"

"It certainly does, Sweetheart. A beautiful job! Where are your shoes? Get your things so we can go. It's been a long day."

After Paige had left the room, he smiled at his aunt. "Well, Sophia, that must have been some conversation."

Sophia sighed. "There is no such thing as small talk with Paige." She shook her head, but the smile in her eyes belied any pretense of frustration or annoyance.

"True."

"Are you so against what she wants to do?"

"Not at all. I just don't want her to do it for the wrong reasons, and I don't want her pressured into anything."

"No one here has mentioned it, except to answer her questions. How do you think her family will react?"

"I don't know."

"Are they reasonable people?"

He thought a moment and finally said, "I think so. I hope so. For her sake."

The aunt nodded.

"Something peculiar happened on Thanksgiving, at the Hamilton's. Andrew's wife, Julia, told me there were some things I should know."

"Yes?"

"I don't know them yet. Santoro is putting the information together. Something to do with the mother's illness and frequent hospitalization and Paige. Especially when she was very young, a toddler maybe, I'm not sure."

Sophia was silent, listening.

"She didn't come right out and say it, but I had the feeling Julia was telling me Martha had hurt Paige."

"Hurt her?"

"Injured her. I don't know how or why. I'm waiting for the files. Santoro said he should have everything within the next week or two."

"She seems fine..." Sophia ventured.

"I know. According to Julia, Paige has no memory of any of it, whatever 'it' is."

"Well, we will deal with what comes. Sometimes the past just has to be the past, Nephew. And who is to say what this child does or does not remember? Maybe she has already come to terms with it, no? She's happy now, and she is in love. She has a good head. Just as important, she has a good heart."

"That she does." Then, "I'll let you know when I know."

The aunt nodded.

Glancing toward the foyer, he sighed. "Let me find Paige. She must have gotten sidetracked saying goodnight to Mama and the girls. We need to head for home."

Snow was falling as they got into the car and sped away. She sat next to him, her head on his shoulder. He kissed her.

"So you had a good day?"

"Yes."

"And a good visit with Sophia?"

"Yes." Apparently feeling no need to elaborate on the discussion with Sophia, she nestled against him, and his arms closed around her. The darkness hid his smile. He loved her so much. She was still part woman, part child, and she touched his heart.

At home, she insisted he have another drink while she prepared dinner. He turned on the news, put his feet up, and drank his scotch.

Paige had watched Dominic, and sometimes Victoria and Isabella, prepare what seemed to be the men's favorite meal often enough that she was sure she could do it now. She sliced the peppers and onions and sausage and put them in a pan with olive oil to sauté. While the griddle was heating, she broke several eggs into a bowl and heated another frying pan. She buttered thick slices of sourdough bread, and set them aside. She scrambled the eggs, then put the bread on the griddle and toasted it. Finally, she filled two plates and took them to the den.

"Well, look at this! What have you done here, my love?"

Paige smiled shyly. "It's just dinner. Do we want wine or beer to drink?"

"Let's have a beer, okay?"

She had done an excellent job of preparing the eggs and peppers and Dominic told her so, at the same time being careful not to overdo it. Approval was important to Paige, but only if it was warranted.

"You wouldn't say that if it weren't true, would you?" She was serious.

And just as seriously, he answered, "No, I wouldn't. I would never do that to you."

This brought a smile. "I didn't think so. Thank you."

After they ate, she cleared the dishes and straightened the kitchen while he showered. In bed, she rubbed his neck and back, removing all traces of the frustrations of the day. When she snuggled against him, he turned to her. "Come here to me."

And she did.

Paige and Dominic decided to sleep in on Saturday and relax most of the day before dressing for the party. They awoke early, made love, and went back to sleep. It was late afternoon by the time they ate breakfast.

The party was formal, after six. Paige had chosen a strapless, floor-length, black sheath. At the hemline was a wired ten-inch ruffle that, upon reaching the slit in back of the skirt, followed the inverted *v* to mid-knee.

Dominic had given her an early present of diamond-drop earrings and a bracelet. She was standing at the mirror trying on black opera-length gloves. She couldn't decide whether to wear them or not. Dominic decided for her, saying, "I like the gloves. Wear them just for the first half hour or so." He was right. They would be an inconvenience for any longer than that.

She then slipped the bracelet over the glove on her left arm, found her shoes and stepped into them.

Dominic always looked good to her, but tonight, in the tux, she thought him exceptionally handsome. He came up behind her and put his arms around her.

"So what do you think, my love?"

Eyeing their reflection in the mirror, she responded, "That she's the luckiest woman in the world."

When Paige and Dominic arrived at the Gianellis, it was like a wonderland. Every tree in the yard was lit with tiny white lights. The porches, upstairs and down, were decorated with large evergreen wreaths tied with huge red bows. There was a fully decorated twelve-foot tree on the front porch. It turned on a pedestal as traditional Christmas music played.

Another tree, equal in size, was centered in the foyer. Garlands of evergreen festooned with red velvet bows strategically draped the staircase banisters. Smaller trees decorated in various motifs adorned tables and mantles. Candles burned everywhere, filling the air with a mixture of cinnamon, vanilla and Burberry scents.

Xavier and Victoria greeted the guests as they arrived. Waiters had been hired for the evening, as well as a photographer. There had been much discussion about a live band, but in the end, Victoria said she felt that was going too far. Xavier, in all their years of marriage, and having heard her use this term often, had never figured out exactly where "too far" was located. Only Victoria seemed to know. At any rate, music played on the stereo would suffice, she said. Besides, where on earth would they put a band?

The photographer, though Xavier knew his wife would be loathe to admit it, had been hired specifically that she might have a picture of Dominic and Paige. So thrilled was Victoria at the prospective marriage of their only son, something she had begun to fear would never take place, that it was a thorn in her side that she had nothing to show friends when she bragged of her son and his lovely bride to be. The wedding was only a little less than a year away, but already Victoria was pulling out long-stored items from Dominic's infancy: a christening gown, bronzed shoes, his baby book. It had been close to ten years since the last grandchild, and Victoria was ready for another baby.

Looking at his wife of fifty years, Xavier wondered if she had ever forgiven him for what had happened with the son. Right or wrong, he knew Victoria blamed, not only him, but Sophia and her husband, Carlo, as well.

His son. At times it was hard to believe this giant of a man was his flesh and blood. Always so smart, even as a mere boy. Serious and quiet and unafraid of Satan himself. When all was said and done, that he was so strong and fearless was a gift, according to Sophia.

Could it be laid entirely at Dominic's feet that there was a part of his life in which he had to make difficult and, at times, what must be atrocious, appalling decisions? Even now, Xavier did not know. Not knowing was a survival technique he had developed years ago, and Dominic seldom discussed with him the facets of his other life. That was how he thought of it. *His son's other life.*

He saw Dominic and Paige enter the foyer. They were a stunning couple. Victoria got their attention and made them pause momentarily. This was the photographer's cue. Dominic just smiled and shook his head, then whispered something to Paige, who in turn tucked her arm into Dominic's and faced the camera again. Connie and Jackie descended on them. They liked their brother's fiancé and had an insatiable curiosity about her.

Connie, precocious hothead that she was, had conceded not long ago that Paige was indeed as nice as she seemed. Jackie thought her brother was too controlling, but Sophia told her to keep this opinion to herself. Paige was friendly, comfortable with Isabella, but without a doubt, it was Sophia to whom Paige was drawn, with whom there was a special bond.

There was no way the girl could know what her life would be like as Dominic's wife. None knew what he had told her. They could only wait and observe. What made Xavier hopeful, though, was his son's demeanor toward Paige. It was obvious that Dominic loved her, and the girl worshiped him.

That she was not prone, even in jest, to arguing or questioning him was a good thing. She wasn't silly or childish, despite her youth. Maybe it would be all right. Suddenly, Xavier was awash with shame at his thoughts. Dominic was a good man, generous with his sisters and their families. His entrepreneurial skills provided the entire family with a luxurious lifestyle.

When Mario and Richard had approached Dominic about opening a sporting goods store, he had not only supplied the financial backing, but had insisted reputable accounting and marketing firms be hired to assist them.

Victoria brought Xavier back to the present, introducing him to Paul and Martha Hamilton and the respective grandparents.

Paige noticed when her family arrived, but she stayed by Dominic, watching them from a distance. There was something about being with the Gianellis that boosted her confidence. She was comfortable among them. Already, as far as they were concerned, she belonged to them, and she wanted her parents, *especially* her parents, to see this.

Though they gave no sign of it, she was sure her family was impressed with the magnitude and opulence of the Gianelli estate. Victoria and Xavier received them warmly, and began introducing them to other members of the family as they made their way to where she and Dominic stood visiting with Tomas and Isabella.

Victoria was a polished and gracious hostess, making sure Paige's brothers and their wives were paired with her daughters and their spouses. She, Xavier, and Sophia ushered her parents and grandparents to the living room, and the children were dispatched to the game room where entertainment and refreshments were available and geared to that age group.

Paul Hamilton watched his daughter move comfortably about the room with Dominic Gianelli. They had taken their drinks and were now seated in an alcove off the formal living room, deep in conversation, just the two of them.

It made him crazy the way they always looked at each other as if the bedroom was their next stop. Paige stuck to Dominic like glue, taking her every cue from him.

The Gianellis spoke glowingly of Paige, how pleased they were with the forthcoming marriage and what a wonderful and welcome addition she would be to their family. Martha and Victoria were already discussing wedding plans. This thing had taken on a life and momentum of its own, and Paul knew there was no stopping it now. His daughter would marry Dominic Gianelli. He wished he could feel better about it. No one else seemed to have the same trepidations he had about the relationship. Maybe he was wrong.

Deep down, he knew he resented the way Gianelli had taken her. In every conceivable way, he had *taken* her from him. *And Paige was his.* Not just his daughter, but his prize. He had raised her, molded her. It had required a firm hand at times, but he had insisted on excellence, would settle for nothing less, and she had delivered. He was proud of his sons and their many accomplishments, but the situation with Paige was different. Their lives put asunder, every day for so long a challenge just to get through it, they had persevered. And they had done so privately. It hadn't been easy. But they had done it.

At twenty, she was beautiful and she was brilliant. He always left it to others to describe her as such, for he was reserved, modest, and he had instilled this in his children as well. Until Gianelli had come along, Paige was concentrating on her career, holding a position coveted by those ten years her senior. Now she was going to walk away from it, as if it were nothing. And nothing was what she thought of his concerns when he tried to express them. Oh, she was polite, respectful. Anything else was unacceptable. That had been drilled into her early on. But she wouldn't budge when it came to Gianelli. Well, neither would he.

All in all, the evening was a resounding success, Victoria decided. Everyone seemed to have a good time. The women had plans to get together and discuss the wedding. It was close to 2:00 A.M. when the last guests departed. Paige and Dominic had said goodnight, but were on the front steps locked in an ardent embrace when she went to turn off the lights. "You two! You're going to freeze to death!" she chided.

"Not a chance!" Paige laughed as they turned and hurried toward the waiting limo. "Goodnight!"

———

In the car, Dominic traced the outline of Paige's nipples through the dress and teased, "Is this because you're hot or because you're cold?" She smiled and ran her hand down the front of his trousers until she felt his erection.

"It's because I want this." She wet her bottom lip with the tip of her tongue, then leaned over and kissed him. "Can we?"

"Not enough time, Zucchero. We'll be home in ten minutes."

"Then, maybe there's time for this." Undoing his zipper, she reached for him, put her head into his lap and took him in her mouth. He leaned back and closed his eyes.

She was getting good at this. He had begun to understand the premium placed on virginity and a lack of experience on the part of the woman. Certainly other things had to be considered. Her youth, her love for him, her desire to please him. Still, teaching her to enjoy the things that were so satisfying to his sexual appetite was both exciting and gratifying. And there was so much more to teach her.

———

Later, when Dominic told her to turn over, Paige reached for the headboard, each hand clutching a rail. Using a pillow to make her bottom more accessible, he straddled her, then leaned down and kissed her neck. "Do not let go, no matter what," he whispered. "Do you understand?"

"Yes."

She recognized that things like this were part of something that excited him, and in turn, they excited her. Always she surrendered herself to him. And it was with complete trust that she followed him down every path, swept up in his desires.

In the aftermath of their lovemaking, she lay in his arms giving him soft kisses. She loved his big chest and never tired of running her fingers through the dark curly hair that started there, then traveled in a line down his abdomen, growing thicker again in his groin. She would lie there, feeling him, tasting him, loving him. She simply could not get enough of him.

She thought of the party and how possessive he had been this evening, more so than usual. She had danced only with him, and he had never left her side. He was always touching her, his arm around her waist, his hand on her back, and she loved it.

Now he pulled her even closer to him, and buried his face in her hair, his voice husky. "I love you, Paige."

"I love you, Dom." She more than loved him. Whatever that was.

And they slept.

Christmas Eve was to be spent with the Gianellis and Christmas Day with the Hamiltons.

Christmas morning Dominic and Paige exchanged presents. He admired the instruments for the Paige One, saying they would go to the marina and install them in the next few days. He could tell she put a lot of thought into the gifts she gave, but more and more, he was learning this was simply who she was.

She had insisted he open his gift first; then she opened the smaller of her packages. It was a gold key chain with an oval nameplate engraved with the proposed wedding date and her name. "Catherine Paige Gianelli - December 1, 1981." When she saw this, a smile lit her face, then worked its way toward an honest-to-goodness grin. "Thank you, Dom. I love it." Fingering the attached keys, she seemed a little self-conscious, but nonetheless thrilled with the gift.

"The keys are to the apartment and to this house, and there's one for Villa Disanti. Symbolic, but I thought they might make up somewhat for me insisting we wait a year." He gave a shrug. "I'll be glad when it's official, too. Okay?"

"Yes."

The second package held monogrammed black ceramic coffee mugs with the initials "DXG" and "CPG" on them. This time, she swallowed several times and blinked back tears before saying softly, "These are the best, Dom. Thank you so much." She went to him then, wrapped her arms around his neck, and kissed him. "You won't be sorry, Dom. I promise."

He looked at her for a long moment. "Don't you think I know that, Sweetheart?" In a now familiar gesture, he touched her cheek, and gently tucked a strand of hair behind her ear. "Where do these thoughts come from, Zucchero?"

A slight shrug and a little smile was her answer, then she kissed him again.

SEVEN

New Year's 1981

Early on, Dominic and Paige had claimed New Year's Eve and the four days that followed as a time for just the two of them, and they excused themselves from all family activities. Monday and Tuesday were long and busy days for both of them, but by noon on Wednesday they were packed and headed for the marina.

The Mallorca had been stocked and was well supplied with anything they might need. They had no plans, no timetable. Dom said they might just drift offshore, depending on the weather. It didn't matter. What did matter were four days and nights to themselves, with no interruptions. As she was putting jeans and sweatshirts into a drawer, it occurred to Paige that she hadn't seen Manetti and Buscliano since they'd left the house. When she asked, Dominic said only that they were nearby but wouldn't be joining them.

It was cold and a light rain was falling, so they ate dinner inside the cabin, but close to midnight, Dominic went to the galley and poured two glasses of wine. They took them on deck, and shared a kiss and New Year's wishes.

When Paige said thoughtfully that she couldn't imagine a more wonderful year, he smiled. "We still have that date at the altar, don't we?"

New Year's Day they took *The Mallorca* out for several hours, letting her drift while they talked or napped in the deck chairs. Paige noticed a couple of boats that seemed to stay some distance from them but were never out of sight. She did not comment on this.

That night, after dinner, he turned off the music, and told her to come sit with him. He wanted to talk to her.

"Paige, where do you think Manny and Buscliano are?"

"On one of those boats that are following us?"

He smiled a little and nodded. "That's right. There are security personnel on both those boats." He took a drink of his beer, then lit a cigar. "Why do you think I employ such stringent security measures?"

She didn't know what to say. She did think about it sometimes, but from the beginning she had sensed that Dominic was a man who would tell you *what* he wanted you to know *when* he wanted you to know it.

"I'm sure you have an opinion, Paige, and I want to hear it." He always called her by name during these discussions. She knew it was important to him that she take them seriously. Then, more gently, he said, "Paige, just tell me what you think."

She was nervous and had begun to fidget a little. Finally, she took a deep breath and said, "You're well known in the business world, and you have substantial influence." This was straight out of a file at the firm. She paused, cleared her throat. "I suppose being a person with comprehensive assets and

far-reaching impact could make you a possible target?"

"Go on. A target in what manner?"

Once again she was at a loss for words and didn't know how to respond. Kidnapping had crossed her mind, but she quickly dismissed it. Not in her wildest fantasies could she imagine someone being able to abduct him. If there were no filters in place, people would be contacting him incessantly, wanting him to invest in a project or contribute to a cause. That would be bothersome, but hardly a reason for security measures that were second to none she had ever seen.

The air in the cabin was hazy with the smoke from Dominic's cigar. He noticed that Paige ended each sentence as a question. This was obviously difficult for her. It was important to Paige to give the right answers. She didn't realize there were none as such. He simply wanted to know what she thought.

Watching her closely, he said, "I'm a man who doesn't like to leave things to chance. Not anything. Do you understand?"

She nodded.

"All right then. Tell me what you understand."

Hesitantly, she answered, "What you said….that you don't like to leave things to chance."

"But what do you think I mean by that?" Being so young, her face read like an open book. Right now, he thought she was feeling somewhat badgered by his persistence. She was biting her lower lip again. "Paige?"

"I think you mean you want to be in control, that you don't like surprises. That you like to allow for all possibilities in any given area and always have a plan, a contingency factor."

"That's right. That's very good. You can understand, then, why the security measures extend to you now that you are with me." It was a statement, not a question.

Again, she just nodded.

"All right. You can see how, if someone wanted to, say…influence my thinking or my actions in some way, they might decide to do it by using you as a means of getting my attention."

"Oh."

"Yes, oh. This is why I keep going over this with you, Paige. I want it fixed in your mind that this is not some quirk of my personality that has to be humored. This is a serious matter, and I want it taken seriously by you. Do you understand?"

"Yes."

"How are you dealing with it so far? You don't seem to mind, but you're a quiet one, and I'm not sure you would tell me." He stubbed out his cigar and took another from the humidor on the cocktail table.

"I'm fine. At first it felt a little awkward, but I must be used to it, because now I don't think anything at all about calling you or Vincente or Manetti."

"You don't find it inconvenient? Too restrictive?"

"No, not at all."

"Good." He lit his cigar and studied her for a long moment. "Paige, are you afraid of me?"

Her eyes widened in astonishment at his question. She would never know how gratified he was by her response.

Her voice was soft, earnest, when she answered. "No, Dom, I'm not afraid of you. I'm a lot of things where you're concerned. I'm in awe of you most of the time. I admire and respect you more than anyone I've ever known, and I love you so much I'm completely overwhelmed by it. But I'm *not* afraid of you." She paused. "Okay?"

"Yes." And for the first time since the onset of the discussion, he gave her a real smile. "One more thing and we'll call it a night. I don't want you to be afraid to ask or tell me anything. Ever. This notwithstanding, there may be occasions when I won't be able to provide answers to your questions. Can you think of why that might be?"

She was thoughtful for a moment. "Because it wouldn't be good for me to know?"

He nodded, watching her face intently. "And could you accept this?"

"Yes."

He held her gaze. "You could accept it and let it go?"

"Yes."

"Why? Why would you do that?"

No hesitation here. "Because I trust you, Dom."

This was another of those times when he felt a stab of emotion, though he gave no sign of it—"Because I trust you, Dom." He loved her so much, and more and more he believed they were on solid ground. He always hoped so, but it was hard for him not to test it. This was how he lived his life, and he took nothing for granted.

He patted the cushion beside him now. "Come here, Baby."

She was in his arms as soon as the words were spoken, her mouth on his. God, she was so sweet.

Friday and Saturday were spent doing the things they liked best. Dominic and Paige slept late each morning and ate breakfast for lunch. They drank wine and made love in the afternoons then napped on deck afterward, *The Mallorca* rocking gently in the winter breeze, strains of their favorite music playing in the background. They fished and talked, played chess and gin and poker, and talked some more.

Dominic awoke early Sunday. The clock showed 4:20 A.M. Paige wasn't there beside him. At first he thought she might be in the bathroom, but when he checked, she wasn't there. His heart was pounding as he took the steps to the deck two at a time. She was standing at the bow, looking up at the sky, arms folded, hugging her body. She was barefoot, wearing only an oversized sweatshirt. The air was still and the stars were brilliant against a backdrop of endless black. There seemed to be no boundary between where the ocean ended and the sky began.

"Sweetheart?" This, softly.

She turned to him. "Hi. I couldn't sleep. I didn't want to wake you so I came up here. Isn't it spectacular, Dom? It's almost as if you could reach out and touch them."

Wrapping his arms around her, he kissed the top of her head. "Yes, it is. It really is." Then, "You're freezing, Baby."

"I'm okay. It's so beautiful, and …" her voice broke "…and I'm just so…so happy." Her voice was barely above a whisper, and she reached up and brushed the tears from her face.

"Hey, what's this?" Now he was wiping her tears with one hand and rubbing her back gently with the other.

"Just overwhelmed, I guess." She tried to laugh. "The night, the stars, you, this time alone. It's all so awesome…so perfect." Moving into his arms, she whispered, "I love you so much." There were more tears. "And I can't believe I'm going to cry about this." But she did.

After a while, he coaxed her back to the cabin and into bed, then held her till she fell asleep. He lay awake contemplating the emotional episode he had just witnessed. She was sensitive, yes, but as a rule, not weepy. Checking, he found her forehead warm to his touch and her cheeks flushed. Remembering the date, he realized it was almost time for her period again. Mystery solved. And he too slept.

When they awoke, she wanted only coffee and a cinnamon roll. He had noticed she favored sweets when it was time for her to start. She stayed close to him and was very quiet. This was a pattern he recognized now.

She put on a long-sleeved tee with a sweatshirt over it and her windbreaker on top of that. Anytime now, he thought.

As they eased *The Mallorca* back into the slip, Paige sighed and rested her head on his shoulder. "Back to the real world."

"We're always in the real world, Zucchero. Our own private part of it is pretty nice, though, isn't it?"

"Very."

Manetti and Buscliano were waiting for them, standing by the car talking to Vincente. The three men watched as their boss and Paige came toward them.

Manetti observed, "He looks good, rested."

The others nodded in agreement. She was good for him. This they all knew. At first, they had worried. How could someone so young, so Americanized, fit into his life? But she did. Nice and quiet. Very cooperative. Never gave them any trouble.

Thinking about the Christmas presents still brought a smile to Manetti's face. The gifts, delivered by Vincente, while discomfiting at first, were appreciated by all. They had waited until the boss came round and had shown him the brightly wrapped packages that had been left for them. What should they do? Giving them an amused look, he had laughed and said, "Why don't you open them?" Mr. Gianelli always gave them holiday bonuses, had turkeys and hams or cases of wine sent to their homes, that kind of thing. The gifts from Paige were an anomaly.

As they approached, Paige noticed that Manetti, Buscliano and Vicente were all wearing the gloves she had given them. She nodded and smiled, but stood back as Dominic briefly went over next week's agenda.

Once home, she unpacked their things and went to the kitchen to make a cup of tea. She found Dom in his office going through messages, and took her place, standing in front of him, his arm encircling her waist. He smelled of aftershave, the smoke from his cigar, sunshine, and ocean air. She took his hand and placed it on her breast. It took another ten minutes for him to sort the messages, but when he had finished he took her in his arms and kissed her. She pressed against him, returning his kisses, wanting him.

"Let's go upstairs." She was peeling her sweatshirt as she said this.

In less than a minute, they were in bed, their clothes in heaps on the floor. Locked in his embrace, she was pressed so closely she could feel his heart beating. Their lovemaking was almost frenzied. She couldn't taste him enough. His hands were all over her. She broke from his embrace and slid down in the bed, taking him in her mouth. He moaned, letting her continue for several minutes, then pulled her atop him. She moved slowly at first, tantalizingly, grinding him into her.

"Is it good, Baby?" He had taught her to look at him while they fucked, and she did so now.

"Yes," she whispered.

She tilted her body forward, quickening the pace of her movements. She bit her lower lip and closed her eyes, concentrating on the moment. "Dom."

"That's it, come on. You're almost there." He grabbed her wrists, pulled her down, and locked her against him. Then, passion overtook her. Her hands clutched at his chest as she cried out, "Now!"

She was still atop him, and her breathing was quick and shallow. "I love how we fuck."

"Tell me what you want, Baby. How do you want to be fucked?"

"Turn me over," she said, knowing this was one of his favorite positions.

He whispered, "Ask for it."

"I want you to turn me over and fuck me."

He had her on her stomach in seconds, and was lying atop her, his hands holding her wrists, his body pinning hers to the bed. Repeatedly, he rammed himself into her, again and again, until they reached the height of their passion and were spent.

When they went to shower, she noticed she had started her period. It took her by surprise, but when she thought about it, she guessed it was time after all. He did not approach her about making love during this time, and she was relieved. Not that she would have refused him, but still... She wasn't sure exactly what rules applied here, and, until she met Dominic, her entire life had been based on rules. Other than the subject of basic reproduction and strong admonitions to "wait," neither Drew nor the Sisters at St. Ag's had ever addressed anything like this. So she left it to Dominic. And, somehow, without having to talk about it, a system had evolved. When her period was over, she came to bed naked. Things were so...so easy with Dominic. And, not for the first time, she thought that knowing him, loving him was like...like coming home.

She watched him now as he brushed his teeth, combed his hair, put on his robe. It gave her a sense of proprietorship, observing him in these personal tasks.

Dominic caught Paige watching him in the mirror. He smiled. "And what are you thinking?"

"Lots of things. That I love you. That we're getting married this year." She sighed. "That tomorrow's Monday and this will probably be a very busy week."

"Something wrong at work?" he inquired, knowing this was not the case. She was simply out of sorts, a little moody, due to her period. It wasn't something easily discussed with Paige, and he didn't press the issue. It puzzled him that she seemed to know so little about her body, things that most girls knew from the age of twelve. And as open as she was to intimacy, to anything he desired in their lovemaking, she was shy about *this*.

"No, I just, I don't know. I guess I'm tired. Not of work or anything. Just tired."

Patiently, he said, "You'll feel better in a few days, Zucchero."

Paige nodded. Sometimes it seemed Dominic knew her better than she knew herself. It wasn't a bad feeling. Later, as she lay in his arms, on the verge of sleep, she thought of this new year and how anxious she was for it to pass. He had kept his promise though. Nothing had changed. They were apart only for purposes of work or when he had to travel, which had been seldom to date. She snuggled against him and closed her eyes.

He kissed her forehead. "Goodnight, my love." And they slept.

EIGHT

Paige—the Early Years

On February 1, 1960, a baby girl was born to Andrew Paul and Martha Grace Hamilton of Long Island, New York. Joining a family of three brothers, Andrew, seventeen, and twins, Matthew and John, fifteen, she was christened Catherine Paige Hamilton. Being the sole daughter, granddaughter, and niece, she was welcomed enthusiastically by the male-dominated family. Her father, a well-established investment banker, provided a comfortable and privileged lifestyle for his wife and children.

He considered himself a conservative, no-nonsense man with a strict moral code, but nonetheless a loving and devoted parent. His wife Martha, a rather spoiled woman in many ways, came from an old New England family that could trace its bloodline back to the original settlers. A true socialite, she had surprised Paul pleasantly by being a proud and attentive mother to the three boys, always participating in their school and sports activities through the years.

When their daughter was born, he was thrilled. They had always wanted a little girl to complete their family. Paul noticed that Martha was rather quiet after she returned home from the hospital, but he thought she was probably tired, more so than with the boys when they were born. After all, Paige came along later in their lives, when he and Martha were forty.

Looking back, he would not be able to pinpoint exactly when the trouble began. Indeed, it was Andrew who had the first suspicions. Martha was cross most of the time, complaining that Paige was a bad baby. The baby did cry a lot.

They took her to the pediatrician, who said she was probably just colicky. He also said that Martha seemed anxious and the baby, sensing her nervousness, was reacting to it. He was concerned that Paige wasn't gaining the weight she should, so he changed her formula and added vitamin supplements.

Drew could hear the baby crying again, and he hurried to the nursery. He entered the room quietly, and found his mother leaning over the crib. She crammed the bottle into the baby's mouth. Paige sucked hungrily, then stopped and began to scream.

"See? You're not as hungry as you thought, are you?" his mother said with what sounded like vicious satisfaction.

"Mother, what's the matter?" Drew asked, keeping his tone mild.

She seemed startled as she turned and faced him. "I don't know. I fixed her a bottle, but she doesn't want it."

Andrew approached the crib, took the bottle from her, and felt the heat from it. It burned his hand. Giving his mother an incredulous look, he told her, "You're tired. Go back to bed. I'll take care of her."

"Just let her cry. It won't hurt her," she said as she left.

Andrew picked up the hysterical baby and held her close. "Shhh, it's okay, Paige. It's okay." He took her into the bathroom, wet a washcloth in cool water, and bathed her mouth and face.

Then he changed her diaper, made sure the formula had cooled sufficiently, and sat down in the rocker with her. At first, she was tentative about taking the bottle, but finally hunger won out and she ate.

Andrew sat looking at his sister. She was a pretty baby, with dark hair and big brown eyes, the lashes long and thick. Six months old now, she was serious and seldom smiled or laughed. She lay in his arms, her eyes looking straight into his. "What are you thinking about, little girl?" He touched her chin, tapping it gently with his finger, trying to coax a smile from her. He rocked her till she fell asleep, then laid her in her crib.

The next day he told his father about the incident. Paul blamed it on Martha being tired and said he was certain she didn't realize the bottle was overheated. Andrew wasn't so sure. He had a bad feeling about it. From then on, he checked on the baby frequently.

He began to feed Paige as soon as he came home from school each day. He would put her in the high chair and get two jars of food. She was always hungry, and she always finished both jars. When he asked his mother if the baby had eaten earlier, her response was usually the same. "Oh, she never eats well for me. She's such a temperamental baby!" All three brothers noticed that their mother seldom held or played with Paige.

Andrew began to feed her breakfast before he left for school, and also her bottle at bedtime. She gained weight and the doctor was pleased. Still, she cried a lot and no one knew why. Sometimes mysterious marks and bruises would appear on her skin. They would eventually fade, but would later recur, and this was a frequent and worrisome pattern.

One Saturday night as Andrew returned home from a date, he saw his mother leaving the nursery. She looked surprised to see him.

"What's going on, Mother? Is Paige all right?"

She sighed, her annoyance evident. "She's fine. Just fussy as usual. She's quiet now. Go on to bed."

Andrew went to his room, but a nagging instinct made him return to the nursery. Tiptoeing to the crib, at first he didn't think the baby was there among the blankets, but then he realized she was not only covered with several, but some were wrapped around her head.

The heaviest blanket was to the outside. After removing it, he found another wound tightly around her face and neck. He picked her up, swooping her from the crib. She gasped for air and finally began to cry.

"Oh, baby, it's okay. It's okay, Paige." Once he had settled her down, he changed her and fed her a bottle, then rocked her to sleep. He spent the night on the floor beside the crib.

The next day, when he could arrange a private conversation with his father, he told him what had happened. But to no avail—Paul was in denial. What man wants to believe his wife could do horrible things to a baby, her own baby?

From then on, Andrew watched Paige more closely than ever, and he let his mother be aware of it. He thought this might offer his sister some measure of protection when he wasn't there. He had always loved her, but now he had a special bond with her. She would smile only for him, and she cried when anyone else held her, even their father, much to Paul's dismay.

Andrew's watchfulness did not keep the mysterious marks and bruises, or the unexplained hours of inconsolable crying at bay. Visits to the doctor provided no answers and were another agony to be endured. Paige would scream every time a nurse came near her. At first, they thought this might be because of the inoculations, but in the end, they determined all the nurse had to do was be in the room with her for the hysterics to begin.

Paige walked at ten months, and any injuries she sustained were blamed on falls from her attempts at navigating the house and the stairs. She had bonded with her father, finally, and with the twins, but their mother could not hold her, bathe her, or feed her without a fuss.

The situation had put a strain on Andrew's relationship with his parents. His mother felt betrayed by his alliance with the baby, and his father thought him far too judgmental of his mother. It wasn't an easy time in the young man's life.

February of '61 brought the little girl's first birthday. Pictures of the event showed a beautiful one-year-old with curly black hair. She was sporting a cast on her left arm and one cheek was badly bruised. According to her mother, she had fallen on the patio.

In March, Andrew returned home from school one afternoon and entered the house to his sister's frantic screams. Bounding up the stairs, he burst first into the nursery, then into his parent's bedroom. His mother was standing over Paige, a large ornate hairbrush in her hand. Paige was lying on the floor, naked, blood spurting from her nose and mouth. There were marks all over her body.

He picked up the injured child and ran downstairs, where he called the police, saying only that he needed help, that his mother had hurt his baby sister. The police were there within minutes, and an officer took Andrew and Paige to the hospital.

When the emergency room clerk asked for their doctor's name, Andrew requested another physician take care of her. He had always felt that the pediatrician, a family friend, was missing something in caring for his sister. There were too many unexplained situations, too many things casually passed over.

Paige kept screaming, and Drew was so upset he was fighting back tears. He wouldn't let anyone take the baby from him, insisting that he had to calm her first. A nurse kept trying to intercede, and this increased both his and the baby's agitation.

Finally, the officer intervened and asked the nurse to leave the room. Drew sat on the edge of a chair, rocking back and forth and speaking soothingly to the baby. "It'll be okay, Paige. It'll be okay."

After several minutes, he told the officer to please ask just the doctor to come in, because his sister was afraid of nurses. The officer complied.

The doctor started an IV, sedated the toddler in order to examine her, and x-rayed her from head to toe.

Finally, the officer asked, "And you think your mother did this?"

Very quietly, Drew answered, "I know she did, sir."

"We'll need more information and a statement eventually. How old are you, son?"

"Eighteen."

"I see. Have you called your father?"

"No, sir."

"Well, why don't I do that for you?"

"Yes, sir."

By the time the officer called, Paul Hamilton had returned home from work that day and found his house in chaos. Martha was under arrest and being put into a patrol car as he drove up. The twins were there, too, confused and upset. No one seemed to know where Andrew and Paige were, or at least, no one was telling them.

The police informed Paul that he could come to the station the next morning with an attorney and discuss Martha's release. Only then did he realize that his wife was going to spend the night in jail. Finally, a man identifying himself as an officer called and said he had taken Andrew and Paige to the hospital. Could he please come as soon as possible to the ER at Westwood?

In the end, he decided to take John and Matt with him. They were already upset, still unclear as to what was happening. When they arrived at the hospital, they were taken to a room where Andrew was sitting, head in hands, beside a sleeping Paige.

Paul Hamilton was a strong man and not given to shows of emotion, but the sight of his daughter and her injuries was too much for him. "My God!"

Hearing this, Andrew raised his head and looked at his father, and as he spoke his voice was full of pain. "She did it, Dad."

And Paul knew his son was right.

Tears streamed down Andrew's face. "I had to do it, Dad. I had to call the police. We can't let her hurt Paige. Not anymore."

Dominic sat in his office, the box of files on his desk. Santoro had sent them over this morning, telling him to follow the dates, that often he would have to read something from each file to obtain complete information about a particular incident. He suggested he start with the ER and police files from March of 1961. Dominic poured himself a scotch, put on his glasses, and picked up the file.

> Westwood Hospital
> Date: March 13, 1961
> Time: 4:50 P.M.
>
> Patient: Catherine Paige Hamilton
> DOB: 2/01/60
> Weight: 17 pounds
> Height: 25"
> Sex: F
> Race: C

Notes:
Patient was brought in by officer and patient's brother. Patient is a female child, one year, one month old, with multiple injuries. According to her brother, the child's mother inflicted the injuries with a large metal hairbrush. Patient's injuries include:

- Fracture left arm (secondary—cast was recently removed)
- Four rib fractures—current (see physician's notes)
- Fracture of left cheek bone
- Severe contusion of left eye
- Concussion
- Contusions on buttocks, thighs, back, arms, chest and forehead

The attending physician's notes read:

- X-ray reveals several rib fractures incurred possibly three to six months ago.
- Fracture of middle finger on right hand—possibly
- six to eight months ago
- Left arm—greenstick—two months old
- Right forearm—fracture—possibly six to eight months ago

Patient is distressed even by appearance of female hospital personnel. Genitalia examined—patient is intact—no evidence of penetration of vagina or rectum. Mother is in police custody. Will recommend the mother be removed from home and child be released to father with provision of visits by Children's Services personnel and counseling for family members.

The police file on Martha said only that she was in custody for the one night. Paul must have called in a lot of favors, because by ten the next morning they were in court. The hearing lasted less than an hour. Martha was to be admitted to a hospital upstate for a minimum of two years. During that time she was to have no contact with her daughter.

There were four pictures of Paige, taken, Dominic supposed, to substantiate the injuries. And even twenty years later they were heartbreaking. In two of them she was lying on her back, obviously sedated. The bruises on her chest and abdomen, the swollen black eye and fractured cheekbone, the marks on both legs were sickening. But what really got to him was the little right hand clutching someone's index finger. It was all you could see of another person. He knew it must have been Drew.

In the other pictures, she was on her stomach. These showed the injuries to her back, her bottom and her legs.

"Christ!" He closed the folder, took a long drink of scotch, and said again, "Christ!"

Normally, Paul insisted his sons take a summer job, but the summer of 1961 would be different. Their job was taking care of their sister. Ever since Martha's hospitalization, they had never left the toddler with anyone else. One of them was available to be with Paige at all times. It made the last two months of the school year difficult, but they had done it. Comparatively, summer should be a breeze with the three boys home all day.

His daughter was sixteen months old now. Andrew had taught Matt and John to feed her, bathe her, and change her diapers. They played with her in the pool as much as possible. Andrew said it was good for her, that she slept better at night. Paul didn't argue. Who was he to question? His sons, for all practical purposes, were raising her. They put her at the table with them for every meal and they took her everywhere they went.

The grandparents and Paul's secretary, Margaret Paxton, shopped for her clothing. The boys took her shopping for shoes and, perhaps due to their age, seemed to think sneakers were appropriate for almost every occasion. They dressed her and combed her hair, pushed her in the swing, and read to her. They would show her pictures from the family album, and soon she could point out her brothers and name them. She could say "daddy" and "bottle" and "Bear," for her beloved teddy bear. She loved music, so her brothers kept a radio or stereo playing. They would dance with her to their favorite songs, and she would laugh with delight.

Paul drove upstate to see Martha once a month. That was what her doctors had recommended. It was difficult for him, having her committed like that, but he'd had no choice. Once it was done, though, a peace settled over him and the household. The boys never mentioned their mother except to politely inquire about her after his visits.

It was a good summer. Her brothers were doing an admirable job and Paige was thriving. Paul came home one evening to find them in the pool with Paige on the diving board. Andrew was treading water below, encouraging her to jump, and just when he said "...and three!" she jumped into the water. She did this again and again until Paul called them to dinner. She barely stayed awake long enough to eat. He told the boys to finish eating and clear the table. He would put her to bed. He carried her upstairs, and while he was putting on her pajamas, she yawned, then looked at him for a moment and said, "Hi, Daddy." He fell in love with his daughter that night. Up to that point, he had felt so tormented emotionally and, spoiled or not, he missed Martha. When he thought about it, he supposed he missed their old life, before Paige. But that was not reality.

The reality was that Martha had injured their child. The reality was that she would be in that hospital for at least two years. And this was reality, too, this lovely little girl, who needed him, needed them all.

"Well, now, it's time for you to go to sleep." He laid her in the crib and pulled the coverlet up. "Goodnight, Princess." He leaned down and kissed her, then turned on the night light.

He had barely made it through the doorway when she called out, "My bottle!"

"I'll get it, Paige. I'll be right back." Going downstairs, he had to laugh. As he walked into the kitchen, Andrew said, "Don't forget her bottle, Dad."

"I've already been reminded." By the time he took the bottle to her, she was standing up in her bed, humming and waiting patiently.

He handed the bottle to her, laid her down, and pulled the covers up once more. "Now then! One more time. Good night, Princess."

She pulled the nipple from her mouth with a loud pop and said, "My music," only it sounded like "moozick." He looked for the little music box and wound it up. He spied Bear at the foot of her crib and laid him beside her. "Good night, Paige!"

Summer passed quickly and it was time for school again. Matt and John were entering their junior year in high school. Andrew had been accepted at Princeton but refused to go, saying he wanted to be close enough to help care for Paige. He would enroll at NYU. There was no dissuading him.

Two weeks prior to school starting, Paul arranged with Martha's parents to have Molly, a domestic who had been with the family for years, stay with Paige while the boys were in school. This gave Paige enough time to get to know Molly and adapt to having her there. Thankfully, it was a smooth transition. Once Paige was assured the boys would return each afternoon, she accepted the new routine. At nineteen months, she was a happy, healthy toddler. The grandparents would visit periodically, but with Paige, the die was cast. She would have little to do with anyone except her father and brothers.

At least now, having spent time with Molly, she would tolerate a hug from her grandmothers, but that was about it. Paul knew it was difficult for the grandparents. To have this long awaited granddaughter refuse their affection was hurtful and baffling to them.

He knew Martha's family, too, was devastated over what had happened with Paige and the subsequent hospitalization of their own daughter. He wondered if their lives would ever be normal again.

By the time she was two, Paige talked like a little magpie, but only at home. She was still quiet around others.

At the suggestion of Martha's doctors and the request of the court, and despite his own feelings about therapists, Paul and the boys began weekly sessions with a psychologist. It gave them the opportunity to express their feelings about the situation and what their mother had done to Paige, but the main purpose was to chronicle Paige's progress and her behavior. The doctor would, in turn, send monthly reports to the court and Children's Services.

Paul provided pictures taken on her second birthday: a smiling little girl, surrounded by her brothers, who were encouraging her to blow out the candles on her cake. There was one of her holding the reins to a small pony. She had leaned her head against the pony's and apparently had no fear of the animal. There was another picture of one brother holding her astride the saddle.

When the summer of '62 arrived, Andrew stayed home with Paige while John and Matt worked at the club as lifeguards. Molly continued to help out and mentioned that she thought it was time to potty train the little girl. Paul now realized that no one had given any thought to this.

He mentioned it to his secretary, and Margaret, who was in the business of solving problems for him, came through again. She bought two dozen pairs of frilly, nylon panties complete with lace and bows. She also bought four potty chairs, one for each bathroom in their house.

"Now, just show her the panties and ask if she wants to wear the pretty panties. Tell her if she wants to wear them she has to use the potty in the bathroom. She's a smart little girl. She'll get the hang of it in no time."

Paul, with a red face, relayed these instructions to Andrew, who, of course, took the matter very seriously and decided the weekend would be the time to do it. Paul wasn't sure this was something one could accomplish in a single weekend, but he wasn't going to interfere. He was grateful Andrew had taken charge.

After breakfast on Saturday, Andrew took Paige, along with a pair of the panties, into her bathroom. "Look Paige." He held up the panties for her inspection. "These are pretty panties. Would you like to wear these and quit wearing your diapers?"

She looked at the panties, then at him. She looked at the potty chair, a new item in her bathroom.

"No."

"No, what?"

"No, thank you."

"Paige, come here." He took off her pajama bottoms and her diaper. He put the panties on her, picked her up, and stood her on the vanity. "Look what a big girl you are. Only babies wear diapers, not big girls. Don't you want to wear pretty panties like big girls?"

She looked at her diaper on the floor and again at the potty chair, as if she already knew somehow it was going to come into play, even though he had yet to mention that part of it.

"Paige, do you want to wear the pretty panties and be a big girl?"

Finally, she answered, "Yes."

"That's good, Paige." He then sat her on the potty chair. He brought several books into the bathroom to read to her, as well as a pitcher of water and a plastic cup. By lunch time, she had drunk several cups of water and peed four times into the potty. Frequently, he would pull the panties up and let her play for a few minutes before seating her on the chair again.

She wore the panties, without incident, when he took her downstairs for lunch. The afternoon was a repeat of the morning and she managed to do exactly what she was supposed to do. Andrew praised her.

That night there was a ruckus when he decided to put a diaper on her. He tried to explain that she would be asleep and might need it. She would have none of it. Finally, he gave up and put her to bed wearing panties.

He thought as long as they were doing toilet training, maybe it would be a good idea to get rid of the bottle. "Paige, are you a big girl wearing pretty panties?"

"Yes." She was standing up in her crib, holding onto the railing with one hand and hugging Bear with the other.

"Well, you're drinking from a cup in the daytime now, just like big girls do, so I don't think you need your bottles any longer. Why don't we just take the baby bottles and throw them away? You're such a big girl now. Okay?"

"I want my bottle."

"A bottle is for babies, Paige, and you're a big girl."

"I want my bottle." Obviously, this was where they parted ways. Maybe the potty training was enough for today. He got her bottle.

The next morning when he went in to get her, her crib was soaked.

"I want my diaper," was the first thing she said, making him laugh. She was no dummy.

He gave her a quick bath and fed her breakfast, and they went back to the mission at hand. They made it through Sunday without an accident, but that night she wanted her diaper and, of course, her bottle.

It took only a few weeks before she no longer needed the diapers at night. A milestone. By the end of summer, she had given up her bottle. Another milestone.

Andrew was in his second year at NYU and the twins were seniors in high school now. Paul still visited Martha monthly. The boys had yet to visit, though it was now permitted. At first, it had surprised him that Martha didn't seem to mind the hospital, but when he thought about it, the damn place was more like a spa. They had pools, salons, a gym.

It was costing him a small fortune and, as much as he hated the thought, the next time her family offered to help, he was going to accept. He suspected they were grateful he hadn't left her. Not that he hadn't considered it. But in the end, he was a man of honor and of conscience. He had meant it when he said for better or for worse.

He and the boys still saw the therapist, but only once a month now. Everyone seemed pleased with his daughter's progress. She would be three soon and was smart as a whip, just like her brothers, he thought proudly. They had taught her card games, Go Fish, Old Maid, and the like, and she was always looking for a willing victim.

They took her to Sunday school and church, but she refused to go into the class with the preschoolers, so she went with the boys into the Young Adults Group.

After a couple of swats from Andrew, she learned to sit quietly. This was something they had begun only recently, but Paul insisted they make her mind. He discussed it with the therapist, and the doctor agreed, saying, "Don't let what happened cloud your judgment or hamper your parental instincts. That wasn't your fault. You've raised three sons and they are obviously fine young men. Don't hesitate to guide her, discipline her. Let her know what you expect. Be consistent."

By April 23, 1963, Martha was allowed overnight visits. Paul would pick her up Saturday mornings and return her to Meadow Lake Sunday evenings. Though Molly usually spent weekends at the Crawfords', Martha's parents, this month she would stay and help with cooking and cleaning while Martha was visiting.

On Friday evening at dinner, Paul tried to think of something to say to the boys in preparation for the weekend, but all he finally came up with was, "Let's try to make your mother feel welcome, okay?" They nodded.

As Andrew put Paige to bed that night, he told her, "Mother is coming home tomorrow. Your mother, my mother. She's been in the hospital for a long time, but she's coming home for a visit. Do you remember the pictures we showed you?"

"Yes."

"Well, I just wanted you to know she was going to be here for two days."

Paige considered this. "Can we read about the horses?"

"Yes, get your book." Drew was twenty now, but felt much older. His feelings about his mother were so conflicted. Until Paige was born, he had thought her a good mother. They all knew she was spoiled, but she was fun and charming too, a pretty woman who enjoyed being the center of attention. But this thing with Paige. Once he had asked the therapist if his mother realized what she was doing when she hurt Paige. His answer had not made Andrew feel any better. "Yes, she knew what she was doing. I don't know if she knew why, but she was certainly aware of her actions."

Andrew was enough like his father that for him there was little room for that indefinable area that hovered between right and wrong, good and evil.

At eleven o'clock Saturday, Paul pulled the Lincoln into the drive. The boys and Paige were sitting on the porch. They had dressed Paige in a black-and- white-checked dress with a white collar and cuffs. The dress had a large pocket appliquéd with a red apple. She wore white lacy leggings and black patent leather shoes. Her hair, now thick and shoulder length, was parted and pulled to one side, held by a black and red clip. She had been running up and down the steps, but when the car stopped and her parents got out, she went to Andrew and crawled into his lap.

One by one the boys greeted their mother, and awkwardly kissed her on the cheek. Paige hid behind her brothers till Paul took her by the hand and brought her to Martha, saying, "Paige, can you say hello?"

Looking at Paul, she answered, "Yes."

"Well, then can you tell your mother hello?" She looked at Andrew, who looked ready to grab her at any moment. Paul held his breath.

Andrew squatted beside Paige. "Princess, just say hello. Okay?"

"Hello."

"Well, hello, Paige. You look so pretty. Did Molly dress you?"

"No, Drew dressed me."

Martha seemed understandably nervous. "Oh, well, that was nice, wasn't it?"

The doctors had warned Paul and Martha repeatedly not to expect too much from the children, and they had been right. The boys were merely polite, and Paige wanted nothing to do with her mother. It was somewhat upsetting to Paul that this didn't bother Martha more than it did. By Sunday evening, she was ready to go back to the hospital, and he was relieved to have the visit come to an end.

Though none of them enjoyed the visit or considered it a success, the doctors insisted they proceed as planned, and Martha spent the next three weekends at home. Paul couldn't see how it was ever going to work out. He and Martha had little to say to one another on the drives to and from Long Island. But that he could always talk about the boys and Paige, he would have had nothing at all to offer. It disturbed him greatly that Martha had never expressed remorse for what she did to Paige. Indeed, she never spoke of it at all. It was as if it had never happened. Well, maybe Martha could put it out of her mind, but he couldn't forget it. He would *never* forget it.

Even after four visits, the children avoided their mother as much as possible. Around her, they were well-mannered but otherwise quiet.

One Sunday afternoon, Paul and Martha were sitting on the porch watching the boys play basketball. Paige was in the middle of everything, as usual. Andrew and she were a team in this current game. When it was her turn to shoot, he would pick her up and hold her close to the basket and she would drop the ball in, squealing delightedly, "I got a point!"

Martha surprised him by asking casually, "How is she?"

"Why, she's fine. You can see that, can't you?"

Ignoring his comment, she said, "She's so pretty. She's smart too, isn't she?"

"Very."

"The boys love her."

"Well, they don't have a corner on that, she loves them more than anyone." Martha flinched ever so slightly when he said this, and he felt a little sorry for her. Still, this was her doing and they were all going to have to live with it the rest of their lives.

Martha was released from the hospital and came home to Long Island in June. Molly was staying with them full-time now. Once again, Andrew would be home for the summer to help with Paige.

Matt and John, having graduated from high school, were taking a trip to Europe, compliments of their grandparents.

As it turned out, Andrew spent his days taking care of Paige, and Molly spent her days with Martha, who seemed not to feel at home there any longer. After a few weeks, Martha returned to the club and began spending time with old friends. She managed to stay away until just before Paul came home from work. Dinners were no longer uncomfortable, but they were still quiet. Either Paul or Andrew would bathe Paige and put her to bed. This ritual now included a bedtime story, as well as her prayers and a goodnight kiss.

When Paul pointed out that Martha would never get close to the children again if she continued to spend so much time away from them, she replied coldly, "They aren't interested in me being close to them, Paul. Let it go." The next day he called her doctor and reported the conversation. The doctor said it was just a defense mechanism. If she didn't let herself care, she couldn't get hurt. Give it time. These things took time.

They managed to get through the summer. Paige could swim now, having mastered both freestyle and the crawl, and Andrew spent an hour each evening in the pool with her. Paul and Martha got in the habit of having a drink and watching them. One night she asked if he knew that Andrew was teaching Paige to read.

He shook his head. "I'm not surprised, though. He's taught her everything. I don't know what I would have done without him to help me."

"You would have found a way, Paul. That's how you are." Her voice was soft, kind.

It reminded him briefly of the old Martha, the one he had fallen in love with so many years ago.

Looking at their daughter, she asked, "Does she ever play with other children?"

"No."

"And the reason for this?"

He wasn't sure how to answer her. "Well, when we brought her home from the hospital, the doctors told us we should stay with her as much as possible and that's what we did. It wasn't easy, but we did it. There aren't any young ones around here anymore. None to invite over.

When she was old enough to go to Sunday school, it upset her to be left in the toddler group. She goes with us on Sundays, and she sits with the boys in the Young Adults class, then we go to the church service."

"And she sits through all that without a fuss?"

"She does."

"That's ...amazing, I guess."

Andrew had wrapped her in a towel and carried her to them. "Tell them goodnight, Mermaid." He had numerous nicknames for her.

She leaned toward her father and kissed him. "Goodnight, Daddy."

"Goodnight, Princess."

"Say goodnight to Mother," Andrew instructed.

"Goodnight, Mother." And she pursed her lips and kissed the air, not being close enough to actually kiss Martha's cheek.

Paul and Martha both caught their breath. Paige had never exhibited any sign of affection toward her mother. "Goodnight Paige." Martha tried to answer casually, but her voice belied her conflicting emotions.

Though Paul argued fervently for Andrew to go on to Princeton for his third year, in the fall of 1963, Andrew was adamant about staying close for one more year in the event his father or Paige should need him. John and Matt would be at Syracuse for their freshman year.

September seemed to pass uneventfully. Molly was there to help with the house and Paige. Martha still went to the club every day just before lunch and returned shortly before Paul arrived home.

She was drinking heavily, and though she would switch from cocktails to coffee the last hour, sometimes the effects of the alcohol were still evident to him. There were little annoyances that became big issues between them. For one thing, Martha decided Paige should be fed dinner early instead of eating with them. He explained to her that Paige always had her meals with them, and he wasn't going to change the routine now. Martha merely shrugged and dropped the subject, but he knew she was displeased.

She began to complain about their daughter's lack of normal behavior—in Martha's words, "She doesn't act like other little girls." One day, trying to find something she could do with Paige, she had offered to polish her fingernails. Paige not only would not allow it, she had hidden behind Molly and wouldn't let Martha come near her the remainder of the day.

Growing defensive, Paul asked Martha who she was to question anyone's behavior. She appeared stunned. He had to admit he had never spoken to her in this manner.

That evening after dinner, he talked to her at length and, in the nicest way he knew, tried to explain to her what it had been like those two years she was away. Later, he thought, "She listened, but she didn't hear. She doesn't want to deal with it. She wants it never to have happened." Why didn't she understand they couldn't just pretend the way she did? He didn't believe they would really get past it, but what choice did he have except to try?

Martha continued spending her days at the club, and it seemed cocktails comprised the greater portion of her diet. He began to take exception to what he considered a lack of effort on her part. She said she resented his close relationship with their children, that they made her feel like an outcast.

For some reason, December was a particularly difficult time for her. She was moody and snappish. Molly commented that Martha criticized the child for the smallest thing. The little girl grew quiet, somber, and was even more standoffish than usual.

Paul and Andrew noticed the change in Paige. Now, she was quarrelsome, fearful about going to sleep. She wet the bed, something that had disappeared along with the use of diapers, but for the past two weeks had been a frequent occurrence. They couldn't understand this.

For several nights she woke up crying, saying she couldn't breathe. Bad dreams? They didn't know. But one night, Paul awakened and found that Martha wasn't in bed. He looked for her downstairs first, thinking she might be having a drink. She did this often now, claiming it helped her sleep. When he didn't find her there, he went upstairs to Paige's room.

Even in semidarkness, he could make out the little body thrashing on the bed as Martha pressed a pillow against her face. There was not a sound except his daughter's feet thumping wildly against the mattress. He crossed the room, grabbed his wife, spun her around, and slapped her vehemently. He picked up Paige and carried her to Drew's room, woke him, and told him to keep her there, that he was taking Martha back to the hospital.

Paul got dressed and, after helping Martha into a coat, put her into the car and drove her back to Meadow Lake, arriving at 6:00 A.M.

As soon as he returned home, he filed a report with the police and notified Children's Services. He didn't know how many times it had happened, but he sensed this was not a one-time incident. Children's Services insisted Paige be examined to determine any injuries. This meant an overnight stay in the hospital, another traumatic episode for her.

Dominic was reading the file from Westwood Hospital. He had come to the part where Paige was three years old, almost four. She had been brought to the hospital and admitted for an overnight stay. The physicians' notes were copious. Evidently, Children's Services was notified that the mother had been readmitted to the Meadow Lake Sanitarium because of further abuse to the child. It was suspected that on several occasions, for at least a two-week period, she had gone to the child's room at night and held a pillow over her face.

The child became hysterical upon admission. No female hospital personnel could be allowed in the room with her. They finally had to sedate her in order to do blood work and x-rays. Upon thorough examination, the child's larynx showed massive contusion, proof she had been choked.

Other than this and bruising on both arms, there was no evidence of further physical injury. The doctor thought the bruises on her arms were consistent with having been pinched.

After tests to assure she had no internal injuries, one doctor had written:

> *I cannot imagine the extent of emotional impairment to this child. She appears fearful of everyone except her father and brothers. Due to past experiences with the hospital and medical personnel, it is impossible to perform even the simplest task. We have been forced to sedate her for every procedure.*

The therapist had written:

> *This has been a dreadful and unexpected turn of events. That after a long period of extensive therapy and counseling and the time spent at home, the mother would again seek to harm the child defies all logic. The father and eldest brother will report to me weekly for the next six months, as ordered by the court and Children's Services. The mother is to remain at Meadow Lake for a period of two years, and is once again forbidden any contact with the daughter.*
>
> *The father has informed me that Paige will be enrolled at St. Agnes's School for Girls. I concur with the father's belief that association with other girls her age and the influence of the Sisters there will be a positive step. I am hopeful for this family, despite this setback. The father and brothers are all strong, intelligent men. They strike me as rather reserved, but loving, as well as decent and responsible. With their help, I think the child will eventually overcome the unfortunate circumstances created by the mother. I am requesting monthly reports from the school regarding the child's progress.*

Part of the notes from Martha's doctor at Meadow Lake read:

> *An unfortunate and unanticipated setback has occurred regarding the patient's progress. According to the husband, patient has resorted to the use of*

alcohol as a means of coping. Patient feels threatened by her daughter, seeing the child as the source of her problems, and blames the child for the rift between her sons and herself. She therefore sees removal of the daughter as a solution to her unhappy situation.

As he lit a cigar and refilled his glass, Dominic tried to sort his feelings. Julia was right about one thing. Now, he certainly felt differently toward Paul and Andrew. And Paige, what a survivor she was, but with such a tormented beginning. That she had grown into the remarkable young woman she was now was truly miraculous.

As they left the hospital, Paul drove and Andrew held a sobbing Paige. Dear God, this had to end.

Suddenly, Andrew said, "Dad, don't go home. Let's get a Christmas tree. Would you like that, Paige? We need a Christmas tree, and we need to take it home and decorate it. With lots of lights. Do you remember the Christmas lights? You always like those." She stopped crying and sat up, looking first at Andrew, then at her father.

"A big tree?" She wiped her nose with her hand.

Paul fished for a handkerchief and tried to answer casually, though tears stung his eyes. "Yes, a big tree, Paige, and maybe...would you like to have a little tree of your own in your room?"

Her eyes wide, she nodded. "Yes, please."

They spent close to an hour selecting the trees, a big one for the family room and a small one for Paige. Then they went for burgers and fries. They watched her sitting in the chair, swinging her feet as she ceremoniously dipped her fries in catsup and ate them neatly.

The waiter made a big fuss over her, but Paige was busy watching the other patrons. "When are the boys coming home?" she asked, referring to the twins. Paul choked on his coffee. She always referred to her brothers as "the boys."

"Well, they should be here a week before Christmas, so that's only about three days from now. Okay?"

"Yes."

"Are we forgetting our 'sirs'? This, from Andrew.

"Yes, sir."

"That's better."

Paul had the thought that Drew was going to make a great dad. He was getting plenty of practice.

John and Matt came home for the holidays and the five of them prepared for a festive Christmas. For once, Paul went all out on decorations and gifts. This had never been their practice, and it was totally out of character for him. He was not a man who believed in excess, but if ever there was a time for change, it was now.

Andrew suggested they invite Margaret for cocktails on Christmas Eve and dinner Christmas Day. Why not? She had been Paul's secretary for so long she was practically a member of the family. She lived alone and would probably enjoy being with others, *and* she loved Paige. Maybe fostering a relationship between the two was a good idea. Margaret could baby-sit if and when they needed her, and it would be good for Paige to know another woman besides Molly.

They had a wonderful Christmas that year. They took Paige to the New York City Ballet to see their production of *The Nutcracker*. She loved it, never taking her eyes off the dancers. She told Paul, "Daddy, I want to do that." And he made a mental note to see about enrolling her in ballet classes.

New Year's came and went, as well as Paige's fourth birthday, and it was time to enroll her at St. Agnes's. This was no small chore.

The therapist and the representative from Children's Services spoke at length to the Mother Superior and the Sisters who would have contact with the little girl.

They were told that, due to her abuse by the mother, the child was fearful of women. Until otherwise notified, touching the child was forbidden, even for purposes of affection. She had never been around children her age. They could gently encourage friendships, but were not to force them. She was very smart. Already her older brother was teaching her to read.

Even after discussions with the therapist and Children's Services, the Mother Superior insisted on hearing from Paul exactly what had happened.

After listening to him for almost two hours, she rose and walked to the window overlooking the playground. Paul joined her. Several little girls were playing London Bridge, some were on swings, and some were at picnic tables having their afternoon snack. One of the Sisters had taken Paige outside while she and the father visited.

The Mother Superior seemed thoughtful as they gazed out at the playground. Paige stood next to the Sister and watched the others at play, her expression one of mild curiosity, but she showed no inclination or desire to join them.

"Mr. Hamilton, do you realize how difficult this will be?"

Hesitantly, he said, "Well, she does have a mind of her own. I can't deny that, but she's well behaved—"

Her voice was gentle as she interrupted him. "Not for us, Mr. Hamilton, for her. She's hardly a typical four-year-old."

"All the more reason to have her here. I've given this a lot of thought. She needs structure and she needs to be around little girls her age."

The Mother Superior was silent, thinking. "I'll do it, Mr. Hamilton, I'll take her. But if, after an appropriate amount of time, I feel it isn't beneficial to your daughter, I won't continue."

"That's exactly what I would expect."

"Very well, let's go see about her uniforms and get her on the bus schedule. You may bring her next Monday, her first day. The bus will collect her after that." Glancing at the forms on her desk, she asked, "What about catechism and mass? I see you are Episcopalian."

"Let her participate to the extent the others do who aren't Catholic. Just do what you think is best."

She nodded and smiled. "I always do, Mr. Hamilton."

Dominic picked up the file from St. Agnes's. The record was lengthy, beginning when Paige was four and ending when she was fourteen. There were pictures from each school year. Reviewing the file was like a brief journey into her childhood, like watching her grow for a ten-year period.

There were volumes written by the Mother Superior and the

Sisters who had taught her all those years. Their concern and affection were evinced in their reports.

> *March 1964*
>
> Paige seems to be settling in. She is a quiet, serious child who is obedient and takes instructions well. To date, she does not initiate conversation with others, but she participates willingly in designated class projects. She is advanced in that her family has worked with her, teaching her to read and do simple arithmetic.
>
> Her vocabulary, as with many children exposed only to adults, is broad and advanced beyond her years. She enjoys art, but had to be encouraged in the use of finger paints. She expressed doubts as to whether this was permitted. Sister Marietta reports that once they convinced her it was allowed and she began to paint, they heard her laugh for the first time.

When he read this, Dominic had to smile. It was so like her. He could almost picture her initial disdain.

> *May 1964*
>
> Our school year is ending. We gave our program for the parents last night. Paige was a butterfly. She is still shy and could not be coaxed into singing or saying a poem, but I feel she has come along nicely in a short time. I am going to suggest our summer camp program to her father in order that she may continue to see some of her classmates.
>
> I feel that no contact with them would set her back. Sister Beatrice thinks Paige is more advanced than her classmates, thereby having little in common with them and that this, in turn, contributes to her shyness and lack of interaction with the

other students. This may be accurate, but I think she needs more time. I notice that she is kind and shares her supplies willingly. She is very observant, and her comprehension and retention skills are excellent.

There has been one disturbing occurrence. After hearing a short story about the Madonna and baby Jesus, she asked Sister Beatrice if she knew Mary was Jesus' mother. When Sister Beatrice told her that was correct, Paige wanted to know if His mother ever hurt Him. I asked Sister Beatrice for her response, which was, "I'm afraid I was so stunned by the child's question, I said I didn't believe so, and tried to distract her by asking if she would help me sharpen pencils." There was no further discussion about this, but I regret we did not handle it more wisely. I did advise the father about the incident. He said she had not mentioned it at home, so perhaps it wasn't something on which she had dwelt. The father is a good man dealing with an impossible situation. That he has remained married to this woman despite all that has happened speaks for itself.

The summer of 1964 passed quickly for them. The boys were home, but Matt and John had summer jobs. Andrew stayed with Paige, seeing that she got to day camp at St. Ag's each day from eight to twelve. He would then spend the afternoons with her, taking her to ballet class at Madame D'Andre's and, at home, swimming with her.

The ballet lessons had proved to be an excellent idea. At first, Madame Andre, as the students called her, balked because Paige was only four. She said she was used to parents who wanted their daughters to dance, but she preferred that the *child* wanted to as well. Taking Paige aside, she asked her why she wanted to take ballet. "I want to dance in *The Nutcracker*."

"Ballet is very hard work. Do you want to work hard?"

"Yes, ma'am."

"What else do you like to do, Paige?"

"I like to swim, and I can be a butterfly."

The woman smiled. "I imagine you make a wonderful butterfly, dear."

That was the beginning of fourteen years of lessons from Madame Andre and a lifetime friendship between the two.

This was Andrew's first year at Princeton. He was pre-med, and the next stop was Harvard. He fretted about leaving Paige, but Paul convinced him they would manage and Paige would be fine.

She was what his father had always called a real corker. She wanted to wear her leotard and leggings all the time. She put her ballet shoes on the minute she hit the house. She danced all over the place, and would put on a show for Molly.

When Madame Andre held her Christmas recital, Paige was one of the stars, and in her family's eyes, *the* star. Her love of ballet won out over stage fright and shyness. Madame Andre had told her to pretend she was the only one there. And she did.

Paul bought her a horse for Christmas that year to replace the pony she had outgrown. She was tall for her age, very slim, and had the marks of becoming a real equestrian. She wanted to name the horse Andre after her ballet teacher, but Paul helped her settle on Andy. Andy was a two-year-old pinto and good natured, used to children. Paige rode him daily, but she was allowed to ride only when Paul was there to watch her.

On a Saturday afternoon shortly after her fifth birthday, she started pestering Paul to let her ride. He was busy with other projects and kept putting her off. Finally, she left him alone. When he realized he hadn't seen her for a couple of hours, he went looking for her. Not finding her in the house or yard, he grew alarmed. Then he thought of the stable. Sure enough, she was on Andy, running her fingers through his mane and talking to him as they made their way back to the barn, Andy in a slow trot.

His emotions ran the gamut, but anger won out and, for the first time, he whipped her with his belt. Not waiting to take her back to the house, he whipped her there in the barn, then made her feed and water Andy and help lock up. As they walked back to the house, she was sniffling but unrepentant, and stomped her feet defiantly, her boots making small thudding sounds.

"Catherine Paige, I do not like your attitude!"

"Well, I don't like yours either!"

Taking her by the hand, he led her to his study. He put her across his lap and spanked her till she began to cry. He stood her up, and asked, "Now, Paige, why did I do that?"

"Because you're mean!"

"Paige, do I need to take my belt off again?"

Pouting, she answered him with a note of defiance in her voice. "No, sir."

Molly was hovering in the wings, and let him know she was frantic over what was taking place. Paul assured her that Paige was in better shape than either of them. He told Molly to feed her dinner and see to her bath. He would put her to bed. He then took some aspirin, poured himself a double, and thought, "I am getting too old for this!"

He had yet to visit Martha at Meadow Lake, though he made inquiries weekly by phone. Her doctor agreed he shouldn't visit until he was ready, until the anger and hurt had dissipated. This suited him. He didn't know when that might be, if ever. Right now, he had three sons in college and a daughter that was a handful, in addition to running a household and an office to boot.

It appeared from the records that Paige had done well until Martha's release in November of 1966. Martha had been at Meadow Lake for almost three years this time, and upon her release, the doctors were certain she would do well. Dominic continued to read the files from St. Agnes's.

> *November 1966*
>
> We have been informed the mother will be released and will return home by Thanksgiving. We have grave concerns. Paige has flourished, and I find her

to be a delightful child. While she remains, at times, somber and is quite the loner in many ways, it is obvious she is content at home and here at school. She excels in every class. The Sisters are exceedingly pleased with her progress in all areas.

February 1967

After less than three months, our worst fears have been realized. Paige has been hospitalized after a fall at the family home. It is my understanding that a concussion, a broken wrist and a broken leg are among her injuries. It is also my understanding that the mother was the cause of the fall. During the past month the Sisters had noticed Paige was withdrawn, sullen at times, unusual for her. We will not visit during her hospitalization. I want St. Agnes's and all connected to it to be a safe haven in Paige's mind. When she returns, she will find us here, unchanged, her desk and her classmates waiting for her.

Dominic didn't know how much more of this he could stomach. He wanted to get through it in one day and be done with it. There was so much more than he had anticipated. God, what was she? Seven now? How much could a child endure? Evidently, a lot.

Martha had been home since Thanksgiving. After her three years at Meadow Lake, the doctors assured Paul that her depression was no longer an issue. She seemed to sincerely want to come home and be a wife to him and a mother to her children. Thanksgiving and Christmas had actually been quite pleasant. Martha still enjoyed her cocktails but, to his knowledge, wasn't drinking excessively. Paige was seven now. She excelled in school, rode her horse as if she had been born on him, and loved ballet. She still had little to do with her mother, but he was adamant she be polite. He had already decided it was too late for mother and daughter to ever have a normal relationship, whatever that was.

Martha had surprised him this time though. She made a real effort, especially where he was concerned. He was wary, but also pleased. Paige was in school all day, and three afternoons a week had ballet lessons, so she was away from the house most of the time when he wasn't there.

This freed him from worry, but in mid-January he thought he noticed a change in moods in both Martha and Paige. Paige began to appear at dinner in a dress rather than her school uniform or jeans. "Doesn't she look nice?" Martha prompted.

"Lovely, she looks lovely."

Paige, her head down, toyed with the food on her plate. Well, all right, so she had to dress for dinner to please her mother. It wouldn't kill her. If Martha was trying to be a mother to her, he shouldn't stand in the way.

Paige seemed sullen, but Paul thought it was because she missed Andrew. He had recently married, and though Paige loved Julia, the newest addition to the Hamilton family, she missed having her brother at home. He was finishing his residency, and he and Julia would return to Long Island sometime next year.

The third week of February, Martha decided to give a party for some of Paige's classmates from St. Ag's. Paul had his doubts about this, but again, it seemed to him Martha was trying to be a mother to their daughter. Martha had always loved parties, and she thought Paige needed more exposure. She didn't understand that Paige was a loner by nature, and all the exposure in the world wasn't going to change her.

On the morning of the party, Paul was working in his office when he heard them arguing. Then he heard Paige announce stubbornly, "First, I'm going to ride Andy, *then* I'll get dressed!"

"You'll do as I ask you to do!" Martha shrieked. It was then he got up from his desk to intervene. He reached the foyer just in time to see his daughter's body hit the tile floor in the foyer, and land with a sickening thud. Martha was on the upstairs landing, her hands to her mouth. Paige wasn't moving, but she was breathing. He quickly phoned for help, asking for an ambulance and the police. Paige's left hand lay at an awkward angle, her left leg was twisted beneath her. He was afraid to move her.

Martha, still upstairs, finally spoke. "She went over the railing, Paul. I didn't mean...she wouldn't put on her dress. She never minds me! I try, but she hates me, Paul, she *hates* me!"

Whether it was or not, it began to sound like whining to him, and he could only think, "If I go up those stairs…"

He heard the sirens in the distance. "You may as well pack, Martha. They aren't going to let you stay."

"But, Paul…yes, I slapped her. I admit that. But I didn't mean—"

"It doesn't matter, Martha. Even if it's true, they won't believe you." And he couldn't be sure he believed her himself.

He watched as they carefully lifted the closed eyelids to check her pupils, immobilized his daughter's arm and leg, and started an IV. He told the officers what had happened, and he never looked at Martha as they took her away. Somehow, he had the presence of mind to tell Molly to notify the children's parents that the party had been cancelled.

Riding in the ambulance with Paige, he was torn between wanting her to regain consciousness and dreading the chaos that would follow if she did. She hated hospitals and doctors, and understandably so.

In the ER at Westwood, once again they sedated her then took her to x-ray. Her wrist, her leg and her ankle were broken, her knee cap fractured. She had a concussion, which for now was cause for the most concern. The bones could be set and would heal, yet again. But she had fallen twelve feet onto a tile floor. This time the concussion was serious.

Out of sheer frustration, the orthopedic surgeon, one who had treated her previously, told Paul, as if he didn't know, that this simply had to stop. The man was angry and Paul understood. God knew what the doctors and nurses thought of him, unable to protect his child.

While they prepared her for surgery, Paul called his attorney and asked him to see to Martha. He didn't know if they would let her return to Meadow Lake, and he didn't really care. He just asked that the counselor handle the situation and do the best he could with it. He had to stay with his daughter.

He called Drew and Julia, then Matt and John. They would be in that evening. He felt overwhelming guilt for what had happened, but for the life of him couldn't think what he might have done to prevent it, other than not to let Martha come home. The doctors had been so certain it would work this time. Had she really intended to push Paige or was she telling the truth? He was so tired, and whatever Martha's intentions had been, she had slapped their daughter, obviously hard enough to knock her over the railing, and she shouldn't have done that. In the end, Martha was undeniably responsible for the fall.

Paige was still in recovery when her brothers arrived. Paul watched as his sons approached the area where he was waiting to speak with the doctors. They were tall, handsome men, these three—smart, responsible, and devoted to this little one who had come so late into their lives.

Andrew spoke first, of course. "Dad, how is she?" Julia was silent, looking on sympathetically. Paul was glad Drew had found her. She was good for him.

Taking a deep breath, he told them, "Her wrist is broken and her leg and ankle, all on the left side. The surgeon is concerned about the growth line factor. Her kneecap is fractured. But the concussion is what they consider her most serious injury."

His sons exchanged knowing glances. John spoke next. "And this happened because...?"

"Because Paige wanted to ride Andy before dressing for the party," he said tiredly.

"What party?"

"The party your mother decided to give for your sister's classmates."

Matt, staring at nothing in particular down the long hallway, said, "Paige hates parties," as if, at this point, it held some significance.

"Yes, I know. I tried to tell your mother that, but it seemed she was making an honest effort to be a part of Paige's life. I felt that if it were possible, I should encourage and support that effort."

"But how did she fall?" This from Andrew.

"I was in my office and heard them quarreling. I got up to see what the problem was, but Paige had fallen by the time I reached the foyer. Your mother admits slapping her, but she says she didn't mean to push her over the railing."

"God, Dad, we thought she fell down the stairs! She fell from the landing?"

"Yes. Yes, she fell from there." His sons looked at him in stunned silence.

The doctors came and spoke to them. Paige would be in recovery another hour, then they would move her to a room. The surgeries had gone well. Her EEG was good. She was stirring somewhat, trying to wake up. They could see her, one at a time, for five minutes. Two of them could stay with her tonight once she was transferred to her room.

Paul went in first. When he saw her stretched out in sleep, she always seemed older to him. She was tall for seven. Tonight, though, she looked frail, the plaster dwarfing her slim body. Her left leg was cast from her hip to her foot, her left arm from her hand halfway to her elbow. A male nurse was in attendance. "Paige, can you wake up? Your father is here. Paige?"

She opened her eyes momentarily, then closed them again. "Paige? Come on, wake up."

Again, she opened her eyes. This time she saw him. "Hey, Princess." He choked and could say no more.

Faintly, she said, "Hi, Dad." She had stopped calling him "Daddy" early on. He was sure it had something to do with the boys always calling him "Dad."

The doctors returned. They checked her vitals and adjusted her pain medication and IV. When they rolled the gurney into the hallway, she spied her brothers. Despite pain and grogginess, this brought forth something close to a real smile. Drew and Julia stayed with her that night.

A week later, Paige was released from the hospital. Once she was home, Andrew had to go back to work, but Julia, a nurse, stayed and helped with Paige. She knew how to handle her without hurting her, and she knew what to watch for in the way of complications. Paul was grateful to have such good help. Before long Paige was up and about on crutches.

The court refused to let Martha return to Meadow Lake and ordered her to spend two years in a state facility for the criminal mentally ill. Paul pushed it to the back of his mind for now. He had to take care of their daughter and somehow repair this latest damage that had been done to her.

Dominic was making headway. He estimated he was three-quarters of the way through the files. It was 4:00 P.M., and Paige would be home by six. He wanted to finish before then. The notes from the Mother Superior continued:

> *April 1967*
>
> Paige returned to school this week. She has crutches but doesn't like to use them, preferring to hobble about on her own. She appears happy to be back with us. She has been keeping up with her lessons from home. Her father advises she will need therapy when the casts are removed, and her only complaint is that she can't dance right now.
>
> Despite all that has happened, I am hopeful for this child. She is strong in character, wise beyond her years. She refuses to discuss her injuries. The other children, of course, are curious. She is polite but uninformative. These weeks away from us have made her shy again, but I believe she will outgrow this in time. She will never be a joiner.
>
> Too much has happened in her young life for her to ever be what one would call a "normal child." She is smart and she copes with the situation at hand, whatever it is. She is a survivor and she touches my heart.

There followed copious notes regarding her progress throughout the years at home and at school. Evidently, April of 1967 till 1973 were good years for the family. Paige's injuries healed and she returned to her classes. She could dance once more.

John married Anne in 1969 and Matt married Bitsy in 1970. Martha spent two years in the state facility and was then moved again to Meadow Lake. She was not released until January of 1973. Whatever happened during those years away from home must have either cured her or, at the very least, convinced her she could never touch Paige again, not if she wanted to live outside a sanitarium, because she never went back.

With the exception of final entries regarding Martha's return home and a few from St. Ag's noting Paige's last year, there were no more files, no further reports of any incidents.

One entry from Sister Constantine and the Mother Superior made him smile:

December 1973

> It seems our Paige has finally managed to do something in the realm of the norm. She has misbehaved. Sister Constantine caught her passing answers to a quiz to Angela Manetti. Their punishment was to clean the altar—polish, vacuum, replace candles, and the like. They came upon the Father's liquor cabinet and helped themselves to his brandy. They sampled most of the bottle and fell asleep in chapel. This was how we found them.
>
> The brandy, as would be expected, made them quite ill. We, of course, had to make an example of them and mete out rather severe punishment, but I am certain it is a story the Sisters and I will enjoy retelling through the years.
>
> Unfortunately for Paige, her father did not find any humor in the incident and punished her further at home. We have separated the girls, but I saw them in the cafeteria today. They are not allowed to

communicate at present, but they exchanged conspiratorial smiles. I, for one, am actually heartened by the incident.

The last entry from St. Ag's was written when Paige was fourteen. The Mother Superior had reported:

> Paige Hamilton is no longer with us. As much as it saddened me to do so, I insisted she be permitted to test out of school. Her father would not allow it at age twelve, but this year I felt it was imperative.
> She is too advanced for us to be of benefit to her any longer. To keep her would be an injustice to the child and her potential.
> I understand she will attend NYU beginning spring semester. I see her alone in this undertaking, as she will be much younger than the other students, but in a few years she will come into her own. I pray she finds her place in this world and, one day, the life and love she deserves. She is a remarkable girl. We shall miss her.

Dominic breathed a sigh of relief, having come to the end of this... this what? He was shocked and appalled by what he had read, and he didn't believe Paige couldn't remember what had happened, especially the last incident that occurred when she was seven. How could she not remember that? The concussion...maybe. Or maybe she had simply blocked the memory. Well, from the age of seven through twelve, she'd had no contact with her mother. She would have been almost thirteen when Martha returned home, old enough to defend herself if need be.

One had to think, even if it wasn't an ideal situation, that at least she wasn't in harm's way from then until she left home. To his amazement, the asthma and the chronic pain in her left leg, which she seldom mentioned, seemed to be the only lasting ill effects she suffered from all her injuries.

Glancing at the monitor, he saw Vincente arriving with Paige.

She had left early this morning and been in meetings most of the day. Quickly, he boxed the files.

"Dom?" She came through the doorway just as he was locking the credenza. She was wearing the black dress she had worn the day he met her. He took her in his arms and kissed her.

"I missed you, Zucchero."

He buried his face in her hair, closed his arms tightly around her. Her mouth found his again and she kissed him fervently. After several minutes of this, she whispered, "Let's go upstairs."

And when he took her, he was tender, loving, then passionate and fierce, as if somehow he could erase any traces of the hurtful past from her body.

NINE

Today was Paige's twenty-first birthday. Dominic bought her a sports watch. She had a thing about watches and had quite a collection. He thought they would probably spend at least part of the day with her family, but Paige said she wanted to spend it with him, just the two of them. And when he asked what she would like to do, she had merely shrugged and smiled. "Be with you, of course."

That wasn't much to go on. He wanted to do something special for her but was at a loss as to what. Then it struck him, and he was pleased with himself. Later that afternoon he told her to wear her dark green dress and her emerald earrings and bracelet. She looked at him curiously but said nothing. Before they left for the evening, he took her black coat from the closet and held it for her as she put it on.

In the car, she was silent, pensive, as she traced the lines in the palm of his hand with her finger.

Eyeing her thoughtfully, he said, "Twenty-one is a milestone, Paige. Feeling any older yet?"

She ignored his gentle teasing. "We've only been together four months, but it feels like longer. Longer in a good way, I mean. I'm not sure time is an accurate measure of maturity, but I think I've grown up a lot since we met." Her look was expectant, waiting for confirmation.

He nodded. "No argument here, Sweetheart."

As the car pulled up in front of Harry's, she turned to him. "I love you, Dom."

"So you know what I'm up to?"

"I do. I love it."

They were seated at the same table where they'd sat when on their first date, his table. Throughout dinner, Paige was quiet, reflective. "What are thinking about, Sweetheart?"

"Only that conversation may be somewhat limited tonight. I can't tell you about myself. You already know *everything*. " And with that, she laughed.

He could only think that what he had recently learned about her childhood was in stark contrast to how the young woman who sat across from him now had turned out. She was confident, completely at ease. From the beginning, he had sensed there was something that set her apart, but he would never have guessed... Did she really not remember? She was so open...so honest with him, and yet...

"Dom?"

"Yes, love?"

"Now, *you're* thinking."

Giving her his full attention, he smiled. "Yes, I am, and you would be pleased." There was no need for her to know, and the lie rolled easily from his tongue.

"Oh, well, in *that* case!"

When they left the restaurant, they walked leisurely, hand in hand, just as they had done before. He thought about that first night, the nervousness she had obviously tried to quell, her shy glances at him when she thought he wasn't looking. And later, telling him she wanted to stay, taking her every cue from him, not knowing what to do next. These memories stirred him no end.

Interrupting his thoughts, she said, "Dom, you're doing it again."

He lit a cigar. "Guilty. I'm thinking we should go to the apartment. Would you like that?"

Repeating an old refrain, she smiled and squeezed his arm: "I'd love to."

Once there, they took their drinks and walked out onto the terrace. "Dom, you know that first night?"

"Yes."

"I was so upset when I thought you were going to take me home." Shaking her head, she smiled at the memory.

"Well, Zucchero, that wasn't my intention, but it's not a problem tonight, is it?" His tone was slightly teasing again.

"And you can't know how relieved I am." She sipped her wine and, looking out over the city, said softly, "This is such a great view."

Standing behind her, he put his arms around her and nuzzled her neck. His voice was husky. "Let's go inside." She looked up at him, and he kissed her.

She slipped the tip of her tongue into his mouth. "I love how you taste, Dom."

He kissed her again, and she pressed close to him, sliding her hand down the front of his trousers.

His voice was gruff. "Inside now. March."

They went straight to the bedroom. As he unbuttoned his shirt, she turned her back to him and, in a well-remembered gesture, lifted the fall of dark hair with one hand, exposing the slender neck. "Undo me, please, Darling?"

"With pleasure."

He watched her undress, and when she was down to only her panties, pulled her to him. Running one finger around the lacy band, he slipped it inside so he was touching the soft skin just above the patch of dark, curling hair. His eyes held hers, owning her. "Are you ready to be fucked?"

"Yes."

"Tell me."

"I want you to fuck me."

He took off her panties, let his fingers explore her. She was ready.

He was never hesitant to unleash his desires, so his passion dictated their every move. As he lay back on the bed, she kissed him, working her way down his body until her head was nestled in his groin. Using her tongue, she was all over him. She took him in her mouth, loving him, tasting him until he groaned, "Not too much of that, Sweetheart."

She stretched out beside him and whispered, "I love you, Dom. I love *us*. I love *this*." Then, taking his hand, she guided it between her legs. "Feel me."

She was so warm and slick, and she strained against the gentle pressure of his fingers, craving release.

His mouth was on her breast, his tongue teasing the nipple, and she moaned softly. He continued to stroke her, drawing the wetness to her bottom.

Reaching for him, her fingers closed around him, and she whispered, "I want you in me. *Now.*"

He fucked her, slowly, deliberately, until she clung to him, drawing him deeper inside her as the moment claimed her and she cried out.

His voice was hoarse with passion as he commanded, "Turn over, Baby."

He pushed his cock into her bottom, trying to be easy with her, but she was responding now, moving with him, and it felt so good. Her fingers clutched at the pillow and her breath came in short gasps till she moaned, "I'm coming, Dom, I'm coming!" He could hold back no longer and he rammed himself into her until he too was spent.

She lay in the shelter of his arms, their bodies damp with sweat in the aftermath of their lovemaking. He kissed her, and asked, wanting to know, as always, "Are you okay, Zucchero?"

"Of course." She traced his mouth with her finger and said softly, "You're so wonderful...and I love you so much."

This was one of those moments when his answer came in a gesture. Pulling her even closer, he kissed her, held her in a crushing embrace. Then safe and warm, and wet, they slept.

Paige awoke early the next morning. Sometime during the night Dominic had covered them, and she lay with her back to him, spoon-like, his arms around her holding her tight against him. Her head ached and her stomach was cramping. Just like clockwork. She could do with a less accurate clock!

Freeing herself from his arms, she whispered, "Let me up, Sweetheart, I have to go to the bathroom."

He yawned and stretched and pulled her to him again. "Not without saying good morning."

She kissed him. "Good morning for you. Not so good for me. Cramps." She sighed. "Didn't I just finish an episode of this not long ago?"

He rubbed her lower back. "I'm sorry, Babe. It's kind of a relief though. It wouldn't do to have you pregnant at this point. Somebody would have my head." He laughed.

"We're still nearly ten months from the wedding. Do you think our luck will hold out?" Her dark eyes were warm with a smile.

"We'll just take whatever comes, Zucchero, and we'll handle it."

A man with his own thoughts about things, Dominic wasn't likely to change his mind. He was against Paige using any form of birth control, pills or otherwise, nor was he interested in using condoms. It was one thing with the arrangements he'd had previously. Precautions were necessary. But with Paige, it was different.

He didn't want that stuff in her body, and had he not witnessed how ill she was each month, he would have had a different opinion about the medications Bernie prescribed for her. The pills helped, but had a sedative effect, and she slept a lot. Fortunately, she needed them only the first two days of her cycle. When they had children, he hoped she could have them naturally. Already he knew he didn't want them cutting on her, for any reason.

The months passed quickly, marked by each holiday. For Valentine's Day, Dominic gave Paige rubies—earrings, choker, and bracelet. That night, they went to the annual dance held at the country club. It was a fund-raiser, always well attended. He wore a tux and she a red evening gown. It was strapless with a full skirt cut on the bias that swirled to the floor. She wore the jewels he had given her. With her dark hair, dark eyes and pale complexion, the red ensemble made for a stunning contrast, and she was beautiful. He noticed all eyes on her as they entered the ballroom, and his hand squeezed her waist possessively. "For Your Precious Love" was playing, and she turned to him. "Shall we?"

He took her in his arms. "Of course."

She loved dancing with him, and followed his every step effortlessly. They were a striking couple, moving gracefully about the floor. As they danced he whispered to her in the way that lovers do, and she smiled up at him, her dark eyes shining.

The Hamiltons and the Gianellis were there. Seated at several tables in close proximity, they watched as Dominic and Paige danced, not once, but twice, before finally making their way to them.

Spying the jewelry his daughter was sporting as they approached their table, Paul Hamilton realized, once more, that this relationship was going forward and at full tilt. It seemed to him they seldom saw Paige anymore. Over lunch with Henry Carson, he had found himself asking about her.

Carson, taken aback, recovered quickly and replied, "Why, yes, she comes in for meetings and presentations whenever we need her. We have her pretty much on the same schedule we've always followed with her. It works well, and she seems satisfied not to have to come in on a daily basis." He hesitated, then continued, "Paige tells me she doesn't plan to work once they're married."

"I'm not surprised. I don't think he would allow it even if she wanted to," Paul said, rather bitterly.

"I don't know, Paul. I realize you're upset by this situation, but I see them together. At first, I had the same sentiments as you, I think, but they seem very happy. He's completely devoted to her. I can't imagine that he won't take good care of her. That can't be all bad, can it? As fathers, really, what more can we ask for our daughters?"

Sighing, Paul answered, "Maybe you're right, Henry. It just happened so quickly. And even after several months, I'm amazed at how little I know about him."

"Hi, Dad!" His daughter's voice brought him back to the present as she leaned toward him and kissed his cheek.

He couldn't resist. "Well, hello, Stranger."

"Oh, Dad, it hasn't been that long!"

Victoria quickly changed the subject by asking Paige if she was shopping for her wedding gown. Looking startled, Paige replied that she hadn't as yet, but planned to do so soon. Her response resulted in a chorus of reasons she should not procrastinate, all espoused by her mother and the sisters-in-law, both current and future.

Dominic rescued her by asking her to dance. "Zucchero, you're going to have to throw them a bone. Choose your gown, select the bridesmaid dresses. I haven't wanted to mention it, but I'm getting calls from my side of the group of wedding planners." As if he knew this might be construed as criticism, he assured her it wasn't, but he encouraged her to do her part, and she agreed.

By the end of the next week Paige had chosen a gown by a European designer. It had a white silk bodice and full skirt. The long fitted sleeves and the yoke were of sheer organza sewn with gold and platinum threads that formed a scattering of dainty rosebuds. There was an overlay of this material on the bodice and the effect was breathtaking. At first glance, the gown appeared strapless, and it seemed the intricate embroidery lay on her bare arms and shoulders.

Only Julia and Isabella were allowed to accompany her that day, and she swore them to secrecy, not wanting to offend the others. They watched as Paige stood motionless, eyeing her reflection in the triple mirror. Catching their gaze, she smiled, a slight blush warming her face.

It was the first time the wedding had a sense of reality for her. She would walk down the aisle of St. Patrick's Cathedral (the Gianellis were adamant about this, and since it meant so much to them, what could she do but acquiesce?), and she would marry Dominic Gianelli. Her heart beat wildly at the thought of it, belying her outwardly calm demeanor.

Having selected her gown, she perused the catalogs for suitable bridesmaid dresses. Paige wanted anything from scarlet to cranberry in color. She preferred a simple, but elegant, strapless style with a fitted bodice and long, a-line skirt. It took most of the afternoon, but the women finally settled on a design similar to what she liked that included a matching wrap. Julia and Isabella thought it was lovely. They would arrange with the others to come for the first fitting in April, with the final fitting scheduled for two weeks prior to the wedding.

Isabella suggested that while they were there, perhaps Paige should choose the dresses the nieces were to wear in the wedding, as well as tuxes for the boys and men.

They did choose a dress, in a style suitable for all the girls, regardless of age, but Paige wouldn't even consider looking at the men's attire, saying that once Dominic decided on his tux, the men and boys could follow suit.

Isabella rolled her eyes and whispered to Julia, "You know what? She's *perfec*t for him!"

Overhearing this, Paige smiled sweetly. "Thank you, Isabella."

Julia listened to their banter. She was heartened by Paige's close relationship with the Gianellis. They loved her, and she had further endeared herself to both families by including everyone in the wedding party. There wasn't a niece or nephew, a sister or brother and their respective spouse, who wasn't participating.

She, Anne, and Bitsy, as well as Dominic's three sisters were the bridesmaids, their spouses the groomsmen. Nieces and nephews would serve as flower girls, ring bearers, candle lighters, ushers, and attendants at the guest register, and some would hand out programs. Dominic's father was to be his best man, and Aunt Sophia, Paige's matron of honor.

Paige had told them she wanted a white cake decorated with red roses, and for her bouquet, white roses, very simple, please. Other than that, she had pretty much left the wedding plans to Martha and Victoria, which pleased them no end.

Paige attended Easter services with the Gianellis, and shortly thereafter began classes in preparation to join the church. Dominic had insisted she discuss her decision with her family. He had Vincente drive her to her parents' house, but he refused to accompany her.

"I told you this had to be your decision. You owe it to your family to tell them what you've decided and why. They may accept it, Paige, or they may not. Either way, you will have done what's right. Do you understand?"

"Of course."

But her heart was pounding and her palms were sweaty when Vincente pulled into the drive. She knew her grandparents, as well as her brothers, would be there.

She spent almost two hours discussing the matter with them, and was relieved that they never tried to talk her out of it. In the end, they seemed to accept her decision, saying it was obvious she had given the matter serious consideration, and what more could they ask than that?

When Vincente came for her, Dominic was there, waiting for her. She told him it had gone well, that her family had no objections. He nodded. "That's good, Zucchero, and now it's settled. How do you feel?"

"Good. I feel good about it." One more step toward the wedding.

Dominic and Paige began to attend weekly Mass and would occasionally attend Sunday services with the Hamiltons. Paige, in her desire to please everyone, had decided to include the pastor from the Episcopal Church in the ceremony, as well as Father Stefano, who would perform the wedding vows.

As for Dominic, with Paige converting to Catholicism, and both churches recommending counseling for couples prior to marriage, he couldn't remember a time in his life when so much of it had been spent in church. Still, he was going to do this right. As with so many things about Paige, her efforts on his behalf and for others touched him.

He had shared the information from the files with his parents and Sophia, all of whom were shocked to learn of the disturbing events.

Finally, his aunt had spoken. "Well, it is done and now we know. To what end? Paige is a happy young woman who wears her love for Dominic for all the world to see. She is caring and generous, but goes about it quietly. She is sincere in her undertaking to be part of this family. I agree with you, nephew, that it's odd she would not remember, but I have to ask, what advantage would there be if she could recall what happened? Perhaps things are best left as they are. She is one of our own now, officially so in a matter of months. We will watch her, guide her, and care for her. We will protect her. I see no reason to speak of this again."

They nodded their assent, but they all knew it was something not easily put aside.

Summer was half over now. Dominic and Paige had spent several weekends, as they were spending this one, on *The Mallorca*, one of their favorite pastimes. She was scheduled to be confirmed the following Sunday. He knew she was dreading, not the rite itself, but having an audience, however small.

Well, she would get through it. This was turning out to be a busy year for them, and especially for her, but she was handling it well and he was proud of her.

He and Manetti watched as she showed Buscliano how to tack. She was teaching him some of the finer points of sailing. A hulk of a man whose build resembled that of a refrigerator, Buscliano's face was solemn as he listened carefully to what she was saying.

Manetti puffed his cigar, then ventured, "Mr. G., in your wildest dreams, did you ever think you would see—?"

Dominic interrupted him. "Never, Manny, *never*." And they both laughed.

"She's a real gem, Mr. G."

"Yes, Manny, she is."

It was mid-August and Dominic had a trip to Europe planned.

Strictly business, and ten days was cutting it close. He might have to be gone as much as two weeks. He would have preferred Paige stay with his parents, but she was hesitant, saying it was a long time and she would rather stay home if he didn't mind.

He hated to leave her, but he had no choice. Repeatedly, he went over everything with her. Only Vincente was to drive her, but in an emergency, Manetti or Buscliano would do so. Each day she was to leave a schedule with Manetti so he would know where she was at any given time.

He would call her each morning at seven and in the evenings at eleven. Yes, of course, she could swim and she could jog the garden paths closest to the house. This was to be her home. She had access to everything in it, but in his office, any mail or messages could wait till he returned.

The night before he left, they went to bed early, wanting as much time together as possible. They left nothing from their repertoire that night. Finally they slept, only to waken a few hours later to find their desires rekindled, and he took her again.

The next morning he was dressed and ready to leave by eight. She was solemn as he told her good-bye, that he would call her as soon as he arrived. She had not asked about the nature of his trip, but at the last moment when Vincente was putting the luggage in the car, she asked, "Dom, will you be all right?"

He set his briefcase down and took her in his arms. "I'll be fine, Zucchero, and remember, I'll call you every day. I almost forgot, look on my desk. That's as close as I can come to an itinerary." Then, "I wasn't going to mention it, but I've been thinking about something. You and I are going to take a trip, before the wedding. A getaway for just the two of us. Don't ask me where, that part is going to be your surprise. Okay?"

He left then, trying not to focus on how lost she looked. He would miss her terribly. This he knew. They had not been apart for more than a few days since they had met.

On the plane, he occupied his mind planning the getaway. Several times Paige had mentioned a vacation her family had taken to Yellowstone Park in Wyoming and Montana. Evidently it made quite an impression on her, because she described its beauty with something akin to reverence. Her face lit up when she spoke of the mountains, the wildlife, the natural wonders of the park, the clear and beautiful star-filled nights.

He had arranged with a realtor to rent a house for two weeks during early October. According to her, the weather was turning cold then, but most of the roads were still navigable. His specifications for the house and its location required some special efforts on the part of the realtor, but she thought she had found just what he was looking for. It would make an interesting trip. He didn't recall having visited the area, though he must have flown over it many times.

As a boy, whenever his family vacationed, it was usually upstate or to Canada, and sometimes to Europe, so this trip would hold something new for him and be a nice break for both of them.

He requested a drink, and after it was served, he opened his briefcase, took out a legal pad and began making notes. The meetings would be held in Messina, Palermo, and Catania on alternate days. He sketched the table to note the seating order.

To my right:	To my left:
1) Lorenzo Agosti	1) Bruno Parelli
2) Fausto Abruzzi	2) Alfredo Campisi
3) Carlo Venito	3) Cosimo Moscati
4) Onorato Feretti	4) Gianetto Gardini
5) Abramo Palotti	5) Vittore Salviati
6) Enrico Torchia	6) Cesare De Luca

Agosti would be the spokesman, with Parelli supporting him. If these two joined forces, the others would follow, so Agosti was his target. He hoped he could reason with him. He did not approve of what they had been doing. Prostitution was one thing, being forced into it another. For the right price and the right conditions, it was easy enough to find women who would willingly sell their bodies. The men needed to change their method of recruitment. How many times must he explain that the fewer laws one broke, the less interference from the authorities?

He could usually persuade them to see things his way, but it did not happen quickly. He committed the sketch to memory, then carefully tore it into small pieces and disposed of it. They were almost to Heathrow. There would be a two hour layover there, the two-and-a-half hour flight to Rome, then the drive to the house at Salerno.

This was an important trip. There was a lot on the table, and he intended to resolve every issue. If he could accomplish this, there would be no need to return for at least six months and perhaps even a year.

In the terminal, between planes, he rang Manetti. He had been away only eleven hours, but he missed her. How was she? She was fine, Manny assured him. She'd been swimming and was now lying by the pool reading a book. Things were quiet. Before nightfall, they would speak to her. When she went upstairs, they would post men at all entrances to the house. Not to worry, they would take care of her.

She was scheduled for a full day at work tomorrow, and would go from there to the studio. She should be back on Long Island by 8:00 P.M.

"You know you're to stay with her."

"Yes, sir."

En route to Rome, he tried to think ahead to the wedding. Not much longer now. He planned to bring her to Italy for their honeymoon. She'd never been to Europe, and it would give her a chance to see the villa, meet some of the people. He was going to have to give some thought to security when they went to Montana. Manny and Buscliano could travel with them and, prior to the trip, arrange for whatever teams were needed to serve as guards and to patrol the adjoining areas. As for the acreage, and the entrances and exits to the property, this was information the realtor could provide. It was his understanding that the closest neighbor was five miles away. There was a large restaurant and general store, Henry's and Millie's, about an hour from the ranch. The nearest town of any size was close to two hours away. He would have the house stocked with everything they needed before they arrived.

The more he thought about it, the more he was convinced this would be a wonderful surprise for Paige, something she would really enjoy.

Reclining the seat, he closed his eyes and thought of her, recalling their night of lovemaking. It was going to have to last him two weeks. What he wouldn't give to have her here beside him. He could do that, bring her over, let her stay at the villa. He would be there evenings. What a temptation. But, no, not this time. He would do what he needed to do, and get back to her as soon as possible. He was tired and managed to sleep until their arrival in Rome.

By the time they reached Salerno, it was two in the morning in New York. Still, he had promised her he would call.

She answered on the second ring. "Dom?" He could tell by her voice she had not been asleep.

"Of course."

"I miss you."

"I know, Sweetheart, I miss you too. I've been having some wild thoughts."

"Really?"

He laughed. "Really. It's not feasible, Babe, but if it were I would have you here in a heartbeat."

She hesitated. "Can we make it feasible?"

He said softly, "I don't think so, my love, but if I could, I would. Okay?"

"Okay."

"Are you doing all right? Everything in order there?"

"Yes, I'm fine. Manny told me I should lock our door when I came upstairs for the night, and I did."

"That's good, Babe. It's just a precaution. No one is going to bother you, so don't be afraid. I know it's a big house when you're there alone. I've already decided we're not going to do this again, Paige, not like this." And he meant it. It was too long to be apart.

"I'm glad."

"Okay, Zucchero, give me something nice to think about. What are you wearing?"

"Should I tell you the truth and say one of your tee shirts, or should I make up something sexy?"

"You do wonders for my shirts, Baby. Anything under it?"

"Just me."

"Uh-oh, I can't take too much of this. Listen, Sweetheart, I'm going to grab something to eat, then take a shower and crash. It's been a long trip and I'm beat. I'll call you again later. You go to sleep now. Okay?"

"Okay." He heard a faint sniffle as she said, "I love you, Dom, and I miss you so much it hurts." There was a tiny break in her voice.

His voice was low, husky. "Zucchero, you are my life, my heart. Don't forget that I love you too."

There was silence, then another sniffle, louder this time.

"Paige?"

"I'm here."

She was definitely crying. "Now, how can I bear to call you every day if it makes you cry? Hmmm?"

Despite the fact that Paige was practically sobbing, she protested, "I'm not crying, not really."

He would give her this one. "Okay, then, goodnight, Sweetheart."

"Goodnight."

Paige lay there in the darkness, the bed so big and empty without him, and sobbed into a pillow. She thought about her life before she met him. Satisfactory at best, but more like just existing, going through the motions.

Getting the apartment had given her a sense of freedom. She didn't know why it was such a relief to move from her parents' house. It was, after all, the only home she had ever known. They thought it was youth flexing newfound independence, but it was more than that. Much more.

Thinking back, she realized she had always lacked....what would she call it? An inner peace? There was something going on inside her all the time, an unease that nagged her, ate at her, robbed her of anything close to serenity.

All her life, she had felt one of two ways. She was either in a goldfish bowl, on display, constantly being monitored by others, or it was reversed, and she was merely an observer, but never a participant. She was an outsider, even within her family. They loved her, but... God! Now, her head hurt. Why, she wondered, when she thought about her family, did she always wind up with a headache?

Turning her mind to a more pleasant subject, she focused on Dominic. She had thought from the beginning he was special, had felt it immediately. But there was a moment, a particular moment when she *knew*, when she had walked through a door and it had closed behind her.

Trying to pinpoint the exact moment was difficult. So many things were special. The first time they made love, the way he held her afterward, the look in his eyes the next morning, were all part of it. But it was when he had said, "You're mine now. You know that, don't you?"

Then, yes, *then*, a feeling unequal to anything she had felt before came over her, and it was wonderful, like arriving at some long sought destination. *She belonged to him.* And, finding comfort in this, she finally slept.

When she awoke early the next morning, she decided she couldn't spend the entire two weeks as she had spent last night. Her eyes were swollen and she was tired. She went downstairs and made a pot of coffee. Taking out a pen and pad, she made a list of things to do each day. She would stay so busy she wouldn't have time to think.

First thing every morning, she would run, then swim. She had to spend three days at the office this week and next. When in the city, she would go to the studio on the way home. Those days would pass quickly. The others she would need to fill with activities. Having promised to spend some time with her family and his, she made arrangements to go to the Gianellis on Saturday and to her parents on Sunday.

In the library, she discovered the shelves were packed with biographies of noted military personnel, spanning centuries. The Civil War had always held her interest, so she decided to start with those, choosing one about Robert E. Lee. She was a history buff anyway, and this would keep her busy.

She would do something nice for Manny and Bus. After ten months, they were a familiar part of her life, and she regarded them as friends. Even the thought of the tapes didn't discomfit her. Indeed, she rarely thought about them. She knew, because Dominic had told her, that the house and grounds were monitored day and night, not only by personnel, but with security cameras as well. He also explained that no one but Manny and Bus were allowed to view the tapes. Only in rare instances would someone else have access to them.

The phone rang and she ran to answer it with a breathless "Hello."

"Good morning."

"Hi."

"Someone is a woman of few words today."

"I'm just having coffee and making a list."

"I see."

"I guess I'll spend Saturday with your parents and Sunday with mine."

"Sounds good."

"Truthfully, I'm just trying to fill the days till you return—then I don't want anyone coming around for a while." She gave a little laugh.

"Touché." Then, "I meant what I said, Paige. We won't do this again, not for this length of time, I promise."

"I'm glad. Are you in a meeting now?"

"We just adjourned. Some of us will go for drinks and dinner, then I'll go back to Salerno."

"Oh."

"I'll call you tonight, Zucchero. You have a good day. Okay?'

"Yes, and you have a good evening. I love you, Dom."

"And I love you."

She hung up the phone, closed her eyes, and uttered a simple prayer. "Please keep him safe. Please." It was on this occasion she would begin praying for his health and well being. If asked, had her life depended on it, she could not have explained why.

Nothing had happened to indicate any peril or impending danger to him, but it would become a daily ritual for her. And as time passed, her prayers would become more inclusive, more explicit, as if God might need detailed information in order to understand and grant her requests.

Deciding she had time to bake something for Manny and Bus, she settled on peanut butter cookies. They were quick, and it was a recipe with which she was familiar. She set them aside to cool and dashed upstairs to throw on some shorts and her sneakers.

For almost an hour, she ran the garden paths. It was really very pleasant. Everything from roses and chrysanthemums to hibiscus was blooming. She thought of Dominic's words, that this was to be her home, and she smiled to herself.

Her home, *their* home. Afterward, noting the time, she had to hurry and dress for work.

By eight that evening, she was back at the house. It occurred to her that she hadn't eaten since breakfast. She got an apple, then put on her swimsuit. The water felt good, and she swam leisurely, lap after lap, until she was tired.

She went upstairs, showered and washed her hair, and prepared for bed. Just as she lay down, the phone rang. She had done it. She had made it through the first day.

The Meeting at Catania

This was the third of their meetings. The first was usually a formality, polite small talk with only a hint of what was to come. The second was more serious—lines were drawn, sides chosen. The discussion this morning had grown heated, voices were raised. This issue of trafficking in women was divisive. Dominic thought some of the lesser Dons were, if not against it, at least ambivalent about it. Still, they had no desire to antagonize Agosti or Parelli. Agosti was defensive, saying he personally did not seize the women. He was only taking advantage of an opportunity when it presented itself. Parelli concurred.

Repeatedly, Dominic pointed out that it was still a risk they didn't have to take. They could recruit all the women they wanted, and successfully so, with the promise of money and a good working environment. When Parelli mentioned that some of the clients' tastes ran to the more sadistic, that they liked the idea of having their way with a woman who was captive and frightened, and were willing to pay a premium for this, he fired back, "If they are good at what they do, they can pretend, can't they? Do you want, if not yourselves, your capos, your lieutenants, any of your men spending time in prison when it could be avoided? Do you enjoy having the authorities breathing down your neck, waiting for you to make the smallest mistake?

"I'm not asking you to change anything except your method of recruitment. There is no limit to the advantages if you think this through. You can recruit them from almost any country. Just do it with no appearance of impropriety.

"Remember the old axiom, you must spend money to make money. Select desirable women. Invest in them. Those who have little will be lured by an attractive wardrobe, a nice apartment shared with others, the promise of money. Those more experienced can be enticed by offers of even higher earnings, a more selective clientele. All this can be achieved within the limits of the law." He paused to let them consider what he had said.

Parelli spoke next. "Don Gianelli, while I understand your desire to keep our business transactions as discreet as possible, and to conduct our operations as legitimately as we can, why fix what isn't broken? To date, we've had little trouble from the authorities. They tend to look the other way with this woman thing. The women are brought to us and we buy them. It's quite simple really."

Dominic nodded. "To date, Don Parelli, to date. Of what you just said, that is the part that concerns me. There will come a day when it will be an issue and not a small one. The other side I see to this is the selection process. You don't really have a choice, do you? And your clients, surely they prefer the more attractive women to the less attractive ones?"

Agosti spoke now. "Attractiveness is part of it, the women's specialties are another."

"And how many of these women, when you purchase them, have 'specialties'? Surely not many. Is this correct?"

They were thoughtful now. Finally, he was making some headway.

He poured another glass of wine and lit a cigar. "Please do not misunderstand my objective. As always, I am here by invitation, your invitation. I am a guest in your home, your country. My country at heart, my family's country by birth. I am not here to make demands, only to listen and advise." He was polite, gracious, never condescending, and this earned him favor among these unlikely peers.

"I've given this a lot of thought and I feel strongly that for you to continue with your current practice will not bode well for you in the future. However, by modifying your approach to the selection and acquisition of your...employees...I think you reduce your risk factor and increase your income potential. I believe it to be a win-win proposition."

Abruzzi was talking to Venito—and this was good—when Campisi ventured, "I cannot argue with what you say, Don Gianelli. The fact is we have to invest in these women after we buy them. They have to be cleaned up, fed and housed."

"Exactly, Don Campisi. So why not make your investment ahead of time and select the women who will bring you the most business. This way, the ball is always in your court. You are always in control." The others were nodding in agreement now, and even Agosti and Parelli were thoughtful.

Finally, Agosti spoke. "Don Gianelli, with your permission, let us break for an hour or so and discuss it among ourselves. There's merit to what you say."

"Of course, Don Agosti, and this need not be decided today. It's worth overnight consideration."

Parelli gave Agosti a sharp glance. Gianelli was letting them know this would be decided by the end of the day tomorrow. There would be some fine points to discuss, and this might take a few days, but Gianelli expected them to see it his way and proceed accordingly. Actually, there really was merit to his suggestion, and one could not quarrel with his success over two decades. He was a Don in the truest sense of the word.

He was also like none they had ever experienced. He was somewhat like his uncle before him, but this one—he was educated, a brilliant man, and a successful entrepreneur in his own right. He gave the appearance of a calm and easygoing exterior, but had proven, when necessary, that he could be ruthless and unforgiving. He thought things through carefully, but once he made a decision, it was done. He did what he had to do, always without regret or remorse. It was rumored he was to be married soon, but so far there had been no mention of this.

It was late when they adjourned for the day, and Dominic returned to the house at Salerno. As much as possible, he attended the meetings, then went home. The wave of left-wing political violence that had started in the late '70s, including kidnappings and assassinations, continued in the area, and he took no chances.

The meetings exhausted him. Slowly, steadily, for twenty years he had done his utmost to steer the regions' Dons toward more law-abiding practices when possible. Of course, some things would always stay the same. Drugs, protection—another way to say extortion—you weren't going to be able to legitimize such practices, but you could operate in a manner that reduced the potential for compromise. Stateside, he was free of any connections to them, as much so as possible, but here, only death would divest him of his association. Even though he accepted no money from them, it was still La Cosa Nostra and he was still *the* Don.

He had missed his call to Paige and decided to ring Manetti. What was it there now? Almost 3:00 A.M.

"Manetti here."

"How are things?"

"Everything's good here, sir."

"And Paige?"

"She's very busy, sir."

"How so?"

Clearing his throat, Manetti answered, "For one thing, she's been baking for us."

"Really?"

"Yes, sir. Monday, it was peanut butter cookies, yesterday it was brownies, and today it's rum cake. I can highly recommend the rum cake, sir."

"I'm glad. What else?"

"Aside from work, she runs and swims, morning and evening."

"But no problems?"

"None, sir. And you?"

"Just the usual, Manny. Thanks for looking out for her."

"Goodnight, sir."

He poured another drink and smiled, thinking of her baking for them. She must be desperate. There was one thing he knew about Paige—cooking was not at the top of her list, so the reported attempts amused him no end. He lay down to nap, setting the alarm so he would call her on time.

By the end of the week, the trafficking issue had been settled. They would no longer buy women from their current provider. That this had taken the greater portion of a week to resolve did not surprise him.

Next on the agenda: a dispute between two regions over distribution practices. In short, someone was selling his drugs in someone else's territory. It served Dominic well that he accepted no form of compensation. There was no reason to favor one boss or one area over another. He could be relied upon to issue fair and impartial judgment. This had eliminated the practice of vigilante justice in most cases. Punishment and retribution were now discussed first and delivered afterward.

Then there was the issue of one who had "turned." He would have little choice in this matter. The man had sealed his fate. He let the local Dons decide the order of things, and it struck him as ironic that a man's life was less important to them than a territorial dispute.

The weekend was a time for socializing. Friday and Saturday evenings he was expected to allow the other Dons to entertain him. After dinner, at the casino, Abruzzi whispered to him that they had arranged a "menu" for him, with several "choice selections."

Dominic smiled, thanked them profusely, but said he could not accept their kind offer. He was to be married soon. There were toasts and boisterous congratulations. They had heard rumors, but one never knew. There were many questions. What was she like? Was she an Italian girl? Where had he met her? Was she compliant? This last, in the States, would have been regarded as offensive, but he knew, here, it was talk among men and was considered important.

"She is American and young, only twenty-one, and she is smart and very beautiful. Una vergine. So she is still learning, but yes, she is compliant." Murmurs of admiration and approval went round the table.

Saturday morning, Paige met Sophia at the church and attended early Mass. As the service ended and Sophia turned to leave, wordlessly Paige made her way to the altar. The aunt watched as she lit a candle, knelt, and prayed.

Vincente took them to the Gianellis, where Paige spent the day. She stayed in the kitchen with Victoria the better part of the morning, visiting and helping bake bread. After lunch, she had tea with Sophia in the alcove the aunt favored.

The girl was restless and had little to say. She looked thinner than when the aunt had last seen her. After finishing her tea, she excused herself, saying she had promised Xavier a game of chess. That evening at dinner, they noticed that she toyed with her food and ate very little, but they did not comment.

And later, when Vincente had taken her home and Victoria fretted about her, Sophia observed, "She is young and in love and she misses Dominic. It is all very serious to her. Presently, she has no appetite, but it will return when he does."

Paige saw her parents on Sunday. Tuesday through Thursday she was at the office, and she spent most of Friday completing a set of studies for a new client.

She didn't want anything to interfere with Dominic's homecoming. He was due back sometime tomorrow. She swam for a while, then showered and washed her hair. She was exhausted and fell asleep with the towel still wrapped around her head.

The phone woke her at eleven.

"Dom?"

"Hey, Baby. Were you asleep?"

"Sort of, I guess. Is it five in the morning there? I keep losing track."

"Exactly, my love. I'll be leaving shortly. I've missed you, Zucchero, more than you know."

Tears stung her eyes and her throat ached. "I may never let you out of my sight again, Dom." She tried to joke, but it fell flat.

"Go back to sleep, angel, and I'll be there as soon as I can. I'm on my way. Okay?"

"Yes, have a safe trip and remember I love you."

"I will. Sleep well, my love."

She awoke early Saturday. Trying to fill the morning by staying busy, she ran. If asked, she would have said she walked or jogged, but she ran. After a futile attempt at relaxing in the pool, she finally went upstairs and began to ready herself for his arrival. She took her time. Having settled on a white halter-top sun dress he particularly liked, and white sandals, she went downstairs to wait for him. She was disappointed when she realized it was only a little after one. She got her book and lay down on the sofa in the den. Within minutes she was sound asleep.

Two hours later, Dominic was home. Entering the house, he called to her and, getting no response, looked out by the pool. He was headed upstairs when he noticed the light in the den.

She was asleep on the sofa, on her side, one hand tucked under her cheek. One bare foot was exposed, the other wrapped in a quilt that covered her legs. He touched her arm. "Paige? Baby?" Her eyes opened, and she flew at him, tears already beginning to course down her face. "Dom!"

He held her for the longest time, neither of them speaking. Then he took out his handkerchief and dried her tears.

She was smiling now. "I'm sorry. I just missed you so much." More tears. "Well, honestly! This is getting embarrassing." She tried to laugh.

He sat down on the sofa and pulled her to him, holding her tightly. "It's all right, Zucchero, I'm here now." After awhile he suggested they go upstairs. Neither of them was willing to let go of the other.

In their room, Dominic removed his coat and tie and pulled her to him again. They kissed, long, lingering kisses, tasting each other. It was so sweet and it had been too long. She unbuttoned her dress to the waist and stepped out of it. As he removed his shirt, she ran her hands over his chest. He took off his belt, and she unzipped his pants, reached inside, and felt him, her fingers closing around him. They took their time, savoring each moment, touching, kissing.

Her eyes held his. "God, I want you, Dom."

"I know, Baby, I know."

He laid her on the bed and took off her panties. Folding her in his arms, he held her for the longest time, telling her how much he loved her. And when he took her, their cries of release filled the silence and echoed in the stillness of the summer afternoon.

Later that night, as she slept in his arms, he ran his fingers over her body again. He could count each rib and her hip bones were sharper than before. She must have lost ten pounds while he was away.

The next morning they had coffee, went for a swim, then together fixed breakfast. He watched as she finished everything he put on her plate. He was home now. She would be fine.

Ten

September passed quickly. Paige had ruffled feathers in both families by announcing she wanted no parties or showers given for her. Puzzled by this at first, when Dominic pressed her for an explanation, he found her reasoning sound.

"I have an apartment full of things. You have an apartment, this house and one in Italy, and they are all furnished with everything anyone could ever want or need. It's embarrassing to even *think* about sending invitations to people so they'll feel they have to buy something for us that we will never use."

She looked away for a moment, and her face reddened as she continued. "And it's different for me than it was for your sisters or for my brothers' wives. I don't have close friends that I feel need to be included in this affair. I thought everyone would be happy just to have the big ceremony. Between the rehearsal dinner and the wedding, I thought there was enough going on. Now, everyone is upset because I don't want a bunch of strangers giving me toasters and clocks. And, for the most part, they would be strangers to me. I'm sorry. If they do it, it will be without me."

It was something no one had considered, he was sure. Even he had not thought of it. It was seldom he did not know what to say, but this was one of those times.

As if reading his mind, she sighed. "And, Dom, please don't look like that. Don't you think I know that I'm different in some ways? I'm fine with it. I don't ever remember wishing I had a bunch of girlfriends." She paused, then added, "I have plenty of friends within our families. It's like having six sisters, and there's your mom and Sophia, and I love them all. I do. And *you*. *You* are my best friend. You're everything to me."

Pulling her to him, he held her, saying nothing. She was right. She was different, and he was thankful. He would speak to Martha and his mother and close this issue for her.

Two days before they were to leave on their trip, Dominic told Paige to pack for cold weather. Jeans, sweaters, jackets, boots. Yes, take some dresses, but nothing light. He was still being secretive about their destination. They would leave October 2.

They were taking his plane, a 1981 Gulfstream III. He introduced her to the pilots as they boarded. Manny and Bus and several of their men would accompany them on the trip and were loading the luggage. The plane was a source of pride for him, and he couldn't resist asking her what she thought once they were in the air.

Looking around appreciatively, she replied, "It's wonderful. I didn't know a plane could look like this."

Indeed, part of it was set up more like a conversation pit, a sort of mid-cabin conference room. The carpeting and the wood trim were beautiful. There was a bar, a lavatory, a closet, a baggage area, and an entertainment center complete with stereo, TV, and VCR. "It's fantastic, Dom."

It pleased him that she was impressed.

They moved to the lounge area, where Dominic opened a bottled of wine. He appreciated the way she never felt the need to talk just for the sake of talking. They were on their second glass of wine and she was relaxing now, her head on his shoulder. He finally told her where they were going.

Her reaction was everything he had hoped it would be.

"You overwhelm me with the things you do for me...for us. I don't even know what to say, Dom."

"Does it make you happy?"

"I'm thrilled. I don't know how to tell you..."

"You just did. You'll have to be the tour guide through the park, you know."

"I can do that. Where are we staying?"

"That's another surprise."

They landed at the airport in Bozeman shortly after 2:00 P.M., where five vehicles awaited them. Manetti, Paige, and Dominic took one Suburban. Buscliano put the luggage in another and followed them. The other six men, in teams of two, drove Blazers. They headed northwest from Bozeman, and reached Henry's and Millie's an hour later. The realtor, Jeanie O'Neal, was to meet them there. She had arranged to have the house cleaned and readied, groceries delivered, and the liquor cabinet stocked.

Two complete sets of tableware and glassware, serving dishes, pots and pans, plus every small kitchen appliance he could think of, he had requested. There was already an entertainment center downstairs, but he had them set up one in the bedroom where he and Paige would be staying. Manetti and Buscliano would stay in rooms on the first floor, while there was a guesthouse where the other men would reside.

Henry's and Millie's was a large, rambling two-story wooden structure that served as a restaurant and general store to local ranchers. In a pinch, there were a loft and three bedrooms upstairs that served as a motel for snowbound travelers.

Two barn-like structures in back of the main building served as storage areas for livestock feed and yard and garden supplies, as well as an assortment of tires. The owners' house was on the same property.

When the five vehicles pulled up simultaneously that Friday afternoon, all the local patrons, mostly late coffee drinkers and a few early beer drinkers, took notice.

First through the door were two men dressed in dark suits,

followed by a couple that caught everyone's attention. The man, who appeared to be middle-aged, was an imposing figure, tall and big, well dressed, also in suit and tie. With him was a beautiful young woman, her black hair and dark eyes a startling contrast to her pale complexion and the white wool dress coat she wore. In a low voice, one of the locals murmured, "Who the hell?"

"Shhh!" It was Millie. "They're the people from New York, I'm sure. Get Jeanie."

"What people from New York?"

"They're on vacation. She's his fiancé. They're renting the Dobson place."

A woman appeared and walked with the owner toward the front of the store where the newcomers stood waiting. She offered her hand. "Mr. Gianelli? I'm Jeanie O'Neal. It's nice to meet you!"

They shook hands, and Dominic introduced Paige. Jeanie provided them with a map and the extra sets of keys he had requested. Spying Paige's engagement ring, she admired it vociferously, embarrassing Paige somewhat, but also pleasing her. Millie's husband, Henry, a tall, thin man in his late sixties with a face that looked like tanned leather, ambled in and introduced himself. He was one of those people you liked instantly.

Manny ordered sandwiches and drinks for the men to take with them. Dominic wanted only coffee, and Paige, a Coke. As they prepared to leave, they thanked Jeanie for all she had done. She wanted to follow them to the ranch, but Dominic thanked her again and politely refused the offer.

The couple smiled as they listened to Manny's exclamations over the mountainous terrain and the wildlife. Paige was thrilled. It was beautiful, it was remote, and it would be just the two of them.

Close to an hour later, they arrived at the Dobson Ranch. The arched and gated entrance to the property was set in a rustic stone fence.

There were acres of huge beautiful trees. The driveway was graveled and the house set back about a mile from the entrance. The ranch house was a huge, sprawling story and a half of wood construction trimmed amply in stone.

Covered patios spanned the sides and back of the house. The stone-paved walkways were dotted with large pots of red geraniums, one of Paige's favorite flowers. A beautiful heated pool, two hot tubs, a sauna, and a cabana, were to the rear of the house, as well as a barbecue pit, and two tables with benches, all made from stone and concrete. Further to the rear of the property, there was a stream with water so clear you could see the trout as they swam to and fro.

As they explored the house and grounds, all Paige could say was, "Oh, Dom! It's wonderful!"

She was right. It *was* wonderful. He had a good feeling about this, and he was glad he had done it. After he took a few minutes to go over things with Manny and Buscliano, it was decided that during the day they would man the front gate and house, with one team patrolling the rear of the property and the other two teams the adjoining acreage on either side. In addition to the guest house, there was a large bunkhouse, so there were adequate accommodations for everyone.

Dominic gave strict instructions that they were not to be disturbed during the day, and no one should enter the house between the hours of 7:00 A.M. and 11:00 P.M., except in an emergency situation. This trip had been devised as time alone for him and Paige. When they traveled, Manny and Buscliano would follow in another vehicle, unless he told them otherwise. The one exception would be the trip to Yellowstone later in the week. Everyone would go then.

By seven that evening, they were unpacked and ready to relax. The security personnel had been dispatched to their respective patrol areas. Dominic lit the fireplace and they sat, enjoying their drinks and watching the orange flames as sparks from the glowing embers escaped and drifted up the chimney. The high, vaulted ceiling of the family room with its wooden beams and the massive double fireplace made the house an architectural gem, as far as Paige was concerned.

"So you like it?"

"Dom, I *love* it. Thank you again...for thinking of it...for everything. I can't imagine how much arranging and planning this took. You're amazing. You really are."

Giving her an anything-but-modest smile, he quipped, "Well, if you say so."

"Do we have music?"

Of course they had music, and they danced slowly to song after song, their bodies pressed close.

She fixed them a late dinner of eggs and toast, and they went upstairs to bed, taking time only to brush their teeth. The second floor, which contained the master suite, covered half the area of the first floor, and their room had a balcony with a view that could only be described as majestic. Later, as she lay in his arms, she sighed. "I think I've died and gone to heaven, Sweetheart. Listen to that."

"What?"

"Nothing! Absolutely nothing! Isn't it wonderful?"

She was right. It was quiet, peaceful, and it was nice. And there was something else nice going on.

Paige, her body straining against Dominic's, was getting as close as she could, and she reached for him. His touch was gentle as he took her hand away and told her, "I have things to do first, Zucchero." He kissed her, slow, easy kisses, taking his time. His fingers found her and stroked her knowingly. She moaned softly. "That's *so* good. It feels so good." She closed her eyes and languished in the feeling until her body tensed and she whispered, "Now, Dom, now!"

Then she slid down in the bed and took him in her mouth, tantalizing him till he could stand it no longer, and he pulled her to him again. She lay beside him as his fingers explored her, slipping in and out, skillfully caressing her, arousing her almost to the point of frenzy and then...then she was *there* and it was so sweet. There was no other way to say it—sweet, almost unbearable ecstasy, and he took her *there* time and again.

Seeing her own passion reflected in his eyes, she knew what he wanted, and she whispered, "Fuck me." With that, she turned over and reached for the headboard.

Dominic was prepared. Taking lengths of soft cotton rope, he tied her wrists. His desires were strong tonight, and he fucked her for a long time.

She was little more than a third his weight and he tossed her about effortlessly. He flipped her over and now, her wrists, still bound, were crossed above her head and she lay on her back, her legs spread. He saw in her face just the slightest apprehension, and this spurred his eagerness. As he lifted her body and brought her to him, he entered her bottom, fucking her forcefully.

This was one of those times when he needed *more*. That was how Paige thought of it. These months had taught her he was a man with an intense and varied sexual appetite. The way he so knowingly manipulated her body had honed her own desires and expectations. He never left her wanting, and even now, even when he hurt her, there was something in his eyes as he watched her that kindled her own yearnings yet again, and once more he claimed her and she cried out.

———

Later, their passion spent, Dominic lay holding her close to him, and he could not have loved her more. He had never loved anyone the way he loved her.

And this, *this* was why. Her love for him was all encompassing, and he knew it. She was everything to him, satisfying his every need. A man required more than consent from a woman, more than just being *allowed*. Paige gave herself over to him and their lovemaking. Embracing, participating, she was there with him.

There was this thing she did sometimes after they made love, and often when they awoke each morning, and she was doing it now. She would kiss him, little kisses, gently tugging at his lower lip, running the tip of her tongue just inside his mouth, and she would lay her hand on his cheek and look at him with such wonder and so much love, it truly amazed him.

She interrupted his thoughts, whispering. "Hey, are you there?"

"I'm here, Zucchero."

"Me too, but just barely." Her voice was soft and sleepy. "I love you, Dom."

"I love you, Baby. Goodnight."

When they awoke in the morning, Paige noticed the red circles on both her wrists and was unconcerned. Indeed, looking at them, she got that *feeling*, and she smiled to herself. She knew last night had pleased him, *more* than pleased him. He was the only man she had ever known, and he had taught her well. What they shared was very special. This she knew.

Over coffee, he gently lifted her wrist, examining it with a slight frown. When he caught her gaze, she eyed him seductively, saying, "I'm a branded woman."

"One more look like that, and it's back to bed for you, my love."

They were sitting at a table in the kitchen. She had turned her chair to face him, and her feet were in his lap, her only attire a long-sleeved thermal shirt of Dominic's that came almost to her knees. She pulled the shirt up, and opened her legs. Holding her mug of coffee with both hands, she took a sip, then gave him a sultry smile.

He looked amused, and said, "You are a wanton little hussy this morning, did you know that?"

Lazily, she stretched one foot and very gently tapped his crotch. "And who made me that way, sir?"

"I think the mountain air does good things for you, Zucchero."

Enjoying their banter, she laughed. "Only you do good things for me."

"Keep talking and I'll have to give you the whole world, not just part of it."

She went to him then, sat in his lap. "You're my world."

So their first day was spent making love, sleeping, and eating. Several times and in that order. That evening, despite the chill, they cooked out on the patio. Dominic grilled burgers, smoked sausages and chicken. Paige made a salad of new potatoes, ripe olives, red onion and ranch dressing. She set out bowls of chips and dips, along with plates of onion, lettuce, tomato, pickles and cheese. There were ice cream and cheesecake for dessert. They invited Manny and Bus and the others to join them.

He watched as she helped serve, refilling plates and bowls, replacing empty wine bottles immediately. She was a good hostess. Totally at ease with Manetti and Buscliano now, she was still a little shy around the others, but she was making an effort to be friendly and to put them at ease. He kept his eye on Paulie de Angelis, because Paulie was keeping his eye on Paige.

Eventually, Buscliano must have noticed because when Paulie finished eating, he was dispatched to the front gate. All in all, though, it was a great evening.

When they were alone again, they stripped and slipped into the pool, the warm water caressing their naked bodies. "This is positively decadent, and I love it."

"I'm glad, Zucchero." She was getting that look, and he insisted they go upstairs.

Sunday was another lazy day for Paige and Dominic. They donned jackets and gloves and took a walk around the property. Monday evening they drove to Henry's and Millie's and sat in a booth watching some of the locals as they danced to the music of a country western band. When the band took a break, Paige asked Dominic for change, went to the jukebox, and made three selections. She returned to the booth, took his hand, and said, "Come on, Darling, let's show them how it's done." He was surprised but he obliged her. "Desperado" began to play. He took her in his arms and they claimed the dance floor.

The next song was "Night Moves." As they danced, the crowd eyed them appreciatively. The last song, "Let It Be Me," put her in his arms again, and toward the end she pulled him to her and gave him a long, lingering kiss.

She asked Dominic if he had seen the way the locals looked at them, like they were some kind of curiosity. He had smiled and shrugged dismissively. But she was feeling mischievous, and decided she would give them something to talk about. And she did. Between the dancing and the impassioned kiss, she set the place abuzz.

Henry and Millie came over to say hello and inquire if they liked the house, then introduced a friend of theirs, a man named Garrett

Grayson. Dominic thought he had heard the name before and that the man looked familiar, but he couldn't place him until Millie said he was their local and only celebrity. That was it—he was an actor and a director. Paige shook hands and said hello, but gave no sign that she recognized him.

Garrett sat down and visited with them for a while. Gianelli was friendly enough, but not overly talkative, and the girl didn't say anything after they were introduced. It was hard for him not to keep glancing at her. She was beautiful. He had watched them on the dance floor, noticed how they seemed oblivious to everything going on around them, their focus strictly on one another. The kiss she had planted on Gianelli had eyes popping and tongues wagging.

Gianelli sat next to her, his arm around her. When, during their conversation, she scooted closer to him and leaned against him, Gianelli smiled and kissed the top of her head. Garrett sat with them for close to an hour, and upon leaving invited them to a party at his house the following Saturday. Nothing fancy, just drinks, and a few of the local folks. He hoped they could come. Gianelli said they would try.

Tuesday through Friday they spent at Yellowstone, a memorable time for all of them. Originally, Dominic had thought they would spend only a couple of days there, but they were having fun and there was so much to see. Paige was having a ball, planning where they would go each day.

They stayed in the old hotel there in the park. The food and the service equaled the atmosphere, which was superb.

On Saturday evening, they went to the party. Paige hadn't been too keen on it, but Dominic had told her they wouldn't stay long. Garrett

Grayson was their closest neighbor, he seemed nice, and they didn't want to offend. Henry and Millie were there and about twenty others who lived in the area. Grayson's place was a sprawling ranch-style house, very masculine, very John Wayne, she thought, or maybe Ernest Hemingway. Jeanie O'Neal spotted them and took them around, introducing them to the other guests until Grayson intercepted them.

Gianelli was dressed in slacks and a sweater, Paige in a long-sleeved black dress that fit her to perfection, accentuating her slim body. They looked out of place among the jeans and boots crowd, but seemed not to notice. When Millie took Paige on a tour of his house, Garrett managed to ask Gianelli about her. He was surprisingly informative, telling him that she was a market analyst and they were to be married in December. He added that she was quiet and a little shy until she got to know someone. She was twenty-one, even younger than Grayson had suspected.

Before the evening was over, Gianelli had invited him to dinner on Sunday, and they had progressed from last names to Garrett and Dominic.

On Sunday, when he arrived at the Dobson ranch, Garrett was startled to see that several portable buildings had been moved in on the property. One was outside the entrance and housed two men wearing suits and ties. They nodded to him, opened the gate, and he drove through.

Halfway to the house was a larger unit where two more men stopped him, politely asked his name, and motioned him onward.

Dominic and Paige were sitting on the porch, dressed much as they had been last night, except that Paige wore a white sweater dress. They watched him approach.

"That's quite an obstacle course you have set up here."

Dominic rose, extending his hand. "Sorry, but it's necessary." This, with a smile but no further explanation. Paige offered him a drink and he accepted.

She returned with their drinks and two cigars on a tray, and Dominic, slipping an arm around her waist, said, "Thank you, Zucchero. You must have been reading my mind." They were both exceptionally gracious and polite people, but not for show—Garrett could tell it was simply habit with them, part of their makeup.

Accepting the cigar with a nod of thanks, he commented on the gold lighter, and Dominic told him it was a gift from Paige, who listened as he and Dominic talked mostly of work, travels, and a little about family.

When Paige had finished her drink, she asked if she could freshen theirs, then excused herself to see to dinner.

They smoked their cigars, the best Garrett had ever had, and he said so.

In the dining room, the table was set with white china on brass chargers and crystal stemware that sparkled. The placemats and napkins were white, and there was a French floral centerpiece and brass candleholders with white candles on either side of it.

Dominic immediately told her, "Paige, the table's beautiful. Truly elegant."

Garrett noticed that she smiled gratefully at the compliment, so he added, "Well, Paige, Dominic just took the words right out of my mouth. It really is beautiful, if you don't mind a second opinion."

"Thank you, both of you."

There was roast, medium rare, with new potatoes in butter and leeks, a garden salad with an oil and vinegar dressing, and a grilled vegetable-mix of broccoli, mushrooms, red and yellow peppers, and onion, and individual loaves of a coarse-grained, honey wheat bread served with orange butter.

Over dinner, Dominic drew Paige out little by little, and she spoke of finishing school early and going to work for the investment firm. She also told him about the *Paige One* and *The Mallorca* and how they enjoyed taking them out on weekends.

When they had finished eating, she shooed them to the den for brandy and cigars while she cleared. Dominic mentioned that she rode and was quite good, actually. She also played chess, poker and gin, and had a sound knowledge of football, baseball, basketball and soccer.

Garrett thought he must have looked surprised, because Dominic laughed and said, by way of explanation, "Remember, she was raised by her father and three older brothers."

When Garrett asked about her mother, Dominic looked toward the other room and shook his head. "She was ill most of the time Paige was growing up. Another story. Some other time."

Garrett spent six hours with them that evening, but driving home he realized that while he had learned a few things about Paige, he still knew very little about Dominic. He *did* know he liked them both. There were times when he thought he had been out of touch with the real world too long, which was why he so enjoyed coming to Montana between films.

And Dominic and Paige—to which world did they belong? At first, they seemed an unlikely couple. But you didn't have to be around them long to realize they were very much in love and devoted beyond question.

At nine o'clock on Monday morning, Garrett stopped by to visit Dominic and Paige.

Dominic answered the door, and looked surprised to see him. "Garrett, good morning. You're out early!"

Seeing that Dominic was still in his robe, he said, "Sorry, you're right. I do get out early."

"Not a problem. Come in. We're just having coffee and discussing the day's agenda."

Paige was sitting in the breakfast nook in the kitchen, sleepy-eyed, her long dark hair tousled. Noticeably braless under a white nightshirt, she had pulled on jeans, but was barefoot. Her thick dark lashes and eyebrows were beautiful, and needed nothing to accent them. Her mouth was downright sexy, with its full lower lip. Garrett thought her as striking as any actress, more so than some.

He noticed Dominic watching him. Well, surely he wasn't the first man to give Paige a second look. He sat down at the table across from her, and Dominic brought him coffee.

Examining the mug, Garrett announced casually, "This is one of mine, you know."

They both looked at him, then at each other, then back at him, puzzled. He wasn't offended, but he was surprised at how little they knew about him.

"It came from my store."

"Oh," said Paige.

"I have a store in town, but most sales are through catalogs. We handle specialty items. Nice things. Anything from clothing to furniture, dishes to jewelry. These mugs came from my store. See the GG on the bottom?"

Carefully, Paige checked hers, then said politely, "How nice. They're very pretty. I believe Dominic had Ms. O'Neal shop for us."

Dominic nodded. "So what do you call it? Your store, I mean."

"River's End."

"That's distinctive. And easy to remember." This, from Paige.

Garrett laughed. "Yes, once you know about it!"

He asked if they would like to go into town, have lunch, and see his store.

The three of them spent a pleasant day, driving to Great Falls, eating barbecue at Garrett's favorite hangout, and browsing at River's End. Dominic encouraged Paige to pick out something she liked and, if she wished, to shop for souvenirs to take back to the family. After careful consideration, she chose more coffee mugs. They were some of Garrett's favorites, with silhouettes of running horses on them. She also chose earrings and a watch, then picked out things for all the nieces and nephews. Garrett couldn't help but notice how Dominic was with her. Words like "possessive" and "protective" were the first to come to mind, but there was something more, something deeper. There was such a ...Garrett searched for the right word...a bond, yes, a bond between them.

It was not a modern-day relationship, not to his way of thinking. Paige definitely deferred to Dominic. No question but that this was a man who would be *the* head of the house. On the other hand, Dominic adored her. Garrett could understand why. He was already given to "what ifs," how it would feel to hold that body, to kiss that mouth. Thoughts of her had crept into his mind as he lay in bed last night, and he let his imagination take him where he knew he shouldn't go.

The sun was setting as they left town to head back home. Paige fell asleep ten minutes into the drive. Once, Garrett heard Dominic ask her quietly if she needed anything. No, not yet, was her response. Garrett offered to stop for dinner, but Dominic said if it wasn't a problem for him, perhaps they should drive straight home.

Back at Dobson's Ranch, they insisted he come in. Dominic poured a scotch for them. Paige said she was going to fix something quick and easy for dinner—she wouldn't be long. True to her word, within forty minutes they were sitting down to eggs and sausage served with thick slices of toast, a fruit salad and coffee.

"What's in this? It's terrific!" Garrett was impressed.

Paige blushed, but smiled appreciatively. "Just eggs and peppers, that's all."

"I've never had it. It's great!" This won him another smile.

Later, having a cigar and a nightcap with Dominic, and feeling very relaxed, he observed, "She's remarkable. Smart, beautiful, sweet, and she can cook. Every man's dream. What else can she do?"

The look on Dominic's face told him he had crossed the line. He didn't respond right away. It was as if he were sizing him up, trying to make a decision about him. Finally, he said only, "I believe that's the first thing I ever said to anyone about Paige, that she was remarkable. So, yes, she is that and much more. She's my life."

He paused, then, in a voice so calm, so quiet that Garrett wasn't certain he had heard him correctly, he said, "And I would kill anyone who laid a hand on her."

Garrett was silent, stunned. Had the man *really* said that?

"Do I make myself clear?"

He had heard correctly. "Yes, of course. Dominic, I swear I never meant to—"

"Excuse me, Garrett. I'm looking for clarification here, not an apology, and I will be the first to say I am...sensitive...where Paige is concerned. I believe it's possible you and I are on the road to becoming friends, and I want no misunderstandings between us. Paige is off limits."

"Well, *of course.*" He didn't know what else to say. "Of course."

Paige joined them, bringing coffee and dessert. The remainder of the evening was passed pleasantly, as if nothing had happened. And as Garrett was leaving, Dominic walked with him to his truck and shook his hand, thanking him for the trip, telling him how much he and Paige had enjoyed the day. If he was out and about in the morning, he said, please stop and have coffee with them.

Dominic returned to the house and found Paige in the kitchen putting dishes away. Seeing him, she smiled. "Almost done here. Are you as tired as I am?"

"I think so, my love. That was a great supper. Garrett was very complimentary."

"That's nice, but he's not the one I'm trying to impress."

He kissed her then, holding her close, murmuring, "You are my life, Zucchero." And they went upstairs to bed.

It was almost nine when he awoke Tuesday morning, and the first thing Dominic noticed was the heating pad clutched to Paige's abdomen. He made sure she had taken her pills, then went to shower and dress. Downstairs, he made coffee, walked outside and lit a cigar. It was a cold but beautiful morning. The leaves had turned and were rustling in the breeze and the sky was blindingly blue and bright.

A little later, Paige, in jeans and sweater and socks, but no shoes, came out onto the patio. He took her back inside and poured a mug of coffee for her. "Are you hungry?" She shook her head no.

"Let's have rolls with our coffee, okay?"

"Okay." She was out of it. Those damned pills.

She ate most of a cinnamon roll, then went to the den and lay down on the couch. He suspected this was where she would spend most of the day. He retrieved the heating pad, a pillow and another quilt and took them to her. Already she was sleeping.

Garrett showed up at 10:30. Dominic poured two cups of coffee, grabbed a handful of cigars, and said they would sit outside and visit, that Paige was sleeping. They passed through the den on the way to the patio, and Garrett watched as Dominic checked her forehead, pulled back one coverlet and straightened another. "Paige, I'm outside if you need me, okay?"

He heard a soft response but didn't understand what she said.

Not knowing if he should or not, he inquired, "Is she ill? She seemed okay yesterday."

Dominic was noncommittal. "She'll be fine in a couple of days, thanks." And he turned the conversation to other things.

They were going back to New York on Saturday, maybe even as soon as Thursday or Friday. He surprised Garrett by confiding that he was looking into buying the Dobson Ranch and the adjoining properties as a wedding gift for Paige.

"Why, that's great!" And he found that he meant it. Despite the discomfort of the conversation last night, he liked Dominic and wanted to get to know him better.

Not once had Dominic or Paige ever asked him about other celebrities, what life was like as an actor, none of the usual things people wanted to know. In fact, they never mentioned anything regarding his work.

They inquired about his family, his ranch, his horses, but that was about it, and it was nice. And as for last night, well, hell, Dominic had called him on his behavior and had every right to do so.

He stayed most of the day. For lunch, he and Dominic made sandwiches and drank beer. Several. They passed the afternoon drinking more beer, smoking cigars and watching football games. That evening he drove to Henry's and Millie's to eat dinner.

Henry and Millie knew he had been spending time with the "New Yorkers," as the locals were calling them, and wanted to know all about them.

"They're a nice couple, going to be married soon."

Millie, annoyed, said, "Well, I know *that*, Garrett. What else?"

He smiled. "What do you want me to say, Millie? They're just people. Very nice people, who decided to take a vacation. He's an investor and she's a market analyst. They met at the office where she works. He's forty-eight and she's twenty-one." He couldn't resist teasing her a little. "Oh yes, those security people with them? They carry guns. Real ones. That's the scoop for today."

Millie sniffed. "You shouldn't gossip, Garrett. It isn't nice." And she left him to visit with Henry.

Friday at noon, they left the airport in Bozeman and flew back to New York. Dominic had called Garrett and told him they would be in touch, but the next few weeks would be busy ones. He left word with Jeanie O'Neal about purchasing the ranch.

Vincente met them at the airport. They had enjoyed their trip, but it was good to be home. Paige made Dominic swear they wouldn't let anyone know they were back before Sunday. That sounded good to him. A little more than six weeks and the wedding would take place. This might be their last peaceful weekend till they were married.

He woke her early Saturday and told her to throw on some clothes, they were going to spend the weekend on the boat. She was delighted. By ten they were aboard *The Mallorca* and rigging the sails.

He waited until evening and told her he wanted to talk to her. The night was cold, but the water was calm and the stars were out. Standing behind her, his arms around her waist, he kissed her neck. "Happy?"

"Very."

"You know I love you, don't you, Paige?"

"Yes."

"Is everything all right? Do you have any questions, or is there anything you think we need to discuss?"

"Everything is fine. I can't think of anything, can you?"

"Hmmm. Maybe just some generalizations. Nonspecifics."

She waited, seeming to know he would continue.

"Do you understand that I do nothing accidentally or impulsively? There are always reasons for my actions or lack thereof. Do you understand this?"

"Yes."

"Do you really? Never just tell me what you think I want to hear."

"Well, maybe 'believe' is a better word than understand, but yes, I believe you're a man who deliberates and doesn't act rashly."

"We touched on it briefly once before, but it's important to me you understand there will be times when you will have to trust me concerning things I won't be able to discuss with you."

"All right."

"I realize it isn't fair, but, again, there are good reasons in place."

"I can accept that."

He hugged her tightly, kissed her cheek. "Your life is going to change. You realize that, don't you?"

"I'll belong to you, officially, and you to me. We'll have papers." She laughed softly.

"Yes, but that isn't what I mean. I'm sure you've noticed I lead a very private life, as much so as possible. Why do you think that is?"

"Because you like your privacy?"

Sternly, he said, "Don't be flippant, Paige."

"I'm not!" she said, earnestly, and with some exasperation. "I don't know your reasons for everything, Dom, but whatever they are, I accept them. Okay? *I accept them.* I came to realize certain things early on, Dom. I love you. Only you. That you come with terms and conditions doesn't change my feelings for you. Doesn't everyone's life change after they marry? I would think so, at least to some extent."

She faced him now. "There is nothing you could tell me, nothing that could be revealed to me that would change my love for you or my desire to spend my life with you. Do *you* understand? I would follow you through the gates of hell, Dom. I would."

He was quiet for a long time, never taking his eyes from hers. Finally, he pulled her to him and held her, burying his face in her hair. By whose grace she had come to him he did not know. Had he really given her an out tonight by mere suggestion and shadowy innuendo? An opportunity to change her mind? He had said as much as he dared, and she remained unfazed. What was he doing? Testing her? If so, she had passed, with honors.

They would be married. This was a closed chapter, never to be reopened. As if she knew his thoughts, she whispered, "I'll always love you, Dom. I'll always be there for you. I promise."

The fragrance of her perfume, the warmth of her body against his were so familiar now, so comforting. He had no concept of heaven, or what it meant. But here, in this moment, with her, it was heaven, *a separate heaven*, apart from all else. Sophia was right. She was his gift.

Eleven

With November came the reality of the wedding for Paige. For so long the wait had seemed interminable, and now it was upon them. On this autumn morning, Dominic was at his office in the city and she at her apartment. He was to meet her at six that evening. There were several things she needed to do, things into which she had put a lot of thought.

For Dominic's wedding gift she had bought a watch, a very special watch. She had ordered it months ago, custom-made, and it was finally ready for shipment. It was a once-in-a-lifetime gift and there was not, nor would there ever be, another like it. That had appealed to her. For his birthday, there was the ring. Like the watch, it was made of gold with black diamonds. Together, they had selected his wedding band, but this ring was special too, engraved with their initials and the date.

Then there was work. She was running an analysis now and had arranged for a courier to pick it up after lunch. Two more weeks, and the fifteenth of the month would be her last day.

Most important today, though, was the apartment. Dominic had asked her about it. Did she want to keep it? If so, it could be arranged.

At first, the thought of giving up this hard-won prize made her a little sad. She had been so proud of it when she bought it, had spent weeks picking out just the right furnishings. At the time she met Dominic, she had reached the point where the apartment was exactly as she had planned, picture perfect. She loved everything about it, and was pleased with herself over what she considered a major accomplishment—her independence from her family.

Telling herself she had exactly thirty minutes to feel bad about losing the apartment, she poured a glass of wine, sat down on the loveseat, and did just that. After she'd finished her drink, she picked up the phone and dialed the realtor. The apartment was a gem, and Paige knew it would sell immediately. The realtor would be there at four that afternoon.

Moving right along, she made a list of her credit cards to be canceled, wrote checks to pay off any balances, and put them in the mail. She called the officer at the bank and made arrangements for her trust fund, available to her on her last birthday, to be transferred back to her father, requesting a copy of the transaction for her files. In a letter she had written this morning, she explained her decision to her father, saying she hoped he would not be offended or think her unappreciative. After careful consideration, she felt it was the right thing to do. She thought he could find more appropriate use for the funds.

Also in the letter, she expressed her gratitude for all he had done for her. And while she realized he had his concerns as a father, she wanted him to please know that Dominic would take good care of her. He loved her very much and she loved him. She closed the letter saying that she looked forward to making him a grandfather again.

She scheduled appointments with the dentist, hair stylist, and manicurist, and for the final fitting of her wedding gown. She ordered gifts for members of the wedding party and asked that the items be delivered to the club where the reception was being held.

Charlie sent up the boxes she had requested, and she began packing the remainder of her clothing, carefully marking the contents of each box. She walked through each room and chose what few items she would keep. Doing these things made her a bit nostalgic, but then she would remember *why* she was doing them and it would make her smile.

The realtor arrived promptly at four and couldn't hide her excitement over the property. Paige told her to feel free to look around, and to please give an opinion as to what furnishings she might leave to sell with the apartment. The rest could be donated to Goodwill or the Salvation Army. The woman handed her a contract, which she set aside for Dominic to review.

Paige continued to pack as the realtor walked through the apartment, exclaiming over every detail, voicing her approval. It was a marvel, she said: the excellent location, the view, two bedrooms, two baths, a spacious living area, a fireplace, and a kitchen with an island. It made her feel good to hear the woman go on and on about how lovely it was.

Dominic arrived a little before six, surprised to find the realtor there, and even more surprised to find Paige methodically packing and marking boxes.

"Are you sure?" he asked her. "I don't want you to do something you may regret later. I know you worked hard for it, Paige. You don't have to give it up if you'd rather not."

She told him she was sure. She felt that somehow three residences were enough for the two of them. Besides, it made her feel good to know someone would be thrilled to get her apartment, probably be as happy as she had been.

"I need a favor from you, though. Please review the contract. It's there on the table. As a matter of fact, please take care of it for me, period. Just tell me where to sign when the time comes, okay?"

He nodded. "Of course." He watched as she turned back to her packing. She seemed okay with it. Heaven knew he didn't need another property to deal with, and he was glad she didn't want to keep it, but he would rather keep it than have her unhappy. The realtor's chatter interrupted his thoughts. He picked up the contract, and they began to discuss the terms.

By eight that evening, the contract had been negotiated, a list of furnishings that would remain with the apartment had been completed, and Paige had finished packing the things she was taking with her. There were a vase and a teapot she took for Vincente to give to his wife. She would explain that she was clearing items from her apartment and she wanted Luisa to have them.

They weren't in the car more than ten minutes when she fell asleep. Dominic told her to lie down, and she did, her head in his lap. "Hmmm. Thank you, Darling," she murmured.

He held her, brushing her hair back from her forehead with one hand. With his finger he traced the dark brows, the straight nose, the bow in her upper lip, the full lower lip, the tiny cleft in her chin. The thick dark lashes fluttered when his finger lightly touched her neck, traced the outline of her collar bone.

Looking at her stretched out on the seat, the small body and the long, slim legs, he thought, as he often did, that she was coltish. She had a black leotard on under the jeans and every inch of her body—the long arms, her breasts—was defined by the clingy material. He never tired of looking at her, studying every part of her.

That she had come into his life at a time when he had all but closed the door on a serious, personal relationship, had not even considered the possibility for years, still amazed him. And while he liked to think he was the sole master of his world, and all that occurred within, some part of him begged the question of her influence on him. Certainly she brought forth feelings of which he had never known he was capable. He had not known how empty his life really was till she went from his arms straight into his heart.

The wedding, according to information gleaned from his sisters, would be a huge and grand affair. He had suspected as much. His mother and Martha, for months now, when not together, were on the phone. He and Paige had seen the invitations only after they returned from their trip, and he had to admit they were elegant. The wedding would be at St. Patrick's on Tuesday, December 1, at three o'clock, with the dinner and reception to follow at Le Mansion on the country club grounds.

When he asked his mother how many invitations had gone out, she was rather evasive, but finally said she thought several hundred. He had yet to mention this to Paige. For him, as always, security was the biggest headache, and this would be a monumental undertaking. Finally, he turned it over to Manetti and told him to do the best he could with it. The waters were calm and there had been no cause for concern, at least stateside, for years, but he never lowered his level of precautionary measures.

Mentally going over his checklist, he found things to be pretty much in order. He would close on the Montana property before the end of the month and, thanks to Paige, the issue of her apartment had been resolved. The villa was being readied for their honeymoon, his tux had been ordered, her rings were ready. Paige wasn't aware of it, but the engagement ring she now wore was a temporary. The set of rings he had chosen actually joined to form one ring with the stone centered between the two bands, creating a unique and exquisitely beautiful ring.

What else? There was the matter of the cost of the wedding. He knew Paul would protest, but he was going to insist on paying at least half the expenses when he could put a figure to them. It was his guess Martha had not given Paul a clue as to the extent of the expenditures. It amused him that Paige managed to stay out of most of the planning, and probably knew less about what was going on than anyone. When questioned about it, she would respond adamantly that she had done "everything I am supposed to do." He had to admit, allowing the others to plan the wedding and reception had given the Hamilton and Gianelli families ample opportunity to get acquainted, and it was working out well.

As the car approached the gates, he shook Paige gently. "Wake up, Sweetheart, we're home."

"Already?" She stretched and yawned, then put her arms around his neck, pulled herself up and kissed him. "I love you."

"And I love you. You've had quite a day, haven't you? What say we do a quick supper, then take a swim before bed?"

"Sounds great." She kissed him again.

She warmed roasted chicken, baked potatoes, and made a salad while he put rolls in the oven, poured the wine and set the small table in the den. As they ate, they watched part of an investigative reports show till he turned it off, saying tabloid news wasn't of interest to him. She agreed.

Later, they languished in the warm water of the pool. He had been waiting for the appropriate time to broach a subject with her, one he rather dreaded, and he still wasn't sure how it had fallen to him to ask her, but somehow it had. She had made it clear she wanted no part of bridal showers or parties, and until recently, he thought the others had accepted her stance on this and dismissed the idea.

"Julia and Isabella want to know if you would agree to an afternoon tea, to be held at your parent's house shortly before the wedding. They want to do something for you."

She looked at him and, shaking her head, gave him a little smile. "Boy, they brought out the big guns, didn't they? Having you ask me."

"Well, it's a dirty job..."

"Ouch! Am I that bad? A tea?"

"Just a few people, that's what they tell me."

"What do you think?"

He shrugged. "It's up to you, Sweetheart. I don't do teas."

Finally, with a deep, resigned sigh, she said, "Oh, I guess. But two hours, no more than two hours. Would you tell them that? And to keep it small, please."

"I'll tell them. You're a pretty good sport, Zucchero."

"No, I'm not. I just don't like to argue." She ducked underwater and swam away momentarily. Circling back, she grabbed him around the waist, kissed his belly, then worked her way up his chest till she emerged, laughing. "Take me to bed."

"You've got a deal."

They went upstairs, and what began as a quick shower turned into much more. Paige, while seated on the bench, found herself at eye level with *that* part of him. She reached for him and fondled the length of him, her fingers gently caressing.

She took him in her mouth and, as his excitement grew, she knelt in the shower to better accommodate him, the warm water spraying down on them. At one point, he told her he was close, but she didn't want to stop. Instead, she sucked harder, taking as much of him as possible into her mouth, her throat. He twined his fingers in her hair, pressing her face into his groin. Then, "Oh God, Baby! Oh!"

Now, Dominic held her close to him, and she lay her head on his chest. His fingers found her, stroked her and she moaned softly, "Don't stop."

When she was almost *there*, he paused, reached for the shower head, and removed it from its bracket.

"Dommm!"

"Shhh. Just a minute. We're not through."

"I *know* that!"

He laughed softly at this. "Turn around, with your back to me."

He began to kiss her, nibbling little kisses on her neck, while his fingers found her again, touching and stroking, exciting her. When she moaned, he took the shower head and held the stream of water close to her, letting it take the place of what his fingers had been doing, and he moved it slowly back and forth.

With his mouth close to her ear, he whispered, "Tell me how it feels. Does it feel good?"

"Yes." Then again, "Yes!" He felt her body tense as she breathed his name. "Dom, now. Oh, Dom, now!" He let the water stream directly on her as she came, until she was still.

He turned her around to face him and kissed her. "So how was that?" This was a first, and he could tell she was a little self-conscious, embarrassed.

She looked at him, then at the shower head, then back at him, saying, "Who knew!" He laughed heartily at this.

Pulling her to him, he held her tight, still laughing. "Oh, Paige, you are something else, Sweetheart! You really are something else!"

The next two weeks passed quickly. They cleared Paige's things from the apartment, which had sold within days of being listed. On the sixteenth, Dominic accompanied her to the office, where she turned in her keys and files. They spoke briefly with the partners, who wished them well. They scheduled their blood tests
 and applied for their license. She got her passport.

Friday, November 20, was the tea. She had grown increasingly uneasy about it, but said nothing. She couldn't have explained it anyway. There were things that hovered in her mind at times. Shadowy things that made her apprehensive, but she didn't know what or why. That was how she was feeling now. She knew Dominic sensed something was amiss because she saw him watching her, studying her. Well, she would go and get it over with. It wouldn't kill her.

After deciding on a pale, mint green dress, dyed-to-match heels and her emerald earrings and bracelet, it was with some reluctance that she told him she was ready to go. They took the Jag today and Dominic drove. She was silent on the ride over and he reached for her hand. "Are you all right, Babe?"

She smiled at him. "I'm fine, thank you. But I'm having a hard time believing my mother can confine herself to a small, family tea." Bringing his hand to her lips, she kissed it. "So, what do the men have planned for the day?"

"The usual, I think. Drinks and smokes."—the men were forever trying new brands of cigars with different tobacco blends. This seemed to be an unending quest, one they all enjoyed—"a lot of conversation, maybe a little poker. Mostly hiding out. Staying as far from the tea as we can get and still be in the same house."

She laughed. "Well, that doesn't sound so bad."

Even before Dominic made the turn into the Hamilton's drive, Paige could see it was lined with cars from the road up to the house and back to the road again on the opposite side, which meant somewhere in the neighborhood of fifty vehicles. She'd been surprised that little had been said about security, but then this was supposed to be a "small family affair." She sighed audibly, but said only, "Oh, well."

Inside, the foyer, living, and dining areas were filled with vases of calla lilies, and white-candelabra-adorned tables and mantles. The furnishings had been rearranged. Small tables covered with white linens displayed an assortment of hor d'oeuvres. Waiters in white coats served drinks. A long table held a multitude of beautifully wrapped packages.

Dominic left Paige with Julia and escaped to the den. It was 3:30.

The first hour she made a real effort to visit with the guests, be gracious. Then, with a slight headache troubling her, she went upstairs to her bedroom to get away for a moment. She used the bathroom, took two aspirin, and decided she should go back before they missed her. As she walked along the landing, her mother called out to her, startling her. "Paige!"

She turned to see Martha coming toward her from the master suite. Her heart began pounding fiercely, and she took several steps backward until her hands felt the wall.

Martha stopped, seeing her daughter's face go pale. "Paige? What is it? We've been looking for you, dear."

Paige, trying to control the rising level of her anxiety, took a deep breath. From the corner of her eye she could see some of the guests staring up at them from below.

"Paige!" This time her mother's voice was more like a hiss. "For heaven's sake, what *is* the matter? Are you ill?"

It took tremendous effort, but she managed to say, "I'm fine, thank you. I just had a little headache and came upstairs for aspirin. That's all." She paused. "Go on down. I'll be right behind you."

Her mother eyed her, seeming puzzled by her behavior. "Come get a drink, Paige, or have Molly make you some tea. You'll feel better. We're going to open your gifts shortly."

Paige made her way downstairs among curious glances from those who had witnessed the scene between her and Martha. She walked past them, through the living and dining areas, and down the hallway to her father's den. As she opened the double doors, she realized there was something very comforting about seeing the men seated there, about the sound of their voices and the scent of cigars and pipe tobacco. Then it came to her. She was safe here.

Paul watched as his daughter crossed the room. All her life the sight of his youngest child had evoked a conflict of emotions within him— love, of course, but love accompanied by so much angst and sorrow.

On closer examination, he decided she looked pale and troubled. As she neared the table where they sat playing cards, Drew leaned back in his chair, and reached out and took her hand.

"Hey, Monkey, you're not supposed to be in here!" Putting his arm around her waist, he hugged her. Then, seeing her expression, he asked, "What is it, Paige? What's the matter?"

Her face flushed and she forced a smile. "I just needed to get away from all the commotion for a minute, that's all."

Paul and Drew exchanged looks. Paige freed herself from Drew's arm, walked around the table, and stood beside Dominic's chair, her hand on his shoulder.

The forced smile was not lost on Dominic, and he checked his watch, "Another hour or two and this should be ending, shouldn't it?"

Paul watched as Paige smiled, gratefully, as if knowing it was Dominic's way of telling her to hang in there, it was almost over. She kissed his cheek and turned to leave. "I'll see you later."

They all watched silently as she left. Then, "Do you think she's all right?" This, from Drew.

Paul said casually. "Of course! You know how she is about things like this." He glanced in Dominic's direction. "She's not fond of parties or crowds. Never has been."

Matt, making no effort to disguise his defensive tone, added, "She just doesn't like having all the attention focused on her, Dad, that's all."

Paul shrugged. "It won't kill her to accommodate her mother for a few hours." Catching the look Dominic gave him, he averted his eyes and concentrated on his cards.

Making her way back to the others, Paige wondered what had caused her panic. The same feeling that had nagged her for years kept returning. In the foyer, she paused and gazed up at the landing, the railing. Her heart was hammering again.

Julia's voice startled her. "Paige? Where were you? We're waiting for you." She seemed to notice Paige's surprise, and she smiled. "You're awfully jumpy today. Don't worry, as the wedding day approaches, it gets worse."

Paige said, dryly, "Thank you, Jules." Maybe she was right, maybe it was the wedding.

It took almost two hours to open the gifts, thank the guests and see them to the door. When the last of them had departed and only family members remained, Paige dropped to the sofa, laid her head back, and closed her eyes.

She heard her mother say, not unkindly, "Well, look at this, one would think she had done all the work!" Paige heard the laughter of the others.

Bitsy and Connie were urging her to come sort through the gifts. They would all help her box them and mark what was from whom. They had kept a list.

It took an additional hour to accomplish this. There were some lovely gifts, none of which they needed or would probably ever use. Her eyes kept going back to the punch bowl, a gift from her mother, the only thing still sitting out. It was elaborate, obviously very expensive. It reminded her of something. Her head was aching again. She noticed that the men had joined them. What now?

"Paige, there were some things we wanted to give you with only family members present, and we want to do that now. Is that all right?" Julia smiled at her, waiting for an answer. "Paige?"

What could she say but, "Yes, of course."

"Well, I'll go first, I guess. This is from Andrew and me." Paige, still seated on the sofa, opened the box and removed two frames, both engraved with names and dates. Inside the first was the picture of her, not quite five years old, wearing the black and white dress, posed on the stairway. "That one is more for Dominic. I promised it to him several months ago." She explained to the Gianellis, "I took that picture of Paige my first evening here, the first time I ever met her."

The second picture, though, was a complete surprise, and Paige loved it. It was of her and Dominic at the Valentine's Day party at the club. The picture was a closeup. They were dancing, their eyes locked on each other.

"Thank you, Jules, Drew. They're wonderful. Thank you so much."

Now, Bitsy was saying, "I guess I'm next. This is from Matt and me."

This, too, was in a frame, but it was a verse. "Do you recognize it, Paige? Of all the gifts Matt and I received, yours was special to us, and we've always treasured it. We couldn't think of anything nicer than wishing the same thing for you and Dominic."

She remembered. She was only ten years old when they had married. Her present to them was a poem she had written. Now they had reproduced it, and beautifully so. The ache in her throat made it difficult, but she managed to thank them.

The card from Anne and John read, "To be filled with happy memories. All our love and best wishes."

This time the box was larger. It was a wedding album, white leather with white on white embossing. Paige ran her fingers gently over the raised letters of their names and the December 1 date. She fought back tears as she smiled and thanked them.

John joked, "With the wedding they've been putting together for you two, you'll be able to fill that album in no time and will soon need another." Everyone laughed.

Connie spoke up next. "You are such a pain to buy for, did you know that?" It was so typical of Connie, even Paige laughed, and it brought her some relief.

"We had to think hard to come up with something special, and, while not original, we're proud of ourselves. Are you ready?"

Paige smiled. "I think so."

"All right, the first item is 'something old,' and this is from Aunt Sophia and Pop."

The box was heavy on her lap. Gingerly, she lifted the lid and pulled back the tissue. It was a Bible, one whose cover was cracked with age, and inscribed on the front was the Gianelli name. There was a faded picture on the cover, reminiscent of a renaissance painting, she thought.

She was stunned by the gift. Someone had painstakingly recorded names and dates of births and deaths of family members since the late 1790's. Carefully, she turned the pages, one by one, until she found, first, Sophia's and Xavier's names, and then Dominic's and his sisters'.

When she spoke, her voice was soft, hesitant. "I don't know what to say...it's beautiful." She bit her lip and started again. "That you would want me...us...to have this..."

She looked at Dominic, and he came to her rescue, saying, "We're honored that you would trust us with such a treasure. Thank you."

Paige said no more, but got up and went, first, to Xavier, and gave him a hug, then to where Sophia was sitting. She put her arms around the aunt and whispered, "Thank you so much. It means the world to me, Sophia. "

The aunt patted her shoulder gently. "I know, Bella, I know."

Connie lightened the moment again. "Okay, enough of that. Paige, open this. I'm giving you something old as well as something new, because you can't carry that Bible down the aisle."

She opened the little box. The first item was a tiny gold filigree ring. Connie explained that Paige was to wear this on the little finger of her right hand. "That's your something old. I've had it since I was a teenager, okay?"

Paige nodded, then lifted the next two items from the box, a garter of white ribbon and lace, and a matching pair of panties. She blushed and held up the garter, but that was all.

Connie protested. "Paige, for heaven's sake, there's not a man in the room who hasn't seen a pair of panties. Let's see them!"

Paige smiled, but shook her head no.

Connie pressed her. "What on earth do you think is there?"

And Paige, her face a deep crimson, but still smiling, replied, "I'm more concerned, Connie, with what might *not* be there."

This brought uproarious laughter, and a hoot from Connie, who proclaimed, "Touché! And by the way, dear, lest you think me cheap, please note the labels!"

"I did notice, Connie." Facing the others, Paige announced, "Dior, both by Dior." She looked more relaxed now.

Jackie was next with "something borrowed." At first, Paige didn't recognize the tiny gold item, until Jackie explained it was an ear cuff.

Excitedly, she said, "Oh, wow, Jackie! I've never had one of these." Paige was intrigued, but Dominic looked concerned.

"You don't have one now, dear. This is a loan, remember? Here let me put it on you." As Jackie pulled Paige's hair back and fastened the cuff on her ear, Dominic spoke up.

"One pair of holes in her ears is enough. What are you doing?"

"Relax, brother, it just clips on and her hair will cover it, but she'll have something borrowed to wear down the aisle." He shook his head.

"Also, since that's a loan, I got you some earrings." It was just like Jackie to tell you what your present was before you had a chance to open it. The earrings were dangling, colored glass beads, like some Paige had often admired.

"Thanks, Jackie, they're great!" And it occurred to Paige that she was actually enjoying herself now.

Isabella, for "something blue," gave her a gorgeous blue topaz cross on a dainty gold chain. She showed her how she could fasten only the cross to her garter the day of the wedding. Then Isabella announced, "One last item, Paige. We all worked on it, and we hope you like it. You and Dominic will add to this over time, but we've given you a head start."

It was an album of Gianelli family pictures, many of Dominic and his sisters as children and young adults: Dom, on his eighth birthday, examining his new bike, then as a teenager, on the beach, his hair dark and wavy, a cocky grin on his face. Each photo was carefully labeled, explaining "who," "where," and "when." This time, the tears spilled down her cheeks. She said simply, "I love it." She kept brushing the tears away, but more would come.

She tried to laugh. "Well, all I can tell you is when something means the world to me, words fail me. And that's how I feel right now. Thank you is inadequate, but it's all I have. So thank you *all* so much, for everything. The gifts are wonderful!"

Dominic had called for Vincente and Buscliano to help with the packages. While they were waiting, he noticed that Paige seemed to have an inordinate interest in the gift from her mother. This had continued throughout the evening, her eyes frequently going to it, studying it. Finally, she got up, walked to the table, and fingered the diamond-shaped crystals that hung loosely from twelve points on the bowl.

Martha brought the box and, after wrapping each cup in tissue, placed them in the bowl. Only when her mother lifted the bowl to repack it did Paige break her almost trance-like concentration and walk away.

Dominic was helping her with her coat when something seemed to catch her eye. He followed her gaze upward to the chandelier that hung in the foyer.

She stared, her focus on the light fixture that had a multitude of sparkling diamond-shaped crystals hanging from each tier.

Dominic looked at the landing, the railing, and the distance to the floor below. It chilled him.

She was quiet on the ride home, holding his hand and tracing his fingers with her own, something she often did.

"Paige, what happened today? Before you came into the den?" This, casually, as if it were of no significance.

"I went to my room for a few minutes. My head hurt a little, and I took some aspirin. As I was about to go downstairs, Mother came out of her room and called to me. She startled me."

"And that's all?"

"That's all that happened...but I was afraid."

"Of what, Zucchero?"

"I don't know. Maybe of her, but I don't know why."

Gently, he said, "And tonight, Sweetheart, a few minutes ago, what was that? What is it about the chandelier?"

"I'm not sure. I think I saw it when I fell."

He held his breath, waiting.

"When I was seven, they said I fell. I think I remember seeing it then."

"Anything else?"

"No, not really. Dad and Drew say it's because I hit my head so hard when I fell." This, so innocently it pained him.

Softly, he said, "I can see how that would be, Zucchero." And he said nothing more. Maybe Julia was right. Maybe it was better if she didn't know.

Saturday morning, Paige called a local charity to say that she would donate a substantial number of items, all new and of value, if they could arrange to pick them up immediately. Setting aside the gift from her mother, she then asked Vincente and Buscliano to move all the boxes to the gate. Someone would be there shortly to pick them up.

She set the pictures from Julia and Drew on the dresser in the bedroom. The Gianelli family album she placed on the sofa table in the formal living room, and the treasured Bible she put on a shelf in an armoire for safekeeping until she could find a suitable place for it.

The wedding album she stored in their closet till after their honeymoon. The items to be worn in the wedding, she placed in a small box, keeping them together.

She made a fresh pot of coffee, filled their mugs, and took them to Dominic's office where Dominic was working. He smiled at her. "Everything going okay?"

"Fine, thank you. Are you hungry yet?"

"I'm getting there. I need another hour or so, okay?"

"Okay. I'll have it ready then."

In the kitchen, Paige took a loaf of Victoria's cranberry bread from the refrigerator and sliced it. She cooked bacon and sausage, smiling because he preferred having, not one or the other, but both. She filled a pitcher with orange juice and set it on the bar. She heard Dominic stirring now, file drawers opening and closing, so she made toast and scrambled the eggs.

When he came into the kitchen, he refilled their mugs and they sat down to eat. She watched him, a slight smile on her face.

Dominic looked up. "What?"

She shrugged, still smiling. "Nothing really. I just like to watch you eat."

He laughed at this. "If it makes you happy, Zucchero, I'm all for it. Want to take the boat out today?"

"Yes!"

"Let's do it then. Noon, okay?"

"Great."

After breakfast, she retrieved their jackets and gloves, and, remembering he had run out the last time they were on the boat, she went to the den and grabbed a handful of his cigars. She laid these things on the hall tree by the front door, then went upstairs. Within minutes she had brushed her hair and done a quick application of mascara and lip gloss. She threw on a sweatshirt and took one for him, too.

Dominic was standing in the foyer picking up the cigars and putting them in his jacket pocket. Seeing her, he smiled. "Thank you, my love." He noticed she was wearing the Rutgers sweatshirt he had bought her. Something he had done on a whim, it had turned out to be a hit with Paige, and she wore it at every opportunity. She was breathless from all her running around, and her youthful enthusiasm and boundless energy were catching. She made him feel young again.

She wanted to take the Jag, so Manny and Bus followed in a second car. On the way to the marina, he told her more about Salerno. She listened intently, her attention focused on what he was saying, the gaze of her velvety brown eyes never wavering. With the sunlight catching her face and the breeze blowing her hair, she was beautiful. *And she was his.*

Later, on *The Mallorca*, with his arms around her as they watched the sun set, he asked her, "So now that it's almost over, has it been such a bad year?"

"No, but it's been a long one. I'm not letting you off that easy." Turning to face him, she kissed him. "But I don't hold a grudge either."

"Well, that's nice of you, Miss Hamilton. Now, *there's* something I can't call you much longer."

"I know. Just eleven more days, then, voila! We're married."

"Are you nervous?"

"About marrying you, no. About the ceremony, very. I've been practicing my vows. I'm still stammering over them and forgetting certain parts. Either that or I say them out of order."

"So we'll practice at the rehearsal, right?"

"Maybe. I'm not sure they let you practice the actual vows." Then, thoughtfully, she said, "I've never seen you act nervous or uncertain about anything."

"Hmmm. Well, that's partly due to age and experience, I think, and otherwise, it just goes with the territory. You know, business persona."

"Good. If you're calm, maybe it will help me not be so nervous."

He slipped his hand under her sweatshirt and fondled her breast. "I think I know how to calm you down. Let's go below."

They made love, then lay in each other's arms as the waves gently rocked them to sleep.

When he awoke, Paige's face was buried against his chest. Kissing the top of her head, he murmured, "Wake up, Sweetheart."

With her face still buried, all he could hear was a muffled, "Why?"

He laughed. "Because the sun is creeping in, even way down here, which means we should be up."

She rolled onto her back and stretched. Then, placing her hand on his cheek, she rubbed it gently, feeling his whiskers, and smiled. "I love you so much."

"How much?"

"Hmmm, so much I'm going to make you coffee."

"And?"

"And bring it to you."

"And?"

"And I'll cook breakfast for you."

"And?"

"And I love you so much." She was laughing now.

They spent the day idly, letting *The Mallorca* drift. They drank their coffee in the morning and switched to wine in the afternoon, as they huddled together, wrapped in blankets, the cold ocean breeze whipping the sails.

He told her more about Salerno and said they would go to Naples and Pompeii if she liked, that he would take her to Rome and Florence another time, but not this trip. She asked if Manny and Bus would go with them.

"No, Sweetheart, there's security personnel in place at Salerno."

"Did Aunt Sophia live at Salerno?"
"As a matter of fact, she did."
"With her husband?"
"Yes, of course."
"But she didn't live there after he died?"
"No, not after he died. Then she came to live with us. Why do you ask, Zucchero?"
"I just wondered. From some of the things she's told me, I didn't think she had always lived in New York."
"No, but she's been here for more than twenty years."
"They didn't have any children, did they?"
"No, there are no children. What has Sophia told you about her life in Italy?"
"Nothing really. Sometimes she talks about when she and Poppa were children. I guess things like that mostly. She's never told me much of anything about your uncle, only that she loved him very much."
"That she did."
Hesitantly, she asked, "Dom, is it okay to ask you how he died?"
There was a distant look in his eyes as he answered. "Yes. Some men killed him."
"Oh. I'm sorry."
He nodded. "Yes. So am I."
She looked thoughtful, but said no more. She had good instincts and she followed them. He stood then, and walked to the bow of the boat. "Come here, Sweetheart." He put his arms around her and held her close to him. "Not that I think you would, Zucchero, but it wouldn't do to ever mention this to Sophia. It's one of those things we never discuss. Do you understand?"
"Yes."
"That's good." Shortly thereafter, they headed for the marina.
They were back on Long Island by seven that evening, and together they prepared dinner. Dominic cooked the steaks. Paige prepared the vegetables and salad. As she saw to the table settings and poured the wine, he thought again how much a part of his life she'd become. She fit so easily into it, as if there had been this space, waiting, that only she could fill.

The week before the wedding they closed the sale on Paige's apartment. She did a final check, and, going over her list, decided everything appeared to be in order.

Her father called to say he had received her letter and spoken with the bank and his attorney regarding the trust fund. He would honor her wishes, though he didn't really understand them, and he wanted her to know the money would be available should she ever need it.

Paige had made a decision regarding the balance of her assets. After arranging with Dominic for Vincente to drive her Wednesday afternoon, she went first to the bank, then to the school.

Seven years had passed since she had left St. Ag's. It looked, even smelled, the same, bringing her a flood of memories. Her throat was tight and she fought a sudden impulse to cry. How odd that only today she would realize what this place meant to her.

The door to the office was open, and the Mother Superior was seated at her desk. Paige cleared her throat and said, "Excuse me."

The Mother Superior recognized the girl immediately and rose from her chair, wondering if she could trust her voice.

"Paige, Paige Hamilton." She hesitated only a moment before going to her and hugging her. "How I have thought of you through the years, my dear."

Paige was lovely, she thought, even more so. What would she be now, twenty-one? Yes, twenty-one. Her father had kept in touch for a while, letting them know when she graduated from college, but they had heard nothing for close to three years. A beautiful young woman, very poised. She was still too thin, or maybe it was the black dress. Then, she noticed the ring.

Taking her hand, she asked, "What is this, dear?"

Paige smiled shyly, but the smile lit her face. "I'm getting married soon. Next Tuesday, actually."

She was well and she was happy! Praise God! "Come and sit. We'll have some tea. I want to hear about this young man."

"He's wonderful." Her face glowed as she spoke of him. "He's a businessman, an investor, very smart." Blushing, she continued. "He's handsome, strong and caring." She bit her lower lip and paused. "He's...not as young as my father would like. People tend to make an issue of the age difference, but we never even think of it."

"Who is he and how did you meet him?"

"We met at work. His name is Dominic, Dominic Gianelli. He's Italian. Well, he's American, but..."

The Mother Superior smiled. "I understand, dear."

"Oh, I almost forgot. I wanted to tell you that I joined the Church."

The Mother Superior looked puzzled. "You joined a church?"

"The Catholic Church, Reverend Mother. Dominic and his family are Catholic. I thought about the vows I would be taking, and I wanted to embrace the things that are important to him and his family. I've already joined the Church, officially, and we attended the instructional classes for couples."

"That's wonderful, Paige." She paused. "As long as it was your decision."

The girl gave her a patient smile. "Yes, Mother, Dominic and his family insisted I give it a lot of consideration, and I did. I feel very good about my decision." Then she turned shy again, and said softly, "I'm looking forward to someday sending our daughters to you."

At this, the Reverend Mother had to find her handkerchief. She dabbed at her eyes. "Well, look at this, would you? This is what happens when age creeps up on you, dear." Regaining her composure, she said, "Paige, it means the world to me to see you like this. All grown up, and so happy. It's what I have always wished for you."

"Thank you. I think I knew that." She seemed to be searching for the right words. "I have...good memories of my years at St. Ag's, safe memories. I wanted to do something to show my appreciation for everything you and the Sisters did for me, and I hope you'll accept a gift."

Then, obviously feeling she should offer some kind of explanation, she said, "Dominic's very..." She stopped, began again. "Dominic will provide everything I'll ever need, Mother. I want to go to him... unencumbered, shall we say. I sold my apartment recently and this... this is mostly proceeds from that. I want St. Ag's to have it. I know you will put it to good use."

With that, Paige handed her an envelope.

Remembering how as a child Paige had shied from public displays of emotion, she said only, "Thank you, dear." They stood, shared a parting embrace.

Immediately, the Mother Superior called for Sisters Beatrice and Constantine and told them of her visitor. She shared her news of Paige, that she had joined the Church and was to be married next week. Yes, she was lovely and happy and well. Finally, they looked at the check. It was for $67,000.

The Mother Superior sat at her desk and made a note in a well-worn file:

November 25, 1981

> A wonderful surprise today. And so appropriate, on the day before Thanksgiving. Paige Hamilton came to visit. She is a lovely young woman, very sweet and poised. She is to be married next week. Another surprise, she has joined the Church. Her fiancé is Catholic. She presented us with a substantial donation, and in that manner, that is so like the Paige we always knew, made it seem as if we were doing her a favor by accepting. I feel our prayers regarding her have been answered.

It was close to 6:00 P.M. when Paige arrived back on Long Island. Dominic was wrapping up last minute details. She knew she had been gone longer than either of them had anticipated.

He was still in his office, and Paige went straight to him. She laid the file folder on his desk and kissed him. "I'm sorry, that took longer than I thought it would, but I got everything done."

"That's good. Let's see, you went to the bank, right?"

"Yes, but I had several things I needed to do there. Let me get us some wine. I'll be right back."

"I'm almost finished here, Babe. Give me ten minutes or so, okay?"

"Of course."

True to his word, within fifteen minutes, Dominic was sitting with her in the den. They sipped their wine while Paige told him about her afternoon.

"Do you want the long version or the short one?"

"Let's start with the short one."

"I went to the bank and then to St. Ag's."

"To St. Ag's? Why?"

"To see the Reverend Mother and give her some money."

He poured more wine and lit a cigar. "I see. How much money did you give her, and why?"

"I think it was sixty-seven thousand. I have a copy of the check there in the file."

"Okay, Zucchero, now I'm ready for the long version."

"I had my trust fund transferred back to my father. I went to the bank to get a copy of the transaction—"

"Excuse me, did your father ask you to do that?"

"No, it was my idea. I thought you would approve, though."

"And I do. I'm sorry. Continue."

"For the past two weeks, I've been paying any outstanding balances and canceling my credit cards, so I wanted to close my checking account and get the final statement on that. I did. It's in the file too."

"That's good, Sweetheart. And then…?"

"I closed my savings account. I took what was there and the proceeds from the sale of the apartment and had a cashier's check made to St. Ag's for that amount. There are copies of all this—"

He smiled. "In the file, yes. Go on."

"I went to St. Ag's and saw the Mother Superior and gave her the check. Then I came home."

She could tell he was thinking about what she had told him, and she waited for him to speak.

"I don't disagree with anything you did, Zucchero, but I'm curious as to why you did it?"

"I thought it would please you. That it was something you would want, but would probably never ask me to do. Because, as I told the Mother Superior, I wanted to come to you, as your wife, unencumbered. Does that make sense? I had to do something with the money that was left after everything was paid, and I wanted it to be used for something worthwhile. So, I thought of St. Ag's."

He was smiling again. "Unencumbered?"

She kissed him. "It's a nice way of saying I have no money, I'm broke. However, I did bring lots of shoes and I don't think I'm expecting."

This brought an appreciative laugh from him. He was amused, yet again, at her wording.

She rose. "I'm going to start dinner. Want to keep me company?"

"I'll be there in a minute, okay?"

"Of course." She knew he would look at the file. He had to know *everything*. Especially where she was concerned.

After she left, Dominic smiled as he recalled her words. "Unencumbered." Paige had a remarkable vocabulary. And her use of it was absolutely charming. "Expecting," not pregnant. Expecting. That had to be a Hamilton thing.

He was still smiling as he picked up the file and thumbed through it. It was all there: the copy of the check to St. Ag's, the transfer of her trust fund back to Paul. He scanned several pages—there it was—$245,000. The amount surprised him somewhat. The final statement on her checking account seemed to be in order, but her savings account puzzled him. Until the end of August of this year, she'd had $43,000, but when she closed it today, the balance withdrawn was only a little more than $9,000. He locked the folder in his desk and went to the kitchen.

"Can I help?"

"Just by refilling our glasses, please."

"My pleasure. What are we having tonight?"

"Lasagna, salad and bread. Okay?"

"Sounds great. I was glancing through the file, Babe, and it all looks in order except for your savings account."

She thought for a minute. "No, Darling, I think it's correct."

"Well, somewhere between August and today you lost about $34,000, Zucchero."

"Oh, *that*. No, I didn't lose it. I bought your birthday present and your wedding gift."

She said this so casually, it took a moment for it to register.

"Hand me that potholder, please, Darling."

Taking it from him, she said, "Thank you. If you put our glasses on the table, I think we're set." She picked up the salad bowl and the dish of lasagna and set them on the table. He was still standing there in the kitchen when she returned for the bread.

"Dom?"

"I'm trying to think of a response to what you just told me."

"Just come to dinner, please. It's ready."

He helped himself to a large serving of lasagna. Then, after a long silence, he laughed. "Well, hell, Baby! No wonder you're broke!"

"Very funny!" She slipped her shoe off, put one stockinged foot in his lap, and gently poked him. "Please remember to show up Tuesday afternoon. I'm in real trouble if you don't."

"You know, Sweetheart, this may be the first time since we met that I have some leverage. I'm going to enjoy the next few days."

She laughed. "Oh, *please!* Dominic Gianelli, how can you even joke like that? I've been putty in your hands from the beginning. I know, and you know, that I'm crazy about you."

He knew he could be cocky and immodest at times, and this was one of them. "Well, yes. Yes, you are." They both knew how this was going to end and they were looking forward to it. "What's the schedule for tomorrow, Sweetheart?"

"Lunch with your parents, dinner with mine. I tried to think of a way to spend it here, just us, but I couldn't come up with anything."

"We'll give them Thanksgiving Day and we'll take Friday and the weekend. How's that?"

"It sounds wonderful."

"Did you enjoy your visit at St. Ag's today?"

"I did. The Reverend Mother was really sweet." She smiled, a bit timid now. "She cried a little when I told her I looked forward to sending our daughters to her." She looked down as she said this, suddenly finding it necessary to carefully butter a piece of bread.

Touched, as always, by the shyness that came over her at times, he responded, "Well, we'll have to do just that, won't we?" And the thought pleased him.

Thanksgiving Day at the Gianelli household was nothing short of chaotic. "There must be something in the air!" This from Dominic.

His mother, overhearing, laughed. "It's the wedding. We've been working with the children, hoping to avoid the appearance of a herd of cattle charging down the aisle on Tuesday."

Paige observed mildly, "They'll be fine, and if not, what's the worst that can happen?"

Connie shot her an incredulous look, shaking her head. "What world are you living in, Paige, and may I join you? The possibilities for disaster are limited only to the number of children involved!"

Unruffled, she replied, "I don't believe that."

Connie rolled her eyes. "The girl's in denial!"

The mood was festive, and Paige enjoyed this lively, animated family who treated her as one of their own.

By the end of the day, though, she would welcome the quiet, more formal atmosphere at her father's house, to which she was well accustomed.

Later that evening, seated in the Hamilton dining room, Dominic must have read her mind because he leaned over and whispered to her, "Quite a contrast, isn't it?"

She smiled at him. "I love your family, Dom."

He winked at her and replied, "And I love you."

"That's all that matters." *And it was.*

On Friday he told her that if he could have half the day, he would be through with work and he would be hers exclusively from then through the honeymoon.

Mid-morning she brought him fresh coffee and asked if somewhere there was an old tarp or paint shroud available, something that could be thrown away.

Engrossed in reviewing a spreadsheet, he answered distractedly, "Look in that large wooden storage chest in the garage. There should be several things in there. It has a hasp on it, but it isn't locked."

After putting on a jacket and gloves, she went to the garage, found a hammer, and retrieved an old blanket from the chest. She took them to the patio off the kitchen, spread the blanket, then returned to the garage for a large box and carried it outside.

It was close to noon when Dominic cleared his desk and mentally declared everything done. He called to Paige, and getting no response, went upstairs to look for her. Not finding her there, he went downstairs to the kitchen. He spied her on the patio, sitting cross-legged, her back to him.

It took him a moment to comprehend what was taking place. Careful not to startle her, he opened the door and walked outside. With a hammer, she was calmly, methodically smashing the crystal punch bowl her mother had given her. Judging from the pile of glass on the blanket, she had already disposed of the cups. The bowl was in several large segments now. She would take a piece, lay a corner of the blanket over it, then pulverize it with the hammer. He could see her only in profile, but she looked composed, tranquil.

He cleared his throat, and said softly, "Everything okay, Sweetheart?"

She turned to him and raised her eyes slowly to meet his. Her gaze was wary, questioning, as if she were fearful he might be disturbed by what she was doing. He made it clear he only wanted to know if she was all right.

Her relief was apparent. "Yes, I'm almost finished. I'm sorry. I thought I could...take care of this while you were still in your office."

He lit his cigar. "Not a problem. Do me a favor, please. Let me know when you're through and I'll dispose of things for you, okay?"

"Of course, thank you."

She went back to the business at hand, and he watched her for a minute before going inside, and he thought, "*Tell someone else you don't remember, Sweetheart, tell it to someone else.*"

Dominic opened a beer, sat at the bar, and waited for her. He did not know on what level she was aware of what had happened, but somewhere inside she knew *something*. Well, he had to give this one to Sophia. She was right. Evidently, Paige, regardless of what she did or did not remember, had her own way of dealing with it.

Years of experience, particularly in the last two decades, had made him a student of human nature.

As a child, Paige's body had been broken, but obviously not her mind or spirit. These were intact, this he knew. That she grew up to be the loving, caring person she was, he could not explain. He knew he was unwilling to give Paul as much credit as he probably deserved.

To him, there was something sadistic about the way Paul had not only brought Martha back to the house to live, but had insisted Paige honor her as her mother. Paul may not have used that term, but it was, in essence, what he had expected.

A part of him, though, understood that Paul, too, had had to survive and somehow run a household in which they could all exist, if not happily so, then civilly. Still, he felt most of this had come at Paige's expense.

On the other hand, analytically speaking, she was strong. Her infancy and early childhood had been a baptism of fire, but she had survived. Some would say, and he agreed, that this was what was important.

He watched her now as she approached the house, and his thoughts turned pleasant. How could jeans and a plaid wool jacket look so great on anyone? She was a beauty and she moved with such grace. *And* she was his.

Once inside, Paige removed her coat and gloves and reached for a coke. Dominic was still at the bar, having a second beer. "All done?"

"All done." She gave him a direct look and, once again, seemed to search his face for questions or disapproval. Finally, apparently finding neither, she asked what he would like for lunch.

"Let's have sandwiches. We'll cook tonight."

He did not offer to kiss her, or hold her, or touch her in any way. She had to know he did not feel sorry for her. And he didn't. He despised what had happened to her as a child, and he despised the circumstances that allowed it, but he did not feel sorry for her, and he knew pity was the last thing she wanted or needed.

She took a roast from the refrigerator and set it on a cutting board for him to slice. "Fries?"

"Chips are good for now, Zucchero. Let's make it easy."

She smiled for the first time that afternoon. They took their plates into the den and watched a movie as they ate. She sat next to him on the sofa, their legs touching. They finished lunch, and she asked if he wanted dessert.

"Always. Why don't I get ice cream for us?"

"Great, thank you."

"Let me guess—vanilla."

She smiled. "I have no secrets from you, Dom."

"That's good."

Later, the movie ended, she turned to him. In one fluid move, she was in his lap, facing him, her knees on either side of him, her arms around his neck. She kissed him, long, unhurried kisses at first, until his erection pressed against her bottom.

Hoarsely, he commanded, "Stand up."

He unbuttoned her jeans and slipped them off, along with her panties. His hands on her waist, he pulled her toward him and kissed her belly. As his mouth moved lower, she pulled back a little, and he laughed. "Still gun-shy?"

She only smiled and began unbuttoning his shirt. This accomplished, she unzipped his slacks and reached for him. Her eyes held his as her fingers closed around him.

"You want it, Baby?"

The beautiful dark eyes were smoldering, provocative, as she whispered, "Yes. I want you."

Quickly, they undressed. "Now, that's better." He pulled her to him, held her, caressed her, and exhorted her to tell him what she wanted, how it felt, and when she was *there*. And he took her *there* twice. Then he said, "Get on the floor, Baby."

He took her, first on her hands and knees, then on her back with her legs locked around his middle. Twice, he took her hand in his and pressed it to her belly and she could feel his cock moving inside her.

Their excitement grew and their pace quickened until, arching her back and straining toward him, she cried out, "Now, Dom! I'm coming, now!"

He felt her tighten around him and, craving release, he surrendered to the moment, letting it claim him, too.

Paige lay in his arms, completely spent, totally happy. Her feelings became words that spilled forth. "Every time, I think I can't possibly love you more, but I do. Every day, I want you more. I love the taste of you, how you feel, how *you* make *me* feel. I love the way you look at me, touch me, talk to me. I love how you love me. It's everything. You're all I love, all I'll ever need. You know that, don't you?"

Wrapping her tightly in his arms, he kissed her and buried his face in her hair. "I know, Zucchero, I know. I love you just as much. Never forget that. You make my life. You *are* my life, Paige. Do you understand?"

"Yes, yes."

Later, as they cooked dinner together, Dominic thought again of how comfortable they were. It also struck him that no one else got to see her like this. Happy, relaxed, confident, talkative at times. They had their own private world, and he liked it that way—preferred it.

From the beginning, she had been content to be only with him, which had forged an immediate bond between them. His mind always returned to that first night and the way she had surrendered to him, not just her body, but all that she was. Their need, their desire for one another, fueled their love.

She had belonged to him since the first time he'd held her, but in a few days, it would be official. It pleased him, eased his mind that there would be little training required, if any, where she was concerned. Already she deferred to him, was accepting of any decision he made. And he recognized it for what it was—a sign of strength, not weakness, that she could trust him implicitly, and he, her.

Saturday morning when they awoke, Dominic asked her, "What would you like to do your last weekend as a single woman, my love?" This, as they lay together, their bodies warm and naked, marked with last night's lovemaking.

Paige reached for him, feeling him, stroking him. "I want you." Somehow, these simple, innocent words from her always stirred him.

"Tell me what you want, Zucchero."

"I want to do this." She slid down in the bed, and her mouth closed around him.

She heard his quick intake of breath as her tongue teased him, and his moans as her mouth moved up and down on him, sucking gently.

And this morning, she did something she hadn't done before. She began licking him, her tongue warm and wet on his balls, until finally she took his cock in her mouth again, but her fingers continued caressing him.

Certainly it was not the first time a woman had done this for him, but with Paige, everything was a first and therefore special. And knowing this spurred his excitement.

Her mouth felt so good on him, but he wanted to fuck her. "Come here, Baby." She sat up, her hair tousled, tumbling in waves to her shoulders, her dark eyes filled with desire. Then, she took his hand, placed it between her legs, and said, "Feel me."

She was hot, silky, when his fingers explored her, and she lay back and closed her eyes, obviously giving herself up to the mounting waves of pleasure. His hands were working their magic now and he could see she was tense, straining toward release. "I'm coming, I'm coming, Dom. *Now!*" Then, breathlessly, she said, "I want you. I want you in me."

"How do you want it?"

"Both ways. I want it both ways."

She sat astride him, his cock filling her up. She leaned forward, her hands on his chest, and moved in a slow easy motion. His finger was stroking her, and he knew she would come soon. Taking her hand in his, he placed it low on her belly, "Can you play with yourself for me? Can you do that, Baby?"

When she hesitated, looked a little uneasy, he told her, "It's okay. Here, just for a minute, okay?" And he placed her fingertips where they needed to be and moved them with his hand. "Just rub like that, okay? While I fuck you. No, don't stop. Look at me. That's it. Keep it up."

Watching her excited him. It took a while, but finally her breath came more quickly and her body tensed, then… "Now, now!"

He turned her on her stomach and pulled her bottom to him. He entered her slowly, trying to be easy with her, but his need for release was growing steadily, and he began to fuck her, hard, then harder, until she cried out. This took him over the edge, and he pounded her until his desire was spent.

As they lay together, their bodies warm and damp, he pulled the sheet over them. Then, as he held her close, whispered how much he loved her, they fell asleep.

It was late afternoon when he awoke, Paige still nestled close to him, still sound asleep. The sun was low in the sky, and the wind was blowing the tops of the trees, their bare branches bending with its force.

As he watched the swaying limbs, he listened to her soft, even breathing. Her back was to him, her bottom pressed against his legs. His arm was around her waist. The scent of them filled the air— her shampoo, her perfume, mixed with the sensual smell of their bodies.

He had never known this….contentment, this feeling of loving and being loved. The sound of the wind and the warmth of her body lulled him, and closing his eyes again, he slept.

Much later, he felt her stirring against him. It was dark outside, and the wind had progressed from a strong breeze to a howling force. "Paige, Baby, wake up."

Lazily, she stretched and opened her eyes. "What time is it?" She yawned and stretched some more.

"Almost seven, and it's Saturday night, in case you've lost track."

"I'm hungry, are you?" She kissed him. "And I love you."

He returned her kiss. "Starving, and I love you."

They showered and went downstairs to make dinner, he in his robe, she in one of his shirts. They settled on having a huge breakfast meal. She grilled bacon and sausage and scrambled eggs while he fixed pancakes. Looking at each other across the bar, they laughed.

He shook his head. "I think this day began with me asking how you wanted to spend the weekend. May I point out you have used half of it?"

"And it was wonderful. We may do it again tomorrow." She was finishing her eggs. "Dom! Do you know what I just realized?" Without waiting for a response, she continued happily, "We have to decorate for Christmas!"

Her excitement made him smile. "But not now. Right?"

"When we get back from Salerno. We won't have much time though. This is a big house!"

It was indeed a big house. Three stories and close to 19,000 square feet. Calmly, he inquired, "Just how much decorating do we want to do?"

Quite seriously, she said, "I'll have to think about it." She was methodically cutting a stack of pancakes.

"Well, you do that. We'll take care of it when we return. There'll be plenty of time. Is that okay?"

"Great! Thank you." She was pouring syrup on her pancakes now, slowly and evenly. She was funny, rather meticulous with her food in that she didn't like for different items on her plate to touch. The eggs and sausage had to be eaten before she would even think of putting anything else on the plate. Taking a bite of her pancakes, she noticed him watching her.

"What is it?"

"I like to watch you eat, too," he teased her.

"You'll get your money's worth tonight then, because I'm starving." She was quiet as she finished the pancakes, thoughtful as she pulled several grapes from their stem. "Dom, are we taking your plane to Italy?"

"No, Sweetheart, a commercial airliner, but a charter."

"Oh. Is the villa as big as this house?"

"I'd say about the same, yes."

"Are there other houses nearby?"

"Other houses, yes, but not close in proximity."

"Can you see the water from there?"

"You can. Salerno is on the Amalfi Coast, overlooking the Mediterranean."

"Oh." Her eyes widened and her expression was solemn.

He smiled. "Oh?"

Softly, she said, "Oh, wow!"

"I think I have some pictures around. Would you like to see them?"

"Yes, please."

"I'll look for them after we finish eating."

They made coffee and took their mugs to his study, where he located a box of pictures. He spread them out on the table, one by one, telling her about the house, when his uncle had built it. There were photos of the villa when it was first under construction, some upon completion, and others taken over a period of years. She said it looked exactly as she thought a villa might look.

There were pictures of Dominic and his sisters as children, then as teenagers, taken when they visited in the summer. His uncle was in very few of the photos, and she asked about this.

His answer was brief, almost curt. "It wasn't his thing." Then, changing the subject somewhat, he asked her, "Are you excited about going? You haven't said much."

"Of course I'm excited, but it doesn't seem quite real to me yet. Let me get through the wedding first, then I'll deal with Europe."

He smiled. "Still nervous?"

"More than anyone will ever know, and I'm only telling you." She moved closer to him now, and he put his arm around her.

He looked at his watch. "I think it's the countdown that's getting to you. Not for much longer though. Do you realize forty-eight hours from now we'll be in the midst of the rehearsal?"

"Yes."

"Then what, the dinner?"

"Yes, the dinner. It's at the club, isn't it?"

"I think so. You and I are probably the only ones who don't know for sure. Will you miss me Monday night?"

"Why would I miss you?" This, with surprise.

"I mean, not sleeping with me."

"Why am I not sleeping with you?" This, cautiously.

"Because it's the night before the wedding. You have to get dressed, have your picture taken, pack for the honeymoon... and do whatever it is that brides do before the ceremony." He smiled indulgently as he said this, but she was having none of it.

"Why can't I get dressed here?" Now, warily.

It was obvious no one had mentioned to Paige that she was to spend Monday night at her parents and go to the church from there. "Well, I guess it was your father who was telling me, but it's my understanding they want you to go home with them after the dinner. The photographer is supposed to be at the house at nine Tuesday morning. Your brothers will be there with their families. They want to take as many pictures as they can before the ceremony.

"Then, when you come to the church, the photographer will do as many of my family as he can before the wedding and finish up afterward."

She did not look pleased. "Zucchero, I don't like to be away from you either, but it will only be for a matter of hours."

Paige frowned as she considered what he'd just told her and he knew from her expression, much as she would hate to admit it, she could not escape the logic of the plan. At last, she said, "Well, all right, but I'm not going with them after the rehearsal dinner. I'm coming here with you. I have things planned. Vincente can take me there afterward. Is that all right? I just have to be ready by nine Tuesday morning. That's what's important. Right?"

He tried to hide his amusement. "I have to think that's reasonable, Sweetheart."

They relaxed with some wine and a game of chess, then went upstairs, taking another bottle of wine with them. They lay together watching a movie, and Paige began to rub his shoulders and neck, working her way down his back. "God, that feels so good, Babe."

Her hands pressed and massaged up and down his body until he closed his eyes and surrendered, letting sleep claim him.

When Dominic awoke Sunday, he knew what he was going to do. Smiling, he gently shook the sleeping form beside him. He no longer remembered what it was like not to have her there with him, a leg entwined with his, her arm around him, or her head resting beneath his chin.

"Come on, Zucchero, we're going shopping today."

Sleepily, she replied, "Okay, but for what?"

"You'll see."

By noon they were among the throngs of holiday shoppers in the city. Telling her he had decided they should have some things that were selected by the two of them, belonged only to them, they shopped for china, formal and everyday, and when they spied some especially for Thanksgiving and Christmas, he insisted they get those also.

He was particularly fond of stemware, and they bought sets of wine goblets, brandy snifters, and champagne flutes. There was a set of sherry glasses, deep green crystal with gold trim, and she selected a beautiful tray on which to display them.

When they were hungry, they ate in the Food Court, and took short breaks in the coffee bars. Their last stop was a shop called Forever Christmas. Just seeing the expression on her face when they went in was enough to make him want to have the entire store gift-wrapped. They selected exquisite glass ornaments, snow globes, music boxes, wreaths, and small table trees trimmed in turn-of-the-century decorations.

But he noticed time and again her eyes returning to the tree displayed in the window. It was somewhere between twelve and fourteen feet high, he estimated, decorated with large, cranberry-colored, hand-blown glass ornaments with gold trim, and gold fabric angels with lit halos. The entire tree was covered with hundreds of tiny white star-shaped lights.

In the car on the way home, he asked if it had been a good day, and she smiled. "Just another day in paradise." She leaned over, kissed his cheek and said softly, "Thank you, for everything, Dom. You do all these wonderful things, and I keep having all these great times with you. And each one becomes another best day of my life, but I'm never able to tell you how much it really means."

"You just did, Zucchero. You always do."

Monday was going to be a busy day for them, but Dominic was determined to keep it from getting too crazy. They awoke early and had a leisurely breakfast. He made a list, mapping out what they needed to do and where they had to go. They could do it together for the most part, he pointed out. They picked up his tux and shoes and a few last-minute items to take with them on their trip. While she had her hair and nails done, he got a trim and a manicure.

By two that afternoon, it was all taken care of and they were back on Long Island. Paige was suffering a mounting case of nerves, and Dominic wanted her relaxed for the rehearsal.

It was very cold outside but, at his suggestion, they sat in the hot tub, sipping wine and enjoying the feel of the warm water coursing around their bodies.

"We're almost there, Zucchero. Are you happy?"

"Very." Her eyes were closed, her head resting on the edge of the tub. "This is heaven, Dom. We need to do it more often."

"We will. Our agenda should be a lot less congested in a couple of weeks."

"I'm looking forward to that." She sat up now, moved next to him, and wrapped her arms around his neck. "I feel so good. *This* feels so good."

"You're right, Sweetheart, it does. But we need to dress and get to the church. Can we just hold the thought till later?"

"Okay. I'm a little hungry. Are you?"

"It wouldn't hurt to eat something before we leave. My guess is dinner will be late. Let's go find something easy."

"Peanut butter is easy," she said, smiling, because she knew what was coming.

Eyeing her, he thought she looked all of fifteen at the moment. "Paige, how many times do I have to tell you, peanut butter is *not* real food?" This, he said with mock seriousness.

She was laughing now. "It *is*, Dom. It's good for you, full of protein. And it's good on bread or apples or celery."

His voice was adamant now. "It's *not* real food." He had learned early in their relationship that left to her own devices Paige would have survived on three things: peanut butter, cold cereal, and ice cream.

This was something he had quickly remedied. He was accustomed to, and believed in, eating three meals a day, and he had been appalled by her eating habits or lack thereof.

Dominic surveyed the contents of the refrigerator and what was readily available. "We'll make a salad, and we can finish the chicken. How's that?"

"Fine, Darling." She turned away, but not before he saw the grin on her face.

He grabbed her. "You think I'm funny? Hmmm? You think I'm an old grouch?" He was tickling her mercilessly.

Unable to escape, she squealed, "Only when it comes to peanut butter!"

"What do you say?"

When she didn't answer, he continued the torture. "Come on, Baby, what do you say?"

"Uncle!"

"That's not it!"

Finally, "Calf rope!"

Laughing, he released her.

Gasping for breath, she eyed him warily. "I don't even know what that means!"

"It means you give up and I let go."

"Someday I'll get even." But she was smiling.

"I'm sure you will, my love. Now, let's eat. "

They were due at the church at six. Dominic wore, as usual, a suit and tie, and Paige a soft pink wool dress. When they arrived, the church was echoing with the sound of children's voices and their parents trying to rein them in. For a good part of the ceremony, they had only to sit, or stand, and observe, and this made them restless.

As they looked over the program, Dominic and Paige eyed each other in amazement, then whispered back and forth in hushed tones, not wanting the others to overhear.

"Maybe I should have taken more interest in what they were planning. From the way it looks, this could last for hours! The detail is staggering!" This, from Paige.

He squeezed her hand. "It'll be fine, Babe. You've made them all very happy."

They turned their attention to the program again, both still amazed at the content. The music for the Prelude was a medley of *Air* by Handel, *Ave Maria* by Schubert, *One Hand, One Heart* by Bernstein, and Paige's favorite, *Canon in D* by Pachabel.

The Hamiltons would be seated in the North Transept of the church and the Gianellis in the South Transept. While Aunt Sophia was Paige's Matron of Honor and Xavier Dominic's Best Man, they were honorary, and would not accompany the others at the altar. Instead, they would be seated with their family.

The Processional music was to be the Allegro Moderato by Handel, and of course, the Bridal March by Wagner. The order of the processional was explained by the priest. They chose to have Dominic and the groomsmen enter, followed by the bridesmaids, the candle lighters, the ring bearers, and flower girls. As the wedding march began, Paige and her father would proceed to the altar.

And that was only the beginning. There would then be an introduction by the Episcopal priest, Father James, followed by the "Liturgy of the Word" delivered by Father Stefano. Prayers, scripture readings, and a homily on the meaning of marriage would follow. After the selected vocals, "I Have Loved You" and "Where There is Love," the wedding vows, the blessing of the rings and the presentation of gifts made by the bride and groom would take place. Paige and Dominic would make their offerings, and the Priest would bless them.

The ceremony would be followed by a Mass service and communion, Communion was to be followed by the benediction and a blessing. For the recessional music Marcello's Psalm 19 had been selected.

They rehearsed for three hours before everyone was satisfied it would go smoothly, but finally it was done and the families met at the country club for dinner. It was after midnight when Dominic and Paige returned home.

Paige was tired, but her excitement over giving Dominic his gifts revived her. She took his hand, led him upstairs, and asked him to sit down. It was so obvious she had planned exactly what she wanted to do, he had to tease her a bit.

"Why do I have to sit down?"

His question startled her. "Well, I don't suppose you *have* to...." Then she saw the smile in his eyes. "Just because, okay?"

"Okay."

She went to the dresser and removed two boxes, giving him the larger one first. "This is your wedding gift from me." She bit her lip the whole time he was opening the box. The first box held another made of brushed metal with Dominic's initials and the date engraved on the top. She watched anxiously as he opened it and examined the watch carefully. It was elegant, very heavy, mostly black in color with some gold. It too was engraved with both his initials and the date.

She was waiting patiently for him to say something. Finally, he said, "It's wonderful, Paige. I've never seen anything like this. It's beautiful."

She was thrilled with his reaction and couldn't help but add, "It is, isn't it? It's made of gold, onyx and black diamonds. I thought they did a spectacular job."

"They did indeed, Sweetheart. It's truly magnificent." Dominic put it on and it fit his wrist perfectly. Paige told him she had measured his watch band when he was in the shower one day.

"And you won't ever have to have another watch, Dom. At least that's what they said."

"Well, I wouldn't want another one, my love, not ever."

"Okay, now. This one is your birthday present." And she handed him the smaller box, which was wrapped similarly to the first.

It contained a ring designed to compliment the watch, and Dominic was obviously impressed. "Sweetheart, this is fantastic. I have to ask where you found these." She smiled and said only that they were made in Europe, and that she was thrilled he liked them.

Then Dominic reached for her hand and said, "Paige, I have something special for your wedding gift, but the more I've thought about it, the more I believe I would rather give it to you when we return. The shopping we did yesterday was intended as a consolation prize for what I'm telling you now. Will you forgive me for making you wait?"

She smiled. "I don't mind at all."

"Aren't you even curious?"

"Not really." Then, seeing his dubious but amused look, she said, "Dom, whatever it is, I'm sure it is breathtaking and I will be totally overwhelmed by it. But right now, that I'm going to marry you is the biggest, most wonderful thing in my life. That and celebrating your birthday. You know what? We need wine, and I almost forgot! We have to go downstairs!"

It was times like this that brought home to Dominic just how very young she was, but he never had second thoughts about the relationship, the marriage.

Paige asked him to pour the wine while she got his birthday cake from the freezer. It was a vanilla and chocolate fudge ice cream cake. By 1:30 A.M. they had eaten nearly half the cake and drunk the bottle of wine.

He lit a cigar and watched as she cleared the plates, boxed the remainder of the cake, and put it in the freezer. She looked like an angel in the pink dress. There was a glow about her—the combination of wine and the excitement of the evening, he supposed. God! He *did* love her, so damn much.

"Sweetheart, come here." He held her now. "Thank you. For the watch, the ring, the cake, for making this day start out so special. This is it, my love. It's officially our wedding day, the day you thought would never arrive."

"Yes." Those dark eyes held his. "I love you, Dom." Then she was kissing him, her tongue finding his.

Minutes later the pink dress had been discarded, and lay at the foot of the stairs along with her shoes. Her stockings, bra and panties trailed from the landing outside their suite to the floor beside the bed.

She lay in his arms now, with her body pressed against him. "Dom," she whispered, "Fuck me."

And when he entered her, she closed around him like a warm, wet glove. He loved her tenderly, then fiercely, until they lay spent and breathless in each other's arms.

Hours later, when Dominic awoke to gentle kisses and her hand on him, stroking, caressing once again, he told her, "Baby, we've got to get you out of here and to your parents house."

Paige didn't stop what she was doing. "I know, but just once more, please?" She took his hand and placed it between her legs, letting him feel how warm, and *oh, Jesus!* how wet she was. She was whispering, "See? I want you in me. I need you. I need you inside me. Please, Dom."

He was always encouraging her to "talk" when they made love, and she was more talkative this morning than she had ever been. *Timing was everything!* She was pressing herself against his hand now. His fingers found her, and he quickly brought her to orgasm. She reached for him again, saying, "I need you in me, Dom. I need you to fuck me now." He did.

Meeting his thrusts, just as she was about to come, she whispered something to him that surprised him, took him over the edge with her, filling the room with their cries of release.

Afterward, as he held her close and kissed her damp forehead, he asked, "Did you just say what I think you said?"

She nodded.

"What made you say that, Baby? Can you tell me? "

"I was so...excited. And I felt like I wanted it. Wanted you to do that. And I just said it."

"That's good, Sweetheart. That's really good. That's what I want you to do." Positive reinforcement was important. It was part of the learning process, and she was definitely learning!

She was kissing him now, the tip of her tongue teasing his mouth.

His voice was firm as he told her, "Zucchero, we have to get dressed. Come on, Sweetheart." He got up, pulling her with him. She threw on jeans and a tee shirt, grabbed her coat and gloves, and as sat on the edge of the bed waiting for him, she yawned.

Dominic came out the dressing area tucking his shirt in and pulling on his
jacket.

Paige looked as though she might fall asleep at any moment. "Paige! Your shoes, Babe, put on some shoes. We have to go!"

She stood up and looked around, then, yawned and said, "Maybe we could get married tomorrow, instead."

"I don't think so, Sweetheart." He grabbed a pair of tennis shoes from the closet and brought them to her. She yawned again as she tied them. Noticing his coat and gloves, she asked, "Are you coming with me?" She sounded pleased.

"Of course! I'm not sending you off by yourself. Come on, Vincente is getting the car."

It was a thirty-minute drive to the Hamiltons and after 6:00A.M. when he walked her to the door, grateful to find it unlocked with no need to ring the bell. He kissed her and told her to try to get at least a little rest.

"I will. You should go home and sleep till noon, Darling. There's no reason you can't."

He smiled. "I may do just that, Zucchero." Then he pulled her to him one last time. "Thank you again, Paige, for everything. I love you and I'll see you at the church. We have a date at three, remember?"

"I remember. I love you so much, Dom, so very much." Her beautiful, velvety brown eyes were soft, sleepy.

"I know, Baby, and I love you. Now, scoot!"

Quietly, Paige opened the door and stepped inside. She had made it just to the base of the stairs when Paul, coming from the direction of the kitchen, addressed her, disapproval stamped on her face.

"Well, good morning, Paige. I was beginning to wonder if you were going to make it."

She forced a smile. "Good morning, Dad. I didn't intend to be this late... this early..." She stopped.

Paul gazed at his daughter. She was lovely, even with uncombed hair and no makeup. The jeans fit her long legs snugly. She was braless under the stretchy tee shirt, which defined her young breasts, and her nipples showed erect through the clingy material. Her cheeks had color and her mouth was full and soft, had an almost bruised quality about it.

Paige hung her jacket in the closet and walked toward him again. He caught the faint scent of her perfume and something else, something familiar to any man. He knew his daughter had just been with Gianelli, and it drove him crazy. She was beautiful and alluring. There was no denying it.

His voice was strained, uncomfortable, as he offered, "I've made coffee. Would you like some?"

She hesitated, and it was obvious she realized he was angry with her. "Yes, thank you, Dad. That would be nice."

They sat in the breakfast nook, silent at first, drinking their coffee.

After watching as she stifled several yawns, he said, "My God, Paige, did you go to bed at all?"

That her cheeks flamed at his question didn't help the situation. She stood, walked to the counter, and refilled her cup. "Dad, thank you for the coffee. I think I'll go upstairs, take my time getting dressed."

She wanted to escape, but he was having none of it. "In a minute, Paige. Come sit back down, please." He knew old habits died hard. She might be twenty-one now, but he was still her father, and though she hesitated, she obeyed him. "I won't keep you long. One last time, I have to ask, is this what you really want?"

She looked at him now with something akin to sympathy, but there was no missing the passion in her voice. "Dad, I want it more than I've ever wanted anything in my life. I love him *so* much. I don't even know how to explain it. He's perfect for me, Dad, he is. I know you don't think so, and I'm sorry you don't feel better about it, but he's *everything* to me!"

More loudly than he intended, he blurted, "He's close to my age! More than old enough to be your father! Don't you realize that?"

The look in her eyes let him know he had gone too far, but she said only, "Yes, of course, I know that, but it isn't an issue for us. I don't know what else to tell you. He makes me happy. We're comfortable together. He's my life, Dad."

He managed a tight smile. "All right, Paige. You'd better start getting ready. The photographer will be here at nine."

Paige stood up then, but made no move to leave. Ever so softly, she said, "Dad, my loving Dom doesn't mean I don't love you anymore. You know that, don't you?"

His heart wrenched. What was he doing to her, this child, who had never hurt anyone in her life? What was he doing?

"Paige, of course I know that, dear. Look, I just have wedding jitters today, that's all. No father ever wants to give up his daughter to another man. I'm not unique in this respect. And I don't doubt your love for him. I wish you well, Paige, I really do."

It was the best he could do, but it wasn't enough, and he lost her that day. In a moment that seemed to last a lifetime, the feelings flashed across her young face: hurt, defiance, then acceptance, and, finally, closure. With a forced smile, she said mildly, "Thank you, Dad."

Upstairs, Paige drank her coffee and soaked in a bubble bath. Using a folded towel for a pillow, she leaned her head back and closed her eyes.

For a brief moment she'd thought her father might...might what? He wasn't going to give even tacit approval to her marriage. From the beginning, he had despised Dominic. And Dom had been so patient, had tried to extend his friendship to her family. She thought her brothers really liked him. But her father was stubborn. She was tired now and her head ached...

She dozed, waking when the water had cooled enough to become uncomfortable. It was almost eight. She readied herself, brushed her teeth, applied creams and lotions, hot rollers, eye makeup, lipstick. Finally, she removed the rollers and brushed her hair, then sprayed a cloud of cologne and walked through it.

At a quarter to nine, Julia appeared to help her with her dress.

Paige was fastening the waist to the full petticoat. Smiling, she told Jules she didn't know how on earth she was supposed to walk through doorways. They got her into the dress, and Julia buttoned the numerous, tiny buttons from the waist up to the neckline on the back of the dress. When she turned to face her sister-in-law, sudden tears streamed from Julia's eyes.

"Oh, Jules, don't cry, please!"

"I can't help it. In some ways, it seems you should still be just a little girl. And here you are, all grown up and getting married. They're happy tears, Paige. I promise."

At the last minute, with Paige protesting that Dom liked her hair down, Julia took a comb and scooped part of it up, causing it to cascade in waves and curls to blend with the rest. "There, now it's half up, half down, we've compromised."

There was no time to argue.

As she descended the stairs, the photographer began shooting. John and Matt had their cameras and were taking pictures, too. Her mother was urging her to smile, but the photographer was saying no, not yet, this was good.

When Drew's youngest, Michael, now eight, called out to her, "Aunt Paige, see my tuxedo?" she turned to him and smiled.

"That's perfect! That's what we want." This, from the photographer.

They posed her in the foyer, the living room, on the porch, and on the lawn. With each brother, all three brothers, their families, her parents, only the children, then the entire family. Finally, shortly before noon, they finished.

Paige stripped, set the alarm for one hour later, and lay down on her bed, grateful for the respite.

Elsewhere on the island, Dominic was just waking up, his first thought being that it was an empty bed without Paige there beside him. He went downstairs to the kitchen, drank coffee, scrambled eggs and made toast. Mentally, he went over the day's schedule. Everything seemed to be in order.

Upstairs again, he set her ring box next his wallet. He picked up the watch she had given him and admired it once more. Then, noting the time, he headed for the shower.

At the Hamilton's, Paige was dressed and ready to go. Vincente picked her up at 1:30 to take her to St. Patrick's. For today, Manetti would drive Dominic. Other limousines were scheduled shortly thereafter to take the families to the church.

Bitsy said Paige's bouquet was already at the church. John had Dominic's ring. Her father and Drew helped her into the car, saying they would see her soon, and Vincente sped away with her.

Their wedding day was finally here.

Twelve

When Paige arrived at St. Patrick's, Manny and Bus were waiting in front of the church. They helped her out of the limo and escorted her into a room off the entrance of the majestic cathedral. She was surprised to see that they too were wearing tuxedos. She told them how nice they looked, then asked for Dominic. Manny replied, saying he and the groomsmen were in rooms in the front of the church, near the altar. He assured her the others had arrived and everything was in order.

The cathedral was huge, beautiful, almost intimidating in its splendor. Everything was on such a grand scale. The ceilings were over 300 feet high, and colossal statues of saints looked down from almost everywhere. The Pieta was lavish, much larger than the one in Rome. There were numerous altars, and the stained-glass windows were breathtaking. Sophia had told her it seated over two thousand people.

She could hear the music as it began. It was the *Air* by Handel, a sign the guests were now arriving and being escorted to their seats. Manny came to check on her, and she asked him to please tell her brothers she would like to see each of them for a few minutes. John appeared shortly thereafter. He seemed pensive as he took in the sight of her. "You're beautiful, Paige. It's hard for me to see my little sister right now—is she hiding in there somewhere?"

"She'll always be around, I promise." She smiled at him, taking his hand. "John, I just wanted—particularly you and Matt—to know how special you are to me. Everyone jokes about me being Drew's girl, but I have three brothers. I love them equally, and I owe them all. For taking care of me, for loving me, for teaching me…for everything." Her throat ached as she swallowed the tide of emotion rising in her. "And now, I'm going to send you away." She tried to laugh. "I still have to talk to Matt and Drew, and somehow do it without tears and a runny nose."

After wishing her happiness, he hugged her and left.

When John got back to the room where the others were waiting, he sent Matt to see Paige. Dominic asked how she was doing. John patted him on the shoulder, saying, "She's fine. You've got a surprise in store, my man."

"How so?"

"When you see her, she'll take your breath away."

Dominic smiled. "She already does that, John."

"Yes, well, you'll see."

Matt returned, and just as Andrew was leaving, Dominic handed him a note and asked that he give it to Paige. They were within twenty minutes of the ceremony now. The sanctuary was filling with guests. From the chancel, strains of *Ave Maria* filled the church.

Drew entered the room where Paige was waiting, and the sight of the light streaming down on her through the stained glass windows caused a lump to form in his throat that made it difficult for him to speak. But at last he managed to tell her how lovely she looked.

Paige took both his hands in hers, "Drew, what can I say to you? How do I thank you for giving up so much of your life for me?"

"You don't have to say anything, Sweetheart."

Tears overflowed her eyes as she spoke. Their father, who had now entered the room, stopped and watched them from a distance as Paige whispered, "You saved me, Drew. I know that."

Drew took out a handkerchief and helped dry her eyes. "Paige, listen, it's all right. Everything's fine, and it's been that way for a long time now. We're all *fine*. This is your day, Honey. Be happy. Dominic's a great guy. Really! You're wonderful together."

This brought more tears.

Drew sighed. "Paige, please don't cry. Let me get Jules. I think you're going to need a quick fix. I'll be right back."

Paige turned away, in hopes that no one would see her, but she was crying in earnest when Julia dashed in, bringing a damp cloth and a makeup bag.

"Paige, we can't have a meltdown now! I sent Drew to the front. Honey, it's almost time! Here, let's fix you. We can't send you down the aisle to Dominic in tears. What would he think!" Paige smiled at this, but more tears welled.

Remembering the note, she opened it now. Dominic had written: "The best days of my life have all begun and ended with you. The day we met, the days and nights we've shared since, and now today, the day I marry you. Know that you not only hold a special place in my heart, but that you are its sole possessor and keeper, that you are truly the love of my life. Dom" This brought another flood of tears.

"I'm sorry! I don't know where all this is coming from." She was sobbing again. Julia looked helplessly at Paul, and he stepped in. Matter of factly, he said, "Okay, ladies. Any more tears and *I'll* be crying. Paige, let Julia fix you up now. Hurry! We have to take a walk here soon." This seemed to work. In a matter of minutes, they were set. The processional music had begun.

Paul looked at his daughter, who, after being so distraught, now seemed quite calm. "Are you okay?"

"I'm fine. A little embarrassed." But she did not look at him.

In an attempt to mollify her, he said, "No need to be. I think all brides cry on their wedding day."

Paige sighed. "That's bizarre, don't you think?"

This was so typical of her, the sort of thing she had been saying since she was a small child. When she'd been crying, Paul had wanted to go to her and comfort her, but he had hesitated. Now, while they waited, he needed to fill the silence. "Paige, do you remember when you were only four, maybe five, and you took Andy out for a ride without permission?"

"Of course, I remember."

"Well, to this day I have a vivid memory of it. You, stomping ahead of me toward the house after I had already punished you right there in the barn. You were mad! Not hurt, not remorseful, and certainly not fearful. You were just plain mad and stomping those feet like crazy!" He chuckled, shaking his head, hoping his daughter would warm to the conversation, but she said nothing.

"You scared the wits out of me that day, Paige. I swear I don't think you've ever been afraid of anything in your life."

Before she could reply, the wedding march began to play.

"Are you ready?" He smiled, reaching to take her arm.

She did not return his smile. "I'm ready, Dad."

The doors opened and the congregation turned in unison to watch Paige coming down the aisle. A loud murmur went up from them. It seemed to her to take forever to get to the altar. She remembered she had been instructed to make eye contact and smile at the guests, but she just couldn't. Her eyes were on Dominic, and only him, so handsome in his tux, waiting calmly, patiently, for her. Her heart was pounding.

Paige and her father were halfway to the altar before Dominic could see her clearly, and he knew he would never forget this moment. She was breathtaking and so beautiful! The dress was elegant, perfect for her. Her dark hair was caught up in a clasp and tumbled in waves to her shoulders. Other than the diamond earrings he had given her, the bouquet of white roses was her only accessory.

As they approached the altar, she smiled at him, and the look she gave him was filled with love. It was then he realized this ceremony that had begun as something he considered an elaborate and extravagant necessity for others, something he would patiently endure for her sake, was much more than that.

He knew how much he loved her, but what he was feeling now was totally unexpected.

Paige seemed to listen attentively, but she never took her eyes from his, as the Penitential Rite was performed followed by the required readings.

The New Testament reading, being given by Tomas, was from Corinthians I. "Love is patient and kind. Love is not jealous or boastful or proud or rude. Love does not demand its own way. Love is not irritable, and it keeps no record of when it has been wronged. It is never glad about injustice but rejoices whenever the truth wins out. Love never gives up, never loses faith, is always hopeful, and endures through every circumstance. Love will last forever. Let love be your highest goal."

The priests now gave their homilies on marriage. For the first time since the ceremony had begun, Paige took her eyes from Dominic's and turned to Father Stefano. He questioned them now. Did they come to marry freely? They did. Would they love and honor each other as man and wife for the rest of their lives? They would. Yes, they would welcome children lovingly from God, and yes, they would raise them according to the laws of God and the Catholic faith.

Dominic found himself profoundly moved by the questions, and even more so by the sincerity of their responses. This was not rehearsed. That they looked to one another, and in unison answered the Priest, was spontaneous.

Paige passed her bouquet to Isabella and turned to Dominic. She was trembling. He took her hands firmly in his and she looked up at him, taking a deep breath before she began. Her voice was soft but clear and rang out in the hushed quiet of the cathedral. "I, Catherine

Paige, take thee, Dominic, to be my lawful wedded husband. To love, honor and obey. To have and to hold from this day forward, in sickness and in health, for richer, for poorer, for better, for worse. Forsaking all others and clinging only unto thee, for as long as we both shall live."

And he responded, "I, Dominic, take thee, Catherine Paige, as my lawful wedded wife. To love, honor and cherish. To have and to hold from this day forward, in sickness and in health, for richer, for poorer, for better, for worse. Forsaking all others and clinging only unto thee, for as long as we both shall live."

This was the point where the Priest was to bless the rings, but instead, he looked to Paige, and gave her a barely perceptible nod. Raising her eyes to Dominic's once again, she began to speak, earnestly and with the conviction of the pure of heart. She was guileless and her words pierced his soul.

> "Dominic, entreat me not to leave you,
> Nor to return from following after you
> For where you go, I will go
> And where you stay, I will stay
> Your people will be my people
> And your God will be my God
> And where you die, I will die
> And there I will be buried.
> May the Lord do with me and more
> If anything but death parts me from you."

It was eerily quiet in the church as she stood there before him, and he thought for all the world, at that moment, if such a thing existed, she truly looked like an angel.

Father Stefano blessed the rings and nodded to Paige.

Again, her voice was soft but clear in the quiet of the chapel. "Dominic, presenting to thee this symbol of my eternal love and devotion, in the eyes of, and in the name of, God the Father, God the Son, and God the Holy Spirit, I now solemnify my vows and with this ring I thee wed."

As she slipped the ring on his finger, only he, who knew her so well, saw the little sigh of relief and the smile in her eyes.

Now, he took her hand and repeated the vow. "Catherine Paige, presenting to thee this symbol of my eternal love and devotion, in the eyes of and in the name of, God the Father, God the Son, and God the Holy Spirit, I now solemnify my vows and with this ring I thee wed."

The presentation of gifts was made and the Priest blessed the symbols. The Nuptial Mass and then Communion were observed, followed by the Lord's Prayer. Father Stefano performed the Nuptial Blessing and the Sign of Peace. The choir sang "Agnus Dei" as well as "Jesu, Joy of Man's Desiring."

It had been a long day followed by a long ceremony. Dominic could tell Paige was tiring, and he winked at her. This won him a smile.

They knelt for the Final Blessing and Dismissal. Then Father Stefano introduced them, for the first time, as a married couple. Paige had been nervous about the Recessional, so Dominic put his arm around her waist and guided her as quickly as he could up the aisle and out to the waiting car.

Once inside, Paige allowed herself to lay her head back, close her eyes, and breathe a big sigh of relief. She had done it! They were married!

"You're not going to give out on me now, are you?" he teased, reaching for her hand.

Her eyes still closed, she shook her head slowly. "No, Darling, I just need a minute to collect myself." After taking another deep breath, she sat up and gave him a shy smile.

"Come here." His look was serious now.

"I don't know how close I can get in this dress."

"Your dress, Zucchero. It's fantastic, and you are the most beautiful sight I've ever seen. All of a sudden I'm grateful for the hours spent with that photographer. Speaking of which, you know we have to go back in shortly to finish the pictures. But this way, the guests head for the reception and it's only family left."

This brought an audible groan from Paige.

"It's almost done, Sweetheart. Hang in there."

"I am. It's just that I've been in this dress since nine this morning, except for a short nap." She looked him over. "You do great things for that tuxedo, Darling."

"Well, we do our best." This, dryly.

She remembered his note. "I loved your message, Dom. Thank you. I'll keep it forever."

Manetti retrieved them, and they went back into the cathedral for more pictures. This accomplished, the entourage headed for the reception and dinner.

When the time came for their first dance, it was to "The Way You Look Tonight." Dominic had chosen it, and he asked if she remembered that it was their first song, first dance. Of course, she remembered. Paige had selected "One in a Million," and they shared a second dance before she took the floor briefly with her father and brothers.

They were starving and the dinner was wonderful. There were three menus from which to make their selections and nothing had been spared. They chose the Chateaubriand in a delicate wine and mushroom sauce, a vegetable medley, hearts of palm salad and sesame rolls. After dinner, they cut the wedding cake, and more pictures were taken. Then a huge birthday cake was brought out with smaller versions on several tables.

They drank wine and champagne until Paige confided to Dominic that the room was spinning and she had a constant urge to giggle.

"Coffee time for you, my love." He ordered for both of them and, looking at his watch, asked when she would like to go home.

"You mean we have a choice?" She whispered this.

"I think so, why not? We've been very accommodating today, and you, my love, are operating on little or no sleep. It's eleven now. I think we can start saying our thank yous and our good-byes soon."

"Wonderful!"

Shortly after midnight, they were in the car with Vicente, headed for home. "I love my rings, Dom. People were commenting on them all evening. I haven't had a chance to tell you, but I think they're beautiful. Thank you so much. You have exquisite taste. You really do."

Looking at her, he smiled and leaned down to kiss her. "Yes, I do, Sweetheart. I really do."

Once home, they went straight upstairs. Paige was anxious to shed her wedding dress. "Do you want to help me out of this, Darling? There are at least thirty buttons back there, few of which I can reach."

"I do, but first, I want to look at you. Is that all right? I've shared you with the rest of the world all day and most of the night, but right now, I want to look at my bride."

This touched her and, as usual, all the more because she knew he was not, as a rule, given to moments like this. She didn't doubt he *felt* them, but she knew it was a longtime habit with him to keep his feelings to himself.

Holding both her hands in his, he stepped back from her a little, his eyes taking in every detail. "You are so very beautiful, Zucchero. I don't have the words to tell you how I felt when I saw you coming down the aisle. You were breathtaking. And Paige, what you said, after we took our vows, sometime would you write that down for me? I want to keep it, always." He was looking at her with such tenderness. "How did it go...entreat me not to leave you...?"

Softly, she continued, "Nor to return from following after you
For where you go, I will go
And where you stay, I will stay
Your people will be my people
And your God will be my God
And where you die, I will die
And there I will be buried.
May the Lord do with me and more
If anything but death parts me from you."

"That's wonderful, Paige."

"Dom?"

"Yes, Sweetheart?"

"I meant it, every word."

"I know. I've no doubt whatsoever about that." Pulling her to him now, crushing her and the dress against him, he held her tight and whispered, "And I meant it too, Paige. You are my heart, my life. *Never* forget that. Do you understand?"

Her face was buried in his shoulder and, nodding her head, she murmured, "Yes, I understand."

Dominic said they should have one more glass of champagne, a special moment for just the two of them. After they finished their drinks, she was quiet, thoughtful. Watching her, he thought she seemed a little timid, at a loss as to what to do next. This reminded him of their first night together and, once again, he wondered if she would always touch him like this. She was so...genuine, so unaffected.

She was biting her lip. "Paige? You're not feeling shy now, are you?"

The instant flush to her cheeks was his answer, and he couldn't help but laugh. "We're the same people we were this morning, Sweetheart. It's been quite a day, and now we're married, but things haven't changed between you and me. We belonged to each other long before today."

"I know," she said softly, still chewing her lip.

"Do you want to tell me what you're thinking?"

A slight shrug was her answer.

"Paige?"

Finally, she said, "I forgot to get anything to wear tonight."

It took everything in him not to laugh aloud. "Well, you know, I've already been having my own thoughts about that."

She looked at him, waited.

"Come here, Sweetheart."

She stood before him. "Now turn around." She complied.

With uncharacteristic patience, he began undoing the tiny buttons. Then carefully, he pulled the top down and she slipped her arms from the sleeves. He lifted the dress over her head and laid it on the chaise. Still in his tux, he sat on the edge of the bed and removed the rest of her clothing. He held her close and kissed her, telling her repeatedly how much he loved her.

And when she whispered, "I need you," he held her from him, and let his eyes sweep over her body. "Now, why would I want you any other way but this, Zucchero?" He undressed, then reached for her and folded her in his arms again.

The feel of their bodies coming together, his mouth on hers, demanding now, filled her up. Paige loved him so much she ached with it. Others only thought they knew how she felt about him. They hadn't a clue. He knew her. He loved her, taught her, and understood her. He was everything to her. Her love for him consumed her and she knew it, was glad for it.

His fingers were stroking her, owning her, and she surrendered to the sweetness of the moment. "Oh, Dom, now…now!"

"Is that better, angel? Does it take some of the edge off?" This, between kisses, as he held her, seeming to sense that her emotions were still running high.

And she whispered. "Again, I want you to do it again." She reached for him, her fingers closing around him. "You're so big, so hard, Dom. I want you in me. I want everything."

She was right. He did know her. He knew what she needed, and he gave it to her, loving her tenderly, fucking her fiercely, till they were spent and lay, in peaceful contentment, in each other's arms.

And in the early morning hours, with the stars still visible in the winter sky, Dominic woke to her caresses and he took her again, her cries echoing in the dark.

Afterward, as he held her, he considered her almost frantic need for him. She was wound so tight right now. The last few weeks had been hard on her. Her father's unrelenting disapproval of their marriage had left its mark. That relationship, whatever it had been in the past, would never be the same again. He did not know, and would not ask, what took place between the time he left her at her parents' door and their arrival at the church. But it was serious. Not once during the ceremony had Paige so much as looked at her father. And at the reception, even when they danced, Paul could well have been a stranger.

And if that weren't enough, what about the past? What must her life have been like after Martha came home? Knowing she wasn't comfortable with her mother, but not understanding why? Pretending for others' sake that all was well?

It must have been a lonely life for her in many ways, being so different, and she *was* different. Were she not, she could not be with him. It was that simple.

But she was with him. And he whispered as she slept, "It's all right, Zucchero. You're mine now and you're safe. With me, you will always be safe. Rest, my love, just rest." He touched her face, her hair, and gently kissed her forehead. She was his prize, his treasure. She was part of his world now, and he would protect her. They would all protect her.

Thinking back on the ceremony and the special recitation from Paige, he could only imagine its effect on those in attendance. It was so direct, so genuine, her vulnerability so obvious. There had been an almost sacrificial quality about it that probably had left many uncomfortable. But one thing was certain. It had left no doubt as to her feelings for him.

Dominic decided to postpone their trip for a couple of days. They could leave on Friday. The time to rest would do Paige good, do them both good. She was better today. They had cooked breakfast and sat on the porch afterward drinking coffee and talking. He told her to put on her suit, they would swim. She still needed to unwind. It was nice, just the two of them, and from now on it would be that way. At least until the babies started coming. The thought pleased him.

He watched her as she came down the stairs in a black swimsuit, the back cut low, very low.

Taking their time, they swam for an hour, then, wrapped in heavy robes, sat by the pool and drank coffee laced with sambuco. At noon, they ate bowls of sweet cream ice cream mixed with fresh raspberries, followed by steaming cups of Amaretto coffee.

As she cleared the bar of their dishes, her back was to him and the scant suit revealed the cleavage of her bottom. Wordlessly, he took her hand and led her up the stairs to their room. He sat on the side of the bed, pulled her to him, and ran his hands over her body, his fingers lightly tracing the crevice between her legs.

She reached for him, felt his erection. Dropping to her knees, she opened his robe and took him in her mouth. She was becoming more adventurous...and more skillful when she did this, letting her tongue explore and caress the entire area, causing him to groan with pleasure. The sight of her head in his lap while she sucked him made him want to throw her down and fuck her.

Gathering her hair in one hand, he yanked it with just enough force to pull her head back. "Stand up."

He removed the swimsuit, tossed it to the floor, and told her gruffly, "Get on the bed."

She lay on her stomach as he tied her wrists, and spread her legs, making herself accessible to him. Her compliance fueled his excitement. He was fucking her now, pounding her. He flipped her over, her wrists still tied, her arms crossed above her head. He kissed her then, gentle, lingering kisses, moving from her mouth to her neck, stopping at her breasts to tease her nipples with his tongue. He worked his way to her belly, tickling, tantalizing her.

"Tell me what you want, Baby. Talk to me."

"I want you to fuck me. *Now*."

"You want to come?" He was still kissing her belly.

"Yes." She was squirming, and her breath came quickly.

"Now?"

"Yes!"

He held her legs apart with his hands as he put his head *there* and kissed her.

"Dommm!"

"What, Zucchero?" He kissed her again, then using his tongue he began to stimulate her clit. She gasped. He worked on her, kissing and sucking, his tongue his tool. At first, she tried to pull away, but before long she was arching her body toward him, and when she came he knew it had been good.

On his knees now he pulled her to him, and her legs locked around his middle. She was hot, wet, and tight, and she drove him wild.

Later, they lay in each other's arms, blissfully content in their oneness.

She whispered sleepily, "You don't play fair, Dom. What happened to 'no' or 'another time?'"

"I thought you needed to try it at least once. Are you mad at me, Zucchero?" This, as he kissed her, stroked her arm.

"Absolutely furious, can't you tell?"

"Do you still love me? I love you."

"Nothing could make me not love you. You're my husband." This last, she said shyly.

"Well, I think it's going to work then, don't you?"

"It has to. You're stuck with me, Dom. I'm not going anywhere."

She was on her side now, her head just below his chin, the length of her body pressed against him. He knew she would be asleep in a matter of minutes. Then, as she slept, he whispered endearments again.

The villa in Salerno had been refurbished in preparation for its new mistress. The grounds and patios were abloom with flowers. The house had been painted, inside and out, the marble floors were polished to a high shine, the windows sparkled.

All the rooms had been cleaned and aired. The master suite had been completely redone, this time with a more feminine touch. The pantries were stocked, and the cooks had prepared a sumptuous meal in honor of the newlyweds.

They were welcomed by security personnel and the domestic staff. Paige surprised them all, including Dominic, by greeting them and responding in Italian. Later, when he mentioned it, she gave a slight shrug and said lightly, "Well, I had to do something while I was waiting for a year to pass." She smiled. "Don't get too impressed. You heard just about everything I know, but I'm learning. I'll get there."

He was pleased with her and wanted her to know. "Of course you will. I think it's excellent!"

Dominic gave her a tour of the house and grounds and was gratified by her appreciation of its beauty.

"So, you like your other home, Mrs. Gianelli?"

His answer was a big smile. "It's wonderful, spectacular!" She stood looking down the coastline at the deep blue of the Mediterranean cast against the white sandy beaches, and the villas below dotting the countryside. It was magnificent. "I love it, Dom. I really do."

They spent the weekend at home, but on Monday and Tuesday he took her the length of the Amalfi Coast from Salerno to Sorrento. Paige said that the zigzagging bends and curves of the coastline, and the villages that looked like scenes from postcards, thrilled her.

They browsed the quaint shops and dined in picturesque cafes. Her interest and her excitement over everything delighted him. She was fascinated by the duomo, the cathedral at Ravello with the six lions carved at the base of the pulpit, and the nearby villas and their elaborate gardens. Dominic told her that Wagner, Verdi and Toscanini were among the artists that had performed there.

She was awed by the beauty of Positano, with its tiered arcades of rose and honey-colored houses balanced precariously above the glistening water. Its history, he informed her, was long and rich, quite strange, and had started a very long time ago. She listened with rapt attention as he explained how, when the Roman Emperor, Tiberius, ruled, he was mistrustful of everyone, even those closest to him. He feared that everyone wanted to poison him. Not wanting bread made with local flour, he commissioned his three-oar boat to go along the coast of Positano and collect flour from the mill there. The mill, now standing for centuries, had been modernized but still ground flour for the locals.

As part of the Amalfi Republic in the ninth, tenth and eleventh centuries, Positano took part in collecting the first written navigating regulations, which sanctioned the rights of seamen. In the tenth century, Positano rivaled Venice as one of the most important commercial centers in the world. By the twelfth century, it had become an enormously rich area. Its ships sailed everywhere, to every port, with spices, silks, and precious woods, all coveted by those in the West. It was at this point that the beautiful Baroque houses were built. Paige never seemed to tire of the sight-seeing or Dominic's commentaries, and this delighted him.

On Wednesday, they visited Paestum and saw the well-preserved relics of the Magna Graecia colonies, three Doric temples on a flowered and grassy plain. The temples were a tribute to Greek architecture, the temple of Neptune being the largest. It was considered the greatest example of Doric architecture in the world. There was the Italic temple dedicated to Jupiter, Juno and Minerva. It was at this site, he told her, that centuries before the Normans had plundered the temple and robbed it of six columns, which were carried away for use in a chamber in the Archbishop's palace in Salerno. The temple of Ceres, which had a clump of pine trees that formed its crown, was small in comparison, but still impressive.

Dominic took her to Paestum at sunset, telling her that the evening shadows gave the magnificent temples a mirage-like effect. And it was true. They seemed to rise out of the dusk on the flat surrounding plains. They took her breath away, and she told him so.

The museum there was splendid. Dominic told her it housed one of the best assemblies of ancient architecture in the world. It was known for its collection of friezes, the decorative bands along the walls below the ceilings with elaborately sculpted figures.

They were having a wonderful time. While he showed her the country during the day, their nights were devoted to satisfying their ever present desire for one another. The scenario for their lovemaking ranged from slow and easy to fierce and frenzied. What she brought to his life continued to elate and amaze him, and her love for him, her commitment to him was unquestionable. This he knew and accepted.

She slept now, in his arms, her body close, one leg entwined with his. He kissed her and she stirred slightly, then snuggled against him again.

Around 1:00 A.M.. Paige awoke. She used the bathroom, then got back into bed, but found she couldn't sleep. As quietly as possible she eased herself from the bed, and walked out onto the balcony. The weather was still nice. They were far enough south that winter hadn't set in yet. The breeze from the water was cool and she could see the waves crashing against the sandy beaches. Below her, the pool looked inviting. His soft snoring assured her Dominic was sleeping soundly. Hesitating only a moment, she tiptoed into the bathroom, wrapped herself in a big towel, and made her way down the stairs and outside to the pool.

She dropped the towel and slipped into the warm water that felt like silk on her naked body. Leisurely, she swam back and forth, again and again. This was heaven. It was *all* heaven. She was deliriously happy, content. She lay on her back, floating, her eyes closed, replaying in her mind the wedding and all that had happened since. Sending up a silent prayer of thanks, her heart was full, her world complete.

Finally, she began to tire and, feeling she could sleep again, made one last lap underwater, crawling along the bottom of the pool. As she entered the shallow end, her hands reached for the tiled rim just as she emerged, breaking the surface of the water.

Suddenly, something like a steel vise gripped her wrists, jerking her upward, and she was momentarily airborne. Her feet slammed against the concrete, jarring her from head to toe. Now Dominic had her by her shoulders and was shaking her. She knew he was saying something, but she could hear only the roaring in her head. Not six feet from them stood two men with guns. Behind them on the massive walls that surrounded the villa were several more.

"Paige! Answer me!" He continued to shake her. "Are you all right?"

"Y-y-yes." Stammering and trembling, she looked at the two men closest to them. One reached to hand Dominic the towel that lay on a chair. He took it and wrapped it around her. Only then did she remember her nakedness. Her husband was leading her into the house, to a downstairs bedroom. She was shivering visibly, and he was rubbing her briskly with the towel to warm her.

"Paige, talk to me! What happened!"

"N-nothing."

"*Nothing?* What were you doing in the pool, Sweetheart? It's three in the morning!"

"I...I couldn't s-sleep."

"You couldn't sleep?" This, incredulously. "Paige, how did you get downstairs? How did you get to the pool?" He was practically shouting at her.

She was confused by his questions and his concern.

Her lower lip trembled, and she was close to tears. "I just w-went, that's all. I th-thought it would b-be okay. I didn't think you would m-mind." She was whispering, and her breath still came in short gasps.

Pulling her to him for a moment, he held her. "Sweetheart, I don't understand. I need to know how you got downstairs. Are you saying you just walked out?"

"Y-yes."

Dominic let her go long enough to run his hand through his hair. He looked both distracted and worried. There was a knock on the bedroom door. It was one of the men. Dominic spoke to him briefly. "Yes, I think she's all right. She said she couldn't sleep and decided to take a swim. Yes, I know."

Turning back to her, he said, "Sweetheart, when I woke up and couldn't find you, the first thing I noticed was that the alarms weren't working. All the indicators were off. The entire system had been disabled."

With her eyes wide and her heart beating like mad, she told him, "I did that."

"Did what, Sweetheart?"

She swallowed hard. "I turned it off."

He was looking at her quizzically, obviously not fully understanding.

"The alarm. I didn't want to wake you, so I turned it off."

He was silent for a minute, studying her, as if thinking about what she had said. "Zucchero, how would you be able to do that?"

"Because it's like the one Dad installed at our house several years ago. I noticed the pad in the pantry that first day when you were showing me around."

"But you disabled the entire system, Paige."

"I didn't know. I thought it was just for the house, like ours was. I'm sorry."

Dominic was still studying her. How the hell? She seemed fine. Evidently nothing had been compromised, and evidently, *somehow*, she had managed single-handedly to shut down their system.

"Wait here, I'll be right back." He returned, carrying her robe and slippers. He put them on her, then guided her to the kitchen where the same men from the pool awaited them.

Dominic seated her in a chair. "Paige, I want you to tell Mr.

Belludi and Mr. Mazeri what you told me, please. It's all right. We just need to figure some things out here."

She nodded to them. "I woke up and couldn't go back to sleep, so I decided to take a swim. I didn't want to wake my husband, so I turned off the alarm."

Wrapped in the white terry robe, Paige was sitting on the edge of the chair, her back straight, her hands folded in her lap. She was biting her lip and she looked small and frightened. He knew his men felt sorry for her.

Gently, Belludi asked her, "Mrs. Gianelli, how is it you were able to do this?"

Again, she explained that the system appeared to be identical to the one they had at her parent's home.

"And the code?"

"I remembered that to disable the system at home there was a standard code you could use, or you could change it, but we never did, so I just tried that and it worked."

The three men exchanged glances. Belludi nodded. "Can you tell me exactly how you did this?"

"You simply spell out 'disabled' by using the letters assigned to the digits on a phone, then press '0' four times."

Belludi looked at Dominic and nodded. "I see. Well, that explains a lot, but I have another question, if I may."

She waited.

"How did you get downstairs without setting off the alarms? You were on the third floor. You had to come down four separate flights of stairs. There are lasers on each landing, which means you somehow got past these..." He paused, giving her a steady piercing look.

"Oh, *that*." Hearing this, Dominic somehow knew it was going to be good. He listened as his wife, wide-eyed and solemn, told them, "There's about a three-second interval between sweeps. I just ran them, that's all."

Dominic, working to suppress a smile, looked thoughtful. "You ran them," he repeated.

"Yes." This, very softly.

Dominic looked questioningly at Belludi as if to ask if this were possible.

Belludi merely nodded, then said, "Thank you, Mrs. Gianelli.

You've been very helpful. I expect we'll be rethinking some things." He smiled now. "If you wish, you can go now. I'm sorry if we frightened you. However, *you* gave *us* quite a scare, signora."

"I'm very sorry."

Dominic spoke then. "Well, I think we've all had enough excitement for now. Belludi, you'll see to everything here?"

"Certainly, sir. And, we'll, ah, be making some changes. I'll let you know."

"Very well." Dominic thanked him, then led Paige upstairs to their suite.

She sat on the bed, sighing. "Well, *that* was humiliating, among other things." She was picking at the covers and digging the toe of one slipper into the rug, not looking at him. Watching her, his frustration gave way to tenderness and affection.

"Paige, it's all right. Really it is. I just want you to promise me one thing, okay?"

Those dark eyes looked up at him. She nodded.

"Anytime you can't sleep, wake me, please. No matter where we are. You and I will take care of any insomnia. Okay?"

"I promise." She still looked crushed, and he decided enough had been said.

"Paige, no one is upset with you. We were just worried. It's important that I always know where you are, Sweetheart. We've discussed this on numerous occasions, remember? I was concerned, not angry. Okay?"

Again, she nodded.

"Do you think you can sleep now?" he asked gently.

This time she shook her head no.

"Well, let's go make coffee. We'll bring it up here and sit on the balcony and watch the sun rise. Would you like that?"

"Yes, thank you." She eyed him solemnly.

"Come here, Paige." She went to him, and as he folded her in his arms, he whispered, "Zucchero, I *do* love you."

And later, sitting on the balcony, just as first light was dawning, she fell asleep, her head on his shoulder. He steered her inside to the bed and laid down with her, and they slept till noon. She awoke with cramps and a backache, and thus they spent the next two days lounging at home, which suited both of them.

Saturday evening they were invited to dinner by Nicolo and Olivia Donizetti, acquaintances of the Gianellis. Their son, Roger, a young man in his early twenties, accompanied them. They met at a local restaurant, La Scala. Over drinks it was mostly small talk, and Paige chose to listen. After the second round, though, Olivia became very friendly with Dominic, smiling seductively at him, touching his hand, his arm, his shoulder.

Each time she went to the powder room she insisted Paige accompany her, and each time Paige returned to the table feeling more subdued. After dinner, Olivia asked Dominic to dance with her. Turning to Paige, she smiled coyly. "You don't mind if I have just one dance with your husband, do you? It's been so long!"

Doing her best to appear cordial, she answered smoothly, "Not at all."

Roger asked Paige to dance, and she accepted. He was actually quite good, and they attracted attention on the floor.

He asked for a second dance, and even though the others had returned to their seats, she smiled, saying, "I think we owe it to our audience, don't you?"

This was a slower dance, and as he held her he whispered, "Pay no attention to Mother, she's had too much to drink. I'm afraid this sort of behavior is just...her way."

"Thank you for that, Roger. I appreciate it."

"My pleasure, Mrs. Gianelli." He smiled down at her.

At the table, Olivia leaned toward Dominic, her hand pressing his arm suggestively. "Aren't the children sweet together?"

The flirting that had amused him at first was now making him a little uneasy. Paige hardly touched her dinner and had been, for the most part, silent the last hour. And as he watched Roger Donizetti on the dance floor with Paige, he found he did not like the attention the young man was showing her. Shortly thereafter, they said their goodbyes to the Donizettis.

As he drove the MG along the winding roads, he kept glancing at his wife. He knew Olivia had annoyed her, but he was also flattered that Paige could be jealous. Finally, deciding to tease her a bit, he asked what she thought of the Donizettis.

She was pensive, then at last, calm and cool as you please, she said, "Well, Nicolo is nice—henpecked, I think—but very nice, and the son is a polite young man and an excellent dancer. As for Olivia, I don't know what to say. She's the first whore I've ever met."

Despite his efforts, the car swerved and it took him a moment to regain control. Not saying anything, he looked at her. She was staring straight ahead, her shoulders back, hands folded in her lap. He wondered what the hell Olivia had said or done. Something. This wasn't like Paige. But before he asked any questions, he needed to think. No, not Olivia. He'd had a lot of women throughout the years, and Olivia had certainly let him know she was interested, but he had never accepted her offers.

Paige cleared her throat. "Dom, when it's convenient, please pull over. I think I'm going to be sick."

Just ahead there was an overlook with a park and picnic tables. As soon as he stopped the car, Paige jumped out and hurried up the steps, across the pavilion to the other side, then down a grassy knoll. She did not make it to the rest area. He had to wait for Belludi and Mazeri. He explained to them she was ill, then ran after her. He stopped at the fountain and wet his handkerchief.

She was standing next to a tree, one hand on the trunk, the other on her stomach. Coming up behind her, he held out the handkerchief. "Here, Zucchero, wipe your face with this."

"Thank you."

"Do you want a drink of water?"

"Not yet, thank you." She was sick again. He went back to the fountain and rinsed the handkerchief. Some of the visitors asked after her. He assured them she was fine.

When she felt better, he walked her back to the car, his arm around her. As they crossed the pavilion, there was a smattering of applause and a few cheers.

Getting into the car, Paige asked wearily, "What was that?"

He gave a mischievous grin and said, "I told them you were pregnant."

"Oh, Dom!"

They were halfway home when he finally asked, "Are you going to tell me what this is all about?"

She shrugged. "I shouldn't have said what I did."

"You don't have to apologize, Paige."

She gave him a clear, steady look. "I'm not apologizing. I'm just acknowledging that I shouldn't have said it, that's all."

More silence, then Paige said, "Dominic, I would be a fool to pretend there hadn't been many other women in your life, and I would be an even greater fool if this was something on which I dwelt. I put it behind me within weeks after we met. I am not asking and I am not accusing. I want you to understand that. But, please, do not ever put me in the position again of having to listen to some woman regale me with stories, whether real or imagined, of her sexual escapades with you." She paused, took a deep breath, and continued. "I am your wife and that means something to me. It's everything to me. I would do anything in the world for you, Dom, but I will not stand still for some woman trying to discuss with me the size of my husband's—"

"Enough!" He scowled. "I won't have you talking like that!"

She looked at him, surprised at his outburst.

Firmly, he said, "What we say in bed is one thing. *This* is another."

As if she needed to be told this! She was only going to say "penis." No point in pursuing it though. She could see he was rattled.

"Dom, I meant what I said. It's none of my business, and I'm fine with that. But imagine how you would feel if some man started telling you stories about himself and me..."

She saw his jaw tighten. *That's right, Darling, it's not a pleasant thought, is it?* She loved him so much, and she knew this wasn't his fault, but she had no intention of going through it again.

He said nothing more till they were home, and then he asked her to sit down and listen for a moment. "You *know* I would never intentionally expose you to something like that. I had no idea of what was going on, Paige. As for anything between myself and Olivia, there was nothing. A lot of flirting through the years, yes, but nothing more. You're young and beautiful, Paige. She wanted to yank your chain and she succeeded. I'm sorry."

She was blinking back tears now, but she just nodded and said softly,

"Okay."

"Okay *what*, Zucchero." Paige blanched at his tone. He probably hadn't meant to sound so cross. After all, she had done nothing wrong, but she knew he hated surprises, and this certainly qualified as one.

She was staring at the floor now. "Just…okay. I wasn't blaming you for what she did. It made me feel bad, and I don't want it to happen again. It was hurtful and, at best, very rude."

For some reason, bits of the passage on love that Tomas had read during the wedding crossed her mind, causing a little ache in her heart. "Love is not jealous or boastful or proud or rude. Love is not irritable, and it keeps no record of when it has been wronged." She was jealous and she was irritable.

Her sadness must have been obvious because Dominic showed concern. "Paige, I can't take away what Olivia did. If I could, I would."

"I know that." She was staring at the floor, still blinking back tears. "This feels like a quarrel to me, Dom, and that's not what I want. I shouldn't have listened to her. It's just hard to hear things like that…" She was chewing her lower lip.

Dominic was studying her carefully now. "Let's put this to bed, okay?"

Relieved, she said, "Yes."

He took her by the hand. "And now, let's put us to bed."

"Yes."

They made love, as always, with abandon and passion, purging the events of the evening from their minds, and as Paige lay sleeping in his arms, Dominic knew it was behind them. And it was.

They spent another four days in Salerno, mostly at the villa, and he went out of his way to be loving and attentive, even more so than usual. He did not want the incident with Olivia to be what Paige remembered most about their honeymoon. She made it easy for him, acting as though nothing had happened. Their lovemaking reached new heights, and he hadn't thought that possible. And the night before they left for home she told him how much she loved the house, Salerno, everything they had done, that it was very special to her and she would never forget it.

Thirteen

They arrived home on the seventeenth, and the first thing Paige saw as they entered the house was the tree from Forever Christmas, the one she had so admired. Set up in the foyer, it was decorated exactly as it had been in the store. She was thrilled and deeply touched.

Dominic was standing there looking quite pleased with himself as she went to him and kissed him. "Thank you, Dom. It's wonderful! I love it! I love *you*. I love you *so* much."

"You're welcome, Zucchero. I love you...and Merry Christmas."

"Christmas!" The mere mention of the word lit a fire. "Dom, we only have one week to get ready, and there's so much we need to do!"

"Slow down!" He laughed. "We'll get it all done. I promise."

They spent the next week shopping and decorating, and Dominic realized that, because of her, Christmas had become special, in a way it had never been before. Seeing it through her eyes gave it new meaning. He actually enjoyed the hours they spent selecting gifts for the family. They bought Christmas cards and stayed up late into the night addressing them, hoping to get them out early enough for arrival before Christmas Day. They cooked meals, read the papers, and watched the news together. They were married, officially a couple, and they were happy.

The living room, family room, and even their bedroom suite had full-sized trees, artfully decorated. Garland was draped strategically on mantles and railings. There were lights on all the trees in the gardens closest to the house. The front gate twinkled with hundreds of star-shaped lights, and there were huge animated snowmen on either side. They delivered the family gifts on the twenty-third. It took the entire day, but it was fun and it was the end of their preparation for the holidays.

That night, they sat with drinks in hand in front of the fireplace and talked about Salerno and the day trips along the Amalfi Coast. Paige told him she was anxious to return. She loved the villa and the time spent with him there.

"No bad memories then?"

"Not a single one, Dom, I promise."

He set his drink down, drew her to him and kissed her, telling her how very much he loved her. She returned his kisses thinking, *my husband, my husband.* She loved the sound of it. And as his kisses became more urgent, more demanding, she gave herself over to the mounting desire that claimed them both.

She stood before him now and removed her sweater and bra. She unbuttoned her jeans and shed those along with her panties, the glow from the fireplace casting its soft light on her naked body.

He reached for her and pulled her to him. She loved the feel of his hands on her, skillful and knowing, loved the rising tide of emotions that swept over her every time he touched her. She wanted him. Wanted him now.

She had come so far in their lovemaking, very seldom hesitant about anything now. She thought nothing of being nude in front of him. Indeed, she would parade around the house as naked and unconcerned as a cat. While she always let him initiate the act, she did not hesitate to let him know she wanted him. She closed her eyes and sighed as his fingers touched her, explored her.

"You want it, Baby?"

She whispered, "Yes!"

"Then come get it."

Quickly, he stripped and lay back on the sofa, tossing the cushions to the floor to give them more room. As she eased herself down on him, she whispered. "I want you so much!" His hands closed tightly on her wrists, holding her steadfastly against him as she moved, fucking him, slowly at first, then harder, faster, until, softly, she said, "Now, Dom." Then more urgently, "Now. *Now!*"

He drew his finger between her breasts. Her body was damp and warm. Tracing a rivulet of sweat down her belly to the patch of dark hair, his fingers probed her again. "Turn around, Baby."

She got on her knees, her hands gripping the back of the sofa, and he stood behind her, his hands at her waist. Drawing her bottom to him, he pushed himself into her. She knew his excitement was mounting because he was rough now, pounding her.

There was something in his passion for her, when he fucked her like this, sometimes to the point where she didn't know how much more she could take, that allowed her own cravings to surface. She gave way to them freely, swept up in the moment with him, crying out as they found release.

Afterward, she lay in his arms, the air around them a blend of scents from their bodies, the crackling of the firewood, the only sound. And this man, who could go so quickly from fierce to tender, who held her now, his mouth soft on hers, this man, who owned her in their oneness—he was her world and he was all that mattered—now or ever.

Christmas gave way to the New Year, and the months passed quickly for the newlyweds. As do most couples, they had settled into a routine. Dominic spent four or five days each week at his office in the city, and Paige remained at home. His early concerns about her being bored and at loose ends were quickly put to rest. She was never at a loss for something to do. She ran, swam, and made good use of the converted bedroom they now called her "studio." Determined to become fluent in the language, she spent at least one hour each day practicing Italian.

She kept abreast of market trends, reading the Journal daily. Though Dominic had told her she could change anything she wished in the house, she kept her redecorating to a minimum. In the formal living room, she dispensed with the velvet-covered chairs and sofas installed years before and replaced them with airy, complimentary florals and plaids, giving the room a brighter, more pleasant atmosphere. Keeping a promise she had made to herself, she was learning to cook some of Dominic's favorite meals.

He made it a point to be home no later than six on the days he worked in the city. They would have a drink, usually wine, and discuss the events of their day. After dinner, they would clear the dishes and watch the news. They got in the habit of a nightly swim, weather permitting. Then they would sit in the sauna and whirlpool before having an occasional nightcap. Upstairs, they would shower and ready themselves for bed, Dom flipping through channels before settling on a movie or a late hour talk show.

Most nights they made love. Paige was always responsive, always wanted Dominic, but she let it be his decision.

Sophia had talked to her about this and explained certain things to her regarding men his age, the pluses and minuses, so to speak, that came with being almost fifty. For this, she was grateful, for it was not the kind of thing she would have known otherwise. But when she thought about it, she couldn't imagine that this was a less active time in his life. If so, she certainly wasn't lacking for attention from him.

Curious, she wondered idly if other couples made love as often as they, did the same things, but there was no one to ask. And even if there had been, she couldn't have put her questions into words. That was unthinkable. Besides, Dominic had been clear from the beginning that what happened between them stayed between them. Well, she was happy, very happy, and she thought her husband felt the same. This was really all that mattered. It always came down to this.

For Paige's twenty-second birthday, they went to Montana and spent a week at the cabin. At least once each month, sometimes more often, Dominic would take her to the ballet or the theater. They would visit their families on alternate Sundays, usually staying for dinner.

He attended Mass regularly, more out of a sense of duty to Paige than anything else. If she could embrace his family, their beliefs, their social mores so thoroughly, then the least he could do was accompany her to Mass. She had changed her whole life for him. Yes, it was the least he could do.

He received word that his presence was required in Italy the first week in April. He toyed with the idea of taking her with him, but decided against it. From the rather sketchy details, he determined it would probably not be an extended stay, five or six days at the most.

Saying only that he had business that demanded his attention, he arranged for his family to stay with her.

Though she never voiced her objection, he knew she bristled inwardly at the thought of having "sitters," but he was more comfortable having someone there with her, and certainly, on this occasion, he needed to be able to concentrate on the business at hand.

Dominic left early the morning of the third, promising to call them often. From the beginning, it was obvious that Paige hated being apart from him. She neither ate nor slept well, and was restless and unsettled. Sophia noticed that Paige tried to stay busy, occupying herself by working in the garden. And once, only once, did the girl volunteer that there seemed to be something about being outside for hours on end, weeding, thinning, and planting, that tamed the demons that haunted her when Dominic was gone.

Seeing her state, the family let her be. Paige was sweet and ever so polite, but she was not happy. Victoria tried to find things for her to do that might take her mind off missing Dominic. This seemed to work at times, but Sophia thought Paige merely feigned interest, and finally suggested to Victoria that she let the girl find her way. These things took time.

They watched Paige, discreetly so. She was given to long periods of silence. After dinner, she would swim, lap after lap, until she was obviously exhausted, then she would say good-night and go to bed.

The aunt watched as Paige made her way up the stairs. She knew it was difficult for her, not knowing the nature of Dominic's absence. And she knew from personal experience that unanswered questions could be hard on a marriage.

The girl was good, though, never questioning the circumstances of these unexplained trips. She neither asked for nor volunteered information. The aunt was gratified to see the love and loyalty Paige displayed to her nephew. She had been right about her. Paige was perfect for him.

Dominic was due home today, late evening actually, from what he had said, and Paige was anxious for time to pass. He had been gone only a week, but she missed her husband. Victoria and Aunt Sophia had been wonderful, teaching her to make Dom's favorite bread, as well as bucatini, a dish with a bacon and cheese sauce called amatriciana.

Poppa had been generous with his praise of anything she had done in the house or gardens. She knew they cared for her, that it gave Dominic a sense of peace for them to be there in his absence. But she was anxious to have him home, to be done with restless days and sleepless nights, to be whole again.

The morning dragged on, and after lunch Paige decided she would work in the garden again. Maybe she could finish by the time Dominic was home. The house was quiet. Sophia was upstairs napping and Victoria was doing her needlepoint. Poppa was reading, seated in a wingback chair in the living room. He merely nodded when she announced her plans.

Around two she came back to the house for a Coke. Poppa

looked at her sweaty face streaked with dirt where she had wiped it with her glove, and teased that Dominic wouldn't think much of the way they looked after her if he could see her now. A few minutes later Paige had resumed her project, digging up the smaller of some bushes and planting them in a new area.

The grounds of the estate covered almost two hundred acres of the most exclusive property on the island. The gardens were divided by decorative iron fencing, with gates from one section to another, and furnished with chairs and gliders, or benches. Some gardens were devoted to specific flora, roses, for instance. Others were colorful blends of a variety of flowers, hedges, and small trees. All were beautifully landscaped.

The garden she was working in now, though, was some distance from the house, almost to the property line, and consisted mostly of evergreens. It was an area, she decided, that could use some color. Already she had planted caladiums. There was enough shade to sustain the sun-sensitive plants. She had brought two large decorative pots of miniature roses from the greenhouse to put at either end of the bench, and had been eyeing a laurel and wondering if it was too big for her to move. She decided to try. It would be perfect in that corner.

Dominic arrived home early, at 5:10, accompanied by his lead counsel, Rudolfo "Rudy" Santoro. After a brief conversation with his parents, Dominic asked for Paige. Only then did they realize it had been close to three hours since they had seen her and, unhappily, Xavier relayed this news to Dominic, who in turn immediately called Manetti and asked him to check the tapes.

Fifteen minutes later, Manetti reported that at 2:20 she had been seen in the gardens to the east of the house, but was evidently out of range from that point on. Only two other men were on duty, but already they were combing the grounds, and he was calling Sal de Angelis to bring in his crew.

At 5:50 Dominic spied Paige coming up the walk toward the back patio. He watched her for a moment—she was fine—then he turned and strode quickly into his office. He opened a closet door and retrieved a wooden paddle. It was close to an inch thick and about twenty inches in length, with a carved handle.

———

Paige stopped in the greenhouse to discard her gloves and rinse her hands and face. Having done this, she proceeded to the house, anxious to shed the soiled tee shirt and jeans, and to shower and dress for Dominic's return.

When she saw him standing in the foyer, it was like the best gift anyone had ever given her, the way she always felt when her husband walked into the room. She smiled as she started toward him, then stopped short.

The look on his face could only be described as thunderous. His jaw was clenched and he was holding some kind of board in his right hand, tapping it lightly against his thigh. She had seen him angry before, though very few times, and it had never been directed at her.

She saw Mr. Santoro in the doorway of the office, and Poppa and Victoria, still in their chairs, their eyes averted.

Looking at Dominic again, something inside her cautioned silence, and she said nothing, just waited.

Finally, in a dangerously quiet voice, her husband spoke. "Where have you been, Paige?"

Something was wrong and she was trying desperately to figure out what it was. "Just in the garden. I've been there most of the afternoon."

"What did you do, Paige?"

His eyes held hers.

"Just worked in the garden," she said uncertainly.

"What did you *do*, Paige?"

She was trembling now, her mind searching frantically for the right answer.

"Tell me *what* you *did*, Paige!" His voice was loud, emphatic, and echoed in the eerie stillness. No one looked up. No one spoke. No one moved.

Paige swallowed and bit her lower lip, the way she always did when she was nervous.

When he spoke, his words were slow, deliberate, frightening. "No one has seen you for over three hours, Paige. You're not on the tapes. *What did you do?*"

Realization swept over her in the form of nausea, and her heart began to race. She wanted to cry, she wanted to run to her husband and have him hold her, she wanted this to go away. She knew none of these was an option.

She took a long breath, straightened her shoulders, and looked Dominic in the eye as she spoke. "I broke the rules."

"And what happens when you break the rules?" His voice was like ice.

"Consequences." Searching his face for a hint of the man she loved, she found only a stranger.

"What kind of consequences, Paige?"

"Severe consequences." And as many times as he had gone over this with her, only now did it sound ominous.

"Tell me about the rules."

She recited what she knew by heart, word for word what he had always told her she must heed. Why did it suddenly seem so simple and why, only now, so very crucial?

"Do I have a choice in this matter, Paige?"

"No." She tried to swallow the nausea that kept creeping into her throat. She didn't know what was going to happen, but she knew it couldn't be good.

"Tell me why."

"Because you make the rules, and if you don't keep the rules, then they mean nothing to anyone else."

He nodded. "Let's get this over with, Paige. Take off your shoes and come here. Santoro, time please."

She did as she was told and walked slowly toward him. Nothing seemed real. When she was within reach, Dominic encircled her waist with his left arm and at the same moment turned her and swung the paddle high in the air. It came down and hit her bottom with such force it lifted her feet off the floor and knocked the breath from her. Again and again, he swung the paddle, always at her bottom and the backs of her thighs.

After the first blows, Paige felt reality slipping away, and she escaped to a place that bore a vague familiarity—as if she had been there before. But she was snapped back to the present by Mr. Santoro, who called out loudly, "Time!"

Dominic stopped hitting her then, but when he let go of her, she stumbled and fell, face first, to the floor, catching herself on hands and knees.

She heard Santoro ask to speak to Dominic, and they went into the office. Moments later, Dominic returned, this time with his belt in hand. Paige had just managed to stand when he grabbed her arm and began hitting her with the belt, not so cautious as to avoid her back and lower legs now.

It seemed to go on forever until, at last, Mr. Santoro called out. "Enough."

Dominic's voice was cold and harsh as he addressed her. "Paige, we'll finish this upstairs." Then he turned to Mr. Santoro. "I won't be long. We still have things to discuss before you leave."

Santoro was shocked... shocked and appalled by what he had witnessed. He hadn't thought Gianelli was serious at first, but it didn't take long for him to realize a timed punishment was being delivered. The length of time depended on the severity of the infraction. He really wasn't sure which rule was being applied here. Men were beaten, yes, but with fists, sometimes other items. Santoro felt sick to his stomach. He didn't believe Gianelli knew his own strength. He could have caused severe injury to her with the board had he continued.

It had taken all the courage Santoro could muster to challenge Gianelli, and he seemed to have taken it well, but he did not allow it to interfere with the business at hand, which seemed to be meting out a hefty punishment for what Santoro considered nothing more than a mistake, a minor error in judgment made by the wife.

He was thankful it was coming to an end. Gianelli would use a switch on her, then it would be over and done. This was an old custom. The switch was meant only for women and children; it was never used on men.

As Consiglieri, Santoro tried to assign meaning to what had

taken place. Was Gianelli making a statement? If so, to what end? Already he was a man feared and respected by all. That he could punish his wife like this! Everyone knew he would do anything for her—that he adored her, worshiped her even.

Finally, Santoro decided this had nothing to do with the organization. This was a lesson for the young wife, and he hoped, for her sake, she learned it well.

Dominic went outside and returned with a long switch. Paige was on the stairway, her right hand clutching the banister, her movements stilted.

He was behind her now, and she turned to look at him. His face was unreadable.

In their suite, he closed the door. "Take off your jeans." His face still expressionless, he watched as her trembling fingers fumbled with the metal buttons.

Then, as he grabbed her and began hitting her again, he shouted, "Damn you, Paige. *Damn* you for making me do this!"

And the words broke her heart, not the deed. She *knew* how very much he loved her. She was his life and he was hers. The unreality of the situation claimed her, and she no longer felt the switch, though it had broken skin in several places now.

He was saying something to her, and she tried to focus. The switch was in two pieces. "Do you remember what I told you about breaking the switch, Paige?"

"That it's over," she answered, shakily.

He nodded. "Get dressed and comb your hair, then go downstairs and apologize for the worry and embarrassment you've caused everyone. I'll be there shortly."

After Paige left the room, Dominic collapsed into a chair, and wearily rested his head in his hands. He had done it. He'd had to. She had put herself in harm's way. As often as he had admonished her about it, she had disregarded his warnings. What if they had taken her? He couldn't let his mind go there, to what they might do knowing how much she meant to him.

Protecting her was paramount, and she had to know this! What had she been thinking? She'd been so good about it until today. Three hours. Anything could have happened. Yes, it had been necessary, and there was more to do.

Once again, Paige did as she was told, but she found it difficult to speak when she faced them. Sophia was there now, but the aunt, ever her ally, said nothing, only gazed at her, her face as unreadable as Dominic's.

She had to start over twice. "I want to apologize to you for the trouble and worry I've caused. I was thoughtless and careless. I'm very sorry, and I hope you will accept my apology."

Poppa just nodded, but Victoria spoke up. "Bella, we know it was just a misunderstanding, that you—"

Dominic, entering the room, cut her short. "Paige has things she needs to do."

Her feet felt frozen to the spot where she stood, and her mind searched frantically for what 'things' he was talking about. Dominic must have sensed her hesitancy because he added, "She needs to prepare dinner."

He then followed her into the kitchen. "You're not to speak to anyone. If spoken to, you may respond, but only then. Do you understand?"

A barely perceptible nod was her answer. He left, saying he would be in his office with Santoro until dinner.

If Dominic could have followed his heart, he would have taken her in his arms and held her, made things right again, but he couldn't... not yet. She had to feel this, remember it, and take it seriously, very seriously.

And in the office, Rudy Santoro waited, disapproval stamped on

his face. But he said only, "I suppose you considered that necessary." Then, "Couldn't you have just warned her?"
Gianelli's answer chilled him.
"That was her warning."

Paige was trembling so much it was difficult to handle the plates, and one fell, clattering, and broke on the tile floor. As she knelt to pick up the pieces, she felt the pain in her back and legs for the first time.

Dominic must have heard the racket, for he came into the kitchen. She saw that he was there but she didn't look up, just continued picking up the slivers of china. She remembered the day they had shopped for it, how happy they were, and tears stung her eyes. After watching her for a moment, he left. Her throat and chest ached with the effort of not crying.

Sophia appeared and set about making tea for herself and Victoria. Paige kept her head down, concentrating on preparing a salad. As the aunt was leaving, she paused, spoke softly. "You forced his hand, Bella. You frightened him, and you left him no choice. Terrible things can happen when caution is set aside, much worse than what happened to you today. It is a mistake to feel too safe, to think that no harm can come to you. Listen to him, Bella."

Paige kept her eyes averted, and her voice was but a hoarse whisper. "I didn't mean to do anything wrong, Sophia. Surely he knows—"

The aunt's voice was surprisingly stern. "He knows his business. He knows what's best for you. Do you think this was easy for him? He loves you—so much so, he did what he had to do. Think about that."

Paige acknowledged that she'd heard, but did not look up as Sophia departed.

Mr. Santoro left and the five of them had a quiet, uncomfortable dinner. Paige had no appetite and managed to choke down only a few bites of food. All eyes were on her, but she simply could not face them. Only once, she looked at Sophia, but the aunt remained aloof, unsympathetic, and this made her feel even more alone. She was glad when they said their good-byes. Dominic was not speaking to her, but relented enough to say he would be in his office if she needed him. The spark of hope she felt was quickly extinguished by the impersonal tone of his voice and the distant look in his eyes.

Long after the dishes were put away and everything was in order, Paige remained in the kitchen with only the night lights glowing. She felt hollow, empty. The marble-topped counters shone in the soft light. It was like being there, but not, she thought. The digital clock read 11:40.

Dominic cleared his desk, turned off the lights, and went upstairs. Surprised at not finding Paige there, he went back downstairs. At first he didn't see her in the dimly lit kitchen, standing there in the semidarkness.

"Paige?"

"Yes?" Her voice was barely audible.

"What are you doing?"

"Nothing."

"Well, come upstairs, okay?"

"Yes."

"Paige?"

"Yes?"

"Are you coming?"

"Yes. I'll be there in a minute."

Paige waited for him to leave before brushing the tears from her face. She didn't want to cry. She thought if she let herself start, she might never stop. She didn't know if the terrible ache in her chest was from trying not to cry or because her heart had taken the real beating.

Finally, she rinsed her face and made her way up the stairs. She could see him, standing there in the darkness, the only light coming through the doors that led to the balcony off their suite. "Paige?"

"Yes?"

"Am I ever going to have to do that again?"

A sob caught in her throat, but she managed to answer, "No."

"Come here."

She went to him, tears streaming. He caught her up and held her tightly, delivering her from a pit of misery. She would never go there again. This much she knew.

"I'm so sorry, Dom, I'm so sorry," she said, over and over.

"Shhh, it's all right, Paige. Don't, please don't, Zucchero. Please."

His mouth found hers and they clung to each other. And when they made love it was with such passion, such intensity, that afterward they fell into an exhausted slumber, Paige wrapped securely in his arms.

The sunlight coming through the French doors the next morning was intrusively bright, but that wasn't what awakened Dominic. Fully alert now, he realized the faint sounds he heard were coming from his wife. She lay on her stomach, not moving. He brushed the locks of dark hair back from her face. "Sweetheart? Are you dreaming? Paige? Are you all right?"

She was saying something he couldn't understand, and he asked her again. She wet her lips and said hoarsely, "Sore, just sore."

He touched her—she felt like she was on fire. He pulled back the sheet and was sickened by what he saw. His heart pounded as he forced himself to stay calm. From her shoulder blades to her ankles was a mass of injuries. He made himself not turn away but instead assess the situation.

From her shoulder blades to her waist, the marks were from the belt and the switch. Her bottom and down the backs of her thighs looked the worst. The board had left this area covered in black and purple bruises, and the bruises were topped with welts from the belt and switch. From her knees to her ankles the same marks, but the switch had broken the skin in places.

"Paige, I'm going to call Tomas." Then, almost as an afterthought, "Pop, too."

"Dom?"

"I'm here, Zucchero. I'm calling Tomas. We need some help." He made the calls.

When Tomas answered the phone that Saturday morning, it was the tone in Dominic's voice that made him ask no questions but pick up his bag and leave immediately. Xavier arrived within minutes of him.

Tomas found Paige lying nude, face down on the bed, her backside a multitude of injuries. He felt nauseous, and he didn't know what to do. Not for something like this.

Finally, fearful of touching her anywhere else, he felt her forehead. It was hot. He took a thermometer and checked her temperature. 102 degrees. "Paige? Can you talk to me?"

"Yes," she said weakly.

"Paige, can you move?" Dominic looked alarmed. *Good!*

"I don't know."

Tomas looked at Dominic, then at Pop, then back at Dominic, and gestured helplessly.

"Do something!" Dominic hissed.

"I don't *know* what to do!" he hissed back.

Xavier cleared his throat. "Let's call Dr. Forchelli." Dominic's face had gone unreadable, but he nodded assent, and Forchelli was summoned.

Forchelli was an excellent doctor with a select clientele, in that there were never any questions involved concerning their illnesses or injuries. He had been an associate for more than twenty years.

While they waited, Tomas suggested they get Paige something to drink. Dominic was frantic to know whether she was all right. He asked her to move her hands, her feet. That she could do this gave him some measure of relief.

At one point, Dominic leaned over and kissed her. "It's going to be all right, Baby, I promise. It's going to be fine."

"I know. I'm just so sore, that's all."

He was afraid it was more than that, but he hoped she was right.

Dr. Forchelli arrived within the hour and Manetti brought him up. He was a tall, slender man with a head of silver hair and a mustache. He dressed in expensive silk suits and soft leather shoes, a handsome, suave gentleman of sixty-three years. He had met Paige Gianelli at several family functions, holiday parties and the like. His training and years of experience kept his face expressionless as he examined her. He asked Tomas a few questions. Yes, she had fever. Yes, she could move, but it hurt her. Forchelli nodded.

"Mrs. Gianelli, do you remember me? I'm Dr. Forchelli. I think the last time I saw you was at Xavier's and Victoria's shortly after you and Dominic married."

She nodded.

"Now what do I remember about you? Ah, your name. You have an unusual name. Paige, isn't it? May I call you Paige?" He was obviously trying to distract her as he examined her thoroughly.

Again, she nodded. Then she wet her lips and whispered to him, "I'm fine. Just sore, I think."

"Hmmmm. Yes. I'll tell you what, Paige. I'm going to give you a shot for pain. Then I'm going to put some gel on your back and legs. It will feel very cold but it won't hurt, and it will numb everything until we can make you more comfortable, okay?"

"Yes."

He filled a syringe, then plunged it into her arm. It seemed to hurt her and he was apologetic.

Soon , Dominic could see her begin to relax. Forchelli waited fifteen minutes, then asked, "Is that better, Paige?"

Drowsily, she answered, "Yes."

"Good, very good."

As he spread the gel on her back and legs, Paige shivered visibly. This worried Dominic, but Forchelli told him she would be fine. It took him half an hour to cover her with the medication.

The doctor's voice roused her. "Paige, do you need to use the bathroom?"

She nodded. "Okay. Dominic and I are going to help you stand up. We'll take it slow. You let us know if we move too quickly. Okay?"

"Yes."

They managed to get her up and walk her to the bathroom, where Dominic stayed with her and helped her. He put one of his shirts on her. "Dom?"

"Yes, Baby?"

"It's okay."

There was a sudden tightness in his chest and his eyes hurt, but he nodded. He was not a man who wasted time and energy on remorse or regret. This was as close as he came.

Softly, she said, "I love you, Dom. You know?"

Again, he nodded.

He helped her back to bed under the watchful eyes of the others. In the end, Forchelli confirmed what Paige had said. She was stiff and sore from the impact of the whipping. The fever was due to the trauma her body had suffered. She would be fine. She needed to rest today, but should begin moving around as much as possible tomorrow. When she could tolerate it, warm baths would help the soreness. In the meantime, he would give her pain medication and more of the anesthetic gel.

The shot was taking effect now and Paige lay on her side, her eyes closed, one hand holding onto Dominic's. She awoke a short time later to hear voices, low and anger-filled. Poppa and Dom were arguing.

"I would have thought that you of all people would understand."

"Por Dios! Where do you think you are? This is Long Island. This is your home. Paige is your wife! She was working in the garden. She opened a fucking gate! Look at her!"

"You know it wasn't the gate! You didn't know where she was for over three hours. No one knew! Hell, you didn't even miss her till I came home! You tell me what could have happened, Pop. You tell me! She could have been anywhere! How long would it have taken to find her, *if* we could find her?"

She didn't want them to argue, and she wanted to tell them so. But she was groggy, and the words wouldn't come. "Dom?"

"It's all right, Paige. Go back to sleep. I'm right here." Then, more softly, "Forget it, Pop. Just go home."

Xavier knew that part of what he felt was anger toward himself. His son was right. He hadn't even given a second thought to Paige that afternoon. All Dominic had asked of them was to stay with her and make sure she was safe. He had become complacent in his old age, and now Paige had paid the price for it.

"Dominic, I'm sorry. I know you didn't want to hurt her."

Tiredly, he said, "Never mind, Pop. Go home. I'll take care of her."

"All right, Son."

Dominic lay down beside Paige and they slept until early evening. He brought her hot tea, saw to it that she took her pain pills, helped her to the bathroom.

For the next week, they kept others at bay. To her family, Paige pleaded the flu, and except for occasional calls to see how she was feeling, the two had their privacy. Though it was bad the first few days, Paige never let Dominic know the extent of her pain. She had brought this on them and she would never do it again, but she was worried about him. The marks and bruises on her body would heal. Indeed, except for some soreness, she was feeling fine. But she thought her husband's wounds went much deeper. She could see it in his eyes.

Toward the end of the week, choosing the time and her words carefully, Paige approached Dominic. He had worked most of the day until late afternoon, finishing around four. She poured drinks and took them into his office. After setting the drinks on his desk, she kissed him. Wanting his undivided attention, she knelt in front of his chair and took his hands in hers. He teased her, saying that if this was a proposal, she needed to remember he had already married her. She smiled and shook her head.

"I've been thinking about it all week, and I have something I want to say." She saw that he was listening patiently. She took a deep breath and began. "I owe you an apology, a real one. You were right, Dom. About everything. Your reasons were valid, and I want you to stop feeling bad about what happened. I've always been...smug... about how much I loved you, and it was acceptable to me that I loved you more..." Seeing his frown, she rushed on. "I knew you loved me. I just didn't think it was possible for you to feel the way I feel."

He said gruffly, "You were wrong."

"I know that now. I also know you did...what you did...because you cared, and that it hurt you deeply." She paused. "You ask so little of me, Dom, and you give me everything. Yet I couldn't do this one thing for you. I won't let you down again, though. I promise." She was blinking back tears now, but at least she had gotten it out.

He pulled her to feet and said softly, "Come here." It had become one of the things she loved hearing most. She sat on his lap, and with his fingertips, he dabbed at the tears that rolled down her cheeks.

Despite what Paige had just said, Dominic felt compelled to further address the issue, but his voice was gentle in reproof. "Do we need to revisit what I've told you from the beginning, Paige? Was there something that didn't get through? We take precautions. *Precautions.* I have my reasons. Isn't that enough? I care about you, about us. I appreciate what you just said, I do. But I'm not looking for an apology, Sweetheart. *I want you to be safe.* I want you to *think* before you act."

And despite his efforts to remain calm, frustration mounted in his voice. "Paige, all you had to do was tell Manny what you were doing, that you were out of range of the cameras. You did know you were out of range, right?"

Those lovely dark eyes were locked on his, pools of sadness as she answered quietly, "Yes, I knew."

Yes, she knew. Well, good. No excuses. Just the truth. Good. He touched her cheek. "You're my treasure. Don't you know that, Sweetheart?"

She nodded, bit her lower lip, and a few more tears escaped. He fished for his handkerchief and dried them. "I love you, Paige. I always love you. I'm sure I don't tell you often enough, but it's always there.

"And I want you to know that—up here..." and he touched her forehead "and in here..." now he touched her breast "—my love for you is constant and unwavering, but I do what I have to do, Paige. I always have and I always will. Do you understand?"

"Yes."

"And Paige?"

"Yes?"

"Just so we're clear on this. Were the results of punishing you more severe than I anticipated? Yes. And it disturbs me that I lost control, something I'm not prone to do. But given the same circumstances, would I do it again? Yes."

Then, tenderly, Dominic touched Paige's cheek, her hair, and his eyes were soft on her. "Because I love you so much, Zucchero."

She nodded and answered solemnly, "I understand." And she did.

There was a phrase she had once heard, and she'd looked it up. It meant "without God" or forsaken. That was how she had felt that night, as if, briefly, she had glimpsed hell. She would never go there again, not if she could help it. She had been careless, casting off his warnings as if they meant nothing, but she would make it up to him.

He offered, "I think we can put this behind us. Come on, let's take our drinks and go sit on the porch."

That night, as she lay next to him, Paige was at peace. Her husband was no longer in turmoil. She had freed him. By taking responsibility for what had happened and telling him she understood his actions, she had made it an acceptable situation for both of them.

Life's road took strange twists, she thought, and this was one of them, for now they were closer than ever, and she realized the depth of his love for her.

As for Dominic, he was secretly proud of the stamina his young bride had exhibited. It had not gone unnoticed by anyone that day that never once had she cried out or begged him to stop. She had taken her punishment without complaint and without question. She was special and she was his. He was more protective of her than ever. She was indeed his gift.

From then on, Dominic's feelings for his wife were more evident, more on display than in the past. Their families, but particularly Sophia, took note. There was a visible bond between the couple that excluded the rest of them.

One would think that after marriage, this togetherness wouldn't be so ...so necessary. Perhaps not for most couples, but Dominic and Paige were not most couples. They were never happier than when they were together.

When he went to his office in the city, he would call her several times during the day. Whenever possible, she accompanied him on trips. He talked to her about projects he was undertaking, showed her studies of prospective acquisitions, and asked her opinion. She advised him on market trends. She was not only a beloved partner, but a valuable one as well.

And the family watched…and waited…and approved. Yes, she was everything they had hoped for...and more.

*Now that you know the beginning,
following along in Book Two as the story continues...*

The Ginaellis have claimed Paige as their own and she will not disappoint them. In Book Two, Paige also finds favor with Dominic's friends and associates in Italy, but an encounter with goverment agents while they are abroad reveals new information about her husband. Danger follows them home to Long Island and the ominous fears she has been unable to dismiss, despite reassurances from Dominic. are realized.